STORIES BEYOND BELIEF 2

SARAH RUTH SCOTT
and SIMON ROBERT SINCLAIR

authorHOUSE®

AuthorHouse™ UK
1663 Liberty Drive
Bloomington, IN 47403 USA
www.authorhouse.co.uk
Phone: 0800.197.4150

Published by AuthorHouse 02/13/2018

ISBN: 978-1-5462-8855-8 (sc)
ISBN: 978-1-5462-8859-6 (e)

Print information available on the last page.

STORIES BEYOND BELIEF 2

The second book that looks at strange events and stories that are most unusual, some of these stories are taken from a lengthier story in order to capture the interest of the reader. The first story is from the cracked porcelain saga about a mental health nurse called Ruth. She also appears in the Harrington curse helping magazine reporters from criminal world investigate a strange phenomenon involving mirrors. The blood trail story follows the original story called blood trail across time involving the hunting down of time travelling vampires. Operation brainstorm is a more futuristic story that looks at a machine that is capable of restructuring the mind, it is designed to help mental ill patients, until it is stolen and misused. Eight skulls of Teversham is a tale about witches who kill a family and terrorise villagers until somebody is hired to hunt them down and kill them.

EIGHT SKULLS OF TEVERSHAM

CRACKED PORCELAIN- KILLER QUEEN

DOUBLE EXPOSURE

NOTHING IS REAL

BLOOD TRAIL PART 2 EVIL OF THE VAMPIRES

THE HARRINGTON CURSE

OPERATION BRAINSTORM

FOR THE LOVE OF CHARLOTTE

EIGHT SKULLS OF
Teversham

SARAH RUTH SCOTT

PART ONE

HUNTED

It was a cold dark night in October with a full moon in the sky; it was the sort of night where no one would venture out unless they were mad or had a cause to. For the village of Teversham was certainly cursed that night, as the villagers hid away in their houses, listening to sound of night birds such as owls, making the occasional sounds amidst the silence. Suddenly the silence was broken by terrible screams coming from the village as the Druids searched for innocent souls and virgins, looking for those they could sacrifice and in the chaos there stood the silhouettes of eight ugly women holding broomsticks all watching the village from a hill. They were eight witches who had stood outside the villagers homes chanting spells and cursing the ground that they walked on. The witches were known as Albelenda, Florina, Babeth, Nabara, Renilda, Rosalinda, Jeliana, and Passara. As they circled the family they swept their broomsticks across the floor making a ring in the dirt "Pity on you for you will die a certain death" Albelenda said speaking for the others "I am Albelenda and you must fear me and my friends, for we seek to avenge those who killed my family. Dread the darkness and fear the ones who will take your lives this very night"

Albelenda was the leader of the witches, she had long black scraggily matted hair a long nose and a wart resting on her chin. The other witches looked similar except for Passara who was shorter than the others and was badly scarred on the left side of her face. Babeth was slightly thinner than the others and Rosalinda was a little larger than the others. Each one of them were as wicked as each other but Nabara was exceptionally bad and hardly ever spoke, but she hated all non witches and wanted any excuse to use her magic and destroy people.

A female villager walked bravely towards the witches and tried whispering to them. Nabara grabbed her by the arm and pulled her toward her saying, "Speak to me if you know what's good for you" Nabara held her firmly spraying her saliva in the woman's face.

The woman wiped her face with her hand that was shaking with fear, as she stood looking into Nabara's wicked eyes.

"Speak!" Nabara yelled

The woman pointed to the last house of the village in the distance and spoke nervously "The family that you seek live there, but please don't harm the other villagers" She said pleading with Nabara.

Nabara raised her wand and pointed it in the woman's face, she had hatred in her eyes, then gave a wicked smile.

"I suppose you want rewarding for your information and betrayal of your friends?" Nabara asked

"No, just for me and my family to be safe" The woman pleaded.

With one swish of Nabara's wand the woman flew in the air and then landed in a heap on the ground.

"I really hate kindness" She said laughing

"That was mean even for you Nabara" Babeth said in disgust.

"Enough" Albelenda shouted "This village of Teversham is about to experience an awakening, at the hands of the witches who have lost so many due to the persecution and constant witch hunts that have taken place around the woods, the Mayor of Teversham town will know what its like to suffer".

"Albelenda are we going to kill all the family?" Florina asked

"Yes, all the Butterworth family must die, Father, Mother and children" She replied

"Yes, kill them all" Nabara insisted.

"When do we do this?" Renilda asked.

"When the moon is full, on this very night" Albelenda explained "We attack on my command, be ready to ride your brooms and approach from the sky" She instructed them all. They all went back into the forest and waited for the clouds to clear from in front of the moon, and then each one of them mounted their brooms and flew into the sky. They were silhouetted by the moon and descended onto the Butterworth's cottage sweeping around it and waving their wands causing explosions. The Butterworth snuggled together all but Fredrick (Eric) who was in the cellar sweeping the floor, one of the explosions knocked the grandfather clock over which landed on the cellar door. The witches entered the cottage and killed the family one by one, starting with the parents; Nabara killed the youngest child Rosa as she lay asleep in her bed. All Eric could hear was screaming and loud explosions; he stood nervously below and wet his trousers in the process. Everything went silent; Eric listened for any sounds that would indicate that the witches would enter the cellar and find him. Suddenly he heard movement the cellar door began to creek open, and the shape of a woman appeared at the door. He began to shake with fear as the figure got closer to him, and then he sighed with relief as the woman spoke.

“Eric, it’s me Martha” Martha was his neighbour

Eric hugged Martha but did not speak, he was in shock, Martha turned to face her husband Basil and began to cry.

“My god, Basil what do we do?” She said trying to make herself understood.

“Let’s take him to our home” He advised

“But how are we going to get him out of here?” she asked thinking about the devastation and all the family lying dead upstairs.

“Cover him in my cloak and lead him out of the front door” Basil suggested

Martha did as he instructed and helped Eric up the stairs into what was left of the cottage, there were gaping holes in the walls, scorch marks and the bodies of his family lying dead around the floor, Rosa was on the bed with scorched sheets over her dead body. Eric was almost at the door when he managed to look through a gap in the cloak and noticed his mother’s body, her eyes were looking up at the ceiling.

“Mother” He shouted and broke away from Martha running to her side, Basil was close behind and caught hold of Eric’s arm.

“Come lad, stay with us” He could see the sadness in Eric’s eyes “Come on, you can’t help them now”.

Martha felt helpless and just wanted to hug him, she wanted to tell him everything would be alright, but in her heart she knew that wasn't true. If the witches knew he was alive they would hunt him down and kill him, he was destined to spend his whole life looking over his shoulder.

Eric remained with Martha and Basil Bakewell and from that fateful night when he was a mere eight years old, he grew up with their son John aged nine, Basil was a soldier who had fought for England. He taught Eric to defend himself, fighting with many weapons including the sword and long bow, he also showed him how to use his skills with a cross bow. Eric became skilful and cunning in fighting, he knew that some day he would have to face the witches who killed his family and avenge them. Eric had nightmares for years about that night, he relived the events although he didn't actually see them killed, He remembered the screams and saw they're dead bodies lying dead everywhere.

Eric celebrated his twenty first birthday in a banqueting hall in the town of Teversham, quite a few people attended including Martha and Basil, it was a fine feast, with various meat dishes, pies and other savoury delights. Eric was delighted by the feast and in meeting so many people, some he knew others were friends of Basil, some of them were soldiers. He was considered old enough to be a soldier, he showed great discipline and leadership skills, and he was proving to be quite skilful with the sword and cross bow, he also learned to ride a horse.

Meanwhile in another town close to Teversham the eight witches decided to terrorise the village, kidnapping children and murdering innocent people. Albelenda led the witches into the town at night and it was then that she was made aware of Eric's existence, she was furious to find that one member of the Butterworth family had survived and ordered the witches to find him. She expressed her feelings as the witches coven sat around the cauldron; she hated the family and would not rest until they were all dead.

A new Mayor had been elected in the town of Teversham and he was keen to find the witches who caused so much chaos in the town and surrounding village. Unusually so Teversham was the name of the town and the village, this confused the people from outside the area. The people all knew about the Butterworth family and how they were slaughtered by the witches, people were frightened to go out at night or venture into the woods. It is said that many a poor soul have been captured, tortured and murdered by witches, people have heard they're chants and awful cackles, the sound of wolves and owls that indicate the presence of night time ghouls and goblins, and the sound of the devils hoofs running across the ground in a frantic effort to capture lost souls. The bravest knight fears to enter the woods and forests of Teversham, knowing that danger lurks around every corner. Only the witches themselves would stay there and live with other creatures of their kind, surrounded by wickedness and growing up to be bad. Lurking in the darkness they go out at night, taking what they liked and worshiping their demon master the Devil, this is what is taught to children and they grow up living in fear of witches. But be aware that not all witches are bad and understand that their magic is not necessarily wicked, it can be used for good, white witches are known to be good witches, they remain pure and refined, or so legend tells us. The purification of their blood is an abomination to the black witch, they consider them to work outside the witches' coven and not worthy to be called witches. None other than freaks or mutants who use the name to show humans that some witches are more human who have feelings for mankind.

Eric the twenty year old man grew up handsome with fair hair and a cheeky smile, He was strong and fearless just as Basil hoped he would be, a fighter with a reason to hunt the witches that killed his family. Eric worked hard mentally and physically, he was injured countless times with swords, fires, wooden sticks and various obstacles used in simulation battles. Finally he was ready to face the witches, but he would not be alone as Basil had mustered an army to help Eric in his quest. But the Mayor had other ideas, he was a fat stocky man with fair receding hair which he combed over his forehead, he also had a fat Roman nose and beady eyes that could just be seen beneath the heavy wrinkles. Mayor William Malet was a cunning man who managed to deceive the people in voting for him as he promised to make the town and village of Teversham safe. But he was a wealthy ambitious man who just wanted to be popular and richer than anybody around him. Malet wanted to gain power by deception and got rid of anyone in his way, it's amazing how many people simply disappeared, no one asked questions for fear of vanishing themselves. The mayor stood waiting in a room for Basil and Eric to appear, he had arranged the meeting weeks before so that it would fall in line with his re election, if they could kill the witches he could be popular with the people and win votes.

A knock came at the door; this was followed by a pause, then another knock at the door, finally the Mayor answered.

“Come in” He shouted abruptly

Basil and Eric entered the room, marching proudly towards the Mayor

“Good day Mayor” Basil says addressing the mayor

“Good day gentlemen” the mayor grunted

“What do you want from us” Basil said bluntly.

“I need you to hunt down these witches and make this area safe again” He said with his eyes glancing from one to the other.

“That could be possible although that would come with a price” Basil said considering his finances and supporting his family.

“I can offer you fifty crowns a head” Malet offered “Mean that literally and that’s me being generous”.

“I agree that’s a good price” Basil said looking at Eric for approval, and then the Mayor.

"But I need evidence that you have killed these eight witches" Malet insisted

"Proof" Basil said confused

"You want us to bring back all the bodies?" Eric asked

"No, just the skulls, eight to be exact" Malet replied

"Eight skulls" Basil said

"Eight skulls to hang on poles around Teversham town" Malet said sniggering

"The eight skulls of Teversham" Basil said wittily.

"It sounds good and it will keep the witches away from Teversham" Malet said "I must agree with that" Basil replied

"Me too" Eric agreed.

The following morning Basil and Eric set off with a small army to hunt for the witches of Teversham, None of them were aware that the witches were seeking to find Eric at this time, Eric had learned to ride and was given a horse called Alestra, it took a while for Eric and Alestra to get along but after a while they were friends.

It took a few days travelling before they reached a cottage where Rosalinda lived, she was sat discussing Eric with Passara, the soldiers listened to what they had to say in order to find out their plans.

"Passara, I think we ought to consider what Albelenda has asked of us" Rosalinda said sipping from a cup.

"What do you mean?" Passara asked

"Finding that young man and killing him" Rosalinda reminded her.

"Who do you mean, Eric?" Passara asked gazing into her cup.

"Yes, do you remember that night?" Rosalinda seemed concerned.

"I was against slaughtering that family, but they killed our relatives and friends" Passara said trying to justify their actions.

"But they didn't kill children, we would never harm children" Rosalinda said remorsefully.

"I agree but Albelenda was insistent and she wants to kill Eric" Passara said sipping from the cup.

"We have to obey her otherwise we could die ourselves" Rosalinda said fearfully

At that moment Basil ordered the attack on the witches, they rushed into the room taking them by surprise Rosalinda was cornered in the room and Passara managed to escape their clutches and ran out of the back door only to be greeted by John and two other soldiers.

“Are you going somewhere witch?” He asked her

Passara stopped and stared at him, she seemed powerless

“Let me go or you will be very sorry” She hissed at him

“I don’t think so” He said holding his sword to her throat “Come with me” He insisted

Suddenly her eyes changed colour, they were yellow and her finger nails turned into claws, she began to growl like a dog and leapt at John. He fell to the ground and began wrestling with her, they rolled about for a while and then one of the soldiers plunged his sword into her side. She jumped off John and another soldier decapitated her with one mighty blow.

When John entered the cottage he noticed that they had already killed Rosalinda and her head was chopped from her body. Basil was holding her head up by the hair and looking around the room at all the other soldiers.

“Behold the head of a witch” He said proudly.

John held Passara’s head up “And another” he said comparing it to Rosalinda’s head “Two skulls and six to go”

They continued their journey with the two heads in sacks, Eric found the whole ordeal a little gruesome and vomited, he had never experienced this sort of thing before. He rode beside Basil and remained silent, reliving the events over and over again, trying to make sense of it. Basil watched him closely showing fatherly concern, he had grown fond of Eric as if he were one of his own, it was painful to watch him go through such mental torture just like the night his family died.

"Eric, are you alright" He asked

"Yes sir, I am" Eric replied

"You witnessed the killing of two wicked witches, who as you heard were after you" Basil explained.

"I know, but why behead them?" Eric asked concerned

"A witch can only be successfully killed by the severing of her head, for some reason it breaks their spell" Basil patted Eric on the back "You will see a lot worse ahead lad"

"I know, I will be alright" Eric said smiling.

PART TWO

JUSTICE

In a cave deep within the forest a group of witches sat by a fire discussing the deaths of Rosalinda and Passara, Albelenda lead the coven as usual she had this expression of distaste like she was eating something sour like lemons. She deliberately kicked the fire and made the other witches jump.

"Damn that young boy Eric, he survives to tell the tale, be fearful for they now come for each one of us" She said pointing her wand at each of them.

"They apparently want our heads" Florina said concerned.

"Our heads" Renilda said clutching her neck.

"Let them try and get me" Nabara said waving her wand sending a bolt of energy from it into the fire and causing an explosion.

"They don't scare me" Babeth said "I will turn every one of them into pond creatures"

"Jeliana you are the spells and potions witch, you can do this" Renilda said looking at Jeliana.

"I can do almost anything necessary, but it's Eric we really need" She said staring back at Renilda.

"We must watch our backs and signal each other if we suspect anyone or are in danger" Albelenda advised them all "We must also seek out Eric and kill him"

"What about the soldiers?" Renilda asked.

"Kill them all" Nabara said

"Kill them all?" Florina asked.

"You heard kill them all" Albelenda said "And whoever gets in our way"

Later the next night the soldiers reached the edge of the woods each one looked at each other hesitant to enter, Eric looked at Basil waiting for him to speak.

"Now then all of you, listen carefully to what I have to say" He looked at each one of them "I know you are afraid, but we have to move forward and hunt for these witches, we need to do this for our families, the Towns people and the Mayor" Basil was also trying to re assure himself that all would be well.

The sound of night life could be heard by them all, the rustle of branches and the snapping of trigs broke the silence, and something was lurking within. Suddenly they were met by a flock of flying bats fluttering around their heads, one of the men yelled as he held his face and fell off his horse. When one of the troops dismounted and ran to his aid he was also struck by something, blood gushed from the first soldiers head; the second soldiers face was burned by something.

Both the soldiers lay dead Basil ordered his men to enter the woods, and so they moved in one by one. Basil led them deeper into the woods, hoping to catch a glimpse of a witch, each sound made the soldiers jump, they expected to share the fate of the two soldiers they had left behind. Suddenly a flash of light occurred and another soldier fell to the ground from his horse, he jumped back onto his feet, "I am fine" he announced before his head split completely in two. The soldiers formed a circle and all peered into the darkness, Eric was the next to be thrown from his horse and lay on his back with his arms and legs spread out, something burrowing out the ground around him, his hand and feet were being held down with bind weed, this was followed by weed creeping around his neck and strangling him. Basil leapt off his horse and began cutting at the weed, he was joined by John who was also cutting the weed.

Eventually they managed to free Eric, but another soldier had already be strangled by another weed, once Eric was free he sighted a witch flying past on a broomstick, and so he grabbed a crossbow and fired at her, she fell down beside a tree, it was Renilda who was lying with the arrow in her neck.

"Now" Basil said "Finish her, take off her head" He said throwing his sword in front of Eric.

Eric was hesitant, but he knew he had to do it, he raised his sword above his head and with all his strength cut Renilda's head from her body.

"That's my boy" Basil said proudly

"Five skulls left Eric" John said looking at Renilda's head

They continued on their journey, by now the heads in the sacks were spelling badly of decayed flesh, it was that bad they all took it in turns carrying the sack. They tried to sleep during the day as the witches were active at night, two of the guards stood watch at all times day and night, this allowed the others to sleep and when they were on the move they used a wagon to sleep in. They spotted a woman on the road, she seemed weary so they let her rest in the wagon, and she offered to reward them when they arrived at the next village. This could have been the offer of food, food for the horses or even money, She had a kind face and seemed genuine, but after a short distance she changed her appearance and the nice lady was non other than Jeliana one of the witches they sought. She kissed one of the soldiers in the wagon and his face became disfigured and he suffocated and died. She hid beneath him until one of the soldiers opened the back of the wagon in order to let him out; he was supposed to be the next soldier resting. She leapt out at him and cut his throat. Basil rode up to the wagon and slayed the witch, with one blow of his mighty sword she fell to the ground and then cut off her head adding it to the other heads.

The next journey took them over a stream and through a valley; they felt vulnerable travelling through such a wide open area, but certainly not as much as the nights spent in the woods at night. But the witches were cunning and used all kinds of tricks and magic in order to trap and kill some of the soldiers, they were truly evil woman with only the desire to kill others not like themselves. They came to another cottage which looked similar to Rosalinda's home, it was quiet and very tidy inside as if it had just been cleaned. Basil entered first cautiously entering through the main door at the front of the cottage, all seemed fine until the door locked itself separating Basil from his men. He continued to walk around the cottage until he arrived at the kitchen; Suddenly knives began to fly out of a drawer and towards him. Basil dived on the ground and hid behind a cupboard for cover, after a while this stopped and he picked himself up, he found himself accompanied by a woman. She had long black hair and a long dark dress; she had a narrow face and a long nose.

"I am Babeth and who are you?" she asked

"I am Basil" he replied

"What kind of silly name is that?" She asked smiling and showing her dirty mouth and the gaps where there was once teeth.

"Why do you want Eric?" Basil asked

"So that we can kill him" She replied.

"He is outside" He said hoping to provide some time to think of a plan of escape.

"I know, once you are dead I will tend to Eric" she replied holding up her wand

"Wait" he said looking into her evil eyes "Can I advise you against doing that"

"Foolish man stop wasting my time" she began waving her wand

Suddenly a arrow shot through the air and buried itself in her chest, it went straight into her heart and she was pinned to a cupboard door.

The soldiers battered the back door down and entered the room; Eric was holding his crossbow and John went over to remove Babeth's body from the cupboard door.

"I will take her outside and remove her head from her body" John said standing behind Eric.

"There goes Babeth" Basil said with relief.

The knights continued on their quest over hills across streams and brooks, their numbers had depleted since they began, so many had died at the mercy of the witches and some were reluctant to travel on. But only three witches remained Albelenda, Florina and Nabara, they were the worst witches who were determined to get Eric. That very night a storm began sending thunder in the sky and lightning that seemed to light up the darkness, this was perfect weather for the witches who took advantage of it. In all the confusion the soldiers were confused by what appeared to be the weather conditions and what was the witches magic, the men thought they were hallucinating as they sighted naked women walking towards them, each attractive. Suddenly one of the soldiers yelled out in pain and other cries were heard all around them, they witnessed strange creatures moving about before their eyes. After the storm had passed, Basil looked around him, only to find a lot of the soldiers lying on the ground, some wounded and some dead. But as he checked everyone was accountable but one man, Eric who was missing, it was thought that the witches had got him at last. Basil gathered the men together and buried the dead, he stood next to John and hugged him.

"The witches have taken Eric" Basil said sadly

"I know" John said with a sigh

"We must find them" Basil continued

"We will Father" John said confidently

The witches had arrived back in their cave accompanied by Eric, He looked tired but despite this he was well, he was tied up and sat near a fire. Nabara stood over him waving her wand at him and snarling, Albelenda and Florina were sat at the entrance of the cave looking out at the countryside. Nabara was angry and continued to tease Eric with her wand, sending sparks in Eric's face causing him to turn his face away from her.

"You are going to die soon" She said sneering at him.

"Why are you doing this?" He asked

"Because you killed my family" She replied

"I did nothing, I was a boy" He said "You killed my family, all of you did"

"They all deserved to die, I hated all of them" She said kneeling down and looking into his eyes "Aww little blue eyes is sad, go ahead cry sad boy"

"I don't need to cry" He replied "The soldiers will be here to rescue me soon"

"That's what you think, we will kill them before they even get near here" She explained "We have magic and we have cunning, we can trick them into walking into a trap".

"You hate families don't you, why is that do you hate children?" He asked.

"We all have children; they are wonderful, except for one child who is a bit of a freak".

"You mean only one child?" Eric asked

"She looks different, sounds different and certainly acts different" Nabara said looking at Albelenda.

Albelenda looked back at her frowning

"Are you talking about my freaky daughter?"

"Yes the one that has no name" Nabara said "The one you keep locked in your cellar, who is only allowed out in the dark in case she shames you"

"Do not speak of her" Albelenda shouted "She is no daughter of mine"

"A freak she may be but she is yours" Florina said

"Yes yours Albelenda" Nabara said "She walks about in this cave like an animal"

"It was a few days before the soldiers got close to the cave, the witches had laid traps all around it, some of them were pits with spikes and snakes others were nets and other devices that would trap, harm or kill them. Nabara was constantly tormenting Eric and repeatedly telling him that she would kill him.

"Your death will be slow" She said "I will drain the blood from your body and make you drink it".

Eric was getting thirsty but he never trusted the witches, thinking that they would poison him, or even give him some potion that would make him ill or hallucinate.

While the witches were out looking for the soldiers Eric was a approached by a pretty young girl who looked about eighteen years old, she brought him a cup containing water and put it to his lips. She never spoke but just smiled and went back into the deepest part of the cave; she did this repeatedly and even brought food for him, assisting by holding the bread to his mouth and feeding him soup with a spoon.

She poured water over his wounds and bandaged them so neatly around his legs.

"Thank you" He said "Have you got a name?"

She shook her head and walked away, all he could see was her silhouette disappearing into the cave.

The witches returned usually discussing the activities of the soldiers

"Did you see those spikes going into that man, like meat hooks through meat" Nabara said laughing

"I enjoyed poking at that man in the net, I burned him to death and listened to him scream" Albelenda said also laughing.

"I saw the man in the pit trying to fight off snakes that didn't exist, so much for my magic making him think things were there" Florina said laughing with them.

"Girl" Albelenda shouted "I hope you have been looking after Eric"

The girl came forward from the darkness, her pale skin shone from the light emitted from the fire.

"God, your so ugly" Albelenda said spitefully "Go away freak you make me sick"

"She is awful Albelenda" Florina commented

"I really don't understand how she turned out like that, she's nothing like me" Albelenda said looking at her reflection in a bucket of water.

"What do you think Eric?" Nabara asked him

"I didn't really see her" Eric said trying to ignore her

"Freaky like you" Nabara continued "Or your family"

As she spoke to him she deliberately set fire to his trouser leg with her wand, watching him yell in agony, then poured water over him.

"This pain is nothing to what you're going to feel soon" she yelled

The soldiers were camped about a mile away, there were thirty left from the fifty that began from Teversham, and some were weak and most of them frightened by the witches' magic. Basil was concerned about Eric and wondered weather or not he was still alive, he felt confident that he was and that seemed to keep him going. Basil had a plan to divide the men into two parties he would lead one and John would lead the other, this would mean that they could search from two directions east and west. This meant that each group would have fifteen men and they could make a sweep of the woods by spreading out, the object would be to meet in the middle. Basil ordered them to break camp and begin their search immediately, his plan was to take the witches by surprise and rescue Eric.

Meanwhile the witches went out in search of Basil and his men, they were hoping that their traps continued to work and reduce the army in numbers. But this time the soldiers were aware of the dangers and were very cautious not to fall into any traps that the witches may have set them. Eric remained calm and hoped that they may stumble upon the cave to rescue him, he sat fidgeting and suddenly felt thirsty, he had hoped that the girl may come to him after all she did cleanse the wound on his leg and offer him a drink. Eventually she did appear but she was holding a large knife in her hand, she moved forward until she was right in front of him, then she walked behind him.

"If you are going to kill me do it now" He said anxiously

She remained silent and stood behind him for a while, she held the knife firmly in both hands pointing it towards his neck, and she was so close he could feel her breath on his neck. And then just as he thought she was going to cut his throat she cut the ropes that had bound his wrists, and then she gave him the knife to cut away the rope around his ankles.

"Thank you" Eric said "You are not a freak, not in my eyes"

"I must rescue my friends" He said walking towards the entrance of the cave

"Thank you for cleansing my leg I will come back for you," He promised

Once he was out of the cave Eric rushed into the forest forgetting that he had a bad leg, it was almost as if it had healed, he felt no pain or discomfort, in fact he felt quite well considering all the brutality that he had suffered. He managed to see the shining of the metal armour from the soldiers as they were walking through the woods, He wanted to shout but he didn't want to alert the witches and give away their position. So he crept closer to them, and then spoke to one of them, they turned around to face him; one of them pointed a sword at his throat.

"Abas it's me Eric" He said

"How do I know it's you?" he said "You could be a witch in disguise?"

"You have a pimple on your" he was interrupted by Abas

"It's fine no one else needs to know" He said with embarrassment.

"Sir" he shouted "Eric is here

Basil turned around and noticed Eric, he immediately ran towards him and embraced him "Son your safe, but how did you get away?"

"A young girl freed me" he said with relief

"Was she a prisoner?" he asked

"No a daughter of one of the witches" he explained "Nothing like them, she was very attractive, she is at the cave up there" Eric said pointing behind him.

"We shall meet the others and find this cave" Basil said

Meanwhile the witches returned to the cave and immediately noticed that Eric had gone, they examined the ropes and noticed that they had been cut.

"Girl, come here" Albelenda shouted

The girl came from the darkness and walked sheepishly towards them, she knew that she would be chastised for freeing Eric and stood before her mother to except her punishment.

"Why did you free this man, tell me" Albelenda said shaking the girl

"Put her in a boiling pot" Nabara shouted

"Let her go home Albelenda" Florina said looking at the girl.

"No" Nabara said "She should be severely punished"

"I say she seems sorry to me" Florina said "Besides she can be dealt with later"

"You're too soft Florina" Nabara said grabbing the girl

"I will deal with her and you will be sorry girl" Albelenda said pulling her away from Nabara.

Albelenda took the girl to the entrance of the cave and pointed into the tree's.

"Go now, get out of my sight freak" She demanded

"Your letting her go?" Nabara said angrily

"Yes" said Albelenda "She will return home and go straight to the cellar where she belongs"

Nabara was not at all pleased and went off in another direction, she was so furious she accidentally met up with some of the soldiers, but they didn't see her and continued on their journey led by John. Nabara decided to play a trick on them and cried out in a child's voice.

"Help me" she paused and then continued "Help me please".

One of the troops raced forward into the bushes shouting

"A child is in trouble"

And then there was silence everybody looked forward into the bushes, but all was quiet, and then the soldiers walked cautiously forward, stepping over trigs. Eventually they came to the place where the voice came from and noticed the soldier pinned to a tree, with his throat cut and his stomach sliced open with all his insides hanging out. Nabara had clearly done this and was planning to do something similar to all of them, she seemed to be worse than ever now, a real psychopath far worse than the other witches, using her power to kill and cause devastation. Nabara decided to wait until night time in order to continue her killings, she liked the thrill of hearing her victims, yell and scream in pain, or their bodies quaking in fear as she tormented or tortured them.

Florina managed to find John and his soldiers and attacked them, she flew into a group of them wildly waving her wand and coursing chaos, leaving bodies lying across the ground. John and the few remaining soldiers hid behind trees, finally one bowman managed to send an arrow into her side causing her to fall to the ground with a thud. John ran forward and raised his sword severing her head from her body.

“Two left” He said holding up her head.

Meanwhile Basil had found the cave with the help from Eric, suddenly they heard a scream.

“That’s the girl” Eric said anxiously “She is in danger”

He raced on ahead of the others, Basil was concerned about Eric and raced after him, but Eric was younger and more active, reaching the entrance in no time. Suddenly he felt a heavy blow to the head and stumbled to the ground holding his head. Albelenda was on top of him holding a rock covered in his blood. Although he was dazed Eric tried to fight her off, she tried hitting him again but this time she stopped holding an arrow that was buried on her chest. Basil raced forward and began hitting her on the head with a rock until her skull split open. Basil had saved Eric’s life and knelt down to help Eric to his feet, but Eric was too weak and fell back to the ground, at the moment Nabara swooped down and attacked Basil sending a fireball into his back and then hitting him across the head with a heavy club. Basil was less fortunate than Eric and died almost immediately. Before he died Basil whispered to Eric.

"Be brave and fight them to the end" Basil faded away before he finished his sentence. John arrived to see his father whispering to Eric, and then watched him die with Eric close to him. Nabara had gone deep into the cave hoping they would follow her, she had wanted to use Eric to trap the soldiers when he was held captive but her screams brought them there anyway. The soldiers did follow Nabara into the depths of the cave, it was getting darker inside as they entered a long tunnel, and suddenly a swarm of bats flew at them. After a short while they disappeared and a bright light came from the distance knocking down some of the soldiers. Some of the men were overwhelmed by the smell of rotting flesh, a nauseated feeling came over all of them, this became more intense as they got further down the tunnel. They could feel a mixture of something soft and slimy along with a hard substance, looking down they noticed it was human remains, victims of the witches, but mainly due to Nabara. Nabara began tormenting them by sending snakes in their pathway, she also transformed herself into a wolf and began hitting some of the soldiers with her claws, scratching their faces. The room began to light up as Nabara set some of the soldiers alight, blood curdling screams echoed in the cave as Nabara picked off some of the soldiers, one of them dropped into a large bath of acid. Eric tried to follow Nabara's trail hoping to trap her into a corner, but she was too fast and managed to kill quite a few of the men in no time at all, making eerie sounds and laughing wickedly. She placed her hand on one mans shoulder and bit a lump out of his neck severing the jugular causing him to bleed to death. Soldiers fired cross bows sending arrows into the air, they were not even aiming just desperate to hit the witch, but the arrows bounced off the cave walls, some landed in them. She appeared unstoppable as she mercilessly killed more soldiers; it was like a blood bath the walls were covered in their blood.

In a last desperate hope to capture her Eric whispered to John and the both ran in separate directions, John shot arrows towards the large bath making a noise. Nabara responded to the noise and rushed towards the bath of acid, and then both Eric and John shot arrows straight at Nabara, she was so overwhelmed that having so many arrows in her that she yelled and fell into the bath of acid. Watching the acid strip the flesh off her body gave Eric an idea, he decided to put all the heads into the acid, thus getting rid of the flesh and stop the odour caused by the rotting flesh. Eric and John looked around them, they were the only survivors, they found fresh sacks and put split the skulls in to three of them. John had noticed that Albelenda's skull had been damaged but never mentioned it to Eric, he was afraid it might affect the reward money.

PART THREE

FEAR OF THE WITCHES

The sun rose the next morning and it was almost as if the witches never existed, Eric and John had the only evidence in three sacks, eight skulls ready to show the Mayor. One thing puzzled them was the Mayors obsession with the number eight, he had a fixation on it, everything he did included the number eight. No one could deter him from that number, not in any sense of the word, in the bible it would signifies resurrection and regeneration, that which is beyond. This may be the reason that the Mayor sought power, he also expected respect and gratitude from the people, and perhaps he expected to be resurrected or regenerated in some way. When Eric and John returned to the Mayor, he was delighted to see them, he greeted them with open arms as if they were his long lost son's, he patted them on the back and congratulated them for their efforts. He opened his desk drawer and produced bags full of coins, Eric and John put three sacks on the table and the Mayor examined each one in turn, he called John over to his side of the desk and asked for his opinion of the one skull with the crack on the head.

"This one is damaged" the Mayor said expecting an explanation

"Eric knows about that one" John said trying to avoid answering the Mayor

"The skull is damaged" He repeated directing his attention to Eric

"Basil hit her on the head with a rock, she is the leader of the witches, she is called Albelenda" Eric informed the Mayor.

"Albelenda" The Mayor repeated "I can almost feel her power" he said looking into the eye sockets "To think she sent fear into the hearts of so many, I almost envy her".

Eric looked at John expecting a reaction, but John just gazed at the skull, the Mayor didn't seem surprised that only the two of them survived, he was glad that they returned safely with his skulls. The Mayor ordered a feast for the return of the two men and in fact he struggled to remember their names, just the deed. He gave a speech without mentioning the two gallant men, for some reason he forgot they even existed, instead he announced that he had taken care of the witches and made the town of Teversham safe again for to walk the streets. He even told the town folk that he had arranged for the eight witches skulls to hang on poles around the border of the town in order to warn any witches not to try to attack anyone again. For a time this worked and everyone felt safe until strange events took place such as food poisoning, crops dying and people suffering from all manner of illness, in fact everything that went wrong was blamed on the witches skulls, they were said to be cursed. Even things such as the miscarriage of babies and sudden deaths were all due to these skulls. Everybody who lived from miles around had heard of the eight skulls of Teversham, people were afraid to visit the town and village for fear of dying from a disease or being cursed themselves. The skulls remained for about two years until the Mayor was advised quite strongly to get rid of the skulls for good.

Eric was still a little annoyed by the Mayor taking the credit for taking care of the witches, John didn't seem to mind as much, although to some degree he felt as if his father should have got some notoriety, like being honoured or a statue erected in his name, or perhaps a statue of him dressed in his uniform. We never even had the chance to mourn properly, each soldier was remembered but no one but Eric or John witnessed their bravery in battle against those wicked witches. The last night that the skulls were around the town they actually glowed red and then green from some light within, by this time even the Mayor agreed that it was a good idea to get rid of them.

The following day the Mayor sent for Eric, he never asked for John for some unknown reason, Eric was pleased to go and see the Mayor hoping for some recognition for assisting to kill the witches. The Mayor stood proudly in front of his desk, soon he began pacing up and down in front of the window, when Eric arrived at the Mayors office, and Mayor appeared to be nervous and sharp.

"Ah, young man" He began "About these eight skulls"

"Yes sir" Eric said respectfully

"I need you to get rid of them" The Mayor said mopping his brow with a handkerchief

"Of course sir" Eric said "And where would you like me to dispose of them?"

"Take them up to the mountains of the north and hide them in a cave" He instructed.

"That way their spirit cannot harm people, did you know the witches feared me, they think I am powerful, even more now, I have the ability to control their magic"

Eric looked at him and couldn't believe what he was hearing, it was as if the Mayor had gone insane, but he was talking about his association with the number eight and the resurrection process, he also touched on his belief in the regeneration process and his association with the occult. Eric was not able to follow his conversation and became distracted by a knock at the door, the mayor seemed reluctant to reply, maybe he didn't want to be interrupted or maybe he was so engrossed in his own chain of thought, that he genuinely didn't hear the door.

The door was knocked again, this time harder with more urgency, this time the Mayor seemed to wake up from his fanciful journey.

"Come in" he shouted

"You wanted me sir" John said standing next to Eric

"Yes, have you brought the skulls" he asked

"All eight of them" John said holding up three sacks

The Mayor took the three sacks and placed them on the table

"These skulls will forever be the eight skulls of Teversham, I have held these skulls and feel their power" The Mayor seemed to go into some sort of trance.

"Sir" Eric said trying to break him from it

"I want you to take the skulls now and bury them in the ground by a cave in the mountains" The Mayor dismissed Eric and John then went to his bed.

The next morning Eric set off with the eight skulls of Teversham, he knew that it would take him days to reach the Scottish mountains, but he had plenty of supplies to take with him. It took days of riding across a rugged terrain before Eric was even close to the mountain that he needed to dispose of the skulls. Eric spent nights thinking of Basil and how he died, he had buried him in the woods and left a heap of rocks there so that he could locate it in future. He felt cheated by his sudden departure as if things had been left unsaid and he had not had the chance to thank him for his help and guidance over the years. He also felt as if John was jealous of their relationship, although John never said anything, his actions seemed to say it all, and also by the way he would look at him when Basil was showing him how to protect himself. Eric appreciated the praise from Basil, Basil was the type to complement the efforts that people made, he admired talented people and those who made the effort to practice their skills and reach a good standard of performance. Eric really showed him how he had mastered the art of sword fighting and accuracy with the cross bow, Basil was certainly proud of him and showed it.

Eric also had time to reflect on the kindness that Albelenda's daughter had showed him, cleansing his wounds and offering him food and water. She never really spoke to him, but her action spoke volumes, she had warm hands and kind eyes, but mostly her beauty shone through like a beacon on the hills.

Unlike the witches who's wickedness made them ugly on the inside and outside, they were so bad they scared each other, Eric was relieved that they were dead and so were the towns folk of Teversham. After travelling for a week Eric finally reached the cave marked with the hoof of Satan on the outside rock, Eric felt frightened as he entered the cave; he felt a chill run down his spine. The place was very eerie with a sense of evil within, Eric looked down into an enormous pit and then stood and looked around the cave with his blue eyes that seemed to sparkle, and he felt the presence of someone behind him. This was not unusual as he had this feeling from leaving the village, he felt like shouting out, but he thought this might attract attention to himself. He opened the sacks and began to empty the contents onto the ground, one all the eight skulls were out of the sacks he arranged them neatly on the ground in a circle. He sat for a while and just stared at the skulls, almost expecting them to move, He felt tired and wanted to sleep, but he had a long journey to make back home and just wanted to bury the skulls and go home. He was about to get his spade out of his pack when suddenly the place began to shake and the sound of rumbling could be heard in the distance, at first Eric thought it was thunder and lightning, the type of conditions that you would expect from a storm. But this was much worse, Eric was experiencing the start of the witches magic at work in the cave, for when he looked back at the skulls they were all lit up, and a green luminous substance began to trickle through the mouth and nostrils, this was followed by a form of electricity or energy travelling from one skull to another. Eric tried to run away but he became fixed like a statue in one position, he felt as if he were in a vice being crushed at one point, at this time he thought that he could see Albelenda.

And then no sooner did he see her, Nabara appeared and began cursing him

"I will finally see you die now Eric" she shouted

"Die Eric and go with your soldiers to your death" Albelenda shouted

After seeing them shouting all eight witches appear and circle around him all chanting "Die" and repeat it several times. Eric became dizzy and felt himself being drawn to the pit, parts of his body became numb and the voices had become louder, He felt the earth moving beneath him and the rumbling continued, slowly he began to drift closer to the pit. Suddenly with one mighty push the witches send Eric into the pit, Eric falls down and lands in some kind of lake containing a thick mixture and a film of mist covers it. The rumbling stops and everything is still, the atmosphere becomes calm and the skulls sink into the earth as if nothing has happened.

PART FOUR

RESURRECTION

The Mayor had wondered why he had not heard from Eric for five years, surly he would have contacted him telling him that he had buried the skulls. He had once heard that the secrets of resurrection lay in those mountains in Scotland and regeneration was also possible but again the answers remained in the caves high up there, but the Mayor never ventured there. Eventually he sent for his soldiers and a small team of explorers to go to the mountains in search of Eric, he never mentioned what he really wanted, but hoped that they would discover the secrets and return to him with the information. He needed to know if it was possible and only then would he venture out into the cave and use whatever information that was relevant to either prolong or restore his life.

The explorers and accompanying soldiers left the town of Teversham, in order to begin the arduous journey to the mountains, John was sent with them to gather information about the cave. They are also hoping to find Eric alive and solve the mystery of his disappearance; this would explain why he was gone so long.

John was leading the explorers who were called Aalef, a small man with a long beard and wearing a hat looking like a Goblin, Malbert was a thin man who walked oddly as if he had some sort of deformity, Gaud was a strong hard faced character who never smiled, finally Balian was the wisest of the explorers, very conscientious and keen on working long hours to discover things. There were few soldiers with them on this trip, it was considered an advantage to use fewer due to the cost of hiring them and because they were travelling light on this trip. It was the Mayors idea to do this, he wanted as few people to know any secrets about the cave, he certainly didn't want the town's folk to have knowledge of resurrection or regeneration.

On the journey John was telling the explorers the story of how, he and his father had battled with the witches, and about the eight skulls of Teversham. He avoided telling them about Eric and his part in their deaths, until one of the explorers asked him.

"What of Eric" Balian asked him.

"Oh, he fought well and at one point, he was captured by them" John explained

"A brave man, was he? Gaud asked "Strong like me"

"Yes, strong like you Gaud"

Malbert was travelling slowly behind them, his horse appeared to be more like a donkey, but he seemed happy to do this.

"Come on Malbert" Gaud shouted back to him

"Yes keep up, we don't want you picked off by outlaws or witches" John shouted

"I am coming, but the scenery is breathtaking don't you think?" Balian said looking around him.

"The only breathtaking thing will be you if you don't catch up" Aalef shouted

Eventually Malbert caught up with them and joined in their conversation, they talked until their throats dried and then it was time to make camp for the night.

In order to boost moral the explorers organise songs around the camp fire, they considered it better than telling spooky stories or boring the soldiers with any more tales of their own journeys exploring places of interest. Gradually the explorers singing began to sound out of tune, and they decided to retire to their tents and sleep, they soon slept leave two soldiers to guard the camp.

Meanwhile south of their camp miles away from the explorers, a witch's coven assembled consisting of seven witches namely Mirabell, Flora, Darnetta, Bittora, Zabal, Grisel and Ricolda. Zabal was the daughter of Nabara and just as cruel. Darnetta was the leader daughter of Florina, she was just as scatty as Florina but as wicked as the rest of them. The daughters seemed to be more powerful than their mothers and demonstrated their abilities by frightening villagers across the glens of Scotland. Zabal stood in front of the other witches and began addressing her audience, by shouting and stamping her feet in rage, she pointed her wand at every one of them.

"I will have vengeance on whoever killed my mother, he will pay dearly for his actions, all of you must help me find him" She insisted

"But, how will we find him, we don't even know his name?" Darnetta asked

"Yes, who is he?" Ricolda asked

"Don't be so negative, of course we will find him" Zabal shouted swinging around "Are we not witches, do we not have the power to find him"

"I was just asking" Darnetta said disgruntled

"We search through the glen in every village until we find him" Mirabell said looking at Zabal.

"Yes, and then we kill all those responsible for her death and for all our Mothers" Zabal said shaking her wand

"It will be like a resurrection of the witches" Mirabell said confidently "We stand for our Mothers all seven of us, as the eighth daughter is missing at present".

"Dear Lamia, the devils daughter" Zabal said "She will be the most powerful of all"

“Where did Lamia go?” Bittora asked

“She disappeared when her mother died” Grisel explained “I suppose she was heart broken”

“She could have been captured by the man your talking about” Bittora said in response to Grisel’s answer.

“She will return when she is ready to join us, no one will keep her for long, she was a freak remember” Zabal said brushing back her long black hair.

“Oh yes, her mother never called her by name” Grisel said “Just, the girl”

“Well, Lamia will return soon and complete our coven” Darnetta said confidently.

“We will be the most powerful witches ever” Zabal exclaimed “And then we will fight the world for supremacy”

The explorers were travelling towards the caves in the Scottish mountains, they had set camp in a forest near a mountain only a few days ride away from their destination. Gaud the biggest member of the team, made a camp fire and he was cooking meat over the flames, the smell of the food enticed all the explorers to join him. John and the soldiers were sat away from them having a discussion on the task ahead, finding Eric and taking him back to Mayor Malet.

“I fear we will be taking Eric’s body back to Mayor Malet” John said

"If he were alive, then he would have returned by now"

The soldiers nodded in agreement, each one were loyal to John as they were to his father Basil. John seemed a little uneasy and tried not to make any eye contact with the Explorers, he was told by the Mayor not to trust them and watch every move they made. So being sociable only complicated matters further, he needed to keep his distance but at the same time observe the explorers from a safe point. He was also trying to find the significance of eight in relation to the Mayor and the eight skulls of Teversham, he was aware of the reference to the bible about resurrection but there was more to this, the Mayor thought so too in connection to Magic and ultimate power. The witches knew about it and kept it a secret within the coven; they were in control of this great power and confident that it would help them to conquer the non magical element of society.

Gauds manners were much to be desired as he tore the meat from a bone with his teeth like an animal. Balian was disgusted by this and wandered off to another part of the camp, he was more interested in finding answers to the disappearance of Eric and the eight skulls of Teversham, so was Malbert who joined him, they had a conversation between the two of them. While Aalef the Jewish member of the team went to sit by Gaud and offered him refreshments.

"We need answers Gaud" Aalef said rubbing his hands by the fire

"We are in the dark in more ways than one" Gaud replied

"What do you mean?" Aalef asked stroking his beard

"I don't trust that Mayor Malet, he is sly and cunning like a fox" Gaud explained "He is definitely up to something".

"I agree" Aalef said looking around at the soldiers "Do you think they are part of it?"

"Yes, I think so" Gaud said also glancing at them.

"I will warn the others" Aalef said standing up

"Do that, they should be aware of it" Gaud agreed.

The morning began sunny and fresh, the men gathered their belongings and continued their journey through the valley, crossing streams and passing a large lake. But by the afternoon the weather changed and storm clouds followed them, like an evil sense of foreboding; it was as if someone or something was following them. The men felt as if they were being guided to the caves on the hillside. This occurred for two days, the supplies were running low and the horses were tired especially the ones pulling the wagon carrying most of the equipment they needed. It was also useful if they needed to bring back Eric's body, should they need to do so, the Mayor was insistent of them doing this in order to prove that he was dead and try to find out what happened by the condition of the body. John was convinced that Eric was alive and had got injured or something otherwise he would have rejoined his family in Teversham. He left home in order to bury the eight skulls of Teversham in the caves and has not been seen since this time, nothing seemed to make sense at this point.

The finally arrived at the foot of the mountain, two of the soldiers remained with the wagon while the rest travelled up to the cave. The storm finally began with the roar of thunder and flashes of lightening in the sky; they just reached the mouth of the cave when the rain came down heavily on the ground and surrounding trees. Three of the soldiers burnt torches and guided the explorers into a tunnel, they passed a large cavity where Eric had fallen, but they were unaware of this so they continued travelling down the tunnel into the depths of the cave. Cobwebs were all around them and the occasional spiders within the web, as they got deeper down bats were moving about startled by the men, they began to fly about. Soon they reached the bottom of the cavity and immediately noticed a solid block of what appeared to be ice, closer examination revealed the shape of a body inside it. Suddenly a flash of light occurred followed by a bang which was something powerful hitting the block, each of them were knocked to the ground and all looked up at the block as it began to melt like ice. The body was Eric, John identified him but stood his distance watching him slowly coming to life, first his chest rose and fell, and then breath came out of his mouth like smoke and his eyes began to open. It was truly amazing seeing him come to life after so long frozen in this substance, one of the explorers touched it.

"It's impossible" Aalef muttered "This stuff kept him alive" he called one of his colleagues over to him "Come Malbert; bring a vessel so that I can capture this stuff".

Malbert rushed over to him and gave him a vessel small enough to take a sample, he filled it and Malbert replaced it in to his bag. The rest of the party gasped as Eric tried to speak to them, John offered him a drink and he appeared to sip it at first and then took it from John and gulped it almost choking.

"It's almost like he was in a woman's womb, growing like a child" Aalef said astonished

"I marvel at the way he is, seeing his skin, he is so silky and his eyes are sparkling" Balian said in wonderment.

"It is like he has been resurrected or regenerated" Malbert said "I have never come across this before"

"This is some kind of magic at work" Gaud said looking at the others.

"We must not tell anyone of this" John said nervously "It is to be our secret".

"I disagree" Aalef said "So many people could benefit from our find"

"I agree with Aalef, this is worth more than gold" Malbert said excitedly.

"No, nobody should know before the Mayor is informed" John said insistently.

The explorers looked at each other and then at Eric, who was holding his head.

"God, what has happened to me" He said groaning

"What exactly did happen to you Eric?" John asked

"I was burying the skulls, and they seemed to come to life, all of them glowed and this green substance came from all the orifices" Eric explained "I was thrown across the cave by something powerful and fell down this pit".

"How on earth did you survive the fall?" Aalef asked

"And, how did you get covered in this substance?" Balian asked

"I don't know, but I am here and well" Eric said "Saved by god"

They started to make their journey out of the cave, when the ground suddenly shuck beneath them, most of the men lost their footing fell backwards and dropped down close to the edge. Balian tried to pull him back with the help of Malbert and Aalef, John appeared disappointed by the rescue, as he continued along the ridge. They soon reached the mouth of the cave, at this point they heard a groining noise followed by sheiks of laughter, this time Balian felt a blow to the head and fell into the pit. No one was able to save him from his fate, but all watched helplessly as his body fell hundreds of feet to the bottom, and then he landed onto rocks, needless to say he was dead. The rest of them left the cave and went back to the camp, the two soldiers were asleep, and John appeared angry with them and began shouting.

"Wake up, what are you doing sleeping?" John said kicking them

"I am sorry sir, but we have been awake all night" one of the soldiers said dreamily.

"Yes, we didn't sleep for fear of the witches last night" said the other soldier.

"Well, get the horses ready we are going back" John commanded

"Is that Eric?" one of them said

"Yes we found him in the cave" John said

Nobody asked anymore questions, but Gaud repaired the wagon wheel and soon afterwards became ill, it was thought it was his heart, later he died after the men had eaten supper. Malbert was found dead in his bed, it was early morning and the men were almost ready to travel, but the most mysterious death was the very next night Aalef supposedly drown near the lake. There were no witnesses and no reason why this would have happened, but it seemed strange that all the explorers who witnessed the so called resurrection died before they could talk about the experience. The soldiers were very nervous, frightened to eat or sleep in case they met the same fate, once they reached home they sighed with relief.

John and Eric went to see Mayor Malet providing him with information about Eric's supposed resurrection, the Mayor appeared to be surprised and arranged for them to join him for a meal.

"So, Eric" He began "Did you bury the eight skulls of Teversham?"

"I tried to, but as I put the skulls on the ground, some sort of powerful witchcraft occurred, they came alive" Eric explained

"Really, that's amazing, so they were powerful" the Mayor said

"I was thrown down a pit by some kind of force" Eric continued "It was as if I were fighting all the witches at once"

"I knew it" The mayor clapped his hands together "Go on, continue your tale"

"I fell down the pit, but it was as if I were travelling in slow motion, I fell to the ground but I had a soft landing and then I blacked out" Eric said "I know nothing until John and his men woke me up"

"I have a sample of the substance he was preserved in" John said showing Mayor Malet the container.

The Mayor snatched it from John and held it tightly to his chest, he seemed to act strangely as John continued to talk to him, it was if he were in a trance.

"All the explorers are dead" John announced

"So, how many people know about what we have discussed?" The Mayor asked.

"Only a few soldiers" John replied "They will remain quiet I will make certain of that"

"Make sure John" the Mayor said with a cunning look on his face.

"Eric, my friend" the Mayor said walking around the table towards his chair

Eric felt a little uneasy as the Mayor placed his hands on his shoulders and continued to speak to him.

"Eric, I need you to do a job for me" the Mayor gripped his neck at the back "I want you to find eight descendants of the witches, and kill them, I want you to bring back the skulls as before"

"Can I give it some thought?" Eric said

The Mayor tightened his grip and his breathing changed becoming more rapid

"I can't tell you how important this is, they are so powerful and I fear they will destroy all of us" He said his voice seemed to quiver as if he was afraid.

"I have no weapons powerful enough to fight them and how will I find them?"

The Mayor released his grip and walked over to a cupboard in the corner of the room; he took a key from his belt and opened the door. Inside was a sword and shield, he took them both out and placed them on the table, and then he pointed to the shield in the centre of it there was a cluster of jewels, he held it up to the light and ensured they shone.

"This shield is the way you will find them, the light will shine in the direction of a witch and they will turn green" He explained "The sword will also glow at the presence of a witch" he seemed pleased with himself "The weapons will also defend you against the witches magic".

"Are you sure of this?" Eric asked concerned

"Yes, I am sure, they fear the shield and the sword" The Mayor said confidently.

"Then I will do it" Eric agreed.

"Good I will reward you" the Mayor said rubbing his hands again.

"When do I go?" Eric asked

"In a few days" he replied feeling more at ease.

Eric left the room with the shield and sword and headed to the stables to join his horse Alestra, while John remained with the Mayor.

"I want you to send the soldiers who went to the cave, they can accompany Eric on this Journey" the Mayor said smirking "They will meet their fate there as for Eric" The Mayor paused "I have further plans for him"

"Is it true about the sword and shield protecting him?" John asked

"No, of course not, but he will think so" he replied "He just needs confidence enough to fight them, but the shield will find them".

"You mean find the witches?" John asked

"The witches will find Eric, the shield will lead them to him" the Mayor said looking out of the window "I will take their power from them and become a powerful wizard myself, immortal and powerful".

EIGHT SKULLS OF TEVERSHAM –

CHAPTER FIVE

CONDEMNATION

It was a sunny morning and a pleasant ride for Eric and the soldiers, riding through the glens of Scotland with the hills and mountains forming a picturesque back drop and contrasting with the green valley and flowing stream.

"This is what I call a magnificent country" Eric said to his horse Alestra "We are indeed fortunate enough to be part of this land, enjoying its scenery".

One of the soldiers looked across at him and then at the other soldiers

"Are you well Eric?" he asked

"That I am Hedrick, I am merely sharing my experience with my trusty companion Alestra" Eric said patting his horse "She has been loyal to me even found her way home when I was stuck in that cave".

"Yes, that was unbelievable, such a distance" Hedrick agreed

"I was gone for a while wasn't I Hedrick?" Eric asked

"Yes you were and John was concerned about you" Hedrick explained "He spoke of you often and feared the worst"

"I really can't explain what happened, I was burying the skulls and I suddenly experienced something pushing me, the skulls were alive and a dark green slime was coming out of their mouth and eyes, the force was so great it threw me down a pit. I travelled down and down, I seemed to go fast and then slowly until I landed in some kind of substance and that's all I remember" Eric said

"It must have been frightening" Hedrick said bowing his head "I remember you recovering and that ice that contained you"

"It was strange, I was scared but then I felt a sense of security as if I was being helped, rather than attacked". Eric explained

"Perhaps a guardian angel was watching over you that day" Hedrick commented

"Perhaps that was so, I have had the feeling that someone has been following me for some time, I speak of many years ago to the present" Eric said looking behind him.

"Is this how you feel now, do we have company?" Hedrick asked concerned

"I do feel a presence, but I can't say what" Eric said shivering.

Eric led the soldiers into the mountains, leaving the valley behind them, they had been riding days before the shield began to glow brightly, it was dusk and darkness was soon upon them, the moon was full and the sound of wolves howling disturbed the horses.

"Witches are present men, be on your guard" Eric said tapping his horse "There Alestra be brave"

No sooner had Eric said these words Ricolda suddenly appeared on her broom flying around their heads, she produced a tornado effect and caused all the soldiers to fall to the ground, the horses all reared up and almost trampled on the soldiers. Eric held his sword and shield tightly and awaited the imminent attack, as Ricolda began throwing fire balls in their direction, the shields proved useless as a defence as did Eric's so called enchanted shield. Ricolda was relentless in her attack upon the helpless soldiers, she dodged the arrows from their cross bows and swooped down like an Eagle after its prey. Soon she had slaughtered all but Eric, who stood alone even his sword was useless. He was thrown to the ground by the force of Ricolda's wand as the power from it blasted him pressing on his chest, she was teasing him and decided to cast a spell that brought about bind weed, which twisted and curled around his arms and legs.

"Not this again" He said as the weed began to loop around his neck and strangled him.

Eric thought he was going to die as the weed tightened up and he became breathless and the colour drained from his face, his whole body was going numb and he felt limp. Grisel had joined Ricolda and assisted in killing the soldiers, she was busy sending electric missiles into the bodies of the soldiers making sure that they were dead, Ricolda flew over to Grisel in order to tell her about Eric.

"Come and see what I have done to Eric" Ricolda said boasting.

"These soldiers are all dead" Grisel said firing a last electric charge at Hedrick.

But when they returned to Eric, he was gone and the entire bind weed was cut, with some areas burnt.

"Impossible, he's gone" Ricolda said astonished

"But how did he escape?" Grisel asked

"Someone has helped him" Ricolda said looking around

"But who, all the soldiers are dead?"

Eric found himself laying on the ground, his eyes were blurred and all he could make out was tall trees silhouetted against a bright sky, he must have passed out. It was now morning, he was surrounded by bushes and when his eyes began to focus he saw Alestra just outside of the bushes. Eric was shocked and bewildered finding himself in this place, after having a near death experience with bind weed, a lucky escape or was he helped by someone. Eric was upset by the fact that the Mayor had lied to him about the sword and shield, they were not enchanted at all, and he began to feel vulnerable and alone. He remembered the things that Basil taught him about self defence and keeping his mind focused at all times. He also reflected on Basil's death at the hands of Nabara, the evil witch that tortured him and the witch responsible for killing Rosa his youngest sister.

Eric walked up to his horse and stroked her mane and began whispering to her.

"We have an impossible journey to make my friend and we could well die"

Eric put his sword away and secured his shield to his horse, before riding on the road again, further into the hills through trees and shrub land. He had been riding for a few hours when he suddenly stopped and looked around him, he could sense the presence of someone behind him as he had done many times before. But as usual no one was there; this led him to believe that he had got some kind of guardian angel watching over him. He had believed that he was going mad due to all the things he had experienced, hallucinating or experiencing a form of paranoia as we would say today. Eric decided to rest for a while, he secured his horse to a tree and settled down on the ground curled up in his warm blanket, as he began to fall asleep, the shield began to glow and Ricolda returned. This time she was alone, as she crept up to him and held the wand in front of her.

"You won't escape this time Eric, time to die" she said holding the wand up in an effort to destroy him with magic.

Suddenly an arrow shot towards her and penetrated her throat, she held it and fell crashing to the ground, dropping her wand beside her, and lying lifeless in a grassy area beside Eric. Eric slept through this and eventually awoke to see her lying face down with her eyes wide open. The arrow indicated that the person who had been following him could be a soldier or someone human as apposed to something spiritual. He decapitated Ricolda and put her head in a sack, constantly looking around him for his stalker or protector.

"Someone is with us Alestra I can feel the presence of someone" Eric said to his horse.

Eric was travelling along a dirt track when he noticed the shape of someone lying on the ground, so he dismounted his horse and walked towards the person cautiously in case it was a trap, he carried his sword holding it firmly in his right hand. As he got closer he noticed the curvy shape of a female, and her long black hair, she was wearing leather trousers and a type armour across her abdomen. As he turned her over, he noticed that she was battered and bruised with scratches on her cheeks, but she was breathing. He went back to Alestra to fetch a flask of water, and then returned to her, brushing her hair away from her face and dropping tiny amounts of water onto her lips. She began to move her mouth and Eric gave her a drink.

She opened her eyes and was startled, her body jumped, Eric was amazed at how beautiful she was, despite her wounds and the dirt on her face. He thought she looked familiar at first, she reminded him of someone, but then she appeared different as she looked into his eyes.

“Thank you” She said “I am Annabelle, but you can call me Anna”

“I am Fredrick, but most people call me Eric” He replied nervously

“I bet I am a mess” She said

“No, not really” He hesitated “What happened to you?”

“I was robbed and beaten by outlaws” she replied “But not raped” she swiftly added.

“I am glad, I mean that you were not raped” Eric felt awkward as he had little experience with women.

“Are you able to ride?” he asked

“I think so although I ache so much” she explained still gazing into his eyes

“Then you can ride on Alestra my horse” he offered

“Alestra what a beautiful name fro a beautiful horse” she commented

“The best” he agreed “Let me help you up” he said assisting her to mount the horse.

“Thank you Eric” she said smiling

“Where are you heading for Eric?” she asked

"I am seeking ancestors of witches who killed my family" he said grabbing the reins and walking beside Alestra

"Witches?" she asked

"Evil creatures, who torture, curse and kill people" he said

"They must be wicked" she said with empathy "Treating people like that"

"I escaped from the witches who killed my parents" he said sadly

"Lucky you, but unlucky them, I am sorry" she looked at him sympathetically.

"I was given a shield and sword, and they are supposed to be enchanted" he hesitated waiting for a response "But they don't work".

"Really" she said negatively

"The shield is supposed to detect witches by lighting up from the green emerald" he pointed to the shield "But nothing, see it is lit up now and no witches in sight"

"Perhaps you need to have faith in magic" she said lightly

"I have no time for magic, it is meaningless to me" he shrugged "Besides magic was supposed to have killed my family"

"It is said that you can only fight magic with magic" she quoted

“I wish I could believe that” he said dismissively.

“And may I ask what of your life?” Eric asked Annabella

“My life?” she seemed on the defensive

“I am from a humble family, nothing special, I fought to defend my cause and believed in self preservation, I get what I want with my own power of persuasion” Annabella seemed very coy in her responses toward Eric.

Eric admired her radiant smile that lit up her face and illuminated her pale complexion, and her eyes had the power of enchanting him, so much so that he felt magnetised to her.

After a few hours travelling they stopped and rested, Eric took the shield from his horse and threw it onto the ground, and then he helped Annabella to dismount.

“That’s no way to treat a shield” she said with disgust

“It is useless, see how it still shines and no sign of witches” He said angrily

“I told you have faith” she said

“I might as well not have it, it’s useless” he said disappointedly

“No, don’t do that” she shouted

Eric looked shocked at her reaction and went back to Alestra for the sword

"Put the sword next to the shield and see what happens" she said

"Nothing will work" he insisted

"Do it" she said stamping her feet

Eric was reluctant at first, but eventually he did what she asked and placed the sword right next to the shield, the shield became brighter and before long an image appeared, it was the remaining witches, all but Lamia who was a silhouette in the background. They were all sat around a caldron, a witches coven discussing non other than Eric, who was watching them in disbelief.

"We must split up and search for Eric in order to find him" Mirabell said

"He should be dead by now" Zabal said angrily

"He is being protected" Darnetta said huffing

"Who is protecting her?" Zabal asked spraying saliva as she spoke.

"Some kind of sorcery if you ask me" Bittora said

"Can't you feel the magic Zabal?" Grisel said looking at her "It is all around you William Malet is behind this I swear".

"I feel it breath it, smell it" Bittora said "And so does Grisel"

"That's you Grisel, the smell" Zabal said nastily.

"Let's not argue amongst ourselves" Flora said "It's Eric that we are after"

"Yes, lets find Eric and end this nonsense" Mirabell insisted.

Eric looked at Annabella and kissed her on the cheek, showing his gratitude

"You are a genius, it worked" he said excitedly

Annabella stood shocked at his reaction

"Oh I am sorry" he said realising what he had done "I got lost in the moment, I didn't mean to, you know, kiss you" Eric was embarrassed

"Kiss me" she repeated

"Yes sorry" he repeated

Annabella turned her head away and touched her lips, then smiled, while Eric was trying to change the subject, finding a way out of the situation.

"We should camp here Annabella" He finally said

"As you wish" she replied still surprised at his reaction

The rested in an enclosed area of the woods, Eric suggested that they stay close to each other in case they are attacked

"I trust you will protect me from your witches" she said

"Indeed I will" he replied

Eric had found a comfortable spot and laid a blanket down one under them and one on top, they lay beside one another looking up at the sky. Eric had his sword and shield beside him, Annabella had her eyes open and began to yawn, she gave a cough placing her hand over her mouth.

"Isn't it beautiful" she said

"The sky?" he replied

"The moonlight sky" she said pointing "I love the night"

"I always think of bad things at night" he said despondently

"The night is wonderful, peaceful and perhaps tranquil" she said sighing

"Goodnight Anna" he said finishing the conversation.

"Goodnight Eric" she replied disappointedly.

Eric stayed awake for a while wondering about Annabella as she didn't exactly divulge any real information about herself, perhaps she had run away from home or maybe she was from a group of travellers or gypsies. But then they had just met and no one give information to perfect strangers, for who can truly be trusted in a place like this. They slept for hours and in the course of the night Annabella had cuddled up to

Eric as if he were a large warm friendly bear. She had her arm across his body and her leg across his; she was so close that he could feel her warm breath on his neck. However once she realised what she had done she moved away from him and gave him some distance, he was surprised by her actions, but remained silent. They still had miles to go in order to reach the mountains, the roughest part of the journey was ahead of them, and the weather was changing, becoming colder. Grisel was ahead of them setting up a trap for Eric, using her wits to arrange his demise. Eric was crossing a wooden bridge high up in the air, across two mountains in order to find out where they were and plan the next route. Grisel had loosened the ropes and weakened the bridge ready for him to cross, all he had to do was walk across it and when he reached the middle it would give way causing him to fall down into the valley onto the rocks below. Annabella had stayed with Alestra while Erica started to work his way across the bridge, Grisel watched as he stepped across carefully until he reached the middle. Suddenly Eric heard something snap and the bridge collapsed sending him down, he was falling, his body was spinning in the air, but then he stopped as if he was floating on air, he landed on a ledge and seemed motionless for a while. Annabella reached down and touched him, she grabbed his shirt and began pulling him up, he pushed his feet against a rock and sprang up onto solid ground. Grisel raced forward on her broom and tried to pull Eric backwards off the ledge, Annabella grabbed the sword and began poking her, eventually Grisel let go of Eric and Annabella stabbed her in the stomach, she fell onto the ground holding her stomach, the sword lit up and sliced Grisel in half, Eric took the sword from Annabella and chopped off Grisel's head.

They continued their journey, it was now getting very cold and it was harder to travel, through the snow, they had been a long way and the months had passed.

"Two witches are dead and six are left" Eric said calculating on his fingers.

"Well done to you Eric" she said sarcastically "Six more witches"

"Are you alright?" he asked

"Frankly, no" she said grumpily "I am tired, sick of this cold weather"

"We need to find shelter" he said concerned for Annabella and Alestra

But this time Bittora was searching for them, she was known as the wolf or the hunter, she could transform herself into wild beasts of any description. Eric went hunting for food for Annabella and himself, he took his cross bow and shield for protection. Annabella was asked to stay with Alestra and watch for witches coming in their direction. Eric crept through the woods when he caught sight of a deer; he aimed his cross bow, and steadied his arm until he was ready to fire. Bittora seized her opportunity and pounced on Eric in the form of a wolf, she began clawing at him and then bit his shoulder, Eric hit her in the face with the cross bow and stunned her, but she came back at him biting him in his side.

Eric continued to fight and then passed out, he was losing blood and too weak to fight, Bittora had her chance to kill him at this time. Annabella was present at this time, she attacked the beast with Eric's sword, she swung the sword and chopped the beast to pieces, she lay in her own blood and as Bittora transformed she chopped her head clean off.

Annabella managed to get Eric to respond enough to put him on the horse and lead him to a cave, when they arrived she helped him into the cave and lay him down. Once he was comfortable she made a fire and collected water in a bucket, she used all the items that she had such as rags and blankets as well as food and water. She began to cleanse his wounds and had to stitch his open wounds with thread that soldiers kept in their bags; she used an ointment from her own bag and then made some soup, hoping that he would wake to eat it. She used herbs and potions to help heal his wounds and control his fever; it took days for Eric to respond to his treatment, Annabella had hardly slept caring for him.

"Please don't die on me Eric" She said mopping his brow "I can't live without you, you have become my life, you must know this" became tearful thinking that he would die. Eric was actually sick for months, he was reflecting back in his mind and dreamt about riding his first horse and then remembered Alestra,

He thought back to his family and his youngest sister Rosa remained his, he remembered taking out with him and playing with carved figures. He woke up long enough to eat and drink, Annabella held up a flask and gave him some water, at that point he thought of the girl with no name who helped him in the cave healing his wounds and giving him water like Annabella, but she was Albelenda's daughter Lamia meaning devil child. Annabella was so much like her in her ways, but she was so different in appearance, they were both beautiful but her features were different. It made Eric feel good being nursed by Annabella; she even sang to him sounding like an angel with her soft silky voice, it was just like a lullaby keeping him calm and relaxed.

As Eric began to improve he felt as if he were falling in love with her, he hardly knew her, but he was felt as if he had known her forever.

Annabella decided to discuss her childhood and spoke of the cruelty that she faced, the worst child abuse known to mankind.

"I was treated badly as a child; my mother abused me in indescribable ways, not just by beating me and kicking me down the stairs, but locking me in a cellar. She hated me and called me names and when I refused to do her bidding she would burn me with hot sticks. I was treated worse than an animal scavenging for scraps of food, her friends were the same and so I ran away from home when I was old enough and fended for myself, it was hard at first but I did it. All I wanted to be was loved and treated as a normal child, not follow in her madness" Annabella looked at Eric for his reaction.

Eric gazed in her eyes and acknowledged her with a nod and a smile

She smiled back "But I have spoken too much and tired you with my chat and you have a long way to go in order to search for the witches".

"My dear Annabella" Eric began to speak

"Anna" She interrupted him by correcting him; Annabella is too much to say

"Anna, I am so grateful to you" he said

Annabella lowered her head and tears began to flow down her cheeks,

"My word Anna why do you cry?" he asked

"No one has spoken to me as nicely as you do, you are so kind and gentle" she said sincerely

"I treat you as I do anyone I care about, I care and I show it" he said

Eric put his fingers under her chin and gently lift her head until her eyes looked into his, they gazed into each others eyes.

"You are the most beautiful woman I have ever met" he said wiping away her tears with his fingers.

"Your lips are generous and your eyes are alive, sparkling by the light of the fire, your skin is so soft to the touch" Eric was aroused by the warmth she sent out to him.

"You are handsome and strong, the bravest man alive" she said in response to his words "I feel safe in your presence"

Eric kissed her on the left cheek, but Annabella wasn't going to let him get away with this a second time, as she kissed him tenderly on the lips, a lingering kiss which took his breath away. They embraced and Eric was able to feel her heart beating fast, she felt so warm and tender, her body smelt fresh like fragrant flowers. Eric was already half naked and so Annabella removed her top, revealing her shapely breasts, her nipples were hard and prominent. He watched her chest rising and her breathing became rapid as she became more excited. Her fondled her with gentle hands and they kissed once more, Annabella removed the rest of her garments and Eric did the same, they both went under the blanket and proceeded to make love, starting with a gentle rocking and synchronizing their rhythm. They became more vigorous and passionate rising to great heights, their body heat could have melted all the snow in Scotland, they made love for hours and then their bodies entwined as they hugged and relaxed together.

"I love you so much" Annabella said

"I love you too Anna" he replied

"I am so happy" Annabella said smiling "I don't want this time to end" she said kissing his chest

"Me too" Eric said kissing her on the forehead

"I can never live without you Eric" she admitted

“I feel the same Anna” he said.

Another day passed as they continued to make love and it was almost as if Eric had forgotten about the witches and Eric’s sworn duty as a soldier to kill the these witches, and take their skulls back to Mayor Malet at Teversham. The Mayor must have been anxious waiting for his trophies and to boast about his efforts to kill the witches taking all the glory. But the Mayor also wanted answers to the figure of eight and the resurrection process, Eric knew in his heart that he needed to continue his quest.

“We must go” Eric said anxiously

“Must we, can’t we stay forever, just you and me” she begged him “Why spoil our happiness for your stupid quest”.

“Anna I must forfill my quest and then we can live in happiness, I promise” he explained.

“But we are happy now and what will it achieve killing witches?” she replied

“They are after me and I can’t exactly hide from them, I must face them and only then can I live in happiness” Eric said trying to get up.

Eric gathered his strength and got dressed ready to face the witches, he was fully aware that he would meet another witch soon and he was not disappointed. He had just made his way out of the cave, joined by Annabella they prepared the horse and began walking down the snowy mountain.

Flora was waiting for them a few yards ahead, above them, she pointed her wand towards the rocks above and blasted a rock causing an avalanche. The snow descended swiftly Eric was in front of Annabella, she noticed it falling and turned to Eric in order to warn him.

"Look out Eric" she shouted

But she was too late the snow was almost on top of him, just then a light shone and a strange canopy formed over them like a giant igloo or transparent ball. Eric touched it and it vanished along with the snow that had covered it. Disappointed that her trap had failed Flora made another attack on Eric this time trapping him in a block of ice, another flash occurred and the ice melted.

Eric recovered and rushed towards Flora who appeared to be dazed, but she waved her wand at him, Eric raised his shield, deflecting a fiery missile omitted from her wand, she fell from her broom into the snow. Eric raced forward and noticed that she was on fire, he raised his sword and cut off her head.

"The shield actually worked" Eric said delighted

"That's good" Annabella said impressed with his performance

"Only four witches left now" he calculated

Annabella appeared to be unhappy about the remaining witches, she was quiet for a while as they entered the forest, they had both experienced so much together in a short space of time. The rest of the day was peaceful and they were able to enjoy each others company, they walked together most of the way holding hands and kissing, having a discussion about the beautiful scenery around them. Scotland was so different to England, not merely for it's landscape, but the mysterious legends that made the place unique, with its lakes and hills, valleys and castles in the mountains and by the sea. It was a place where the Druids lived and practiced their religion, where the brave Scottish tribes fought for land and where witches hid from others who threatened their existence.

It was night time and the sound of wild life was present, owls and other night creatures came out, this also brought about the wrath of Darnetta, she made her presence known by swooping down upon Eric and Annabella, throwing fireballs in their direction, Eric held his shield in front of them and the fire bounced off both the shield and surrounding trees. She attacked a few times and then stayed in mid air sat on her broom and cursing Eric, spitting as she spoke.

"Foolish man do you think that you can escape my wrath, I will show you my fury and burn you to death" she threatened

She made another attack, but this time Annabella fired the cross bow hitting her leg, she spun to the ground hitting a tree as she fell, her eyes gazing at Annabella.

"I know you" she said but before she could say any more Annabella sent an arrow into her throat.

"Kill her" Annabella shouted

“I think you have done it already” he replied

“I mean cut off her head” she said eagerly

Eric grabbed his sword and cut off her head with one blow, Annabella sighed with relief “I thought she had cast a spell on you”

“She did try to control me” he admitted “Did she recognise you?”

“No, why would she?” Annabella asked

“I thought she knew you” he said puzzled

“Well, she didn’t okay” She said sharply

“Are you angry with me?” he asked

“Never, ever look a witch in the eyes” she advised him.

They travelled towards the cave where Eric was once captured, Eric felt uneasy as he approached a nearby wood.

“I need to rest” Annabella said holding her head

“I agree, we need to rest” Eric said leading Alestra to a tree and securing the reigns.

They made camp and prepared food, but Annabella hardly ate, she appeared unwell and her thoughts seemed distant, she removed the blanket from the back of the horse and lay it down. They snuggle up close in the blanket and began to kiss, but Annabella turned her head away from him, she seemed sad and tearful.

"What's wrong?" he asked

"Sorry, it's nothing" she replied

She gazed up at the stars and soon drifted off to sleep, Eric stayed awake for a while concerned about Annabella, he tried to analyse her behaviour, by piecing together the day's events, but nothing was obvious. She was a mystery at times and not the type of person to discuss all her feelings, at least that's what he thought. He found it difficult being in a relationship and he was always told that women are such complex creatures, very hormonal as we say today.

Later that night the silence was disturbed by Mirabell as she searched for Eric swooping down searching for his camp, she was looking for the camp fire that would indicate someone was in the area and that person could be Eric. She noticed both Annabella and Eric lying on the floor and sent a bolt of lightening from her wand down at them. It managed to strike Annabella who reacted by yelling, she was injured, Eric was trying to put out the fire that was caused by the lightening. While Annabella brushed away the scorched in her shirt, Eric ran to collect his sword and shield, Mirabell sent more lightening towards him but he managed to dodge them. He held his sword up ready for her next attack, suddenly the sword lit up and a bolt of lightening seemed to come from it and hit Mirabell knocking her to the ground, her broom landed by Annabella's feet. Eric raced forward with his sword and shield in hand Mirabell pointed her wand and sent a fireball at Eric, it deflected off the shield and he was close enough to cut her down with his sword. Eric cut off her head, he dropped his shield and sword and then ran towards Annabella, he knelt down and opened her shirt.

"I thought you were wounded?" He asked trying to find the burn.

"It was nothing" she replied

Eric watched his shield light up and an image appeared, it was Zabal sitting in a cave, Eric recognised the markings on the cave wall drawn by Lamia, Zabal was sat by a fire.

"I know that place" he said "That's the cave where the girl lived"

Eric knew that he was to face the most evil of witches and at a place she knew well, he was prepared to face her knowing he was at the end of his quest, with only two more witches to find. He knew the eighth witch would be the most powerful and challenging. They packed everything in order to return to the cave where he had been captured and tortured, it was only a short ride away.

When they arrived near the cave Eric looked at Annabella and offered her the reigns to the horse.

"Take care of Alestra I will find Zabal" he said "I don't want you to be in danger"

"I can handle danger, just because I am a woman" she said

"My love I know you have been through so much, but I don't want you to see Zabal" he explained

"But she will kill you" she said concerned

"But I have my sword and shield" he replied

"But they won't protect you against her" she said

"Trust me, I will defeat her" he said kissing her on the lips.

Annabella whispered in his right ear, which puzzled him.

"They get inside your head" she said

Eric walked away and never looked back, her words stayed with him and seemed to echoed on his mind as he entered the mouth of the cave, he could hear her voice repeatedly, ***they get into your head.***

Eric walked down the darkest part of the tunnel and suddenly came face to face with Annabella.

"I thought you were staying with Alestra?" he asked disappointed

"But I wanted to be with you" she said kissing him on the lips

"But you agreed to stay away and whispered in my ear, saying they get inside your head" he quoted "What did you mean?"

Annabella looked strangely at Eric and then smiled "Who is Annabella?" she said laughing and watching his lips turn blue.

Eric looked in horror as Annabella turned into Zabal "We do get into your head" by the time Eric had recovered Zabal was a few yards away from him

"Curse you Eric for killing my mother, you will suffer for that" she said sending electric charges towards him. Some hit his shield, others hit the cave walls, but some hit him. Eventually he fell backwards and hit his head on the wall, and knocked himself out, Zabal flew towards him and took his shield throwing it down the pit.

"Now you will die" she said aiming her wand towards his head

"No, he won't die, you will not kill Eric" Annabella said

"Lamia, so you did survive" Zabal said "the freak child, what happened to your face?"

"I changed it so that Eric would not recognise me" she said

"So are you going to slap me or are you stronger than you look" Zabal mocked her

"I have the strength to defeat you Zabal" she replied confidently "I shall end your cruelty"

"Who are you?" Zabal asked

"You know who I am, you have said it, I am Lamia the devil child" Annabella said

"You are a freak traitor of witches, you have killed your own kind" Zabal said angrily

"There are good witches you know and we care for people, we live for the good of mankind" Annabella said checking that Eric was breathing "I was called Lamia by my mother Albelenda, but I changed my name to Annabella along with my life"

"You are a witch" Zabal shouted

"I am my own person and a white witch" she replied

Zabal sent a bolt of lightening at Annabella, she dodged it and returned a flash of lightening from Eric's sword, sending Zabal flying across the cave. Annabella was younger and faster and continued to move around the cave as fast as lightening, dodging every missile that Zabal hurled at her. Zabal transformed herself into a wolf and Annabella did the same, they fought wildly scratching and biting, and then Zabal became a snake. Annabella set fire to the snake and tossed it down the pit, she was just about to help Eric when Zabal appeared by his side holding a dagger to his throat, laughing as she press the blade against his flesh.

"Surrender Lamia or watch Eric die" Zabal threatened

"I surrender Zabal, please don't kill him" she pleaded

“Guess what Lamia, I still want to kill him” Zabal said making his neck bleed

“You right Zabal, how silly of me I have been” Annabella said “I thought I loved him, but guess what, I don’t”

“What?” Zabal asked confused

“Kill him” she said watching the expression on Zabal’s face.

Zabal released Eric from her clutches and he fell to the ground,

“We could be powerful together” Zabal said “Rule the world”

“Yes, we could” Annabella said “If I let you live”

“What do you mean?” Zabal asked confused

Annabella produced a cross bow from behind her back and for a arrow into her forehead, she looked shocked at Annabella and fell to the ground, Annabella picked up the sword and chopped off her head.

She knelt over Eric and shook him by the shoulder, she began to open his eyes, and she decided to sit beside him for a while. She felt sleepy and closed her eyes for a while, but as she drifted off Eric awoke.

“Annabelle, wake up” he shouted

“We need to clean these skulls and take them to Teversham” Annabelle said

"Wait, there is one more witch to find" Eric remembered.

"Then we must clean the skulls we have and then bathe in the lake, and then consider about the last witch" she suggested.

They travelled down to the lake and both stripped naked and swam in the lake for a while, afterwards they lay naked on the bank and made love. For a while they had forgotten about Eric's quest and lived for the moment, relaxed in each others arms admiring the view. Eric noticed the shield was glowing and stood up quickly, looking around him, he became very anxious and searched for his sword.

"Anna, a witch is approaching, where is my sword"

Eric felt the cold steel of a blade touching his throat, it was his sword which Annabella had taken and held it to his neck, it shone under the sunlight.

"You know who I am, don't you Eric?" Annabella asked

"Oh god" he muttered

"I am Lamia, the girl who supposedly had no name" she said "I changed my name as I also changed my appearance, now I have to kill you"

"But you love me" he said confused "Don't you?"

"Yes" she said hesitating "But you would kill me, I am the eighth witch"

“I am so mixed up in my head” he said in despair

“We mess with your head” she said “I don’t want to kill you”

“I am your stalker, the one who followed you and protected you, ever since you were with me in that cave years ago, I loved you then and ever since. I deliberately messed myself up and lay near the road, every time you thought a guardian angel was with you, that was me, I have saved your life countless times. I used magic each time, I broke your fall down that pit and preserved your body, I revived you, resurrected you and returned your horse to Teversham. It was all me and no one else, I stopped you falling from that bridge and nursed your wounds, I brought you back from the dead using herbs and potions which are in my bag, I did all this because I love you”.

“I suppose that means something” he said

“God” she shouted “I can’t kill you” she said giving him the sword “You will have to kill me”

Eric cast the sword into the lake and held her firmly in his arms “My god Anna, so god help me I love you and I will never hurt you”

“So, what now?” she asked

“We find another skull” he said “So how did you change your face?”

"By Magic" she said "Pure and simple, I cast a spell on you when you turned me over on the ground, I wasn't really attacked and robbed, I played with your memories too".

"We could take one of the original skulls" Eric said "No one will know"

"Let me go and get one" She insisted "I can control the magic"

Annabella returned to the cave and dug up one of the skulls, it was her mothers damaged skull, fractured by Basil hitting it with a rock, she put it in a brown sack and raced back to join Eric. They took time to travel back to Teversham as Annabella didn't feel well, she soon discovered that she was with child (Pregnant) and judging from their time together, she could have conceived just after Eric had recovered from the fever a few months ago. When they finally did return the Mayor was eager to see them, he was alerted as soon as they arrived, and ordered their presence. They entered his office wary of his devious ways, expecting him to ask a lot of questions, using subtle means of interrogation I order to get answers about the resurrection and solutions to the figure of eight.

"Sit down Eric and friend" He said "And who is she?" he asked rudely.

"This is Annabella" Eric replied "My friend, lover and companion"

"And what of the skulls?" he asked

“All present” Eric said offering him the sack containing eight skulls

“Perfect” the Mayor said rubbing his hand together.

“What now?” Eric asked

“I want you to take these to the cave and bury them along with the others” The Mayor insisted

“But, don’t you want to display them?” Eric asked

“No, the town folk would not approve, they don’t want the witches magic here in Teversham, causing miscarriages and the pox amongst other things”.

“I understand” Eric said glancing at Annabella.

“You have done well Eric and you shall be rewarded by myself”

Eric attempted to pick up the sack containing the skulls, but the Mayor clung hold of it. “I will get John to bring these to you when you are ready to depart”.

Eric stood up and Annabella followed him to the door, the Mayor looked at her disapprovingly before she left.

John entered the room through another door and sat himself down, the Mayor was looking out of the window at Eric and Annabella crossing the street.

"I seem to know that woman from somewhere, who is she?" he asked

"She is his woman and she with child" John said

"His child I presume?" the Mayor asked

"Yes, of his making" John replied

The Mayor laid the skulls across the table in a neat line, and checked each one in turn, and then he grabbed one of them and held it up.

"Eight skulls and how many did I ask for John?" he asked

"Eight" John said puzzled by his question

"Then why has he brought me seven?" the Mayor asked walking towards John

"Seven?" John asked nervously.

"He has brought back one of the original skulls" He said angrily

"How do you know" John asked

The Mayor shoved the skull in front of his face "Remember this one?" he pointed to the crack in the side of the skull near the eye socket "Cracked, this is Albelenda's skull"

"Yes, I remember us examining it" John remembered the day they looked at it.

"So, that leads me to wonder why Eric brought this one back" he paused "And where is the eighth descendant, the missing witch".

"Perhaps they didn't find the eighth witch" John suggested.

"Or perhaps he did" The Mayor said pondering returning back to the window

"But I need eight for completion"

"Wait, are you suggesting that Annabella is the eighth witch?" John said

"Can you think of any other answer?" The Mayor said disgruntled

"Shall I send for them" John asked eagerly

"No, I have another plan" The Mayor said "I will follow them to the cave and then we will take care of them there"

"You mean kill Eric?" John said concerned "He is like my brother I can't do this"

"My dear John, we kill the witch and maybe the spell will be broken and Eric will be himself again" the Mayor smiled wickedly.

CHAPTER SIX

ALL FOR LOVE

Eric was in the stables with Annabella and his trusty horse Alestra, he was preparing for his next quest to bury the skulls in the cave of witches. One of Eric's friends gave Annabella a horse for the journey and supplies for the journey. John entered the stable and showed Eric the sack of skulls, Eric took them off him, John had a strange look in his eyes.

"Here are the skulls that you gave the Mayor" He said

"Thank you John" Eric said noticing the concern on his face

"Is something troubling you John?" Eric asked

"No not really" John said looking at Annabella

"I do worry about you John" Eric said "Watch out for the Mayor he is not to be trusted"

"I will watch for him" John said wanting to say something about Annabella.

“Safe journey” John said hugging Eric.

John left the stable and Eric walked over to his horse Alestra, he stroked her mane and spoke to her.

“My faithful Alestra, brave and loyal, we have been to many places together, shared adventures and experiences” he said

He checked Annabella was well and packed for the journey; he helped her saddle the horse and check supplies.

“We need to make sure that we have everything Anna” he said

“Including the skulls” She replied

Annabella and Eric set off on their quest to bury the skulls in the caves of Scotland and with it their past, pain and misery that darkened both their lives.

They had been riding for some considerable time before Annabella complained about feeling sick and tired, she looked pale and her mouth was dry with chapped lips. It was as if her body was fighting against the child within, perhaps it was part of her mother’s evil inside her, and her goodness was trying to reject it, like an alien being. She began to projectile vomit, clearing her body of the badness within, as she thought as she stepped from the horse and continued being sick in the nearby bushes. After a while she remounted her horse took a drink from her flask and wiped her mouth, she nodded at Eric and smiled.

“Are you able to carry on Anna?” he asked

"Yes, I think so" she replied "What was the Mayors name?"

"William Malet" he replied "Why do you ask?"

"He was known to us, an evil man, cunning and ruthless, please don't trust him" she said looking at Eric "He wants to be a powerful warlock"

"He is a witch?" Eric said "I thought he was involved in the occult somehow"

"He has limited abilities and wants to process the power of the witches and the secret of the resurrection" she said "And regeneration"

"So, that's why he wanted to kill the witches"

"Yes, He wanted the witches killed all of them including me" she explained

"So, that's his game, what about the significance of eight and his obsession for that number?" Eric asked

"According to the bible and other old documents eight represents the resurrection, but it is all about regeneration and rejuvenation an art which my family perfected. The potion is active in the cave, I used it to bring you back, it can be found in a green vessel, inside a wooden box. I restarted your heart with a bolt of lightening from my wand, and the fluid that you were preserved in kept you young".

"I feel as if you have told me everything, but I feel as if I still know nothing" he confessed

"If the time comes you will remember and you will act accordingly" she reassured him.

The next morning, the mayor ordered the soldiers to mount their horses ready to ride, they were given instructions to kill Annabella the witch and arrest Eric, the Mayors instructions were very explicit, to kill her in the same way as the other witches were killed by beheading her. It was his way of killing their magic and making himself seem powerful and popular with the people although he hated them.

Eric and Annabella entered the forest, they both dismounted in an area sheltered by trees with long branches and many leaves decorating each branch with various shades of green. It so secluded and so far away from the problems associated with Teversham.

"We are close now Anna" Eric reassured her "We just need to bury the skulls and then we are free to live are lives as we desire"

"Not exactly" Annabella said lowering her head

"What do you mean?" Eric asked

"The skull I picked up was damaged" she said

"But that belonged to your mother, she was hit on the head with a rock" he explained

"I know I saw her die" she paused then continued "She was evil and needed to die"

"Why would you give him that skull?" he asked

"So that he would follow us to the cave and then I could rid Teversham of him" she said clenching her fists in rage "He has to be destroyed along with his evil".

"Anna do you realise what you have done?" he said angrily.

"Yes, he will realise that he will never be immortal or powerful as he desires, William Malet the great warlock" Annabella said with relief

"In that case we need to get to the cave quickly" Eric said anxiously

"I love you Eric" she said hugging him and kissing him on the lips

Eric looked at her puzzled "I love you too Anna" he said returning a kiss

At that moment Eric's eyes widened as he felt a gush of air pass his left side and Annabella gave a heavy sigh and fell to the ground, Eric knelt down and noticed an arrow buried in her chest. Moments later Annabella died, Eric held her and tears came from his eyes, he looked up at the trees and shouted.

"Why" he began rocking her in his arms pressing his head against hers.

Suddenly a group of soldiers appeared and ran towards Eric; John stood behind him and put his hand on Eric's shoulder.

"Stand aside Eric while I remove her head" John said raising his sword

"No" Eric shouted "Leave her alone, you have already killed her" he said guarding her body with his own.

"She has put a spell on you" John said

"No, we are in love and she is not wicked"

"Then if you won't let me finish this, you must die first" John said attempting to stab Eric with his sword

Eric had his sword at hand and blocked John's attack, John was knocked to the ground by Alestra's hoofs as she reared up and kicked him in the chest. John rolled over on the ground and quickly recovered, he got up and attacked Eric again, this time he managed to wound Eric, the soldiers stood watching the fight by John's orders. Eric was bleeding from his side but he continued to fight, John was getting weaker from his wounds and eventually Sercombe dropping his sword.

"Eric, why are we doing this, we are brothers, what would father say to us now?" John said gasping

"You killed Anna, why did you do this?" Eric shouted angrily

“The Mayor ordered me to, he said you were enchanted by her love” John explained “I am so sorry Eric”

Suddenly a arrow spun into the air and landed into John’s body, John fell to the ground and Eric ran to him and knelt beside him.

“Forgive me Eric” John said taking his last breath and dying.

Before Eric could attack the Mayor, the soldiers held Eric and one of them struck him on the head with the handle of his sword. When he recovered he was in the cave lying next to Annabella, fortunately nobody had beheaded her, and she seemed so peaceful lying on a blanket.

Eric looked around trying to focus on everything around him; the mayor stood watching him with a smirk on his face, he walked over to Eric and pointed to Annabella.

“She is Lamia, the daughter of Albelenda, and when I return from the pit I will behead her and finish the power of the witches for good” he said

“You are mad” Eric said “You will never succeed”

“Who will stop me?” the Mayor said mockingly “You?”

“They get inside your head” Eric said pointing to his own head

The Mayor shrugged him off and turned to address his soldiers

"I want eight of you to come with me and two to remain with these two, any trouble and you have my permission to kill them" The Mayor said leading them down a tunnel leading to the foot of the pit.

Eric noticed the wooden box that Annabella spoke about, it was close to the soldiers, he knew he had to find a way to distract them. He waited for a while trying to think of a plan, at this time a storm had began outside and strange noises came from the pit, flashes of light from the lightening lit up the cave and the roar of thunder caused the soldiers to jump and quake with fear. The ground began to shake and all the skulls began to rise up, a green substance poured out of the skulls and the bodies of each witch attached themselves to the skulls. Their souls were alive once more and they attacked the two soldiers as they tried to escape out of the cave, the witches worked jointly and used their powers sending electric bolts into the soldiers bodies. The men burnt away bit by bit, their flesh disappeared from their bodies leaving skeletons soaking in the rain just outside the cave entrance. Eric lay waiting for his fate, he thought that he would be the next to die, but the witches left them and entered the pit, before long there was a loud bang and yelling, screams could be heard from men.

Eric rushed to the wooden box and found the potion that Annabella had mentioned, she had described everything perfectly and Eric even followed her instructions on how to revive her. He put the vessel to her lips and tilted her head back, and then he used the substance and poured it over her body. Massaging her body with the substance and took the wand out of the box and held it to her chest hoping to recharge her heart like a defibrillator, but it failed. He tried again this time, he aimed it at her chest from the cave entrance and a bolt of lightening shot out, it was so powerful it threw him across the cave into the wall.

Eric heard more noises and saw the Mayor coming out of the tunnel with a look of horror on his face, he seemed disturbed and held a sword in his hand belonging to Eric.

"Stand aside I want the witches head" he shouted

"Do you know the significance of the number eight?" Eric asked

"The power of the resurrection?" he replied

"I know of that power" Eric said holding his hands up

"Tell me" the Mayor insisted

"I can do better than that" Eric said standing to one side "I can show you"

"What do you mean" the Mayor asked

"Behold" he said moving enough for the Mayor to see Annabella standing there

"Lamia" he gasped

"Back from the dead, just like me" he said smiling

Annabella was gleaming and very much alive, she raised her arms and a light emerged around her, the Mayor stood with his mouth wide open, while Eric took the sword out of his hand.

“But she had an arrow in her heart” he said

“That crumbled and fell like dust on the ground, she has been resurrected” Eric said happily

The Mayor threw a knife at her and it bounced off her chest and onto the ground, he snarled and ran at her, but she pushed her back with a great force of energy.

“I have poured that liquid on myself so I am invincible” he said

“That substance is nothing but Olive oil, we used it the last time we were in this cave, in order to refresh our skin” Eric explained

At that moment the ground began to move as before and the witches returned

The Mayor looked around him and saw all the witches together, he looked at Annabella “Save me from these witches” he pleaded

Annabella picked up her wand and pointed it into the air, she spoke calmly and clearly the words from a spell.

“Tamara lemus kathara” the cave shook and the whole place echoed with the sound of thunder.

Eric landed in her arms and remained there until it was all over, the Mayor fell into the pit, yelling as he fell and landed onto rocks breaking almost every bone in his body. Most of his blood poured across the ground, and no one mourned his death, he would soon be forgotten in Teversham least of all for his greed and corruption.

"Is that the end?" Eric asked

"No, my love, this the beginning"

The town and village of Teversham lived in peace; the witches of Teversham were a memory and soon became a story passed down generations like other folk tales, of course like any story things were added on and changed to suit the age.

As for Annabella and Eric they travelled north further into Scotland, they settled down in a cottage and had a daughter they called Rosa after Eric's youngest sister and they lived happily ever after or did they?

CRACKED PORCELAIN

Killer Queen

INTRODUCTION

Ruth is a psychiatric nurse who has faced dangers and lived through nightmares from her past. She had lived with a man named Malcolm, a once kind and loving boyfriend who was slowly revealed to be a murderous psychopath. Discovering her sexuality, Ruth left the man she thought she loved for a patient called Pamela, Malcolm, enraged and rejected, pursued both Pamela and Ruth. In a battle for their lives, the girls pushed Malcolm out of a window and he fell to his death, but not before he killed Pamela with a knife, thrusting it into her abdomen. The knife was supposed to kill Ruth, but Pamela jumped in the way to save her, it was Pamela's final act of love for Ruth. But what happened previously was nothing compared with her latest experience, when she was being pursued by yet another psychopath with evil intent.

A young man stands posing naked in front of a full length mirror, he has one of his favourite Queen songs on his C.D player called 'Bohemian rhapsody' and he is miming to the song and practicing dance moves almost like a ballerina. He is room appears tidy for a man, and displayed posters of Freddie Mercury everywhere. He was evidently a fan of Queen by the amount of songs he was playing and by the way he mimicked Freddie Mercury's moves, as he would have performed them on stage. But this young man appeared to perform in a more feminine way as if he had been observing a young woman's movements, he used his arms and legs like a mime artist and his body seemed to float on air. He was a slim youth in his mid twenties who was dancing to Queen he had short brown hair, large brown eyes with a rather unusually soft smooth complexion.

It was a summers evening in the early part of the week, the streets were quiet and only a few people were roaming about. Amongst these people was Ruth a slim woman with long dark flowing hair and large brown eyes. Ruth had a look of melancholy that some would mistake for sadness. Although she would have every reason to be sad judging by her tragic past living with a psychopath called Malcolm who murdered her mother and her girlfriend amongst others. Ruth is was mental health nurse who worked in the local hospital, on an acute mental health unit, dealing with all kind of conditions from bipolar, schizophrenia and clinical depression. Ruth had been deep in thought when she was suddenly distracted by a speeding car passing by playing loud music. She jumped and then returned to her thoughts, unaware that someone was following her. It was the young Queen fan who moved with a feminine walk using his hips to propel himself and wriggled his behind as he moved along. He had headphones on playing 'Queen' a song entitled 'You're my best friend'. Ruth entered a bar and joined a few friends, after a few seconds she walked the bar with one of her friends and ordered drinks. The youth stood at the bar, removed his headphones and stood close enough to hear their conversation, but remaining silent. Ruth was discussing relationships, making it known about her sexuality by her choice of words and from her tone of voice.

"Look Kathy, I don't care what people say at work; they all know that I am a lesbian, why should I hide it? The whole world knows after my appearance on TV and radio as well as the press" Ruth said

"Ruth, remember that was when you were in modelling now you're back in nursing and all that's behind you." Kathy said concerned.

"I might have stopped modelling but I haven't stopped being a lesbian, that's me and my sexuality" Ruth explained to her friend.

Kathy was a blonde woman with shorter hair and built slightly larger than Ruth, she was listening intently to Ruth along with the youth who by now had bought himself a drink. He kept glancing at Ruth's beautiful face, watching her mannerisms then making similar movements as if he was deliberately copying her. But was this young man a stalker or had he got a more sinister thought in mind? He had sat down and made a point of staring at her, if Ruth had not been so busy maybe she would have noticed him watching her and felt uneasy. Ruth was too occupied and engrossed in her own thoughts and conversation to be bothered with anyone else. Ruth decided to dance with some friends on the dance floor, she was demonstrating how active she was and full of life. She was dancing for a while, with the young man watching her, but he was distracted by a woman passing comment about her in a very negative way. She was making reference to Ruth's sexuality and her past as a model on television, commenting on how she didn't like her. At that moment, the young man was distracted by the sound of a Queen song called 'It's a kind of magic.' It was the backing music for a magic act performed by an illusionist which lasted an hour. After a while the young man left the bar and headed down the street, but he continued to mimic Ruth's movements and when he arrived home he practiced them in a mirror to the Queen song 'I want to break free' played loudly. Talking with his mouth and hands as Ruth did, even giving a smile as if to express empathy and then looked away as if to get distracted. Usually she would then play with her hair and tighten her lips clutching a pen in her mouth, with a reluctance to continue speaking, allowing others to have their say. Ruth was very expressive with her eyes, mouth and the way she held her head she also used her hands in order to express herself, and so he had many things to copy but the young man seemed to master it all.

The next morning, Ruth picked Kathy up for work. She was sat in the car looking in front of her at a busy street. She was relieved that she was not in the crowd as she particularly hated crowds of people and the closeness of strangers. She felt intimidated and very vulnerable when people brushed passed her- especially men. The typical stereo type, fat men with horrible sweaty bodies and eyes that undressed women. Like the evil Malcolm's of this world, horrible perverts, who used women to provide them with their own sexual needs, no matter who they hurt. She felt secure in her car almost as comfortable as being in her wardrobe, that dark and solitary place that she was safe in, as long as she remained silent hidden away from her abusers.

Kathy made her jump as she suddenly opened the door and shouted Good morning. She was so bubbly and bright where Ruth took a long time to revive from her slumber and confessed to being grumpy in the mornings.

"Did I startle you sorry Ruth?" Kathy asked, sorting out her bags.

"It's okay Kathy, I was deep in thought" Ruth said smiling.

"You're worried I can tell. What's troubling you?" Kathy asked, concerned.

"The usual thoughts I suppose. And nightmares" Ruth replied.

"Come on Ruth, we discussed this, you must think positive and believe in yourself". Kathy insisted. "What happened was not your fault and you must move on for your own sake"

"I know your right I hear your voice in my thoughts and try to be positive" Ruth began to drive away.

"I read something that you wrote about some time ago saying, if you visit your saddest place you will find me there, amidst the broken wings and lost souls. Hold back your tears for your memories lie like peaceful doves in a tree, so peaceful, so white and pure. Remember those broken wings and lost souls, those forgotten dreams and ambitions that once captivated your heart, yet a glimmer of hope, flicker of light appears in the darkness taking you into the light, far from the dark and solitary place. New hopes, new dreams and a bright future await me, my positive thoughts and warm heart goes forth into the light." Kathy read the words from a sheet of paper.

"My words and you kept them" Ruth said holding back the tears.

"Yes to remind me that you can think positive, I will quote these words whenever you're negative" Kathy said firmly.

"Thank you Kathy" Ruth replied

"Don't mention it" Kathy said dismissively.

On the radio Queen was performing Radio Gaga, Ruth smiled remembering this tune from her training days, her first encounter with mental health being chased by an elderly male patient who was suffering from bipolar.

They arrived at the hospital and parked the car near a wall; Kathy was the first to step out of the car followed by Ruth who swept her hair back from her face with her hands. Kathy laughed as the wind blew it back into her face, smugly smiling because of her own short hair and the fact it was more manageable than Ruth's long hair. Ruth loved her long hair but it was less manageable in rough weather and awkward to tie up while on the ward. Close by the same young man who had watched Ruth in the bar continued to watch her and he was also amused by Ruth's actions, trying to mimic her while playing his favourite Queen music

'You're my best friend'. He watched them enter the building on the mental health unit; he seemed to wait for a while in the car park before entering into another building.

He had entered Accident and Emergency and wandered into the toilets, he sat in a cubical and proceeded to expose his arms, he was a thin man who looked effeminate and timid. He produced a small knife from his shoulder bag and held the blade against his wrist, with a deep breath he cut across his wrist once and then again until he began to bleed onto the floor. He sighed with relief and watched the blood trickle onto the floor. Shortly after a pool of blood surrounded his feet and drifted under the cubical door. He heard a door shut and two people were talking, young female voices he had entered the women's toilet. Suddenly one of them screamed having seen the blood, the other woman shouted out.

"Hello can you hear me, are you alright" She said

"She could be dead" The other person said expecting a woman to be in the cubical.

"Lets get help quickly" One woman said to the other

The receptionist quickly calmed them down and alerted security who ran into the toilet to deal with the situation followed by a nurse. One of the security guards pushed open the door and escorted the young man to an available cubical in casualty. The nurse dealt with his wounds after a doctor was satisfied they were superficial cuts, she asked him questions about how he was feeling and soon discovered that he was suffering from clinical depression.

"So what's your name?" The nurse asked.

"Colin" He replied

"I'm Kim" she replied washing his arm "So Colin why do this?"

"I wanted to end it all, nothing to live for" Colin said, wincing in pain.

"So how long have you felt this way?" Kim asked.

"For quite while now. Ever since my parents were killed in a car accident" Colin responded, avoiding eye contact.

"Sorry to hear that Colin, I will get some help for you, maybe you can discuss this with a psychiatric nurse" Kim said bandaging his arm

After a discussion with the psychiatric liaison nurse, Colin agreed to be admitted onto the mental health unit for assessment. Colin seemed pleased to be there and even more so when he saw Ruth walking down the corridor towards him.

"Hello Colin, my name is Ruth" She said smiling, "Come with me and we can talk about your stay".

Colin sat in a room with Ruth, spending most of the time watching her mannerisms. He was interested in her eye movements and the way she used her hands to express herself. She spoke with her hands and her fingers seemed to move about like a musical conductor, and seemed to touch her hair a lot. She seemed aggravated by her hair being tied back and seemed to fidget constantly as if she was uneasy being sat down.

"I like your eyes" Colin said staring at her large brown eyes.

"Thank you" Ruth swiftly replied, trying to steer the conversation back to the interview.

"You have long shiny hair and lovely teeth" He continued

"Can we just stay focused on the interview please Colin" Ruth said feeling very uncomfortable.

"I am sorry I didn't mean to embarrass you" He said looking away.

"Colin where are your parents?" Ruth asked

"They are dead, killed in a car crash" Colin said looking out of the window onto the ward.

"Colin that's not true is it?" Ruth said sternly "Why are you lying?"

"Yes they got crushed in the seats like melons" He insisted speaking coldly in a detached manner as if he didn't care for them.

“No they are alive and well, I spoke to them earlier” Ruth watched Colin’s eye movements which told her that he had avoided the truth and he was being deceitful

“Why are you lying to me Colin?” She asked trying to get his attention “Are you upset with me because I stopped you talking about me?”

“No I just hate them” He looked back at her “I can’t help saying things about you because you are beautiful” Colin admitted.

“I am flattered but I need to be professional and you are a patient” Ruth said trying to explain the rules about patient and staff involvements. She felt so uncomfortable because he just kept staring at her, and she thought that he was undressing her with his eyes. He spoke frankly to her expressing his thoughts and feelings, but Ruth could only relate such things to her past. He may have been complimenting her but his words only made her feel more uneasy. She was also so shocked at the cold way he referred to his parents as being dead, and without giving any response when she faced him with the truth about his parents being alive and well.

“I don’t fancy you, it’s not like that and I know that you are a lesbian” Colin said bluntly.

“Well, that’s my personal business and my life Colin” Ruth said defensively “You have no right to judge me”

"I am sorry, really, but I am really not happy and I want to change my life. Even my parents" Colin said coldly "They disgust me, I want to be like you."

Ruth felt a shiver running down her spine as Colin related his feelings about his parents and his school life. He spoke about everyone having no eyes and of how he had nightmares of blinding everyone so that only he could see. He discussed many things, nothing positive. It was as though he could only see the bad in everyone, all but Ruth. He referred to a time that he was playing cricket and got into a fight, he was hit on the head with a cricket bat. The incident was recorded as accidental, although Colin insisted that it was a malicious attack and he was suffering from concussion. This was one of the many problems at school according to Colin, he claimed to have been bullied because of his feminine ways.

Ruth finished the interview feeling mentally drained, she was tired and even her speech was slurred when she was relaying the entire conversation to Kathy.

"Colin is clearly besotted with you," Kathy said smiling.

"Oh come on Kathy he's a patient. And besides, he's living in a fantasy world" Ruth said unconvinced by his explanations.

"Ruth I am joking he is psychotic and has a warped mind, he is unhappy and relates to you for some reason" Kathy appeared satisfied that Colin was just depressed and lonely.

"So I can relax then? Just not worry about another possible psychopath like Malcolm trying to ruin my life?" Ruth said with a sigh.

"He appears to have a psychosis but I wouldn't worry about your safety" Kathy reassured Ruth.

The following day Ruth was back on the ward going about her duties as a nurse, the usual activities took place such as handover from the night staff to day staff and reporting on each patient including Colin. No problems were reported, no violence or suicides, nothing to really say of significance. After a quick handover the night staff went home while the day staff took over the care. But throughout Ruth's twelve hour shift Colin had been watching her every time she was in view either on the ward or in the office. He studied every movement from her walk, gestures and posture; he listened to her speaking and instructing the staff to carry out duties. He continued to do this every shift that she was on; she was oblivious to this and hardly ever came in contact with him until one day. Ruth was passing his room and overheard him talking to himself and looking in the mirror, behaving just like her, every movement was exactly like hers.

"Now listen to me. You know what to do so carry on all of you." Colin said.

A shiver shot down Ruth's spine upon hearing and eventually seeing him impersonating her. All she could think to do was wait anxiously for Kathy. When she arrived Ruth told her everything.

"Ruth are you sure about this, or is it about the other day when he appeared to fancy you?" Kathy said in disbelief.

"For fuck sake Kathy he is freaking me out" Ruth said angrily.

"Calm down Ruth, he is harmless, don't go by past experiences you're becoming paranoid" Kathy said trying to reassure Ruth that Colin's actions were normal for a patient at least.

"He is probably tormenting you or teasing you and your letting him get to you" Kathy explained "He's a healthy young man in his mid twenties, who has a crush on you".

"I wish he would just have a fucking crush on someone else." Ruth said looking out of the office window onto the ward.

"You ought to feel flattered, not insulted" Kathy said while watching him walking down the corridor.

"I just feel as if there is something else about him that we haven't seen yet" Ruth said watching him look at her from a distance.

"See that's what I mean. I really don't agree Ruth. It's your paranoia" Kathy dismissed Ruth's claim and started writing notes.

"And he keeps playing Queen songs that I used to love them until he started performing to them acting like me, 'We will rock you' was playing in his bedroom and he was performing like me, with every gesture…I hate Queen now."

After being treated for a month, Colin left the hospital on Fluoxetine (Prozac) He appeared more positive and able to cope with life a little better or so the experts were led to believe, Ruth reserved judgement and felt a little easier when he had finally left the hospital. She felt his eyes on her each time she was on duty and she couldn't relax at anytime at work, even her home life was affected when Cheryl was out visiting family Ruth simply couldn't be alone which was usually her way of unwinding. She went to a bar with friends more frequently; this was because she had a feeling something was going to happen at some point and craved company.

Everywhere she went she noticed every Queen song stood out more than usual, it was as if he knew where she was going and arranging for these songs to be played. Songs such as a 'Crazy little thing called love' which was quite apt at this time for Colin.

In the meantime Colin was in his apartment looking in the mirror, talking to his reflection. "Oh Ruth you don't know how alike we are. Don't worry I will protect you from harm my darling" Colin leant forward in the mirror "But I am Ruth I will protect me".

He had studied her make up from seeing her out at night in local bars, he applied it so perfectly applying each brush stroke and other appliance with ease. Then he stood up and walked just as he had observed, over to the drawers across the room. Out of the draw he pulled out a long dark wig and mutters to himself.

"Perfect" his voice was eerie as he played with it wi.
hands just like Ruth does.

He had photos of her from her modelling days all around the mirror; each photograph had been chosen showing her flowing hair and soft silky complexion. Unblemished looks that were specially designed to appear good by photographers, Ruth used to marvel at how they made her seem so flawless. Ruth considered herself like cracked porcelain she was modelling attractive on the outside yet scarred on the inside due to past abuse. This was one part of her life Colin was unaware of her abuse or most of her past, although he read about Malcolm in 'Criminal world' magazine. Malcolm the psychopathic killer who was once in a relationship with Ruth, the man that killed Pamela's mother and ruined her life by abusing her and leaving her with all those memories to deal with. Raping and killing her mother in front of her eyes, no one should ever experience that or being raped by another man present. Ruth's girl friend Pamela was later killed by Malcolm in a fight, where Pamela attempted to save Ruth's life.

Colin sat for hours in front of the mirror and continued speaking and mimicking Ruth, he was having a complete conversation with himself as Colin then as Ruth.

"Kathy who gives a fuck that I am a lesbian its my life and I will live it how I want, no one should be harmed for how they were born. Any fucker who does try to harm them, I will deal with them".

"But Ruth you will get in trouble" Colin responded

iscrete, I will pursue them in darkness
” He replied as Ruth producing a knife
nd tear without a care, half a pound
ce, half a pound of treacle this is the way I
a knife, I bleed you like treacle”.

Colin prepared his outfit dressing like Ruth in a pair of dark jeans and a white blouse then put on a small black leather jacket. Then he walked towards the door and opened it placing the handbag neatly over his shoulder before leaving the apartment. With one hand on the door, Colin turns to the mirror by the door, smiling Ruth's smile and speaking in her voice “Dressed to kill” He remarks leaving the apartment and going on the hunt for victims that disliked Ruth. Colin walked for a while before seeing the woman in question, he waited for the opportune moment and when she was alone in a dark alley, he stopped her and spoke like Ruth.

“Do you know who I am?” He asked

“You're that gay Ruth” She replied “I would know you anywhere”

“Oh very good” He said sarcastically “So you don't like gays?”

“Wait are you trying to pick a fight, are you drunk?” She asked

“Fuck you bitch I am sober, but I don't like you” He continued

“Look I am not against gays each to their own as long as you don't bother me” She sounded nervous and began walking backwards against a wall.

"You fucking liar I know what you really think" He began fidgeting and pulled a knife from the handbag.

"I told you I don't want trouble, I just want to go home" She said in a quivering voice

Colin put the knife to her throat and forced the blade across her neck cutting her deeply and then stabbed her in the abdomen. She dropped to the ground landing at his feet; he could feel her body still moving for a while then nothing. After a short while he walked calmly away as if nothing had happened, he seemed to make it obvious that people saw him walking down the street deliberately bumping into people. He took his ear phones out of his handbag and proceeded to play the Queen song 'Killer queen' as he walked confidently down the street.

Colin went on to meeting other women armed with his sharp kitchen knife which he concealed in his bag wrapped in a thick cloth. He took one woman down a alley and questioned her about hating Ruth, she stood confused and certainly didn't expect to die.

"Why don't you like me" He said impersonating Ruth's voice

"I have nothing against you, just your sexuality" She replied

Colin got close to her and waited for his moment to strike, the woman began to edge away from him and said that she found the conversation boring and tried to get away. At that point he got close enough to slit her throat, making sure he severed the artery and watched her bleed to death before he casually walked away. Later he led one woman to his apartment and killed her in a similar manner; she spoke against Ruth in a pub one night overheard by Colin. He spent some time talking to her before killing her and dumping her body. He always played the Queen song 'Another one bites the dust' after killing each one at the end of the week he had killed several women.

The following week the murders appeared on the news and in the papers causing a lot of people to discuss the incident. Ruth was going to work it was Kathy's turn to pick Ruth up from her apartment. Ruth was late and looked particularly tired as she entered Kathy's car, she slumped into the seat wearing dark jeans and a white blouse with a spec of blood on the sleeve. Kathy didn't notice it as it was on the opposite side to where she was sitting in the passenger seat.

"Morning Ruth did you have a rough night?" Kathy asked looking at her tired eyes.

"Oh yes how did you know?" Ruth asked

"Well you look awful" Kathy said honestly

"Oh thanks Kathy that what a lady wants to hear in the morning" Ruth said feeling hurt.

"You a lady don't make me laugh" Kathy replied laughing

"Well shit to you Kathy dear" Ruth said almost smiling

"You see that's what I mean" Kathy continued "The gob on you"

"You wouldn't have me any different" Ruth said smiling.

"Well at least I got you smiling" Kathy said driving along to the hospital

When they arrived Kathy mentioned the murder and hoped that Ruth had seen the news too, but Ruth hardly ever switched the television on in the morning. She never even had the radio on that morning.

"I just caught a glimpse of the news this morning Ruth so I just heard it was a murder near you, down some alley". Kathy explained "But now they have found more bodies"

"I haven't heard anything" Ruth replied "A bit scary though".

As Ruth stepped out of the car Kathy noticed the blood on her sleeve, she couldn't take her eyes off it and made it obvious to Ruth that she had seen it.

"What have you done Ruth?" Kathy asked

"Oh shit I must have caught my arm on some broken glass" Ruth said hesitantly.

"So when did you do that?" Kathy asked concerned.

"I don't know" Ruth replied abruptly "I am okay"

They entered the hospital finding that everybody was discussing the murder; Ruth was surprised by the presence of police who were questioning people in the area. She was surprised as two officers approached her one of them grabbed her arm and noticed the blood, without hesitation he arrested her and they led her to a police car.

"What the fucks going on?" Ruth shouted

"Your under arrest" One of the officers said

"What on earth for?" Ruth yelled

"Just come quietly" Said the other policeman

"Read her the rights" one officer said

When they arrived at the police station Ruth was taken downstairs and locked in a police cell, she remained there while the police pieced together evidence enough to officially arrest her. Ruth sat thinking about previous events, she realised that the blood on her blouse was from her leg. She had scratched it badly in the night self harming from night terrors, but the police wouldn't believe this. She needed either Kathy or her girl friend Cheryl to be there in order to confirm her story, although even Kathy suspected that she was somehow involved in the murder.

After a while Ruth heard someone at the cell door and the sound of keys unlocking it. Two officers stood outside and eventually entered the room; they led Ruth out of the cell, up the stairs and into a small room with a table and four chairs. To her surprise Kathy was sat in one of the chairs, she gave a sigh of relief and greeted her warmly with a hug.

"Kathy what's happening?" Ruth said desperately.

"You are being questioned for that girls murder" Kathy replied "But don't worry I know your innocent".

The police officers sat opposite, the one introduced himself, he was a large fat man with odd teeth and bad breath.

"My name is detective George Mills and this is my colleague Gary" He said introducing his colleague who was a little smaller than him and had a kinder face.

"Gary switched on the tape while George quoted the date, time and details of the suspect and introduction to interview. George also had a package in his hand and seemed to be clutching it as if it was going to escape, he also had a smug look on his face as he proceeded to interview Ruth.

"Now we could make this as easy or as hard as you like Ruth" George began "I mean if you cooperate we can be finished and the job will be easy".

"Where were you last night?" George asked

"I was at home for a while and then I went for a walk to Sankey's bar" Ruth said calmly.

"Did anybody see you there?" Gary asked "it's a big place but nice"

"Yes it is nice and I was there with my friends Gloria and Sheena".

“What time did you leave?” George asked

“About 11pm I needed to get home in order to go to bed, as I was up early for work” Ruth said looking at George then Gary.

“We need you to go with a female officer and get changed out of those clothes, we need to examine them” George said

“What’s going on am I being accused of murder? Ruth asked

“Ruth just cooperate please” Kathy pleaded

Ruth stood up and took some clothes from Kathy, she then left the room with a female officer. Soon after she returned dressed in some of her other clothes, she seemed less relaxed and less willing to cooperate.

Gary switched on the tape and the interview resumed Ruth tried not to give George eye contact as he resembled her father’s friend and her abuser.

“So would you mind telling me where you got the blood on the blouse?” George asked

“It’s from my leg I scratched them in the night” Ruth explained

“Oh, you mean when you were struggling with Janet?” George asked

“Janet?” Ruth asked puzzled.

“The woman you murdered” George said

“I didn’t murder anyone” Ruth said shaking

“Oh you mean it was an accident” George continued

“No I mean I never met her or had anything to do with her” Ruth said looking at Kathy

“Well we have witnesses who say you had an argument with her months ago in non other than Sankey’s bar” George sat back and again seemed to have a smug expression on his face.

“I remember an argument with a woman who insulted me, she was with a group of women who had been drinking” Ruth recollected.

Gary edged forward and looked into Ruth’s large brown eyes, he was watching her expressions and eye movements as George was questioning her.

“I can understand you feeling angry and upset, possibly humiliated by what she said, maybe you had good cause to fight with her. But then it got out of hand and you killed her, no one would blame you for getting upset. What did she say to you?” Gary asked

“She was going on about my sexuality, saying that I was a lesbian who flaunted my sexuality on TV as a model with my friend Pamela” Ruth explained

“What a waste you’re so beautiful, so I bet you were angry” Gary said trying to extract more information out of her.

"Thank you and yes I was fucking angry" Ruth replied

Kathy touch her hand and looked at her as if to say stay calm, but she felt her sweaty palm and her fingers were shaking.

"Is Kathy your girl friend Ruth?" George asked watching Kathy trying to comfort her.

"No, she's my friend my girl friend is Cheryl she is probably waiting for me outside this room" Ruth said glancing at George.

"Why can't you look at me when I am talking to you Ruth, is it guilt?" George baited her.

"No not at all I find you repulsive and fucking rude as shit" Ruth said almost spitting in his face.

At that moment she proceeded to vomit, Kathy grabbed a rubbish bin and tissues from the desk. Ruth continued to retch and brought up copious amounts of fluid that made Gary move away from the table.

"This is normal for Ruth" Kathy said rubbing her back

"I'm okay" Ruth said "Sorry Kathy"

At this point the officers decided to stop the interview for the present time they switched off the tape recorder and went out of the interview room. They continued to discuss the case walking down the corridor; Gary seemed unhappy and reluctant to continue interviewing Ruth.

"George something seems wrong about this case" Gary said walking into a nearby office "Ruth doesn't seem like the type of person who could kill someone"

"What a load of crap Gary, she is a typical psycho killer, a real bunny boiler" He insisted "You just fancy her, she looks at you with her big brown eyes and you are in her spell"

"Bull shit George, she has feeling you know and did you see how nervous she was?" He asked almost pleading her innocence "She doesn't seem strong and powerful enough to over power women"

"Nut jobs seem to gather up the strength to do anything mate" George continued in an arrogant manner "I reckon we will have her confessing when we go back"

George was given an envelope by one of the female officers, he looked at her as if she had two heads and then opened the envelope. Gary thanked her and watched as he pulled out half a dozen photographs and spread them across the table.

"Sick bitch, look what she has done to these women, now do you think she is innocent?" George said angrily "Let's get her to confess"

George marched back into the interview room followed by Gary, both of them seemed fuelled up for another interrogation of the accused

"Shall we continue?" George asked rubbing his hand together

"Why not go for it big boy" Ruth said "Do your worst you obviously think I am guilty."

"Are you okay Ruth" Gary asked "Only you seem frightened" he seemed genuinely concerned

"Oh, are you playing good cop bad cop, very cute" Ruth said with tears forming in her eyes "You are fucking pathetic, honestly, one who acts like a prick and the other complements me"

"We need to show you a tape from C.T footage see what you think" George said placing the envelope down on the table and putting a video into a player.

The video showed a figure walking down a street near the crime scene; the person was walking along with a hand bag over the left shoulder and touching her face with her left hand. It was dark and the street was dimly lit with a few street lamps, she stopped for a while looked around and then continued.

"This is you isn't it?" George asked

"No certainly not" Ruth replied "But it looks like me I must admit".

"It is you I am sure of it and so were witnesses who saw you out that night" George said

"I haven't got a handbag like that" Ruth said noticing the white handbag

"And if you look carefully that person is carrying it over her left shoulder, and using her left hand to do things". Kathy said pointing.

"So what does that mean?" George asked in a highly intellectual manner.

"George the person on the video is left handed, he is also a male" Gary pointed out to George who looked disappointment.

"It is not apparent from the outset but watch his walk and the general mannerisms" Kathy said as George reversed and reran the tape.

"Colin" Ruth said "It has to be Colin"

"Ruth that's ridiculous" Kathy said dismissively.

George presented Ruth with a series of photographs taken of the victims, he placed them strategically across the table "Do you recognise any of these?"

Each photograph made Ruth cringe, some of the bodies were cut to pieces and covered in blood, they were hardly recognisable, but Ruth did point out a few of them "I know this one and this one I argued with them in clubs and pubs"

At that moment a knock came at the door, almost immediately afterwards the police woman enters the room. She took George to one side and he seemed to get annoyed by what she said to him.

He walked back over to Ruth and leaned over the table, giving her the pleasure of his foul breath. Ruth waved her hand in front of her face and turned her head away. George seemed uneasy for a moment before speaking, loosening his tie and giving her a poor excuse for a smile.

"Well it seems your innocent and I must apologise" George obviously wasn't used to apologising and being humble, however he was presented with evidence of her innocence on a paper which her squeezed tightly in his hand.

"I would however appreciate your help with my enquiries as you seemed to know Colin Bailey" George said trying not to look at Ruth

"How does fuck off sound" Ruth said angrily "of all the cheek of this excuse for a man"

"Ruth we have to help" Kathy said abruptly "It's our duty"

"Why the hell should I help them with what they put me through" Ruth said frowning at George "He has been a real bully and you want me to help him?"

"Because you're the stronger person and we must stop being obstructive and help find Colin" Kathy paused for a moment "Wait a minute we never mentioned Colin's surname".

"Oh he rang asking what was happening to Ruth, when you mentioned Colin we realised who he was" George explained

“So you were right about Colin” Kathy said to Ruth “I am sorry for doubting you and I should have listened to you in view of past events”.

Kathy also realised why Ruth vomited and walked over to George, she looked him up and down then stared into his eyes.

“Ruth is right you are a creep” Kathy winked at Ruth then sat her down and comforted her “its okay Ruth, I understand. But finding Colin will save lives”

They both explained about Colin and the way he behaved, discussing about him being obsessed with Ruth and copying her mannerisms. It was obvious by now that Colin in his own mind wanted to become Ruth and modelled himself off like her, he even dressed like her. But what was worse he killed the people who were likely to harm her; Janet was only one of many victims discovered while Ruth was in the police cell. A total of nine bodies were discovered in various locations around Manchester and the greater Manchester area, Colin dressed as Ruth and went on a spree of murders trying to justify his actions by saying Ruth was defending herself. But who really knows what is in the mind of a killer, he was not sexually attracted to her, neither was he a homosexual or transsexual in the true sense of the word. Ruth could except any type of sexual preference and mixed with all genders, frequenting the gay village for fun. She was in a lesbian relationship with Cheryl but failed to understand Colin who dressed like her and killed people because they offended Ruth. What was worse Colin remained on the streets and could attack someone else at any time, only Ruth could stop him killing again or could she?

Colin used music to help motivate himself to go out and kill more women, his favourite being 'Another one bites the dust' and it always seemed to be songs by the pop group Queen. 'Another one bites the dust' and 'Don't stop me now' was his favourite songs, although 'We will rock you' was the one he played most with killer queen as his second choice. He was speeding in his car when he used to play 'don't stop me now' and by all accounts he was having such a good time as the killer queen. But he used these songs to fuel his anger and enhance his excitement prior and following his murder spree.

The police raided Colin's apartment and discovered all the photographs of Ruth and then found photographs of Colin dressed like Ruth, it was clearly evident that Colin was the murderer posing as Ruth. Much as Colin tried to simulate Ruth he still couldn't fully disguise himself as a female, it was sad but he really wanted to be Ruth for some reason. With this in mind he was still on the streets somewhere and even though Ruth felt safe, he was unpredictable.

Ruth was being watched by the police as she tried to lead a normal life, they knew that he would have to contact her at some stage, either at her apartment, at Emma's house were her step mother Diane once lived or at one of the bars that Ruth frequented. Ruth just had to be herself and wait for Colin to contact her, she was like bait on a hook sent into the water to catch a fish. She was moving about for weeks before something happened, then one night she entered a club with some friends, her girlfriend Cheryl joined her. She seemed relatively happy, joking with her friends as she walked through the door. After she had been there for a while she got up to dance as usual joined by Cheryl, Kathy sat with her friends Sheena and Gloria. Ruth was unaware of the police presence as they were dressed in plain clothes, George was busy eyeing up the girls and commenting to his colleagues about how they looked in a chauvinistic manner. But no one was aware that Colin was present, standing in a dark corner, watching Ruth dance in her usual energetic way. He was wearing a long dark wig and a black dress, mimicking Ruth, he was quite relaxed until a Queen song started playing. 'I want to break free' encouraged everyone to start dancing, but Ruth left the dance floor upset.

"Ruth you used to like this song" Cheryl said confused

"I have gone off it" Ruth said walking back to her friends

"Is that because of Colin?" Cheryl asked

"Maybe" Ruth replied abruptly "Sorry I am just going to the toilet"

"I will come with you" Cheryl offered

"No, I want to be alone" Ruth insisted, looking at her friends and then walking away.

She entered the toilet and Colin appeared dressed like Ruth. She felt like she was looking into a mirror looking at her own reflection.

"I have missed you Ruth, have you been avoiding me" Colin said locking the toilet door.

"Colin, where have you been?" Ruth said nervously "I was arrested because of you"

"Oh you know here and there" Colin replied "And call me Ruth after all I am you now, I killed as Ruth and now I have become you. Tell me, do you like what you see?".

"I don't understand" Ruth replied "I am no killer, why do you portray me as such?"

"My dear, I was protecting you, I killed for you. I have solved your problems by killing your enemies" Colin said coldly

"But why dress like me, I don't understand?" Ruth asked

"I am you, don't you understand. I have been you for a long time, and quite frankly. Well, there is no room for both of us and so one of us must die" Colin produced the knife from his white handbag which was wrapped in a bloody rag.

"You know the police are aware that you murdered those women, how many did you kill, four or five?" Ruth asked glancing at the door then back at him.

"Well, nine or is it ten now" Colin said coldly "But that doesn't matter it's just a numbers game. You should be grateful your enemies are dead, it's just us now, but alas one too many.

"Do you intend to kill me?" Ruth asked "After all you did say one too many"

There was a silence while Colin looked into a mirror "Uncanny isn't it, how much alike we are I practiced being you for months and even on the ward when they gave me that electric shock treatment I suffered to be like you. Do you know what it feels like to have electricity surging through your body?"

Colin noticed her edging towards the door and jumped in her way, he held the knife to her throat and let the blade touch her flesh. He managed to puncture the skin holding the knife so tightly and blood trickled down her neck.

"One cut will end it all" He said grinning "Oh Ruth with so much beauty, so much love and compassion, a beacon of hope shining in the darkness, you are lighting the way for so many lost souls."

"But why be like me, what have I got that you want?" Ruth asked trying not to show her fear, but her body language betrayed her as she started to perspire and shake. Then she remembered in her training never show the patients that you are frightened.

"Don't make me angry or I will cut you like the others" Colin shouted "You who have beauty, love and not afraid to express yourself, you who are a lesbian but fights for your gender, you ask why be like you, when you are a living legend" He said holding out his hand and slicing open the palm of his right hand. "This is your blood not mine share it with me" He said wiping it across her face then onto her right shoulder. "This is yours I want you to have it, let our blood flow and become as one"

At that moment the door handle started to move, then came a male voice colin grabbed Ruth tightly around the waist with one hand and held the knife to her throat with his free hand.

"Ruth it's the police were coming in" The voice was that of the policeman George.

The next thing they heard was the door being rammed open by some heavy object, it took a few hard bangs before the door burst open and the police came rushing in.

"Stay back" Colin shouted "Or I will kill her"

George was the nearest to Colin "Come on lad it's all over, hand me the knife"

Colin hesitated "One of us has to die, there is only one Ruth"

George noticed Colin relaxing his grip and taking the knife away from Ruth's bloody neck, "That's it lad relax and let Ruth go"

Suddenly George rushed forward and Colin stabbed him in the shoulder, his large body fell with a thud to the ground. The other officers stood frozen to the spot watching George rolling about on the ground. Colin looked at Ruth and she stared at him for a moment trembling, he raised his knife pointing it at her.

"This is the end Ruth" His eyes widened "I did say one of us had to die"

At that moment he pointed the knife at himself and plunged it deeply into his stomach making sure it was enough to cause a fatal wound, he pulled out the knife and repeated his action. He fell to the ground and Ruth kicked the knife away from his hand. She knelt down beside him and bent her head down his mouth listening to his final words. Her eyes widened as she managed to catch his words and then take his final breath.

"There is only one Ruth and she is you besides who wants to live forever" Colin said before his death.

Kathy was standing close by with Cheryl and other friends each looking at Ruth, Kathy moved forward to comfort her, then Cheryl took over and led Ruth out of the nightclub. All the emergency crew were outside Ruth was helped into an ambulance with Cheryl while the others stood and watched them leave.

Amazingly Ruth did attend Colin's funeral, he was cremated and at the ceremony the family played a song that Colin always wanted for his funeral service called ironically 'Who wants to live forever' by Queen

Ruth soon recovered and she was asked to get involved in the Manchester pride festival scheduled for the end of August, by that time she would probably feel better and able to cope with one of her worst fears, which is crowded places. The festival was a busy place and Ruth was used to the gay village as Cheryl and her frequented bars there. Ruth enjoyed dressing up and she would be in familiar company and amongst friends, she loved the parade and interacting with everyone there. Of course gay pride is world wide and both her sister and she were in the New York festival last year. But the biggest problem Ruth had to face was her frequent nightmares, if only she could master them then she could live a relatively normal life. Ruth put the radio on and the Queen song played as Ruth lay down and closed her eyes 'The show must go on' how very apt.

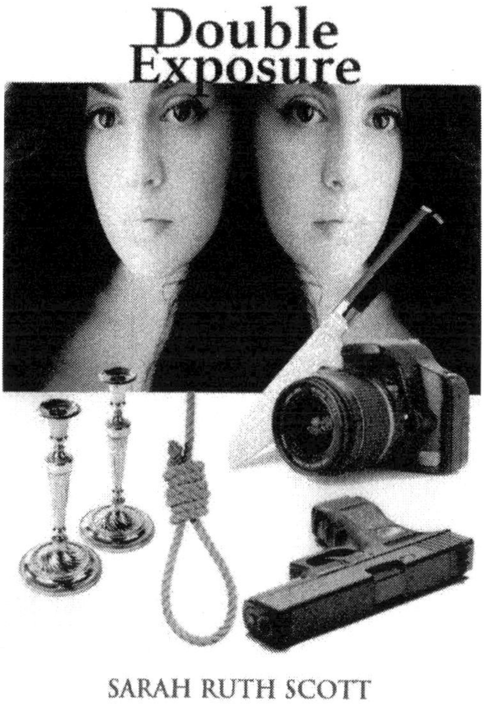

DOUBLE EXPOSURE

Criminal World

Criminal world is a magazine dedicated to investigating crime all over the world; the reporters and photographer gather details of crime from victims, police records and criminals themselves. The team take steps to ensure that the public are provided with detailed accounts of events with graphic pictures that questionably cannot be compared with any other crime magazine.

Samantha King is a reporter who joined the team from the Australian office of Criminal world she is courageous and determined to get what she wants. She is also outspoken and uses her beauty to get what she wants, unfortunately she tends to offend people with her bad language and temper.

Fiona Ellington is one of the reporter's who is also a daughter of the editor, who is strong-minded and a force to be reckoned with as she immerses all her energy into finding a good story. Her life is criminal world and anything else in life takes a back shelf including love and marriage.

Stuart Elliot was a photographer who spent a few years as a wedding photographer and then ventured into the world photographing models moved into the area of crime when he found himself actually photographing a murder as it happened.

Daniel Harrison another reporter that used to work in war zones, he had a history in the army and used it to help him on location in remote areas. He achieved many things in his younger life recognising an opportunity for a story an every moment. He was said to even sleep with a notepad in his bed.

Many other people worked for criminal world of course and the main offices employed computer experts and retired scientists surprisingly enough. It was a thriving concern and the connections with other areas of expertise helped to make the magazine more accurate and credible. The World Wide Web or Internet serves as a valuable asset for criminal world in order to receive vital information for the magazine.

MISSING IN SCOTLAND

One of the main premises for criminal world was based in central London close to Piccadilly Circus. It was inside a tall building on the fourth floor with a bronze plaque outside indicating exactly where to find it. On the fourth floor was a door with a design of the world decorated on the glass saying 'criminal world magazine' opposite

Samantha entered the office walking gracefully down the corridor with her head held high, she seemed a confident woman with so much inner strength. She had long brown hair, which shined beneath the artificial florescent lights. She looked about thirty having young radiant skin that was slightly tanned. She wore a tight dress black dress that complimented her slim figure, catching the eyes of any man passing. But although she seemed confident she had a rather sad expression as if she were carrying the world on her shoulders.

Samantha walked through another door and found herself in a waiting area. A young man sat at a desk looking at a computer screen. Samantha gave a gentle cough to draw his attention then repeated a cough, eventually he responded.

“Yes can I help”. He paused as he gazed at her beautiful face.

“I am Samantha I am your new reporter” Samantha said confidently

“Oh right” The young man said still staring at Samantha

“Would you mind not staring and finding Fiona?” Samantha said feeling uneasy

“I will ring her now” He said smiling

He picked up the phone and tapped out the numbers, he appeared rather clumsy as his fingers seemed to randomly press buttons.

“Have you got any identification please?” He asked her

Samantha produced a driving license from her handbag will this do it has my photo “I’m afraid I’m not topless on it” she said sarcastically

“Yes fine thanks” He said sheepishly

He finally got through to Fiona and began to speak

“Is that Fiona, I have a Samantha King here for you, your new reporter” He paused then pointed to one of the seats opposite “Can you sit there please, she will be with you soon”.

Samantha sat and crossed her legs, her dress rose up her leg slightly and she quickly pulled it down. The young man had noticed but pretended not to and proceeded to knock over a pot of pens.

Fiona walked in she was a slim blonde woman around thirty-five years old, very attractive, but appeared to be very serious. She shook Samantha by the hand and smiled "I am Fiona".

"Come with me she beckoned Samantha" then looked at the young man

"Hadrian you need a tissue you're clearly drooling" Fiona said passing him by

"I want to know what you're going to do with your erection?" Samantha asked in a low voice after she passed him.

Fiona chuckled at what Samantha had said

"Hadrian is really harmless, he is rather special you know" Fiona said smiling.

Hadrian had tried to ignore their remarks and looked back at the computer muttering, "You don't want to know the answer to that one".

Fiona took Samantha through the main work area where most of the staff was concentrating on their tasks, people were walking about and some were talking on the phone she could see them picking up the phone and saying 'criminal world can I help you' this happened so many times. Some heads turned and seemed curious to know who was passing they entered the editor's office; he was sat at an untidy desk searching for something.

He looked up as they entered the room "Oh you must be Samantha from Australia"

"Yes sir" She said politely

"Manners as well, I am Bill not sir, we are more informal here". Bill said still searching amongst his papers.

"Ok well welcome to criminal world London" Bill continued

Bill had short but thick hair and a handlebar moustache; he was quite tall with a large stomach due to alcohol consumption this was known as a beer belly.

"Bill what are you looking for?" Fiona asked

"My cigarettes" Bill replied

"But you don't smoke anymore" Fiona insisted

"I do since your mother came back home" Bill remarked

"But Dad you have to be patient with her" Fiona said sternly

"She's hard work since her breakdown" Bill said finding his cigarettes

"OK I will visit tonight" Fiona agreed

"I hope you enjoy working with us my daughter will show you to your office" Bill said putting a cigarette in his mouth

Fiona gave a cough and pointed to the no smoking sign on the door, Bill took it out of his mouth while she left the office, and then returned it to his mouth.

Fiona led Samantha out of the office to a room nearby their were two desks there inside a spacious office, near the one desk stood a large filing cabinet and a plant on the top in a very decorative pot. The leave hung down the sides of the cabinet in long green strands, pictures were on the walls of other countries and one photo stood out it was of Fiona standing under the New York office with the criminal world logo above the door. She was standing with other members of staff all smiling and seemingly happy together.

"Nice picture Fiona is that New York?" Samantha asked

"Yes I used to work there" Fiona said reluctant to talk about it

"Did you like it there?" Samantha asked

"I was there three years until I lost my boyfriend in a shooting" Fiona said sitting at her desk

"I'm sorry" Samantha realised she had touched a raw nerve

"I am too Paul didn't deserve to die like that" Fiona suddenly stopped talking and turned on her computer.

Samantha didn't pursue the conversation and proceeded to empty her box of office equipment. She made use of every available space and put everything neatly away. Everything she had matched and she even lined books up neatly on a shelf.

"So have you got anyone?" Fiona asked Samantha

"No the last creep cheated on me" Samantha said continuing to count and line up all her pens.

"Waited until I was on an assignment and pissed off" Samantha said bitterly

"What a bastard" Fiona said in surprise

"Too fucking right took some of my fucking stuff too" Samantha went on.

"Men, they are just a load of tossers". Fiona smiled

"Too fucking right" Samantha said watching a man knocking the door.

"Oh Dan you're here, back from sunny Spain I see". Fiona said looking at Samantha.

Daniel Harrison had worked in war zones as a reporter and was an ex army man, He was thirty-six, muscular with short hair and a roughed face. He seemed quite arrogant on first impressions and seemed to hide a more sensitive self.

"Ladies may I say sunny Spain was excellent and I achieved all I needed to in a few days, one major story in the bag". Harrison boasted

"Well that's good" Fiona gestured to Samantha behind his back tosser.

Samantha tried to keep a straight face and just nodded, Harrison was oblivious to they're gestures and continued to boast about his new story from Spain. The phone ringing interrupted him and he decided to leave the office.

Fiona picked up the receiver "Hello" She said "Yes she's fine, he has just left here ok bye" Fiona said putting down the receiver

"That was Dad he was looking for Dan and he said he hopes your settling in ok". Fiona said looking across to Samantha.

"Yes everything is fine, no problem". Samantha said reorganising her pencils

"Have you got OCD by any chance" Fiona said tutting.

"Obsessive compulsive disorder Sorry I do have it a little" Samantha admitted

"So have you had any interesting stories in Australia?" Fiona asked

"Yes a few murders, but mainly missing persons and kidnappings" Samantha said

"Good well you will be sent everywhere from here" Fiona explained

"I read about one you wrote called 'cracked porcelain' about two models Pamela and Ruth lesbian women being pursued by a psychopathic killer that was a good story".

"You liked that one poor women were both abused as children that's why I called it cracked porcelain it was mainly about Pamela and her being abuse as a child it happened to Ruth as well but Pamela was a child model protected by her disabled mother".

"And what about Jodie the Goth girl" Samantha asked

"Yes poor Jodie got accused of a brutal assault on a young girl, she's in jail right now, but personally I think she's innocent" Fiona said

"Wasn't she bullied at school?" Samantha asked

"Yes learned to defend herself and suffered for it" Fiona said

"Meaning?" Samantha was asking for more information

"Well when she took up self defence classes she only wanted to protect herself but she was drawn into fights and lost control". Fiona explained

"So you understand Jodie?" Samantha asked

"Yes I do, its all about understanding Jodie and others" Fiona replied

"My stories involved murders in the outback's of Australia and city crimes in places like Melbourne and Sidney" Samantha explained

Samantha followed up a few local stories around London before venturing further, she was eventually sent to Scotland on a missing person story. It was quite usual for a simple story to turn out to be major news; Samantha usually got assigned to such stories. She was asked to travel to a small place near North Berwick, close to Edinburgh and stay at this castle near the sea; she was to go with Stuart Elliot the photographer.. The missing person was Susan Macgregor the niece of a wealthy landowner called Gordon Macgregor. Both Samantha and Elliot were to pose as distant relatives, who are up in Scotland on vacation visiting uncle Gordon who happens to be an old friend of the editor Bill.

Samantha and Elliot set out by car and travelled through on the motorways of England until they reached the Scottish boarder. Samantha made Elliot swear not to sing on route after hearing him singing Scottish songs at the start of their journey. Even their taste in music varied so much and Samantha was not a very tolerant person, threatening to insert the radio into his anatomy. Elliot put it down to her time of the month but Samantha put her attitude down to her recent separation and her ex boyfriend being an asshole.

Samantha and Elliot arrived in Edinburgh at 16.00 hours and caught the train to Berwick

While at the station the other guests arrived in couples are as individuals, an eccentric couple waited on a bench the man wore a plain shirt, braces and a dickey bow with shorts and his partner wore a pale pleated skirt and a white blouse and pumps. They both had straw hats and between them stood out from all the other guests. Beside them stood a slim woman with short blonde hair she edged towards the couple and started to speak to them.

"I take it your waiting for the minibus?" she said jovially

"Yes" the man said "Going to Macgregor's castle and the haunted weekend"

"My name is Sharon" the slim blonde woman said

"This is my wife Sylvia and I am Reginald or Reg" He said extending his arm to shake her hand.

"Have you done this before?" Sylvia asked

"Yes many times I go all over the country searching for ghosts". Sharon admitted

"Oh that's nice have you ever seen any?" Reg asked

"Oh yes many times its so exciting" Sharon replied excitedly

"We have been a few times but not seen much" Sylvia said disappointedly

Samantha and Elliot were in close enough to hear the conversation

Samantha whispered to Elliot "We are in for a fun packed weekend with them" she said sarcastically

They catch the minibus to Macgregor's castle travelling through miles of countryside over a bridge and through woodlands. The guests were discussing previous ventures on the way until they reached their destination seeing the castle on the side of a cliff overlooking the sea. It was like a picture postcard the whole scenery was beautiful and the castle was well kept. The castle was a typical fairytale building such as seen in a Disney movie with high towers and walls with narrow windows that would have been used for bowmen to shoot their arrows at their enemy

They were taken to the main entrance and led into a main hall and asked to sit down on the many chairs that were placed neatly in one big circle. It was then that Macgregor made his entrance from another room; he was wearing a kilt and the rest of the attire typical of a true Scotsman. He was a tall man with ginger hair and a long ginger beard he was quite portly and had rosy cheeks and a slightly bent nose.

He introduced himself and explained about the rules of the household

"You are free to roam the castle but you are not allowed to go into that room" he pointed to the room by the main staircase "That room is private and I want all your phones and any other devices and I will lock them in my safe until you leave". He looked at each of them "This is a special weekend of ghost hunting and so no contact with the outside world". He noticed Samantha and smiled "We dine at six o'clock or 18.00 hours, so we will meet in the main dining room". He pointed down the corridor "My servants will show you to your rooms and settle you all in, after which feel free to explore these rooms".

A few men who looked hard took Samantha and Elliot to their rooms and menacing one of them had a short beard and a rough voice. The other never spoke but just made grunting sounds each time the other man spoke. After settling in Elliot knocked on Samantha's door, she fastened her clean blouse and headed for the door.

"Oh it's you" Samantha said sounding disappointed

"I get the distinct impression you don't like me" Elliot said smiling

"Nothing personal I don't like men at the moment" Samantha replied

"Ok I believe you" Elliot said

"Look if we are going to have to work together don't get in my fucking face ok" Samantha said abruptly

"Ok that suits me" Elliot agreed holding his hands up. "Anyway Macgregor wants to see us in the study". Elliot said heading towards the stairs

They managed to find the study and knocked on the door after a few moments waiting for a answer they went in. The room was virtually empty with a few pictures and a desk but the most curious thing on the desk was a board game Mystery murder game and figures set out on the table in various rooms as if someone was playing the game.

Elliot noticed the game and began to touch the figures

"Please leave them alone!" Macgregor shouted

Elliot jumped and dropped the figures

"I'm sorry but no one knows who put this here or why and so its evidence" Macgregor seemed worried

"Interesting and intriguing" Samantha said bending to look at the figures

"I suspect that we are the figures and part of someone's game" Macgregor continued

"Why do you say that?" Elliot asked

"Because I found a card beside my bed with a picture of a man in purple on it" Macgregor said "And before my niece went missing a card of a woman in blue was by her bed.

Samantha noticed a portrait on the wall "I like your painting its you isn't it?"

"No its my identical twin brother John, he slept in the room that you are staying in lass" Macgregor said almost smiling.

"So who are we?" Samantha asked

"You're my cousin from London called Samantha and you lad are Stuart another cousin from London" Macgregor explained

"So we are on vacation?" Elliot asked

"Yes and don't tell a soul" Macgregor insisted

"Of course not" Samantha agreed.

"So lets go and eat" Macgregor said leading them into the corridor and then into the large dining room.

They met other people in the dining room who were introduced by Macgregor, the room maids and servants were walking about and Elliot made a point of observing them. On the way to the dining room each one was a suspect for kidnapping no one escaped his notice. Samantha had also suspected one or two people mainly male staff as she was going through an anti male phase in her life. Her previous relationship with Derek caused her so much heartache she was ready to castrate any man at this point.

Macgregor introduced his guests to Samantha and Elliot, firstly my friend Janet the friend from Inverness. She was a tall thin lady with short dark hair and a pale complexion. A vicar who was from Aberdeen, he was a short bolding man who seemed to look over his glasses like you would expect a teacher to do. He was quite portly with chubby cheeks like a hamster he kept looking over at Samantha across the large oblong table. Macgregor sat at the head of the table the entire cutlery shone and the glassware sparkled, the servants came into the room and served each guest with a hot soup dish.

Both Samantha and Elliot were amazed at the banquet and at the way things appeared to be organised. Macgregor obviously enjoyed entertaining his guests, he also made a point of making them feel comfortable in his presence.

"I am pleased and delighted to have you all here and hope your stay will be comfortable" Macgregor said addressing everyone "I do hope my niece Gillian will return safely with us, I would like you to meet her as she is the apple of my eye". Macgregor looked around the table at all his guests in turn. "You are in the castle of Macgregor home for generations of Macgregor's so don't be surprised to see a few ghosts occasionally". Macgregor seemed serious when he referred to the place as being haunted.

Samantha was more interested in the large ring that he was displaying on a finger on his right hand. The ring had a ruby inset in the centre of the ring, which shone like a red light. Macgregor noticed her looking at it and smiled at her in a strange manner as if he could read her mind.

"This ring has been passed down the family through generations" Macgregor was addressing Samantha who was two seats away. "Its as beautiful as you my wee lassie and it will never come off".

Samantha smiled and began to blush "Thank you" she said looking down at a bowl of soup in front of her, then at Elliot, he just smiled and picked up his soup spoon and began to scoop up his soup. Samantha had a very delicate manner, which indicated that she had been to functions like this before. She knew exactly how to behave and displayed such elegance like a lady of the manor. Elliot however was much more down to earth oblivious of the other guests behaved more like a caveman in some cases.

Samantha could here conversations around her discussing Gillian's disappearance and Janet was sitting next to her wearing a purple dress, she seemed very observant pointing out items in various rooms. She particularly curious about Samantha and examined her like person buying a vase or other interesting objects.

"So Samantha" Janet began

"Call me Sammy most people do" Samantha said smiling

"Ok Sammy where are you from?" Janet asked curiously

"I am from London" Samantha replied

"Yes but I can detect another accent there" Janet said in a probing manner

"Well I am originally from Australia" Samantha revealed.

"So you are related to Gordon" Janet said

"She's my cousin" Gordon quickly interrupted.

"I see and I am a friend of Gillian's, we were at school together" Janet said watching the servant put her main meal in front of her.

"Game pie my favourite," the vicar said smiling.

"I aim to please Charles" Macgregor said cheerfully.

Samantha felt nervous next to Janet but was not able to understand why; something told her that she was hiding something or not quite who she seemed to be. She was also still curious about the mystery murder game on the study table that apparently just appeared there. No one knew why it was there not even the servants, but it had been there since the disappearance of Gillian a few days ago.

Samantha and Elliot were sat in the study with all the other guests, listening to Macgregor telling ghost stories. He seemed quite intent as he related each detail his eyes seemed fixated on the portrait of him as if something was wrong. He then looked at his audience then focused on Samantha's large brown eyes. He explained about his ancestors who lived in the castle and who according to himself haunt the many rooms and corridors each night. He was so convincing it was almost as if he believed his own stories and was relaying real events. This was all part of the performance with sounds and visual activity provided by a clever man hidden in a control room, Macgregor's missing brother had created the whole show years before in order to entertain the public. Now Macgregor had his audience and he was like the master of ceremony, circus master and storyteller all in one.

"Well ladies and gentlemen if you look and listen we have the weather giving us the atmosphere for my ghoulish stories" He pointed to the window where a storm was taking place, thunder and lightning followed by heavy rain.

"I must tell you the story of Angus Macgregor" He began with a solemn look on his face. "Who's wife was gravely ill, she was suffering from a painful illness stricken with fever and as pale as snow" He looked back at Samantha and smiled "She was very beautiful and a true lady, but her illness aged her and her hair turned white.

Samantha felt uneasy as she listened to his story almost as if he was talking about her but then she knew deep inside she couldn't have been.

Macgregor continued his story "Angus watched his wife as she began fading away but was attracted to a maid who gave him pleasure. They he was having an affair carried away by his weak will and obsessed with one so young and fair. However on his wife's dying day she beckoned him to her side and whispered in his ear saying I know and repeating I know. He began to shiver and became enraged sending the maid off but she walked up the north tower and threw herself off plunging to her death. She returned from the dead to haunt him shouting and screaming at him, you are a wicked man you will die a horrible death. Sure enough he did as he fell down the main stairs near the entrance hearing her words over and over again, he was crippled and had pneumonia and true as her words were he died a horrible death".

Macgregor pointed in the direction of the north tower "Every night you can see a white figure falling from the tower and on the stairs a floating shape moves down the stairs as for Angus you can hear him in his bed gasping for breath and you may even see him somewhere within the castle".

"What a chilling tale" one of the guests said shivering

Samantha looked at her in disbelief then whispered to Elliot "They take it all in don't they". She said smirking

Macgregor looked at the large antique grandfather clock standing by the wall and continued with another tale.

Angus had a younger brother called John who was in the woods at night when it began to rain; he sheltered under a tree and was suddenly struck by lightning. He survived but became mentally impaired he was so bad that he killed his wife by stabbing her to death with a knife, she was found by a servant in the library. Sometimes you can hear her screams or see her walking covered in blood. He walks about too with his menacing eyes and hunched up body moaning as he moves around the corridors at night. You think your safe until he suddenly catches you and stabs you over and over again, you can tell when he is about to attack because before he does you hear the striking of the clock at the midnight hour".

At that moment the clock struck and everybody jumped including the sceptical Samantha, each person looked at the clock but it was only Eleven o'clock.

"But that's not all" Macgregor said continuing his story "John died after killing his wife by shooting himself and blowing his brains out, you can clearly hear the shot every night almost in every room" He paused then yelled "Bang!" at the top of his voice, he then roared with laughter as they all jumped again.

After Macgregor had successfully scared the guests especially Sharon he left them to tell their own ghostly tales. Sharon kept jumping at every sound and saying 'what was that' even when no one else heard anything. Sharon had already stated that she had heard voices and spoke to them saying 'If your there contact me in some way, make a noise or something'.

Meanwhile he called Samantha and Elliot to one side wanting to speak to them in private. "I need to discuss Gillian" He said in a solemn tone

"Gillian went missing during the last haunted weekend. Before she disappeared she claimed that she could hear voices, as you know we set up the atmosphere for the ghost hunting by elaborate sound and visual effects".

"So it could have been one of these sounds?" Samantha asked trying to make sense of it.

"No this was nothing like our pranks, it was voices of command telling her to do things" Macgregor explained

“So was she ever assessed mentally?” Samantha asked concerned

“No never” Macgregor replied

“You think she may schizophrenic?” Elliot asked

“Yes maybe” Samantha replied searching for a rational explanation for her behaviour.

“I suppose it is possible” Macgregor admitted

“My mother was schizophrenic” Elliot said reflecting back on his past

“I had a friend who was schizophrenic and she used to have audible hallucinations she tried to drown out the voices by putting headphones on and playing music, this worked for a while but nothing works perfectly”. Samantha said concerned.

“What was Gillian wearing when she went missing? Elliot asked

“She was wearing patterned T-shirt and blue jeans”. Macgregor said giving a loose description of her attire, he produced a photograph from the inside pocket of his coat and showing Samantha and Elliot.

“She’s pretty” Samantha remarked

“And where was she when you last saw her?” Elliot asked

“In the library looking at books” Macgregor explained

“Can we go there?” Samantha asked eager to find out more information.

“Yes of course” Macgregor He made his excuses to the other guests and took Samantha and Elliot into the library.

After a careful search of the room Samantha and Elliot were satisfied that nothing was unusual in the room. Elliot examined every inch even the walls for any signs of another exit like a false panel or section leading to a secret passage. He felt as if he was being watched and did notice tiny object, which could have been a camera in the corner of the room.

“What’s this Gordon?” He asked

“Oh that’s part of our elaborate equipment that we use for the ghost hunting, we project images in the room to give the elusion of a ghost the sound equipment is concealed in a few false books”. Macgregor explained

“Very clever” Elliot said

“So you make people believe that ghosts exist” Samantha said

“Yes its all part of the fun and thrill of the weekend” Macgregor said playing with his ginger beard with his fingers.

Samantha was attracted again by the ruby ring again as she saw it sparkle.

Samantha asked to see Gillian’s bedroom, it looked just like the other rooms even to the point of having a fireplace and wall panels. In the middle of the room was a four-poster bed with red silk sheets like Samantha's bed. There was no sign of dirty footprints or blood and according to Macgregor there was no sign of a struggle. Elliot examined the wall panels and around the fireplace hoping to find for a secret entrance or doorway. Nothing seemed obvious and everywhere was spotlessly clean like all the other rooms, which eliminated a possible, escape root in the area. Samantha thought that Elliot had been watching too many movies and had an over active imagination.

Macgregor led them out of the room and locked the door behind them; Samantha and Elliot decided to have a walk outside around the immediate area, examining each window and doors for any clues.

"Something doesn't add up" Samantha said

"Like what?" Elliot said bewildered

"Come on Stuart didn't you think Janet was odd asking questions like a detective or something?" Samantha said looking at another window

"I think you have a lot of imagination" Elliot said heading for the conservatory door.

"Fuck you Stuart why can't you see it are you fucking blind" Samantha said angrily

"Sorry but you're the reporter, I am merely a photographer" Elliot explained

"Well I know there is something about all this that doesn't make any fucking sense and that Janet knows something". Samantha insisted.

"I can appreciate that Sammy but why get so upset?" Elliot said checking the conservatory door.

"Because no one fucking listens to me, I don't know why I waste my breath honestly" Samantha said walking back towards the main entrance.

"Perhaps if you didn't swear or get stressed it might help" Elliot said hoping to get through to her about her attitude.

"Well I am sorry but I can't help it, I feel so fucking stressed" Samantha was certainly acting very emotional like she was hormonal.

"Ok I get it, but we need to be rational and think about this clearly".

"Yes I know sorry let's go back inside".

Samantha and Elliot entered the main door and began walking up the stairs when they noticed everyone rushing about frantically.

"What's happened" Samantha asked

"It's the vicar he was found dead in the study with marks around his neck, it looks like he has had a rope around it" Janet explained

They all entered the study and noticed the vicar on the floor with a rope around his neck; next to his body were a mystery murder game card with a picture of man in purple on it. The police arrived soon afterwards and interviewed the guests and staff. Janet spent a lot of time with them before they left; she then spoke to Samantha and Elliot in the library.

"Ok who are you two, you go outside snooping why?" Janet asked abruptly

"So who the fuck are you?" Samantha asked

"I am a under cover police detective searching for Gillian" Janet explained

Elliot looked at Samantha and back at Janet, he seemed a little confused at her explanation.

"We are from criminal world I am a photographer and she is a reporter" Elliot explained

"Reporters your kidding right, so what have you discovered?" Janet asked

"That this is a creepy castle, probably haunted and nobody is who they seem". Samantha replied.

"Well that's a fact" Janet said looking around the library

"I can't help feeling that we are being watched all the time" Samantha said also looking around.

"I know I have had that feeling since day one" Elliot admitted.

"Fuck now I sound like that daft bitch Sharon who jumps at every sound and sees things moving in the darkness". Samantha said jokingly.

Meanwhile in a secret room a figure sat watching them on a television screen, the screen was one of many that showed various rooms in the house. The pictures changed revealing more rooms including the bedrooms one of the rooms had a girl on a bed with her hands and feet tied to the bedposts. The girl was quite still and appeared to be asleep after a while she changed positions. On the desk near the television screen was a mystery murder game card with a picture of a white lady on the front.

The person picked up the card and examined it, then placed it back on the table near a card with a picture of a red lady.

Samantha went to her room which was close to Elliot's room, Janet had left them and joined Macgregor in the study. Samantha went into her bathroom and began to have a shower hoping it might relax her so that she could sleep. She was washing herself when she thought that she heard a noise in the room. It was as if something heavy had been dropped on the floor making such a noise that it could have been easily heard above the sound of the gushing water in the shower. She switched off the shower wrapped a towel around her and went into the bedroom.

When she got there she noticed the tall lamp stand was on its side on the floor, it was heavy consisting of mainly brass and could only have been pushed over. Samantha decided to lock the door in case someone had entered the room and perhaps stolen something. After checking all her things she discovered nothing was missing.

Samantha turned main light off and put her side lamp on turning it to a dim light. She put on her eye mask and tried to settle down for the night. She began moving from side to side trying to get comfortable and eventually she fell asleep. She was unaware of being watched by an infrared camera the observer seemed fascinated by her as she lay sleeping. He then stood up and walked towards the door dressed in a black jump suit and brandishing a torch.

The panel opened leading into Samantha's room after a short pause the figure emerged into Samantha's room clenching the torch. The figure walked towards the bed where she was sleeping and placed a mystery murder game card of miss scarlet on the table, then reached out to touch her. The figure grabbed her shoulder and shook her; Samantha pulled off her mask and thrashed out at the figure. The torch fell on the bed and she used it to hit him on the forehead and he fell to the ground. She then shone the torch in his face and gasped in horror as she saw his face looking at her.

"For fuck sake Stuart, what the fuck are you doing" Samantha said hysterically

"Ouch I found a secret passage" Elliot said holding his head

“So you decided to come in my fucking room and scare me” Samantha went to hit him again and realised what she was doing “How fucking smart was that?”

“Found this card near the secret panel, I thought I saw a figure in the passage” Elliot pointed to the wall “I thought he came from here”.

Samantha looked at her hand and noticed blood then looked at his head

“You’re bleeding my god it’s running down your face” Samantha said worried

She held out her hand touching his face “Here sit on the bed” she advised him

“I will get something to clean you up”. Samantha said rushing to the bathroom

She returned with a damp flannel and a towel “Let me deal with it” she offered

She began dabbing the wound with the flannel and cleaning his face

“Ouch that bloody hurts” Elliot exclaimed

“Man up it’s only a fucking scratch” Samantha said continuing to clean the wound.

“It still damn well hurts” Elliot shouted

"Shhhh for fuck sake shut up everyone will here you" Samantha said in a low voice

"I didn't mean to scare you Sammy, but I had to warn you" Elliot whispered

"Ok I understand, I had a visitor before who obviously meant me to have this card" Samantha said looking at the mystery murder game card of a woman in red "I guess that's me" She said concerned

"Yes the person could have killed you" Elliot said with equal concern

"The noise from the lamp stand falling must have made him rush off and he exited through the secret exit. I heard it crash to the floor when I was in the shower it landed by that wall". Samantha pointed towards the wall

"My god you were lucky Sammy" Elliot said

"We need to stick together Stuart for our own safety" Samantha said concerned

"Oh I would be safer with you" Elliot said holding his head

"I am sorry really" Samantha said smiling and sounding so sincere

"Ok what have you got in mind?" Elliot asked

"You sleep here with me but on the side of the bed near that wall" She pointed to the wall where the secret panel existed.

"Ok" Elliot agreed

"But don't get too close and no touching ok" Samantha insisted.

"Understood" Elliot said with a smile.

Elliot lay on the bed facing the wall while Samantha lay with her back to him smiling to herself as if she really wanted something to happen. But Samantha was so mixed up at this stage her emotions were surging like engines in a race waiting for the flag to indicate go.

Meanwhile Sharon and another guest were walking around the ground floor near the study unaware that the killer was watching them on his screen. He was holding a remote control and opening the passage doors close to where they were walking. "Hello" Sharon said, "let me know your there give me a sign" Suddenly a door opened and Sharon vanished into the study someone covered her mouth and plunged a dagger into her back. The other guest took no notice of her thinking that she was doing her usual over dramatics and annoying sounds. Then she entered the dining room and saw the outline of a figure that she thought was part of the ghostly pranks until she felt a heavy object hit her on the head. The figure hit her viciously several times until she lay limp beside one end of the table. Sharon was cut to pieces in the study with a large sharp knife and the killer's hands were covered with blood. Then a calling card dropped with a lady in pink on the front of it and the bloody knife was placed next to it.

During the night Samantha was moving about restlessly and Elliot was just turned on by her presence in the bed. Eventually she turned towards him he felt her warm breath on his chest and she moved her head on the pillow close to his face. Elliot had turned his head towards her but kept his eyes closed then she pressed her cheek against his. Breathing onto his face she was now cuddled up to him and could feel his body heat as she pressed her lips against his and began kissing him. She had lost control perhaps she was thinking about someone else as her fingers began to wonder around his back. He returned a lingering kiss and his hands wandered up and down her back and started fondling her buttocks. She removed her top and they both continued kissing for a while before becoming completely naked and enjoying each other's bodies. They had totally lost control by the time they were kissing each other's body and made love unaware that they were being watched by the infrared camera.

By morning Samantha and Elliot were embraced naked in a comfortable position, the sun was shining through a crack in the curtains with a beam of light drifting across the bed. Samantha was actually lying on top of Elliot with her head on his naked chest gradually her eyes opened and she began to focus on the hairs on his chest. She stayed perfectly still trying to understand what she had done and why, as nothing made sense at all. She had obviously lost control of her emotions and he being a man took advantage of her feminine weakness. Foolish moments that she would no doubt regret and have to explain the best way she knew how. The embarrassment and humiliation and now lying naked on top of a work colleague, what was she going to say to him when he awoke. She finally pulled herself away from him and looked beneath the bedclothes at her naked body then at him.

"I did dream all this right?" Samantha said to Elliot as he began to wake up

"God not unless I did too" Elliot said just as surprised

They were both acting like virgins encountering their first sexual relationship

"No I mean it was a mistake, a foolish mistake" Samantha said trying not to give him eye contact

"Yes a moment of weakness" Elliot said trying to reassure her

Samantha put her hands to her head "Fuck me this isn't happening"

She began staring into space her eyes were wide and her mouth open, Elliot tried to touch her in order to comfort her.

"Just don't" She pushed his hand away "Just don't touch me ok".

"We need answers Sammy" Elliot said trying to change the subject

"Answers, I am fucking freaking out and you want answers, you are unreal" Samantha said hysterically

"No you don't understand I mean about the abduction and the murder" Elliot said

"Oh that well go and get washed and dressed and then come back here ok" Samantha said hiding under the sheets.

"Ok" Elliot said pulling back the sheets on his side of the bed

Samantha turned her head away trying not to look at him, while he put on his clothes.

"And Stuart don't mention this to anyone" Samantha looked at him for a reassuring reply

"Honestly I wont mention a thing" Elliot sounded sincere as he unlocked the door and left the room.

An hour later a knock came at Samantha's door and Janet stood waiting, Samantha opened the door expecting Elliot to be there.

"Ok I am ready" Samantha paused and looked at Janet

"Sammy I need to speak to you" Janet breezed past Samantha

"Come in" Samantha said sarcastically

"Another guest has been murdered, a calling card left this time a man in purple" Janet said moving up to the bed

"When was this?" Samantha asked

"Last night and I think it was your colleague Stuart" Janet said looking around the bed.

"Impossible" Samantha said dismissing Janet's theory

"May I ask how you deduce that" Samantha had her arms folded in a defensive gesture.

"Oh come on Sammy you must admit he has been snooping all over this castle" Janet insisted

"You can't accuse him he's innocent" Samantha insisted

"How do you know?" Janet asked

"I just do" Samantha answered swiftly

"He slept here last night didn't he?" Janet smiled

"What makes you say that" Samantha said innocently

"Because his socks are on your bed and there are fair hairs on the pillow on this side need I go on?" Janet said picking up a sock with her fingers.

"Alright he did so what now you fucking accuse me" Samantha said upset about being discovered with Stuart.

"Nothing but tonight we can all explore this castle for clues" Janet insisted

At that moment a knock came at the door, Samantha opened it and Elliot stood fully dressed. He entered the room acting as if the night before had never happened, and then he noticed Janet standing by the bed.

"Good morning" Elliot said cheerfully

"There has been another murder" Samantha said before Janet could speak

"Oh was that with a calling card?" Elliot asked wondering why Janet was looking around the bed.

"Yes I suspected you but you were apparently occupied all night" Janet said looking at Samantha

"Oh yes I was all night" Elliot said looking at Janet and then Samantha

"So why don't we go for breakfast?" Samantha said wanting to leave the room in a hurry.

Janet swept her hands threw her dark hair and smiled at Samantha she knew that she had embarrassed her and gathered from Samantha's response that she regretted the night before and just wanted to put it behind her.

"Oh I was left a card too with a purple man on it" Elliot said

"So we have all had one now?" Janet said "But how is this person entering the rooms?" she continues

"Secret passages I found one last night" Elliot boasted

"How romantic you entered Sammy's room via a secret passage and that's why you have a bruise and gash on your forehead, she wasn't expecting you". Janet said teasing them.

"Lets leave it shall we" Samantha said dismissively

Janet wanted to catch the murderer she suspected everyone but considered this one to be a clever psychopath who knew the castle well. Also this killer might have an accomplice as the bodies seemed to be being moved from one place to another. Evident by fibres on the shoes and blood stains by the walls which also meant that there was secret doorways and corridors around the castle once used as an escape route for the occupants during invasions centuries ago.

That night Janet had discussed exposing the murderer to her police colleagues they needed to be discrete in order to capture the murderer. She had arranged to set a trap for him by hiding police in certain locations within the castle disguised as servants. The killer seemed to strike at night when other activities were going on and so it was considered the best time to set a trap. The killer was obsessed with board games and mystery murder was his favourite game. He had left the board game in the study on a table. Occasionally he moved the pieces around according to who was murdered and where. The weapons matched the murder weapons used each time making it obvious that the killer had planned his or her murders to detail.

"We are dealing with a violent psychopath who could be anywhere in this damn castle, just be careful".

The weather that night was stormy, thunder and lightening with heavy rain. Samantha and Elliot entered the secret passage from Samantha's room both carrying torches fighting away cobwebs and feeling insects crawling on their body. They were both dressed in dark clothes as if they expected to be tumbling in the darkness finding answers to this mystery.

"Didn't you find Macgregor acting oddly?" Samantha asked

"Yes a little I suppose" Elliot replied

"And he wasn't wearing that special ring" Samantha said tripping over

"Are you alright" Elliot said concerned

"Ouch fuck I can't find the torch, it must be broke" Samantha said searching around with her hands.

Elliot shone his torch towards her "Here grab my hand lets stick together". Elliot said holding out his hand

"This changes nothing Stuart, I am still not happy with you" Samantha said grabbing his hand and standing up.

They continued down the passageway until they reached a door, Samantha had been clinging onto Elliot's arm and let go as he opened the door. They had reached the roof and were heading across a narrow pathway to another door.

"We are on the roof" Elliot shouted

"No shit" Samantha said sarcastically

"Well let's go or we will be here all fucking night" she continued

It was very slippery with the rain pounding on the roof and water drifting onto the path forming a river before them. Elliot slipped a few times but Samantha managed to keep her footing until they had almost reached the door. Suddenly she slipped and a few bricks crumbled away and disappeared off the roof. Samantha was slipping through the gap, she began to scream sliding almost to the edge of the roof clinging hold of bricks. Elliot caught her by her arms and tried pulling her up still slipping himself.

"Find a footing come on I am slipping" Elliot shouted

"I can't fucking move" Samantha said trying to grip hold of another brick

"Come on Sammy" Elliot shouted in desperation

"I am going to fall" Samantha shouted

Samantha suddenly felt a ledge with her feet and began to climb up, Elliot pulled her the rest of the way and they both fell back onto the tiles. Elliot found the torch and they continued across the roof holding on to each other.

"I think I am going to find a new career this job is fucking dangerous" Samantha said in anger

They entered the door and walked down some steps into another secret passageway.

"Right hold my hand Sammy" Elliot said

"Not likely" Samantha said still moody

"So we don't lose each other" Elliot replied

"Ok just for that reason" Samantha said grabbing his hand

After walking a short distance Samantha was actually grabbing Elliot by the arm, she was so close he could feel her breath on his neck and her heart beating.

He was reluctant to comment in case she started shouting and swearing at him.

He came across a panel with a catch on it, which released the door mechanism; he pulled the catch and the panel opened into a bedroom. Lying on the bed was Macgregor's niece she had auburn hair and was wearing a green dress, she was awake and looking up at the top of the four-poster bed.

Samantha and Elliot raced over to the bed Elliot was trying to untie her legs while Samantha untied her arms.

"You must be Gillian" Samantha commented

Gillian nodded and looked down at Elliot who was holding the rope that he had removed from her feet.

"Who did this?" Samantha asked

"Uncle Gordon" Gillian replied in a weak voice

"We need to go" Elliot said anxiously

"Can you walk?" Samantha asked Gillian

"Yes I think so" Gillian said swivelling round on the bed

"Let's find Gordon and the other guests" Samantha said eagerly

"No" Gillian said "Why don't we find out what's really happening and enter the secret passage, we may catch Uncle Gordon before he kills again.

"Good idea" Elliot said eager to catch the killer

"Well alright" Samantha agreed "I just want this whole fucking mess over with".

"Excuse Sammy she is very hormonal" Elliot explained

"Fuck you Stuart" Samantha said heading towards the panel

Elliot looked around for the catch on the panel, suddenly it opened and they began to enter the passageway. Elliot led the way until Gillian made the suggestion to follow a thin faded line on the wall which she claimed she made when she was being lead down there from the library.

Meanwhile another victim had been murdered with a heavy spanner the killer hit her several times on the head, in a vicious attack and showing no mercy as he caved her scull in. The woman's dress was covered in blood and she was being dragged like a sack of potatoes along another part of the passage and left in the library along with a calling card with a picture of a woman in white.

No sooner had the killer left the library than Samantha and Elliot entered. Seeing the body they had a quick look and then re entered the passage. While this was going on the killer stuck again this time attacking a man with a candlestick using the same force, as before determined to make sure he was dead. He hit him several times with blood spraying all around him as he obviously severed the archery in his neck. He struggled with this body leaving him in the conservatory and placing the weapon beside his body.

A hand reached forward to touch Samantha's head it was covered with blood grasping at her hair then got disturbed. Samantha and Elliot were alerted by the sound of a gun shot which at first sounded like one of Macgregor's elaborate sound effects then another shot was fired sounding different. They all followed the direction where they thought the sound was coming from Gillian seemed eager to get there first.

They arrived at the main control area in the cellar and were astonished to find six monitors displaying various views of the castle. Suddenly they noticed Janet and a few others walking along a secret passage and behind them a well-built man shaped like Macgregor. He managed to catch up with them and attack one of them without the others noticing.

"My god he's picking them off one at a time" Elliot said anxiously

"They must be close to here by now" Gillian said looking around

"Look at all this stuff" Samantha said pointing to the board game

"But this is not the control room Macgregor used that was near the study not here in the cellar" Elliot said confused "why have two rooms to do this?"

"Obviously he wanted us to know about the one but not this one" Samantha explained.

Gillian picked something up from under the table and stepped back watching both of them. At that moment Janet appeared with two men and stand beside them each one looking at Elliot.

"So it was you" Janet said "Using Sammy as your accomplish very smart or are you"

At that moment a man appeared "Well what do we have here?"

Janet looked at him and frowned "Gordon I have your killer" she said confidently.

"Is that so" He said coldly "Well have I got news for you"

"I have been following them and they have been at the scene of each one" Janet said

Gordon raised his arm revealing a revolver "Well guess what?"

"You're the killer but how?" Samantha asked

"I used this remote control to operate all the doors and entrances I also followed you all at all times, those catches don't work and never have done. I have been in control of this game all the time and sadly all of you have come to your end" Macgregor smirked evilly.

"But how did you do this all alone?" Elliot asked

"He didn't" came a voice from behind each turned to see Gillian with a gun

Elliot turned to see a spanner flying in the air towards Macgregor's head, he swerved to avoid it coming hitting his head. Despite his efforts caught him on the temple and he fell to the ground groaning and holding his head. As this happened Gillian responded by shooting at everyone wildly, after a few seconds she realised that she was out of ammunition. She then pulled a knife from a sheath and proceeded to lash out at anyone close catching one of the men at the same time Macgregor charged at them too. There was a confusion of arms and legs everywhere, people were bleeding and eventually both Macgregor and Gillian were lying on the floor in handcuffs. During the scuffle on the floor Gillian had attempted to grab Macgregor's gun but couldn't quite reach it. It was thought that Samantha may have hit her at this point preventing Janet from getting shot. At one point Gillian had tried to stab Samantha in the chest but fell forward narrowly missing her throat.

Two of the men who were police officers had been shot but not seriously wounded while Elliot managed to cut his hand. Samantha had thumped Gillian at one stage but may have been trying to attack Elliot as she was still annoyed with men due to breaking up with her boyfriend. Janet looked at the killers then at Samantha not knowing what to say.

"Thank you Sammy, sorry I accused you of all this" Janet said shamefully

"You're welcome and its ok" Samantha said smiling

Janet smiled back and then told the police officers to take the prisoners away.

She then took other policemen and searched the cellar for bodies, during her search she discovered Gordon Macgregor bound and gagged in a corner. He explained about his brother John who had gone missing years ago, during Gordon Macgregor's absence when he was in Greece John must have installed all his elaborate equipment including a separate generator to power everything. The idea of operating monitors to watch everyone was clever although using a remote control mechanism to operate panel doors to the secret passages suggests a planned operation and the murder game could only be the work of someone evil and a dangerous psychopath, a person with no continence but an intelligent man.

By the time the forensics arrived and everyone was questioned it was morning. Macgregor had switched off the generator and disconnected the other systems so that only the lights and boiler system and any other necessary electrical equipment operated in the castle. The door panels on each of the walls were taken off while the police searched all over the castle for other bodies. Skeletons were found in various places including a vault and it was thought that John had been killing people for years mostly with the aid of Gillian. The one puzzling thing was that she was tied up at times Elliot saw her on the monitor tied to a bed. It was never explained why unless it was to lead Samantha and Elliot into the room as a diversion while John carried on killing. The other puzzling thing was that John never had a motive for murder; he just enjoyed murder mysteries and games.

The following morning turned out to be sunny with clear skies with a no rain forecast for at least three days. This was a welcome sight after all the storms and additional artificial storms over the last few days. Samantha vowed and declared that she would never enter a castle again except for Edinburgh of course. Elliot actually enjoyed the experience and being shouted and sworn at by Samantha.

Gordon stood outside looking at his castle when his surviving guests came out, He spoke to each one in turn feeling guilty about his Brother John's behaviour. But no one blamed Gordon and knew the full story of how John had gone missing and that John tied Gordon up then replaced him in order to get about the castle and middling with the guests.

"I am grateful to you Stuart, you have a Scottish name to be proud of" Macgregor said shaking him by the hand.

"Thank you Gordon" Elliot said smiling

"And my beautiful guest Sammy, god bless you" Macgregor said kissing and hugging her,

"Thank you" Samantha said rolling her eyes and fighting her way out of his ginger beard. She also noticed the ruby ring that she admired on his finger.

They started to walk towards the minibus when Samantha turned and walked back towards him "Just one thing Gordon who was the ghost image in my room last night?".

Macgregor looked puzzled and so she continued to describe what she saw

"It was a woman wearing a ballroom gown with a diamond clustered tiara"

"Heavens my dear I don't know all the sound and visual systems were turned off last night so there wouldn't be any we ghosties from me".

"You're sure?" Samantha asked

"Absolutely" Macgregor said seriously

With that Samantha looked up at her window and a woman waved down to her.

After the castle experience Samantha and Elliot decided to return to Edinburgh for the tattoo. The experience was worth it and just happened to be the one of the most spectacular experiences of their lives.

NOTHING IS REAL

In The Beginning

It was a bright sunny day in a village in France in the nineteen forties, I found myself running down a street in a army uniform, with the sound of rifles and artillery, explosions going on all around me. I saw soldiers being shot and bodies lay across the street wounded or killed by the enemy, I spotted Germans running for shelter in buildings and decided to pursue them. As I entered the building I held my machine gun tight and walked cautiously inside, listening for every sound and watching for anyone jumping out at me. I heard the sound of gunfire and entered the room there before me was a German soldier staring at me and holding his rifle up to shoot me. I froze on the spot and watched as he pulled the trigger unable to fire at him with my machine gun, it was a matter of seconds before I realised that I had been shot and fell helplessly to the ground. I questioned whether or not I had been killed but then I awoke from a dream, It felt so real to me, I felt a pain in my stomach and looked down searching for blood stains on my pyjamas. My throat hurt so I must have yelled out at some point, maybe it was the reaction of being shot, all I know is that if that had been a console game it would be fantastic.

My mother entered the room concerned; she was wearing red pyjamas which only exasperated my situation.

“Daniel what’s wrong?” She asked

“I had a nightmare” I replied not wishing to explain myself.

“You were yelling and making such a noise I thought we were being burgled” She said with her dark hair in a mess and pyjamas ruffled up, looking like Amy Winehouse.

“Honestly mother I am fine”

I must say my parents really worry about me, they I am obsessed with console games as if I am part of a game or something. It is quite bizarre how they think, How can I possibly be part of an animated game that couldn't be real, but then if I wanted to think that way then as John Lennon said in his lyrics to the Beatles song Strawberry fields 'nothing is real'.

My perception of life is that many things in life could be part of someone's dream or the figment of their imagination sometimes fuelled by alcohol or drug abuse. Many writers who create such fantasy books such as Lewis Carol's Alice in wonderland must have been high on something I should imagine, in order to create such characters as a mad hatter, crazy rabbit that at least is my theory. Imagine if everything was animated in some way and nothing was real, the concept of us all being controlled by someone or something above our own intellectual plane. I would like to think that I am making my own decisions and have the capacity to plan my life for what it is worth.

My parents brought me up to think in certain ways, they guided me and set rules as a way to recognise right from wrong, in a similar way school rules were said to do the same thing. So I was brought up by family values and peer pressure and base my morals on both factors, drifting through life fairly balanced between the two hoping to fit into society with this in mind. I wonder how many people could say that about their life based on their background, it would depend on your own views of the nature or nurture debate and learned behaviour. Also we need to look at broken families and where we grew up, what country or location within a place, the urban setting or ghetto.

I am perhaps fortunate enough to be part of a nuclear family consisting of mother Sylvia and Father Robert with a brother Andrew and sister called Samantha.

My mother was over protective and tended to smother us with love, my father wanted me to exceed, to excel in education and become prosperous, so that we would have a richer life than he had and have everything we dreamed of. He used to sit us on his knee while he was on the computer in order for us to get familiar with format and general operations of the computer and internet surfing the web. I even had a children's lap top that taught me the basics about letters, numbers, mathematics, and word building. This helped to increase my vocabulary and spelling skills, I became top of my class in most subjects which pleased my parents and made me popular at school. I went from school to college where I met my girl friend Kim Lewis a clever girl with long dark hair and hazel eyes and generous lips, she was slim and dressed casually but smart. She had a strong personality forthright and opinionated, who would fight for any good cause and be the leader of a campaign. But she had a loving side so warm and compassionate, loyal and devoted to me in every way. I considered myself very lucky to have someone like her in my life, she could read me like a book, some even said she controlled me like a puppet.

I felt a little more freedom at college, I was not under so much pressure to get things done and found that I was able to pace myself; I could plan ahead more and found time to relax with Kim. We used to go to the Cinema together and frequently take walks through the park; I enjoyed our many intellectual conversations or debates.

KIM

I was in the right frame of mind for playing my games, I was the mega gamester untouchable by my college friends and Kim agreed that we should spend a few wasteful hours playing games especially in a competitive way. Kim went more for fantasy games with wizards and witches, while I played more army games and aliens although we both played some of the Batman and other action hero games. I imagined her and my friends in some of the places David Spencer was an alien and Arnold Crutchley was a action hero. David was my inspiration has he was quite inventive with an incredible imagination, in fact he was instrument in the creation of my games. We were playing games one afternoon when he came up with a few ideas that I was really impressed with. He looked at a book by Sarah Ruth Scott called 'Blood trail- across time and then showed me the sequel 'Blood trail – evil of the vampires which I read in a matter of days. I was immediately intrigued firstly by the main character Siena a vampire who was seeking a way to become human again, but being pursued by slayers and vampires. Then her boyfriend Jack an innocent bystander who had become involved in this adventure because of falling in love with Siena. But many characters emerged from this story Carina was the strongest and most admired as a vampire slayer who befriended Siena, clad in armour and weapons to kill vampires she was beautiful with long dark hair and a slender figure, a little like Kim, I could imagine her fighting vampires and leading slayers into battle. Swirling her sword and kicking her enemies to the ground, then offering them a fatal blow to the head or torso, then putting one foot on their chest and holding up her sword in victory. That night I dreamt of Kim in this role, she was my true heroin, I yelled out in my sleep and Kim sat up quickly with a frightened look on her face.

"God, Daniel" She was breathing swiftly her chest was rising

"Oh I feel weird, what's happening?" I said grabbing her arm

"You frightened me, what's wrong? She asked

"I was dreaming" I explained I could still see her in armour, but as I touched her it disappeared and all I felt was her heart beating fast. "My god, I am so sorry"

I said embracing her; she was so warm her flesh was so soft against mine. I felt compelled to make love to her at this moment, she also felt amorous but I felt not for the same reason as I was still fantasising about Carina. That was one of my passionate nights with the thought of 'Blood trail' from that story thanks to my friend David. All I can say is thank god I didn't bite her or trust a stake into her heart, or find myself in a coffin like a vampire I had read about.

"Daniel you have an incredible imagination" Kim said to me as we were strolling through the park.

"It's not all me" I replied "David helped me with ideas and fascinating books"

"Are you telling me that blood trail is a book?" she asked inquisitively

"Yes, blood trail are books by Sarah Ruth Scott, about vampires travelling across time and abducting humans from everywhere harvesting their blood"

"Sounds interesting" She admitted

"The slayers try to capture them and stop their blood thirsty activity" I explained in detail.

"So you want to create a game of this?" she said "I am intrigued"

"Kim its just an idea, nothing more" I added

"It feels real" She said shuddering

"Sometimes I think nothing is real" I said looking around the park

"Nothing is real?" she repeated "what kind of statement is that?"

"Exactly what I said" I said looking into her eyes

“I am real and you are real” she suddenly did a twirl “all of this is real, the trees, the grass, the sky”

“How do you know?” I said in a profound manner

“My senses tell me, I can hear, see, smell, touch” she said smelling flowers and then hugged me kissing me tenderly on the lips “and taste” she said laughing

“I believe you, my theory is blown” I had to admit defeat, but I still had nagging doubts running through my mind, did we truly exist?

We continued walking in the park and share more philosophical thoughts, spanning subjects such as creation and the big bang theory to the meaning of life and the nature verses nurture debate. Nothing was resolved but we reached a common ground in that we considered that some things are inherited from our parents other things influenced by society or external sources. The principles that are presented to us, such as morality and behaviour are inherently demonstrated by others who seem to have the most influence on our lives. We copy such behaviour subject to our own desires and needs; this allows us to be favoured by the majority giving us permission to perform in a favourable manner. Society accepts us for this reason by having good manners and showing kindness to others, however to follow another path leads to anti social behaviour and therefore one is rejected from society as a deviant or rebel. This is known as being a conformist by simply following the rules or law lay down by men, there are many parables that can explain this some are written in the bible as told by Jesus.

Religion plays its part in conformity as each religion lays down commandments or rules to follow said to be guides to keep us on the straight and narrow figuratively speaking. Some religions take things to extreme and history has shown what the consequences can be in that direction. The lack of obedience leads to punishment even death. So if we are born with a conscience and a choice of following good or bad, why are we punished if we do badly? Isn't this considered a contradictory in terms, given a choice of direction and then corrected for going the wrong way? Both Kim and I became entangled in a philosophical web of intrigue and decided to choose what we were going to eat instead of scrambling our brains with such an eye brow discussion.

"So what is your culinary delight?" I asked her politely

"Fish and chips I think" she replied

"Food for thought" I replied wittily "for your indulgence"

"Very droll Daniel" she said smiling, still perplexed by their conversation about life, as Kim had never dwelled so deeply into such a subject that required so many answers to so few questions.

I merely took this in my stride and continued to think of the answers to the universe and fathom them out by myself, but it wasn't long before I too felt hungry and could only concentrate on food. This led me to think how much time people contemplate on in depth theories of life, prompted by reading books, watching programmes on television or in conversation. Wouldn't it be nice to have all the answers at hand like surfing the internet, using tools like google search and finding out about the meaning of life.

We reached a café that I eloquently named greasy Lil's due to the fact it had grubby windows and plastic table cloths that you could write your name in the lingering grease. The staff dressed in well worn aprons which were decorated in faded flowers, these seemed to match their drabbled hair styles. On a positive note the food was cheap and seats were reasonably comfortable. Myself and Kim sat waiting for our well prepared gourmet of delight which consisted of chips slopped on a plate with mushy peas and a recently deceased fish. Kim swore she saw the tail move, but I put that down to what may have been crawling underneath it. We had our meals and made a swift exit out of the door and into the local market, Kim felt uncomfortable all afternoon thinking of the café. We passed a fish mongers hours later and she was physically sick seeing the dead fish with eyes peering at us. We decided return to our university campus apartment building; Kim went for a shower and freshens up while I went to check my emails on my computer in my apartment. We met later to watch a gig from a local band, which was amazing and well worth wasting a few precious hours of our time. We walked across the campus and I deliberately avoided mentioning my philosophy of life although it was burning my brain, somehow I thought that Kim wanted to discuss our relationship. She seemed so bubbly that night, as if her heart was going to burst, her eyes sparkled in the moonlight and her generous lips seemed so moist ready for kissing me. We stopped and kissed under a tree with the dim lights from nearby buildings shining through gaps in the curtains. She melted me with her warm lips and the closeness of her body next to mine, I felt that I found the girl for me; she was in my heart, my soul and every part of me. I realise men rarely discuss the way we feel about girls, but I would burst if I didn't say these words and convey to the world how we as men truly feel. I know that Kim appreciates me being open about my feelings and true to her, and that means faithful to the end.

"Do you really love me" Kim asked

"Why of course I do" I was confused at these words "Did you even need to ask?"

"No, not really but I am not used to men being so honest" she said looking into my eyes.

SABRINA

My creative work helped me to create a blonde girl called Sabrina; I originally drew a picture of her as far back as art class at school. I suppose it didn't mean much to me back then, just another drawing that I kept in my art folder. But years later I painted her on canvas for a art competition, I painted her soft complexion, blue eyes and tried to create an angel. When I finished she virtually came alive, she seemed to detach herself from the canvas and just stared at me with her blue sparkling eyes. She was my fantasy who one day would be a character in my games, that at least was my dream, but she was only known to me at this point. I won the art contest and Sabrina my fantasy portrait was exhibited firstly at college and then at the local art gallery viewed by thousands of people. I was so pleased with my work, my tutor advised me to change my direction and enter art school, but my heart was set on creating games that people would be amazed at and want to play all day long. If I could create the type of characters like Sabrina in my games I would be happy, I would like to control not only movements but emotions such as sadness, anger or love.

My experience with Sabrina didn't stop here I began to see her everywhere; I saw her crossing a street, on a bus and even naked on a train. I began to wonder whether I was becoming obsessed with her or her image, as I was the only one who could actually see her was she an elusion a figment of my imagination. Or did this person really exist, maybe other people could actually see her, but refuse to get involved with her or the situations. I was happy to keep her to myself at this point as I was not ready to share her, perhaps this was selfish but I must confess she fascinated me, I must confess I had become obsessed with her image.

One thing concerned me, when I saw her naked on the train I wanted to hold her, kiss her and make love to her. I was alone on the train and had the opportunity and the inclination, but one thing held me back the thought of Kim waiting for me at the University campus. Kim was my saving grace, my faithful girlfriend who kept me on the straight and narrow, I usually turn to her for guidance but for some reason Sabrina remained in my head for a while. I had to keep in mind that nothing is real, that way I could maintain my sanity at least for a while if I think of life as one big game with my friends as the characters in the game, and with me in control. Sabrina is my fantasy girl and what can I say she appears everywhere, I created her as a character in a few games introducing herself as a action girl or heroine.

EDUCATION

My education began at home with my father who helped me with my home work, by showing me how to research what I needed. I was always at the top of the class and by the time I left school I had ten GCSEs which were English literature and language, maths, biology, chemistry, physics, history ICT, and global citizenship. I went to college and took and passed A' levels in English language, maths and computing. My mind was always on gaming and the thought that one day I would create the perfect game, a virtual reality game that could be mistaken for reality so that the player could actually feel as if he/she could be in the game and live it as I seem to do right now. When I went to university I was beginning to gain practical experience in creating programs and software. I was learning how computer systems worked at a detailed level, the whole concept of controlling programs had become a reality and I was at the helm, like steering a ship, directing the ship on its course with the appropriate knowledge necessary. I was given a problem to solve using a kind of program or be given a computer system and replace it with something more effective or efficient, this involved planning and actually creating it using my skills in the best way possible. But in order to forfill my dream as creator of games I had to know how to write programming codes such as 'Java' or 'C++' I needed to have knowledge of the creative process such as planning, implementation and testing. I also needed to know how games are designed in a way to create an enjoyable experience for the user. I realised that I required a personal computer (PC) software to create it, and a virtual reality headset in order to test it. There is an extensive amount of software available known as integrated development environment (IDE) so I knew I could choose an effective software to suit my needs, I practiced with a few at university before purchasing my own. Technology was advancing all the time and companies were creating workouts for people to use with virtual reality (VR) headsets, frames were made to move about with people in them while watching themselves fly around in the air. The game simulated them on hang gliders or imitating birds in flight, the motion provided them with the feeling of gliding in the air, while the VR sets provided them with the visual aspect of flying motion at altitudes with mountains, trees and rivers beneath them. The scenery could be changed by the user and the gamester is in full control of their movements with hand levers and buttons.

My first year at university consisted of watching gigs, playing games and attending parties, Kim was a party animal so we used to gate crash anyone's party as long as booze was present we attended. We never took drugs or anything that was considered mind altering; after all I was already living in a fantasy world in my dreams and on various games in my past time. I remember relaxing one evening playing a game called Speculate; it was a complete fantasy that involved entering various lands collecting gold from trees and diamonds from the sky using various jump moves and equipment available. I had trouble focusing after leaving the game, everything was blurred and things around the room began to shine like I was still in the game.

Kim rushed towards me as I began to yell and freak out in the chair

“Daniel!” she exclaimed “What’s wrong with you?”

“I can’t see properly, everything looks weird” I replied

“In what way, tell me?” She asked anxiously.

“I don’t know, I can’t explain it, nothing seems real” I said shaking my head

“What game was it?”

“I was playing ‘Speculate” the one where you have to anticipate the moves and trap the diamonds in a box, but the diamonds spread and glowed blinding my eyes” I explained the best way that I could.

Kim seemed to understand having played the game herself and struggled to follow the sequence of the game for the same reason, but she didn’t suffer the same effects.

“You need to rest from these games Dan they are getting to you big time” Kim advised.

"Maybe your right, I need to rest and switch off" I agreed.

After a while I began to recover, my eyes focused again and I felt more comfortable. But I began to experience more and more nightmares of being trapped in games, some of them were quite vivid and explicit especially when Sabrina entered them, she seemed quite loving and clung to me as if she never wanted to let me go. I felt that she was insecure at first, but then as I got to know her within these games she was more possessive.

SIGNS

It should have been obvious to me, but from my earliest experiences I was seeing things such as my time in Blackpool when I saw words written in the sand saying 'Nothing is real' it didn't mean anything to me until I was on the train travelling through the mist, the windows were steamed up and suddenly the words appeared 'Nothing is real' I never mentioned it to Kim until we were in London and I saw a bus pass by us with the same words 'Nothing is real'

"Did you see that? I ask with surprise

"What am I looking at?" She replied

"On the side of that bus" I pointed to the bus that had stopped in traffic

"It's a holiday advertisement; do you want us to go on holiday?"

"No, I was referring to the writing" I prompted her

"Nothing like a holiday in Spain" She read from the banner

"Nothing is real" I said puzzled

"Where are you reading?" I asked looking at the same bus

"What is wrong with you are you dyslexic or short sighted" She said jokingly

I shrugged my shoulders and passed it off as nothing, but with my previous experiences of seeing these words I was convinced it was a sign. I never mentioned it again until we attended a funeral and I saw the same words above the cemetery gate, 'Nothing is real' these words seemed to haunt me for some reason, but I avoided telling Kim in case she worried about me. She might have thought that I was going insane and perhaps she would have been right, maybe I was hallucinating and becoming psychotic. These signs may have been a warning that I was suffering from some sort of mental illness, I could have lost control of reality and those words 'Nothing is real' was an indication that I had lost control.

I was in my second year at university and my studies had become more intense and the course was entering a very difficult area of programming and the placements felt like hard work with my other activities such as the nightmares that kept me awake and visual hallucinations.

I was sat up in bed one night having had a nightmare; Kim was lying on her side facing me, fast asleep breathing gently across my naked back. I was admiring her beauty; she had such soft flawless complexion which was unusual for a girl of her age, I would expect some acne or some abnormality. She was like some of the characters you see in games such as Sabrina my fantasy woman, She seemed to glow just like a new born baby full of innocence and free from corruption. She opened her eyes and struggled to focus, her eyes sparkled from the light of a small bedside lamp that made her blink, and then she licked her lips and spoke to me in a rough voice.

"Have you had another nightmare?" she asked

"Yes, as per usual" I replied

She put her arms around me from behind and rested her head on my back placing right cheek on my shoulder.

"Dan, what am I going to do with you?"

"Search me, I really don't know" I replied

"Perhaps you need a complete rest from games for a while and see if these nightmares subside" She advised.

"Perhaps your right Kim, they feel too real and part of my life" I said in agreement.

Kim seemed relieved at my words of agreement and kissed my back, I turned to face a empathetic face her eyes showed sincerity and her lips expressed tenderness as we kissed, they were warm and generous as she pressed them against my face covering my lips, wet and moist which surprised me as she had just woken up. But then I noticed a glass of water by her side on the table, she had taken a drink prior to hugging me. Her long covered part of her face and she brushed it back with her hand and gazed at me sweetly as she removed her top revealing her cute breasts, her nipples were prominent, raised by her excitement she was ready to make love and wanted to take the lead. She continued to kiss me passionately on the lips and I found myself being aroused by her and realised why I loved her. Soon we became naked and made passionate love, I felt as if I had entered another game this time involving sexual ecstasy with every rhythm of our bodies moving like a stream flowing smoothly through the rocks and falling down hill following the contours of the bank. Then flying like a bird into the sky with the wind beneath their wings, and then swooping down towards the green valleys and the swaying branches of the trees leading to the woods. Kim gives a deep sigh of relief and clings to her man and hold me so very closely as the earth vibrates and thunder sounds, lightning lights the sky and the earth submits to the elements welcoming them as her friend. We both lay on the bed entwined reflecting on our experience, both feeling exhilarated by our venture and both feeling satisfied by each others power of affection and deep affection for each other, we were so much in love. After this we both fell asleep and I began to dream of Kim firstly as a beautiful princess and the as an angel glowing as an image of perfection.

I did enter a game but it was running smoothly with Kim literally by my side, we were riding horses hers was black and mine white. It appeared to be in slow motion until we were being chased by knights in shining armour, they seemed to be riding faster than us and were getting closer.

We could here the hooves as they hit the ground at great speed, shouts from the horsemen echoed through the valley, the men were shouting at us until suddenly they were forced to halt as a giant dragon appeared. Mounted on the dragon was a blonde haired girl waving a sword and shouting out in rage "Destroy the knights one and all of them" the girl was Sabrina she was rescuing us from our fate, the dragon opened his enormous mouth and began spitting fire onto the knights. They were engulfed in flames and were burned to death, they're armour became ovens and they cried out in pain as they soon became ashes. Sabrina smiled at me and then flew away on the dragon leaving us bewildered and safe enough to continue our journey through the valley. I awoke and found that our bodies were still naked and entwined, satisfied at this I went back to sleep and dreamt on, with more fantasies in my head this time I was racing in a car across a desert. I was happy enough travelling along with the radio playing away at high pitch, my open top car with the rush of air breezing through like a hurricane. Suddenly I was being pursued by police cars with their sirens sounding, I was on the run and the police were determined to catch me. I reduced speed when I noticed a road block ahead, and then I decided to speed up and head straight towards the road block, guns fired and I lost control of the car, it began to roll and roll into a sandy area. I tried to get out of the car but I was stuck, my legs felt heavy and numb, I gradually worked my way free and fell out of the car. The next thing I know I was awake and lying on the floor, Kim was awake and watching me struggling to my feet.

"I must have fallen out of bed" I said looking at her naked body

"I was underneath you and you cried I can't move I am stuck" She reminded him "So you pushed me away"

"Sorry I was in a car, trapped my legs were numb" I said

"They were probably numb because they were under mine" She said smirking

"I am sorry Kim, you must be fed up with me" I said feeling low in mood

"Come here" She beckoned with her finger sounding very masterful

"Am I in trouble?" I asked

"No more than usual" She said smiling

I sat on the edge of the bed; she grabbed me by the arms and pulled me towards her hugging me "What the hell do I do with you?"

The next morning Kim was up, washed and dressed, walking around the kitchen preparing breakfast acting as if the night never existed. I walked into the kitchen my body wrapped in a dressing gown; I walked over to her kissed her on the lips and then sat down on a chair by the table.

"Would you like breakfast Dan?" she asked

"Yes please, a bacon sandwich and a cup of tea would be good" I replied

"I like a man who knows what he wants" she said grinning

"I better today, so relaxed and ready to study" I said looking at a book on the table entitled 'Nothing is real'

"Where did you get that book?" I asked anxiously

"It's my book on psychology the nature nurture debate, remember?" Kim explained

"Oh yes of course" I said pretending to remember what she had said; I didn't want to alarm her after what we had discussed previously. She seemed so happy and I wanted to avoid shattering her day by telling her I was still seeing things like the same sentence everywhere DILEMMA

It was a nice sunny day everything seemed fine and I was thinking particularly positive, I had created the ultimate virtual reality game called 'Blood trail' from the book by Sarah Ruth Scott. It seemed like I had reached as close as I close as I could get to perfection, the characters stood out as if they were real and I could communicate with them normally. The locations seemed real and as I played each aspect of the game I really felt as if I was there in the story, I controlled each character as if I were the gamester experiencing it for the first time. I had my virtual reality headset on and control console in my hand, I was set to play the game fighting vampires using the usual buttons to attack and dodge my opponent. I had created each level following the story that Sarah had written so well, I was able to create it to every detail and I played it through as if I was reading the words from her book. I had even used one of my cubicles to isolate myself from the outer room and prevent anyone from disturbing me, it worked I was able to concentrate fully on the story and felt it was completely real. The vampires opened their mouths and revealed their fangs, some flew over me and some appeared in changing rooms and toilets from time portals just as the book explained. Carina who was the leader of the slayers fought many of the vampires with the main character Siena, these characters were hard to create as they seemed larger than life and I had to form their personalities from the book. Carina was from the future hunting vampires through time, while Siena an ex vampire wanted to make a mends from past transgressions by pursuing vampires who had caused harm to her family and avenge them. I played for hours hoping to defeat the vampires and end the game that I had created, it took hours to play it properly and I could imagine people would get enjoyment out of it and spent day even weeks to finish the game.

I left the booth dazed and tired from the hours of playing, I struggled to walk to my settee and flopped on it like a lead weight. I fell asleep and dreamed about vampires and all the characters in the game, as usual everything felt real as if I was actually part of the game. I was the character Jack who was Siena's boyfriend I had to rescue Siena from the vampires in the future, they wore protective suits so that they could go out in the sunlight and kidnap victims from various locations in time using a time portal. The slayers had to create weapons that could penetrate the armour and destroy them, this was eventually achieved and the vampires were chased across time. I was experiencing being attacked and defending myself the best way possible with the use of weapons and tactical manoeuvres, I eventually found myself in a corner unable to move and one female vampire looking like Sabrina my fantasy girl stood over me revealing her fangs and plunging them into my neck. It was at that moment I woke up and noticed Kim peering into my eyes looking concerned.

"Daniel, what has happened to you?"

"I had a nightmare" I said trying to focus on her

"No, I mean the blood coming from your neck" She replied

"Really" I said touching my neck and looking at my fingers "My god, I am bleeding"

"Let me get something to help stop the bleeding" she said leaving the room

She returned with a bowl of water, towels and a dressing pack, and then she knelt beside him and began to wash his neck.

"It looks like scratches; you must have done it in your sleep"

"I was defending myself from vampires" I replied

"Is that what the two puncture marks are?" she asked

"Really?" I asked in disbelief

"Yes, you must have stabbed yourself with your nails" she said dabbing at the wounds.

"I played the game that I created from 'Blood trail- across time' you know the book you were reading" I explained

"Yes, it's a good book about vampires harvesting humans across time" she said

"I have perfected the game and it's ready to be sent to the company Tetron universal, my first game"

"You have worked hard Dan it should be successful"

The next day I arranged to go to the company to sell my ideas and hopefully begin to make money from the game, I anticipated complications from the start with new ideas and convincing the company that my game was a sellable commodity. However I was actually introduced to the director of the company and one of the top designers of Tetron, I was taken to a large room and my game was set up and played on their console. It was an instant hit with them and they arranged to put it in production immediately, we then negotiated a deal and the figures were astounding going well into the thousands to begin with, plus shares in the sale of the game. It was as if they already knew about me and my work, I felt as if they had looked into my past and decided to see me for that reason alone.

Time went on and I was beginning to feel very strange as I continued to played games as if I was meant to be part of them, I was also experiencing trauma from fights and car crashes it was so odd. Kim was concerned about this and suggested that I had a break from the games. We went away for a while in order for me to relax and take a long rest from work, it also gave us time to be together and work on our relationship. I think by that she was hoping that I would propose marriage to her and I know that would make her happy. But I also knew that I was being driven away from the very thing that would eventually would drive me to madness and that was the feeling of being part of a game with its elaborate network of thoughts and concepts that confused my mind making me feel as if I was living in a game and nothing is real. Kim was very clever and knew exactly what was happening to me, she was able to read me like a book, her thoughts were always rational and she had a sound concept of reality. She was my link to sanity and kept me on the straight and narrow, so by virtue of this I was loyal to her and I was ruled by her words of wisdom.

I eventually received information about my game 'blood trail' telling me it was in production and I even had a job offer from Tetron universal inviting me to join their company and produce games for them as an employee. I considered their offer and soon replied, I was interview by the same staff and I was given my own office and laboratory in which to work comfortably. I was in gaming heaven and in my element creating games from books that I loved so much I even met Sarah Ruth Scott who wrote many books that I loved. She was happy about my work and that her characters were coming to life in my games. After a short while 'Blood trail' came out as a game and a movie, my life was changing rapidly I married Kim and we transferred all my equipment into my new home and I was able to work from my office or home, Kim ensured that I rested and separated my work from my marriage, this meant vacations abroad and being happy with Kim. We even spoke about starting a family having children together and bringing them up in normality, Kim was involved in criminal psychology and knew about the dangers that were present in society, bad influences and how corrupt the environment was. She had dealt with the most evil and devious members of society and knew what to expect, but even she was surprised at times in her professional field. I had also experienced such people at college and university. PLAYING THE GAME

During the time that I was creating games from a thing called artifial intelligence (A.I) I used it in order to send messages to the gamesters. I was a way to initiate positive thinking and stemmed from Kim with her positive reasoning, it was also based on strategies to prevent people from contemplating suicide used on mobile or cell phones. This involves paths, dangers and strategies, but in games it prevents the individual from becoming addicted to the games that they play, a type of fail safe mechanism was installed which was activated with stress sensors that detected responses to certain situations within the game.

Kim was asked to try this device and play the game 'blood trail' she agreed as it was to her advantage to help change society by altering the thought process in games. It works by sensing stress in players for example by heart rate, sweat glands and the force on the controls. Kim wanted to see whether they reacted to the other characters in a similar way by use of aggression or fear, it would depend on the sensitivity of the machinery as to whether it causes the console to switch off at the right time and prevent melt down of the user. So it's Kim verses the A.I device and she is willing to test her intelligence against the A.I in order to survive and alter its thought process in favour of the human race.

Kim entered the cubicle, I fitted her up with all the equipment such as the virtual reality headset, body straps and controls, she was ready to play the game. I left the room once all the equipment began to work and the game was about to begin, I shut the door and waited for the light to go on indicating that she had began to play the game.

Kim started to get stressed as she played as the character Carina the vampire slayer, she began fighting vampires, I was able to connect the game to my second control panel in the next cubicle and observe her playing the game. She was doing well fighting vampires, until she started to talk to the character that Sabrina portrayed, something seemed to happen at this point as if she had lost control and her pulse began to rise, the instruments indicated that she was stressed and Sabrina stabbed her with her sword. Although Daniel didn't see the light go out he left his cubicle in a hurried manner, he forced the door open and entered Kim's cubicle. She had vanished and in her place was someone else, Sabrina sat in a corner looking dazed and confused, she glanced at me and then looked away.

"Who are you?" I asked

"Sabrina I think" She replied looking back at him then down at the floor

"No, you can't be" I replied trying to see her face properly under her blonde hair

"Why can't I?" She continued

"Because I created you, you are not real" I said trying to apply simple logic to the situation "I made you, you are out of my head"

"I am artificial intelligence and yes you created me, but Kim brought me to life" she said pointing to the console

"So, where is Kim?" I said angrily

"She is in the game, trapped I think" she said "I have replaced her here"

"But your not real, you're a figment of my imagination" I insisted

Sabrina stood to her feet and walked towards me, she stroked my arm

"Does that feel real to you?" she asked "Can you feel it"

"Yes I do" I admitted

She moved her head close to mine and gazed into my eyes

"What do you see?" she asked

"I see a woman with blue eyes" I replied "Now they are brown" I said watching them change

She moved closer and kissed me tenderly on the lips

"Do you feel that" she asked

"Yes I do" I gasped "You are real, but how is this possible?"

"Do you need any more proof?" she asked stroking her fingers down his cheek

"No, but I need answers, like how you became real" I said

"What do you wish to know?" she asked

"I just want to know how Kim disappeared and you appeared" I said still feeling anxious

"I don't know what to say I am here with you" she said

"I really don't know what to say" I was lost for words I just stared at her in disbelief

"What about, hello Sabrina" she replied

"Hello Sabrina" I said reluctantly

"That sounds nice, so where do we go from here?" she asked

"Wait a minute" I said swiftly

"What's wrong, don't you like me?" she asked disappointed

"Yes, but what about Kim?" I said pulling away from her

"Kim, I am afraid that she is history" Sabrina said dismissing her

"What do you mean history?" I asked her bluntly

"You lost Kim in that game" she replied pointing to the console

"No, I can't have lost her" I said tearfully "She can't have gone"

"I would like to think she is still here, but look around you, do you see her?" she looked around and shrugged her shoulders "No Kim"

"You have me confused" I said looking around

"I am only stating the facts" she said "I can't help what has happened"

Sabrina was lying, she had contacted Kim within the game and they shared information about me, Kim also worked within the network reaching Sabrina's artificial intelligence discovering her plan to dispose of her within the game. She had successfully trapped Kim and at this point may even have destroyed her, Sabrina had all the skills it took to lure her into a trap, she was very manipulative and the most devious person known to man.

Despite my efforts I was unsuccessful in locating Kim, she had disappeared without a trace, I had seen her in the game and now she had vanished and then the game was over.

Sabrina had settled down in my home making herself comfortable, helping herself to my food and using my amenities, I felt as if I were being used by my own creation or fantasy. I had to confess that she was like a breeze of fresh clean air, but did this mean that I had lost Kim and gained a woman that I could only describe as my fantasy. I was living in a strange world where nothing was real, even the person who shares my home; this was through my own creative mind. Now I was confused I was getting outer body experiences and visual hallucinations, my whole concept of life was changing with the presence of Sabrina. I must confess was excite by the very prescience of her, her incredible body and mind, the way she moved and captured my imagination, she was what I desired but feared to behold, like the untouchable crown jewels. I admit I was weak and stupid with no sense of decency, I had become besotted by her charm and beauty and unable to control my emotions. I have to confess that I even made love to her and I was intoxicated by her love and what we shared at this time, it was moments of stupidity because no one could replace Kim. I felt guilty being with her and at betraying my only true love, with someone who I had created for my own personal desire all those years ago when I did a portrait of her during my educational days. In effect I had created my own Frankenstein with all the attributes of my dream woman prior to meeting Kim, she was as near to perfect as possible, but Kim was real and had something that I could never create, free will and the need to love me unconditionally.

One morning I found myself in bed with Sabrina, it was evident by the fact that we were naked that we had made love; I stepped out of bed and crept into the bathroom, I used the toilet and then went to wash my hand at the sink. In front of me was a mirror with the word written in lipstick 'Nothing is real' this disturbed me and my heart began to beat loudly in my chest. I became breathless and my eyes blurred I looked again in order to take in what I could see on the mirror, it was clearly written and stood out clearly. I realised that this was a message that appeared in so many places before such as in the sand, above a cemetery gate, on a bus and a hot air balloon. I had seen it time and time again everywhere but didn't understand it until now, I was experiencing some kind of crises and it was due to gaming. I failed to heed the warning that were there from the start, I was in danger of going insane due to being obsessed with games and my creations had finally caught up with me, I was experiencing visual hallucinations that were part of the games I had put together. But Kim was trapped in a game and it was my entire fault, after all I had sent her there by my own selfish desire to contact the artifial intelligence that existed within the console. I rushed back to the bed and tried to wake Sabrina from her sleep, but she was sleeping too deeply, I tried again but to no avail and so I left the room. Sabrina opened her eyes and smiled cunningly, she had pretended to be asleep and she was no doubt planning her next move which was to find Kim and kill her or destroy the game. By eradicating Kim, Sabrina could stay in the real world with me and live as a human while Kim would be no more not even in the gaming world.

I rushed into the cubicle that Kim had entered before and where she had disappeared nearly a week ago, for some reason time was so irrelevant to me. I suited up and put on the virtual reality headset, I was already anxious and my heart rate increased read by the pulse oxicmeter on my finger, I began to sweat profusely. I entered the game holding the controls firmly in my hands, shaking slightly as I began to start the game. Alarms were activated and I ignored them continuing to find the character in blood trail known as Carina the vampire slayer, I knew that was the person that Kim was controlling in the last game she played. Sure enough Kim appeared and she was fighting a vampire in the demo, I pressed the controls to choose a character and chose Carina, and then I started to play the game operating the character fighting the vampire, using weapons and dodging blows. Sabrina entered the second cubicle and immediately took over the vampire character, but she was actually her in the game fighting Carina or Kim as she appeared to be. It was all very confusing but Kim was actually fighting Sabrina, I had lost the use of the controls and it seemed the battle was about mind control rather than physical strength and ability. Kim was beating Sabrina at this point but as they battled on Kim began to weaken, she had used most of her mental strength and was relying on the rest of her physical energy to combat her opponent.

"You can't beat me Kim your mind is too weak" Sabrina said

"I can match you Sabrina besides you are merely a figment of Daniels imagination" she said waving her sword

"Daniel is mine, I have much to offer him" Sabrina replied

"I will never win Sabrina, I am human with a human heart that will always win" Kim said surging forward to attack

Swords clashed and they both moved across the room with a back drop of a castles grand hall, they fought on a large table, and then jumped off and moved over to the stairs, finally Sabrina weakened and Kim delivered her final blow, followed by a wooden stake to the heart. She plunged the stake in deeply and watched Sabrina disappear into dust. Soon after Sabrina appeared fatally wounded on the cubical floor, I knelt down to her and helplessly watched her die.

Once Sabrina disappeared Kim returned lying dazed on the floor, her body shaking and peering up at me.

"Kim" I shouted

"Where am I?" she asked trying to get up

"Steady, you must be weak" I said helping her to sit up

"Where have I been Dan?" she asked looking round

"In the console playing a game" I explained

"No wait, I was defending you, I spoke up for you" she paused then continued "Yes, you were with Sabrina, she told me you made love to her" she said pointing

"Well yes" I confessed "But she enticed me, seduced me and I was weak, even vulnerable" I said trying to defend myself

Kim rose to her feet and slapped him across the face "Bastard"

"Kim, listen to me" I said stepping back "I am the victim"

"Bullshit" She said attacking him again "You are a man with a mans desire, don't pull the weak and vulnerable card, it won't wash"

"But I thought I had lost you" I said pleading with her "Please forgive me I don't want to lose you"

"We will discuss this tomorrow, I want to sleep on it" she said leaving the cubicle.

IN REALITY

The next morning my friends David Spencer and Arnold Crutchley came round to see my new creation and experience the new game 'Blood trail' I was naturally apprehensive as I had so many problems with the equipment. However I wanted to show off to them, ever boastful me who had many to succeed far beyond their wildest dreams by getting closer to reality as you could get. Arnold had landed a job in architecture and David was a computer repair guy with his own business, unlike me the inventor of games and a computer wizard. Arnold had in toe his Asian girlfriend a beautiful girl named Wania meaning gods gift, she was certainly that, she was gorgeous with a likable personality. We talked for a while and then they entered the cubicles, Wania waited outside with me watching the games from my monitor in the lounge. David entered the game first as a character called Jack, he played the opening story explaining that Jack was in an art gallery admiring a painting, when suddenly a girl leapt out of the picture. It was Siena who knocked him over and fell right on top of him, the story progressed showing how they fell in love and then slayer came after her. Siena was a vampire who was running away from her master Count Vermont, in order to be free from the vampires and even asked god to change her back into human form. Her wish was granted as long as she agreed to destroy the vampires. David was happy to be Jack and played merrily for an hour, things seemed to go well until he was surrounded by vampires and his heart rate began to rise.

Kim entered the lounge and noticed that both cubicles were being occupied

"Daniel what are you doing?" she said angrily

"I am letting my friends experience the games" I replied

"What's wrong?" Wania asked

"It's not safe, Daniel knows that" Kim said alarmingly

"Nonsense its fine" I said trying to reassure Wania

"No it isn't, its dangerous" Kim insisted

"What does she mean, dangerous?" Wania said anxiously

"They are fine I can see them" I said pointing to the screen

"Kim what do you mean?" Wania said hoping to get an answer from Kim

"Tell her Daniel, tell her how I almost died" Kim said standing in front of me and blocking my view.

"What" Wania shouted "Stop it now, turn off the machine and let me get to Arnold"

"Arnold is fine" I said pushing Kim away from the screen

"I want to see him" she insisted running to the cubicle door

"Fine, I will let him out" I said opening the door

"You see, he is fine" I said pointing to Arnold clad in his suit and virtual reality headset "This is the integrated development environment or I.D.E"

"That was brilliant, but why did we stop?"

Wania gave him a hug "I thought you were hurt" she said shaking

"No, it's a really cool game, well done Dan" Arnold said patting me on the shoulder

"Lets see what David has to say" Kim said trying to open his cubicle "It's stuck"

"Let me try" Arnold offered

Arnold struggled to open the door, while I went to find something to force it open, I returned with a screw driver

"This should do it" I said forcing it into the gap and breaking the lock, the screw driver got buried into my hand, I pulled it out but to my astonishment there was no blood. The door opened and to everyone's surprise David had vanished.

"Where is he?" Arnold asked

"I really don't know" I replied looking round

"He can't have just vanished" Wania said bewildered

"This is some kind of trick" Arnold insisted looking for a secret door or panel

"Tell them Dan" Kim demanded "Tell them where David is"

"In the game" I reluctantly replied "He is stuck in the game"

"Holy shit" Arnold replied in shock "Actually in the game?"

"Yes, and he is in danger unless Dan gets him out" Kim said looking at me

"Let me see what I can do" I said suiting up

"What are you doing?" Kim asked

"Attempting to rescue David of course" I replied putting on the V.R headset

"You are putting yourself in danger" Kim said tearfully

"I can control this thing after all, I created it" I said pushing them all out of the door.

Soon I found myself in the game I was a male colleague of Carina's called Gareth the slayer, I tried to find David by entering various room and time portals. I eventually found Jack wounded on the floor in some kind of castle that I had created; he was unconscious with blood coming from his abdomen. I checked the wound and applied pressure to the wound in order to slow the bleeding allowing him to regain consciousness and return home. But before that happened I had to fight off a few vampires, this was part of the game and for me to free him from the game I had to make the ultimate sacrifice, which was to replace him with me.

Hopefully he did get home, unfortunately I will never know as I could not tell from my perspective, I was limited with what I could see or control. When I managed to free Kim, it was from the outside in the cubicle using the controls and equipment at hand. Now I am helpless merely a pawn in a game of chess or toy soldier being manoeuvred by a child, probably a poor comparative but the only one that I can think of at this time. I can only hope that one day someone will free me from the artificial existence, I am at presenting an animated state and living in a unreal world surrounded by my own creations. I can fight off vampires and vanish into walls, doors and do the strangest things I never thought possible.

Imagine that you are here with me, travelling through a three dimensional pathway, imagine theres no heaven it isn't hard to do as John Lennon would say or nothing is real, strawberry fields forever. My voice is now echoing as if I am in a cave or tunnel I see a light shining in the darkness on a wall and written on the wall, what a surprise 'Nothing is real' I know that it is obvious to me. Although at one stage I never considered it so, but the writings on the wall, was I destined to be here, in this place. Maybe I can find the answer to the meaning of life or what the universe is all about, is there a god does he exist, is there an all powerful creator who can dictate how we live our lives. Didn't I do that in a small way creating games and forming characters like Sabrina, the one who came and went in my head, she was even alive at one stage and talking to me, I even made love to her how real was that?

So where are the vampires now? Did I kill them all? I am dressed so oddly clad in armour and ready to defeat my enemy, I wait for Carina who will help me fight them; she is the bravest woman I know. But she is not real just a made up character from the book 'Blood trail-across time' by Sarah Ruth Scott, a writer who made these characters known to me and I made them real. I created this game, the best virtual reality game ever, with so many parts to it and a story line to follow. I have travelled through the game countless times and now I am in it.

I thought back to the time when David and I played on a zombie game and were chased by zombies or rather our characters were, but you can imagine we felt as if we were in the game. Or when I began to create 'Operation brainstorm' a mind altering machine called brainstorm invented by a Norwegian scientist Doctor Jon Ulrichsen, it was from another book by Simon Robert Sinclair. The machine was created in order to cure brain diseases by operating on brain cells and restoring them to normality. In the game terrorist stole brainstorm and kidnapped the scientist, the object was for a special agent to protect Ulrichsen's daughter and find the terrorists. I had not quite perfected the game, but it was almost finished and it would no doubt have been a best seller.

I don't know how long I had been here having no concept of time, all I can say is it has been a long time and I was feeling strange. I had no feelings of hunger, no desire to use the toilet, I had been stabbed and yet felt no pain or anguish, my whole body appeared to be detached from me as if I were dead. Perhaps I am a ghost and passed away without realising, maybe I am in denial, or not crossed over to the spirit world. Or is my body in shock from the transitions of inanimate to animate matter or vice versa, that being an example of how I feel about the situation. I refer to the real person and a cartoon character by use of technology, but in a more advanced form crossing the barrier of human logic, unfolding a new dimension that can transform from one to another at will. My thoughts were interrupted by an army of soldiers marching past me this continued for a moment and then they vanished, they were followed by a children's choir who sang divinely like a group of angels on a cloud, and then silence and the light that I had originally seen shining on the wall moved and shone onto a woman. It was Sabrina looking radiant wearing a white silk dress her long hair was blowing as if she were on a cloud in a breeze, her skin seemed soft and flawless just as I had painted her as a student.

"Where am I?" I asked anxiously "Who am I?" I said reaching my arms out

Sabrina never spoke, but merely looked at me

“Please tell me, am I dead?” I said desperately

Although she was there I felt completely alone and wanted answers, I had been alone with my own thoughts, but now I was faced with someone else who I considered a fantasy.

“Am I real” I asked her

“Touch yourself and answer me” she finally said

I reached down to feel my stomach and my hands vanished inside me

“Oh no” I said feeling around “I can’t feel anything”

“Exactly” she said “You are not real”

“But I was real” I said convincing myself

“You have never been real” she said coldly

“But my past and that I have achieved” I said trying all the more to convince myself.

“I did try to tell you nothing is real, remember?” she said prompting me to think about her words “I was not quoting John Lennon’s lyrics from his song Strawberry fields forever by Lennon and McCartney”

“Nothing is real” I said

“Nothing is real” she repeated

"I am not alive or ever been alive" I said lowering my head in shame

"How does it feel to be a figment of someone else's imagination? She asked

I raised my head and shouted "Kim"

I thought that she would rescue me from my nightmare, then I repeated in a low

weak voice "Kim.

BLOOD TRAIL

PART TWO

Evil Of The Vampires

CHAPTER ONE

THE HARVEST

It was a warm winter evening and all was calm and peaceful, Siena was preparing to go out with Jack visiting a local restaurant. She began applying the make up and suddenly saw something in the mirror, it was her reflection but as a child. She looked so sweet and innocent combing her hair and singing to herself, but then she changed into a vampire. Siena jumped and almost fell off her chair, yelling and waving her arms about. Jack was in the room and noticed her reaction, he ran towards her and hugged her.

"What is it?" Jack asked

"A vampire in the mirror" Siena said panicking.

"Siena don't be silly they don't have reflections do they?" Jack said reassuring her.

"No we don't" Siena thought for a moment "No they don't"

“You have been cured it wouldn’t be you anyway” Jack said positively.

“So what was it some kind of warning? Siena asked

“We killed all the vampires remember including Count Vermont” Jack explained “Everyone died all but that weasel Bramble who fled to the woods”

“Yes your right they did” Siena said calming down “And I am no longer a vampire”.

“No so why don’t you carry on getting ready, we are supposed to be celebrating the day we met twelve months ago” Jack said kissing her on the lips.

Once they were ready they walked out of the door, Siena did her usual thing of looking up and down the street before leaving the building. Then looked up at the sky where she noticed a full moon shining brightly above, she clung hold of Jacks hand and then grabbed his arm.

“Siena your very nervous tonight” Jack said feeling her pinching his arm

“It’s a full moon” Siena said still looking up.

“You are not a vampire” Jack insisted “You’re just like me, or maybe not just like me”

“I can’t help feeling something is going to happen” Siena said looking at Jack.

They continued walking down the street towards the restaurant unaware that a figure was behind them, it was the shape of a man who was keeping a safe distance away.

Siena and Jack entered the restaurant and were taken by the waiter to a suitable table by the window.

"I really can't believe that it's been a year since we met, I can still remember clearly you jumping out of the picture from that time portal" Jack said looking up from his menu.

But Siena was not paying attention; instead she was looking out of the window expecting something to happen.

"Siena are you listening to me?" Jack asked

"Yes of course" Siena said looking at the menu.

"I said, I can't believe that it's been twelve months since we met" Jack repeated himself.

"Oh yes the time portal thing" Siena said still not really paying attention "Fell into your arms"

"Oh good I am glad you figured that one out" Jack said sarcastically.

"Look I am sorry but something is going to happen tonight" Siena insisted.

At that moment they both heard sirens and noticed vehicles with flashing lights passing them by outside the window.

"Coincidence" Jack said dismissively.

"Really, you wouldn't believe it even if it hit you on your dumb head" Siena said getting up to leave.

"Siena, where are you going?" Jack said with surprise

"Out there Jack to see for myself" Siena said heading for the door.

"But, what about our meal?" He said

"Shove it Jack I am no longer hungry" She left the restaurant and walked toward the area where the vehicles went.

A crowd of people were circling a body in what was once considered a quiet and peaceful side of town. Siena pushed through some of the crowd and noticed a girl lying on the ground, her body was pale and lifeless as if she was drained of blood.

Jack noticed Siena and stood next to her; he looked at body in front of him and then glanced at Siena.

"Now will you believe me?" Siena said angrily.

"A traffic accident, why would you think that was about you?" Jack asked

"Oh Jack you idiot look at her neck, look at the puncture marks" Siena pointed.

“She has been attacked by a vampire” Jack said not thinking.

Almost everybody heard what was said, people began to talk amongst each other speaking about vampires as if they didn’t exists and that Jack was some sort of mad man.

“He said she has been bitten by a vampire what an idiot” She said

“He ought to be locked up” Said a man laughing.

Jack walked away embarrassed with what he had said, he was unable to speak due to the shame and humiliation. Siena ran after him shouting, trying to get him to stop and face her, but he kept on walking.

“Jack stop please” She shouted.

The suddenly she felt something hit her in the shoulder, she fell to the ground with the force of the impact. Jack looked back to see her fall down, he then noticed a vampire looking right at him with her fangs showing. She was about to attack him when something shot past him, it was a stake fired from a bow that hit the vampire and she disintegrated.

“Siena” Jack shouted.

He knelt down to help her, then noticed the blood seeping through her dress

“Jack” Came a voice from behind him

Jack looked round "Tom, but what are you doing here?"

"I followed these vampires coming through a time portal, I got one coming through and followed this one who was coming after you" Tom said pointing to the remains of a vampire cloak.

Jack looked back at Siena "She has been wounded"

"She needs help" Jack shouted "Somebody help us"

Tom placed his hand on Jack in order to reassure him, while Jack put pressure on Siena's wounds. The police and ambulance arrived at the same time, the ambulance crew began helping Siena while the police questioned Jack and Tom.

"So what happened to this woman?" The officer asked

"She was attacked by another woman" Jack replied

"Where is she now" The officer continued

"She vanished" Jack said not knowing what to say

But Jack was more concerned with Siena's condition and was eager to get to the ambulance, the ambulance crew were busy stabilising her condition and wanted to know how she had sustained her injuries. She had an abdominal wound that needed attention, it was caused by a sharp instrument like a knife.

Siena was also reluctant to answer questions she just explained it as an angry woman running through a crowd, who attacked a woman and killed her, she tried to help the woman and also got attacked.

Jack went back to the apartment with Tom, he packed a few items for Siena and they went by car to the hospital, Jack felt guilty for not believing Siena when she explained about feeling vulnerable and feeling that something was going to happen to her. But Jack considered after the death of the evil Count Vermont that it would be an end to the vampires and that they could live their life peacefully without the threat of death looming over their heads. Neither of them felt that they needed to watch one another's back for the rest of their life, hiding in shadows on the streets at night.

CHAPTER 2

FAITH RETURNS

Siena was in a single room away from other patients, staff seemed to be in and out of the room regularly checking that Siena was safe. A policeman sat outside the room and watched the corridor for any suspicious characters, Jack and Tom had not arrived and Siena was concerned for their safety. Siena was tired but as she was drifting off to sleep a bright light appeared in the middle of the room, as the light became dimmer an angel appeared dressed in white with blonde hair and carrying a large key around a rope round her waist.

"Faith" Siena said in a weak voice

"Siena I am sorry to see you like this, but when you killed Vermont, you left a few vampires alive and they are trying to avenge their master" Faith explained

"But we thought that we destroyed all of them" Siena replied

"Some escaped in a time portal into the future, they are stronger and have protective suits and helmets like dragons or demons" Faith tried to describe them emphasising their armour all dressed in black.

"So what must I do?" Siena asked

"Go into a time portal into the future find their weakness and destroy them, if you don't the human race will continue to be threatened by the evil of vampire" Faith could see the look of fear in Siena's eyes.

"Siena you will not be alone, watch for a blue angel known as Serenity she will guide you" Faith spoke these words and vanished

At that moment a nurse entered the room walking right up to the bed on her right hand side.

"Who were you talking to?" She asked

"No one I must have been talking in my sleep" Siena said hoping the nurse would believe her.

"Well you must have had quite a conversation" she continued "Oh yes, you have visitors Jack and Tom"

Jack entered the room full of apologies making so much fuss of Siena as he hugged and kissed her.

"So sorry my love, please forgive me" He pleaded.

"It's okay Jack there is more to tell" Siena said explain about Faith

CHAPTER 3

DARIUS LARICK

It was in the year 2190 in a castle much like Count Vermont's overlooking a mountainous region, within the castle walls lived an army of vampires led by Darius Larick, Darius and his brother's Radius and Matthias swore to avenge their ancestor and former Master Vermont by killing Siena and all those who helped her. Vermont had discovered time portals in various locations of the castle and moved through time, in the future he found Darius castle and discovered far more time portals using pictures to cover them up around rooms. It also made it easier to locate them. The main hall was the main area where the vampires travelled back into the past and harvested humans from various times and used their blood to survive.

Darius paced up and down the hall with a menacing look on his pale face, he was displeased and made all his followers know it.

"How many times have I asked you to get Siena and her friends and you just make excuses" He ranted

“But master we have tried” one of the women replied

“Natasha, I want no excuses, get me that woman now!” Darius insisted

“Jessica go with her and don’t forget to wear your protective suits” He advised them.

“Matthias go with them and make sure she is returned here unharmed” Darius instructed “I want to kill her myself”.

“Yes Darius” Matthias said leading Natasha and Jessica into the time portal

“Radius continue the harvest, we need more humans” Darius ordered.

“But we have just returned with many humans” Radius replied

“Silence we need more, send our armies to every location, the toilet cubicles, changing rooms in stores, barns woods and graveyards. Find me humans everywhere harvest the twenty first century and bring them back here now” Darius became very angry pointing to the many paintings in the hallway.

The vampire army prepared for their journey through time wearing their protective suits so that they could venture out in the daylight, without being destroyed by the sunlight the helmets allowed them to see out but protected them from harm. The helmets appeared to resemble demons to frighten their enemies and the body armour also served useful to prevent them being attacked by weapons. The vampires of the future had proven to be more dangerous than their ancestors and they were determined to be the master race, rulers of their age.

The vampires proved successful as they entered woods capturing humans in daylight, entering graveyards both day and night. But more astonishing was their bold attempts to apprehend people from toilet cubicles and changing rooms at busy times in shopping centres. The time portals were everywhere, vampires abducted people by coming through a time portal in a changing room and pulling or dragging them straight back through time.

A barn became a brilliant place to transfer humans from the twenty first century as was a cave in Derbyshire's peak district. People were going missing all over England no one was safe, the vampires took advantage of their ability to cross over through time ever increasing their harvest.

Meanwhile Siena was relaxing trying to get some rest in hospital, Jack and Tom returned to the apartment. All was quiet and Siena began to think about what Faith had said about the future, helping mankind as if she were a vampire slayer and for that matter where were the time portals. She spoke of them appearing in odd places such as toilet cubicles and changing rooms, how strange is that and perhaps beyond belief.

At that moment the door opened and two women entered the room wearing protective black suits that glowed emerald green in the dark, they both wore helmets but by the shape of their bodies in these suits they were definitely female.

"Jessica grab her" Natasha instructed

"She's a fighter" Jessica said trying to stop Siena struggling.

"We need to put her out" Natasha said taking an instrument like a taser gun from her bag.

"Hold her while I use this" Natasha continued "Matthias we need your help" she shouted.

Eventually Siena passed out and Matthias carried her into the female toilets, Natasha and Jessica followed behind him. They entered the second cubicle and vanished behind the cistern into the time portal and returning to Darius.

Jack and Tom returned to the hospital amongst the chaos police, nurses and other people running about. Jack entered Siena's room and noticed her missing the bedclothes were on the floor and all the equipment that she was attached to was dismantled. Then he noticed a blood trail leading to the door and followed it out of the room, he caught Tom's arm and shouted.

"Follow me Tom!" Jack led Tom into the female toilet

Tom had noticed the blood trail and assumed it belonged to Siena, they tried the first cubical but more blood led to the second cubical.

"Jack in here" Tom shouted

A woman entered the toilet "Excuse me this is the ladies toilet" she said entering the second cubicle and finding it empty "I must stop eating cheese, its causing hallucination's"

Jack and Tom went through the time portal and arrived in a strange room full of dolls, each doll looked realistic some resembled famous singers of the twenty first century others were just like Barbie dolls dressed in various outfits. One doll looked gothic with jet black hair and black lip stick, wearing dark clothes mainly dresses. Tom picked one of them up but dropped it when it spoke moving away from it walking backwards.

"It won't harm you, it's not real" Jack said reassuringly

"It's evil magic or witchcraft" Tom replied

"It's a toy doll" Jack said laughing "We have many kinds in our century, they could have got them from the twenty first century".

"Whatever you say" Tom replied

"Let's go and find Siena" Jack said heading towards a door

They walked down a corridor with stone walls either side, the corridor seemed to go on forever, and finally they reached the end noticing a large hallway in front of them, people were talking and others were appearing out of paintings. Vampires were bringing humans back from the past each of them were bound with leather ropes, every one of them looked frightened, but there was no sign of Siena. Jack and

Tom remained hidden until everyone had left the hall, they moved cautiously into the hallway and then down another corridor. Jack noticed another blood trail and thought it might be Siena's blood, it led into a room Jack went in but Tom hesitated.

"It might be a trap Jack" Tom said concerned

"Nonsense it's fine I think it's another time portal" Jack replied

At that moment Tom was pushed into the room and a door slammed shut behind him.

"One day Jack you may listen to others" Tom said disappointedly

A face appeared at the door, the man seemed pleased with himself

"Now I have Jack and Siena, I will be able to avenge my master" Darius said laughing

"How do you know me?" Jack asked

"A little man called Bramble told me of you, he is right here do you wish to see him?" Darius asked pushing Brambles face up to a key hole in the door.

"Bramble you sly worm always willing to betray others" Tom shouted

"Yes Bramble you're a murderer killing Laura" Jack shouted

"Get your stinking body away from here" Tom shouted

"Well Bramble you're not very well liked" Darius said "Perhaps Siena will greet you more favourably"

"Keep away from Siena!" Jack shouted "I am warning you"

"Such empty threats Jack, you have no weapons you are defenceless and you threaten us" Darius said goading him "You will die soon enough I will feed you to my children"

Siena had been taken to another part of the castle far away from Jack and Tom, she was alone, but in a nicely decorated room with a four poster bed and red curtains all around it. She wore a fine dress and her hair was platted neatly, she was able to see Darius on a monitor on the wall.

"Do you propose to kill me" Siena asked

"Call me Darius" He relied "Frankly I admire your courage"

"Darius Larick" She said calmly "I have heard of you, leader of the vampires"

Darius had dark thick hair which he swept back and revealed scars on his cheeks and chin, his eyes were menacing and his complexion was pale almost white.

"Count Vermont needs to be avenged and some of my flock are from his castle, they want you to die, but you should die the death of a vampire, driven into the light to disintegrate. Your death will be slow and painful as the vampires wish it, but we need to change you back into a vampire first and then execute you". Darius explained.

"A will be vampire once more?" Siena asked "I am to be bitten again"

"Yes and starve for a while then your boyfriend Jack can join you and be the first to be drained of blood by you" Darius smiled "You will destroy him and then we will destroy you"

Siena walked around the room thinking, her thoughts returned to the days her mother used to read stories to her, while her father was out hunting vampires. She and her sister woke up many nights hearing wolves crying out with owl and other wild creatures making noises. Sometimes storms kept them awake the sound of wind blowing through trees or thunder banging in the skies, and heavy rain thrashing again the windows. But then Siena missed the walks through the meadows and stepping through streams with her naked feet, the sun beating down upon her as she rode her horse into the village. All these memories and no one to share them with she was alone, sad and feeling helpless, then she remember Faith and all she said to her.

"God I need you now help me fight this wickedness" she prayed

Suddenly the room was filled with a blue light and an angel appeared she was dressed in blue, a long dress even her hair was pale blue. She looked amazing, her face expressed a calmness never seen before and instantly she made Siena feel good.

"I am called Serenity I am an angel sent to help you" She said

"Faith spoke of you in the future" Siena said

"Time has no relevance to us, we are timeless" Serenity replied

"I wish I could say the same" She said looking into her blue eyes

"You seem different to Faith" Siena observed

"We appear differently to all mankind, they see what they want to see or understand, we can be white, black, brown look like any nationality, race or creed" Serenity demonstrated by changing her appearance.

"That's amazing" Siena said surprised

"Even animals if it is necessary" Serenity explained with another demonstration as a white cat followed by a dog.

"Now I am really freaked out" She said shaking her head

"But you want to know how to defeat the vampires" she said bringing Siena back to reality "Firstly you need to escape from here"

"That's impossible" Siena said negatively

"Have Faith Siena and believe in miracles for one is about to occur" She said making the door open with the wave of her hand.

"I will be stopped by vampires" Siena said looking towards the door

"You will be invisible to them, just follow my blue light which will lead you out of the castle and to Carina the vampire slayer". She said reassuringly.

"Follow the blue light and that's it?" Siena said apprehensively.

"Trust in god and follow the light, don't take your eyes off it for one minute or you will be seen" Serenity advised.

With those words Serenity disappeared followed by a blue ball of light resembling an orb, it began moving forward towards the door. Siena followed it as instructed and it continued down the corridor past the main hall and towards the main door, the door opened and she was free. Although she had escaped the castle, she was still not safe and so she continued to follow the blue light into the woods, even now she was transfixed on the light which travelled through the trees and suddenly disappeared.

"Great the lights gone out, did the battery go or something?" Siena said baffled.

"Siena" came a female voice

Siena turned around slowly and came face to face with a woman wearing dark armour and long dark hair, she was attractive with dark complexion and hazel eyes.

"I saw the guiding light and was instructed by an angel to look out for you" She said extending her arm forward with her hand open "I am Carina"

Siena shook her by the hand "I am obviously Siena"

"You are either brave or stupid coming here to fight with us against the wicked vampire leader Darius Larick" Carina said smiling.

"I would probably choose stupid as I am no warrior" she replied

"I would say brave, we can teach you to fight, besides your name is legend in history" she said hoping to instil confidence in her.

"I sincerely hope your right Carina" Siena said smiling back at her

"Let us go and meet the rest of my soldiers" She said leading the way

As they walked along they were joined by other soldiers both male and female each carrying weapons.

"The vampires don't tend to challenge us too much as we have weapons that they know are harmful to them, they generally keep their distance. Carina explained and then paused for a moment "However now you are with us they may try to attack us in order to get you back"

At that moment the sound of branches breaking broke the silence and vampires were instantly upon them, encircling them some flying like bats.

"Stand your ground men" Carina instructed

The vampires attacked using swords and other bladed instruments, swinging them and hitting their enemy. Blood spurted in the air and the sound of clashing steal drowned out the cries of wounded soldiers from the opposing armies. It was a battle to the death and no one at this stage was winning, not until Carina took out her weapon and shot one of the vampires blasting away the armour from his chest and exposing his body to daylight. He immediately disintegrated and Carina used the same weapon on another vampire, and then continued to use it until the vampire realised they would be defeated and fled.

"That will teach those evil bastards" Carina said confidently

"You really showed them Carina" a male soldier said

"Yes another victory to us I think" Carina boasted

They travelled further through streams and a forest until they reached a modern building, Carina placed her right hand on a panel and a light shone into her right eye. The door opened sliding to the left and allowed everyone in, the section that they were in was a main control area with a series of machinery including computers and armoury. People were walking about everywhere some in white boiler suits each seemed to have a purpose or job to do, it was more high tech than Siena expected but then she did originate from the Seventh century.

Carina led Siena into a large conference room where she debriefed her army, making sure that Siena was included in the meeting.

"For those who do not know, this is Siena" she put her arm around Siena

"She is a legend from the seventh century who destroyed Count Vermont and made her name in history as a vampire slayer" Carina continued "We have the honour of being in her presence at a crucial time in our champagne to rid the world of these evil vampires"

"What makes you think we can trust her, after all she has been with these vampires" one man protested

"Gareth, how dare you question my judgement, have I not always led you all well, protected you and defended all of you no matter what you have done"

"Yes madam of course, but she has been with Darius Larick himself" He continued

"Look!" Carina shouted exposing both sides of her neck "Do you see any puncture wounds, scars or indications that he has turned her into a vampire, I have on good authority that she is one of us".

"A blue angel wasn't it" He mocked "She was once a vampire who was turned into a human"

"Step forward Gareth!" Carina commanded

Gareth was a large man with reseeding black hair and a face full of scars, he was a muscular man with skin like leather.

"Touch Siena, feel her neck, check her teeth and please expose her to light, you can even get a mirror and see if you can see her refection". Carina encouraged him to test her knowing that she was not a vampire.

Gareth examined her neck as instructed and then proceeded to open her mouth

"Are you satisfied" Carina asked him

"Yes okay I was wrong about her, but I am only saying what the rest are thinking" Gareth admitted

Carina became enraged at his remark and struck him in the face with her studded gloved fist, this was followed by a kick to the throat.

"How, dare you challenge me like this, do you all think of me this way, I have offered you a solution to the evil of the vampires" She watched Gareth wiping the blood from his face and struggling to talk "Let that be a lesson to all of you not to undermine my authority or question my judgment"

"So what now Carina" one of the female soldiers said reluctantly for fear of being attacked

"Now" Carina hesitated feeling that she had actually gone too far "Now we rest and consider our next move".

CHAPTER 4

NATASHA

It seemed like an eternity that Jack and Tom had been imprisoned, they had had many conversations but had exhausted every subject and became silent. Darius had listened in and was disappointed because none of the subjects were relevant to him and his cause.

"Natasha my dear, you must convince Jack that Siena has died and console him, make him trust you and he could provide you with valuable information" Darius explained

"Yes of course master" Natasha said in a humble manner

"Damn, what was that blue light that led Siena out of here, how the hell did she escape my clutches" Darius lifted his head and spread out his arms "Let the greatness of our kind defeat the human race, let us harvest more souls and drink the blood of our victims".

The main hall filled with human bodies "Feast to our future take the blood from these people". Darius commanded watching the vampires swoop down upon a crowd of screaming humans.

The vampires pinned their victims down and pierced their necks with their sharp fangs sucking their blood and draining them of life. The vampires would not rest until they had feasted enough to satisfy their needs, all that was left was limp carcases sprawled all across the hall.

Both Jack and Tom heard the cries and could see on the monitor what had occurred, so many deaths all for the sake of blood, these people had come from the twenty first century, abducted and brought through the time portals. They knew that in time it would be them who would be victims and they had no way of fighting them unarmed. Their fate rested in the arms of the vampires who had no love for humans, their only desire was to feast off humans and drain them of their blood. Suddenly they were both disturbed by the opening of the cell, a number of vampires wearing armour entered the room, Tom rushed forward to fight them off but they were too strong and pushed Tom over. They wanted Jack so left Tom on the floor and dragged Jack out of the room, Jack was too weak to fight them off and went along with them quietly. He was taken to the same room that Siena once stayed, the vampires dropped him on the bed like a sack of potatoes, and he was curled up in a foetal position all alone and vulnerable.

After a while the door opened and a woman walked in dressed in a long flowing silk dress, she walked up to the edge of the bed and watched him for a while. Then she walked closer to him and touched his head with her hand, stroking his forehead and whispering down his ear.

"Jack are you awake" She asked

Jack opened his eyes to the most beautiful woman that he had ever seen, her eyes were hypnotic just like Siena's used to be when she was a vampire, she was slim with a flawless complexion and flowing blonde hair. She was like an angel and yet could have been the devil in disguise, charming and seductive, with a type of cunning grin that told Jack to be cautious.

"Who are you?" He finally muttered

"I am Natasha, I need to talk to you" She said sitting on the bed

"I am afraid that I have some bad news for you" Natasha began to look sad

"What is it?" Jack asked

"It's about Siena" She continued diverting her eyes away from him

"Siena where is she?" Jack asked concerned

"She is dead" She replied not wanting to face him

"You're lying you're a vampire, she's not dead" Jack said in disbelief.

“Why would I lie?” She said calmly

“But how did she die?” Jack tried to find reason with what she had said “Did you kill her?”

“No, died from her wounds, we tried to save her after all she was once a vampire” Natasha was trying to reason with Jack “We wanted her alive”

She looked at Jack with tears in her eyes holding him and watching him crumble in her arms, she kissed him on the right cheek and gazed into his eyes.

“Jack please be brave you must survive, I can help you, look into my eyes” she said beginning to hypnotise him. “Feel my love, my compassion tell me what you are feeling right now”

Jack began to murmur but not make any sense, he felt out of control as his body began to weaken and he fell back on the bed. Natasha watched his heart beating beneath his chest and his neck was exposed and ready for her to bite.

“Let me kiss you” She said revealing her fangs

Natasha was close to Jacks neck, she had punctured his neck when suddenly she was disturbed by another person in the room, Natasha drew away from Jack with spectacles of blood on her teeth.

“Natasha leave him for now we have other work to do” the person said

"Jessica what are you doing, Darius wants me to seduce him for information" Natasha said angrily

"But it is Darius who sent for you" Jessica replied

"Damn and I was just enjoying myself" she said cursing

The next morning Jack woke up and began to look around the room, then he touched his neck as it felt so uncomfortable. He could feel the puncture wounds made from her fangs and began to panic, he struggled to his feet and looked in the mirror only to find tiny holes with hardly any penetration. But he could still have been converted into a vampire but he was looking at his own reflection in the mirror. So no evidence of being a vampire and he didn't feel weak as if he had lost a lot of blood, maybe he had a lucky escape this time although he couldn't imagine why.

Natasha looked angrily at Darius "Why did you stop me!"

"My child I merely wanted you to seduce him not change him into a vampire" Darius said calmly

"I was getting somewhere and he would be a worthy adversary against the slayers" She replied "You don't trust me do you".

Darius became furious and struck Natasha knocking her to the floor, she began crawling away from him, wiping her mouth as she went.

"No one disobeys their master, I will not hear of it" Darius watched her leave the hall and turned his attention to Matthias.

"I am in command and will be respected" He said waiting for a reaction from Matthias.

Darius took a goblin which was filled with fresh blood and drank from it, he passed it to Matthias who too drank from it and in turn offered it to Jessica.

"We drink the blood of human's in a pact to destroy all slayers" Darius gazed around the room at his followers.

Each person nodded in turn acknowledging their agreement with their gestures, and then they all began to converse.

"Matthias you are my most loyal subject, tell me what do you think of Natasha?" Darius asked.

"She is not to be trusted"

Later that evening Natasha returned to see Jack, she appeared nervous as she stood in front of Jack, he was apprehensive after her last visit and backed away from her "I just wanted to apologise for my actions"

"But you bit me what was that all about?" He asked "I have puncture wounds on my neck, am I now a vampire or what?"

"No" she replied "I didn't even suck your blood"

"So why have you returned?" Jack asked

"Come closer I need to tell you something" she beckoned.

"So that you can do the same again or worse" he replied

"Trust me I want to help you" she said trying to get closer.

She whispered to him "Siena is alive"

"What?" Jack asked with disbelief

"Look at me please" Natasha pleaded "Siena is alive, she escaped somehow"

"I don't understand" Jack was trying to make sense of the situation

"I want to help you" Natasha repeated

"Then help me to escape" Jack still didn't trust her but he considered that he had nothing to lose.

"Okay, but tell me that we would have been good together and kiss me just once passionately" she appeared to be genuine when she made her request.

"Alright just once and that's it" Jack agreed

"Just once" she said kissing him on the lips

Natasha pulled away and moved towards the door, the monitor had been disconnected and Natasha hit the camera with a weapon that she had dropped on the floor near the door.

"Come quickly" she pleaded "We don't have much time"

Jack ran towards her and followed her into the corridor, he paused for a moment "I need to help Tom"

"There is no time, come on" she said becoming anxious

"Not without Tom" Jack insisted

"Very well" she agreed

They went to Tom's cell and freed him while the vampires were still feasting, Tom was relieved that Jack was back and hugged him.

"Thank god you're safe" he said smiling "But who is she?"

"She is our escape plan, get out of jail free" Jack said smiling back

"Come on" Natasha pleaded

They headed down the corridor and towards the door, but as they opened it, the light shone in and Natasha ran back into the corridor. Jack ran into a room and took a bed spread off the bed, then returned and covered Natasha up.

"Right, now let's go" Jack said

They raced outside and headed into the woods, they seemed to travel for hours and before long it began to get dark. After a further two hours they reached Carina's base and confronted the slayers, Natasha expected hostility as she was the enemy and as a vampire she was a predator.

"Why is she here?" Carina asked

"Natasha helped me escape" Jack explained

"But she's a vampire" Carina said

At that point Siena came in the room and ran straight towards Jack

"Jack!" she shouted "You're alive and Tom" she noticed the puncture marks on his neck "What's this Jack, what happened?"

"It's not what you think Siena" Jack said in his defence

"It's a bite, a vampire bite" Siena said concerned

"I did it but he's okay" Natasha admitted

Siena slapped her across the face so hard that she fell backwards

"Why is she here?" Siena shouted "She is a vampire who even attacked you"

"But she helped us escape" Jack explained "Maybe she can help us"

"No way, not possible" Gareth said "I don't need a vampire helping me, it's bad enough with Siena here"

"Who is the big guy?" Jack asked "Why is he so pissed off with Siena?"

"Because I am an ex vampire" Siena said dismissing Gareth

"And who are you?" Carina asked Tom

"I am a vampire slayer from the seventh century" Tom said "I was like you Gareth; I thought Siena was an evil vampire until I saw her kill Count Vermont. Now I feel the same about Natasha, but as Jack said she helped me and she has knowledge of the vampires and the layout of the castle".

"So we can rescue the humans in the castle and destroy the vampires" Jack said

"I can destroy the time portals too" Siena said positively

"Wait a second" Carina said turning towards Siena and Jack "It's as simple as that, we have a lot of planning to do"

"While you are planning people are dying, doesn't anybody care" Siena said holding back her tears "They are murderers and harvesters of humans from the twenty first century, they drain them of blood and discard their carcases like wild animals" she said looking at Natasha.

"We can't just go in there and attack vampires" Carina replied "It would be suicide and as for rescuing humans that too requires planning".

"Each day we waste another life is lost, they drain the blood from humans and destroy lives" Siena said disturbed.

"Oh, so you never did this Siena" Gareth shouted "You never sucked the blood out of a human as a vampire"

"Yes, but I was confused and deeply regret what I did" Siena said defending herself.

"You still did it" Gareth went on "Lives were lost so that you could live"

"That's enough Gareth this is getting us nowhere" Carina butted in "Natasha knows the layout of the castle so let's start there"

"Natasha is going to help us?" Siena asked feeling uncomfortable in her presence

"Well she helped me escape" Jack said defending her

"She also bit you or have you forgotten that" Siena said pointing to his neck

"We discussed this and the circumstances which led to this" Jack said

"Oh and that makes it alright, she can just go around biting people at will, or does she fancy you" Siena turned her back on Jack and walked away.

The next few days consisted of training to fight the vampires, Siena wanted to use Natasha as a punch bag in order to practice kick boxing, but Carina kept Natasha away from her. In fact Natasha stayed with Carina in order to plan the attack on the castle and help the humans in captivity, she was conscious of Natasha's fondness towards Jack, but needed her to get them back into the castle.

Natasha caught Jack going back to his room in the evening, he looked tired and was about to rejoin Siena.

"Jack" She whispered "Please don't return to the castle it's too dangerous"

"I have to I need to help the humans" Jack replied

"But you know the danger and we could go somewhere else together" She gripped his arm "Let's forget all these people and start again"

"Natasha you know I can't do this I am with Siena" he explained

"I want to be human, seek god like Siena did" she gazed into his eyes "You told me she made a deal with god to be human"

"Siena had to do so many tasks and destroy Count Vermont" Jack said stepping away from her.

"Then I will destroy Darius" She replied anxiously "And tell you the secret of the time portals"

"Wait, you know the secret of the time portals?" Jack hesitated

"Yes it is all about a girl called Lily, she holds the secret" She said waiting for a response from Jack.

"Lily a girl with ginger hair and pointed ears about seven years old?" he asked

Natasha laughed "Sorry but you haven't quite grasped the concept of time travel, little Lily is twenty now and continues to travel through time".

"All this time, so she grew up?" Jack asked

"Naturally" Natasha replied "We don't stay children forever"

"But it seems like five minutes since we went there" Jack said astonished

"She discovered the first time portals and knows how to close them, that's how we come to travel from place to place" She explained

"But what about Lily is she now a vampire?" Jack asked concerned

"No, no one will harm her because of the time portals, if anything happened to upset her metabolism it could affect the portals and restrict vampire movement" she said "But Siena should know that being a vampire"

“Ex vampire” Jack remarked “Maybe it was not known by the seventh century vampires, she didn’t appear to know about time portals when we first met and she came from one then”

“Lily likes dolls she gathers them from various locations in time and brings them back here to her dolls room, some look so real, some talk” Natasha explained “Find the dolls and Lily is close by like a dolls trail”

At that moment the door opened and Siena stood looking cross at them both, Jack picked up her signal and said goodnight to Natasha.

“So, what did she want, was it to bite your neck again?” Siena asked sarcastically

“As a matter of fact she was telling me about Lily” Jack said not wishing to say anything about Natasha’s desire to run away with him.

“Lily?” Siena asked “How does she know Lily?”

Jack explained to her about the time portals and the dolls, she appeared to be listening and absorbing the information until he mentioned her age.

“Twenty that’s impossible we left her a few years ago” she said in disbelief

“It is something about time travel and portals” Jack tried to explain

"Nonsense she is trying to trick you and I wouldn't be surprised if she doesn't try to seduce you again or try to carry you off somewhere" Siena said as if she had heard their conversation.

"Well she is trying to help us enter the castle and rescue the human prisoners" Jack said in her defence.

"I don't trust her, she is out for her own desires" Siena said "But you take it all in like a sponge, both you and Carina"

The next night the slayers were ready to go to the castle, Jack had related to Tom about Lily and the time portals. Tom reminded Jack about the dolls room and how the dolls looked, Jack was so anxious about Siena he had not noticed the dolls expressions or voices. I was almost as if the room was alive, and all due to Lily who had collected and dressed them so elegantly. Siena remained quiet watching Natasha's every move in case she betrayed them, although she trusted Jack with her life she considered him a little gullible at times. She cast her mind back on the time when she wanted to turn him into a vampire and attempted to bite him, he was shocked at the time and he felt uneasy in her company for a time. Woman are a complex sex most of the time but enhanced when they are also vampires with a motive in mind, Siena could see this and was acting upon her instincts being cautious of Natasha.

They arrived at the castle, Natasha managed to get inside and let the slayers in, and they crept down a dark corridor towards the dungeons. Natasha led them down some stone steps spiralling around a wall, everyone seemed uneasy until they reached the bottom, suddenly there was shouting coming from the dark.

"Attack them!" the voice shouted

Vampires seemed to appear everywhere attacking the slayers, Natasha turned on Siena knocking her to the ground and hissing at her showing her vampire fanged teeth and clawing at her with her sharp nails. Matthias stood watching his vampires as they slaughtered many of the slayers, they had all been ambushed and betrayed by Natasha who managed to arrange the trap for them. Siena was injured but determined to fight back with all she had, with blood on her clothes and blood dripping from fresh wounds, kicking Natasha and causing her to stumble, Carina lurched forward and administered the final fatal blow piercing her chest with a stake and watching as she disintegrated. She turned to Gareth and ordered the slayers to retreat, not many survived on this occasion as they ran into the forest.

"Damn!" Gareth shouted "I told you she would betray us"

But no one even replied to him just let him rant on to himself and calm down as he travelled home licking his wounds like lion after a feast. When they arrived home the other slayers help them bath their cuts and encouraged them to rest. Some of them mourned their friends and relatives who died so gallantly in the castle, while the vampires feasted on the human's blood and celebrated their victory.

It was weeks before Carina planned another rescue mission into the castle, in fact the vampires thought that the slayers had left the area. They sent vampires out to investigate but they were cautious due to the weapons that the slayers possessed. They were far superior to their own and unbeknown to the slayers could wipe out the vampires with one swift attack, so the vampires concentrated on their harvest and continued to abduct humans from the twenty first century. They at least knew how vulnerable they were and how easy they could snatch them and return them to the castle via the time portals. Meanwhile Carina set up a training program for her remaining slayers teaching them how to defend themselves including Siena and Jack. She also educated them in the new weaponry using swords, guns containing special chemicals in the bullets and a type of hand grenade that would blast away their armour. They had armour that was taken from dead vampires that was used for target practice, when the armour glowed green, it was an indication that their bodies were protected, the green glow was a formula used to seal and protect the vampire bodies. If it failed to glow then the vampire was vulnerable as the demonstration proved, the armour merely contained the fluid like a jar protects the products within. A blast from the specially formulated bullet smashed into the armour and released the fluid and a small grenade would also blast the armour. Spiral blades ripped through the metal but were less effective than the bullet or grenade, this was used at closer range.

A month passed Siena was becoming quite a warrior virtually matching the skills of Carina who was a modern Boudica or Joan of Arc, they also became close friends which didn't please Gareth as he was still apposed to Siena and failed to trust her even though she fought so gallantly in the last battle. Siena and Carina practiced fighting together and often shared a meal even Jack felt left out and spent his time with Tom discussing combat strategies. But Siena's real challenge was against Gareth as they fought in a ring using weapons and hand to hand combat. Gareth nearly killed Siena striking out with a sword, Tom stopped him and Siena actually caught his arm and held a sword to his throat.

"If I wanted to kill you I would have done before now" She had broken the skin on his neck "But I think you're a great warrior and under that rock of muscles a nice man"

Gareth bowed his head and actually smiled and then looked at Carina "Maybe I was wrong about her"

Carina smiled back "You big soft Gorilla" she said winking at Siena

Later everyone assembled in the main area and Carina addressed the audience

"My fellow slayers we have been through much together, we have battled with the evil vampires and been betrayed by Natasha, this time we will be ready to defeat the them and free the humans that are captured. There harvest will be over and the time portals will be sealed preventing any of them to ever harvest again, this will end the evil that they have bestowed upon us and we shall be free once more".

"Let us do battle and then celebrate our victory together" Gareth said proudly.

CHAPTER 5

THE FINAL BATTLE

It was a dark and dismal night, the moon was full and an army of slayers had said their fair wells to friends and relatives as they made their way to the castle for the final battle, hopefully to end the evil that has fallen on the human race. But the slayers are equipped with new weaponry and have been training for this final conquest against the vampires even though the vampires have black protective armour that gives off a glowing green light like emeralds. They also use electrical charges like taser guns powerful enough to stun people, they used these to capture humans in the twenty first century. But will these match the mighty weapons that the slayer had, it was highly doubtful as they possessed weapons that could blast away their armour and destroy the vampires in one single shot. One of the slayers went out one evening and hunted down vampires using such weapons and destroyed them this is what the vampires feared but never anticipated a full assault on the castle.

The slayers entered the castle using the north and south walls, Siena and Jack went with Carina while Tom went to the south wall with Gareth. The plan was to infiltrate the castle from both ends and meet in the great hall, and then when the vampires were defeated they would release the prisoners and return them to their own time. The plan was going well Gareth and Tom had destroyed the vampires from the south section and was heading towards the great hall. Some of the vampires led by Radius and Jessica fled through one of the time portals, hoping to escape their ultimate fate. Darius was busy fighting Gareth, while Matthias was battling with Carina, Siena was fighting off some of the female vampires close by. Few vampires were left but one managed to fatally wound Tom penetrating his back with a sword, he dropped to the ground and Siena ran to his rescue, but he was too late Tom was already dying. Jack saw what had happened and also ran to his aid, Jack held his head from the back of the neck.

"Have we beaten them?" He asked

"Yes, we are the victors" Jack replied

"Please say hello to Lily for me" Tom said

"Come on Tom, you can say it yourself" Jack replied

Darius flew towards Jack after he had wounded Gareth, Siena aimed her gun at Darius and blasted a hole through his armour and he disintegrated. Carina continued to fight Matthias and finally defeated him with a few shots using her special bullets, he too disintegrated into dust.

The slayers had finally defeated all the vampires in the castle and the humans were freed and sent home via the time portals. Siena and Jack knew their next journey was through the time portal in search of Lily and hopefully close the time portals for good.

CHAPTER 6

IN SEARCH OF LILY

Siena stood beside Carina both tired from the battle and both looking around

“I never thought I would see this, standing here surrounded by the armour of dead vampires” Carina said

“I was beginning to think we would die” Siena admitted

“Some vampires escaped” Carina seemed concerned

“Don’t worry Carina we will find them” Siena said confidently

“I will have this area guarded twenty four hours, no one will return here” Carina said determined to stop the vampires returning via the time portals.

“I am sure they won’t come back” Siena said looking at the paintings

"So what will you do now?" Carina asked her

"Find Lily and secret to the time portals" Siena replied "Then seek the vampires that escaped"

"Well, I wish you luck Siena" Carina said embracing her "Thank you" she said kissing her on the cheek.

Siena and Jack slept at the castle that night in order to rest before finding Lily, Jack was very restless in bed while Siena despite being tired found it hard to sleep. Her mind was active and drifting back to her experiences in the seventeenth century, surviving in Vermont's castle as a vampire and running around with her sister Emma as children. During the time she was reflecting on her past a bright blue light glowed in the room and Serenity the blue angel appeared so stunningly beautiful dressed in a long blue dress.

"Siena you have done well to defeat the evil reign of the vampires" she said

"But I was helped and some still live" Siena said humbly

"You will find them; they went into a time portal some to the seventeenth century and others to the twenty first century" she replied

"I will search for them and destroy the rest of the evil" Siena said

With that Serenity vanished and left Siena feeling brighter and able to sleep, despite Jack thrashing around and mumbling in his sleep. Clearly he was still fighting vampires as he occasionally yelled out punching the pillow with his fists.

The next morning Siena and Jack said their farewells and headed for the doll's room in order to find the time portal and seek Lily. On entering the room they noticed the doll's, Jack was more attentive and remembered that Tom considered them evil because they moved and spoke. This time one of the dolls moved and spoke strangely to them as if it knew them and wanted to give them a message.

"Like a person within a person, fictitious people within a dream" she said

"And nightmares keep you awake, and no one will hear you scream" said another.

"Hidden away in a fortress tower so high upon a hill" Siena said

"The lost poet" Jack said realising it was a quote from the lost poet.

"Lily read that poem" Siena said remembering her sitting at the camp fire.

"She is in the tower" Jack said realising what the doll's meant.

"A trapped talent within a cell" Siena quoted "You're right but which portal is it?"

"The picture over there of the tower, that's it let's go" Jack said excitedly.

They entered the time portal and found themselves landing on the hard stone floor of a room that was dark and mysterious.

"This floor is filthy I feel so dirty" Siena said complaining

"Clearly someone hasn't mopped or dusted recently" Jack agreed.

"So where are we?" Siena asked

"I don't know but it's creepy" Jack said deep voice

"Jack that isn't funny" Siena replied nervously

"It could be the tower where the lost poet used to write" Jack said pondering

"Oh how horrid!" Siena shrieked

"What?" Jack replied

"I can feel something over my face like a cob web or something" She spitted something out of her mouth "I can taste it"

"How horrid" Jack said teasing her

"Jack stop it and look for a door" Siena insisted

"Found it" Jack said happily

"What was that bang?" Siena asked

"My bloody head, I hit it on the door frame" Jack said rubbing his forehead

They entered a dark corridor Siena held Jacks hand and they proceeded to walk down slowly, watching out for obstacles in their pathway.

"I hate this Jack" Siena said her hands were sweating and she was quivering.

"So do I" Jack admitted

They walked further and suddenly Siena let out a scream as something dropped on her head, she was becoming hysterical, it was wet and slimy and seemed to drop from the ceiling. Jack tried to identify it but it was too dark to see it clearly but it was motionless, if it had been living it was dead now.

"What the hell was that?" Siena asked Jack

"I don't know but it isn't living" Jack replied kicking it "Lets move on"

As they journeyed on they saw a light ahead of them, Jack began to wonder whether or not he had been dreaming this experience, he had questioned whether the time travel had affected his mind and distorted every thought he had, he was unable to differentiate fact from fiction. Reality from dreams which made him think even the vampires were unreal, perhaps the whole experience with meeting Siena in the art gallery was a dream. But this would mean Siena didn't exist and the here and now was a dream or nightmare. As they entered the lighted area Jack noticed paintings on the wall and realised they had arrived in Vermont's castle but it appeared deserted, Siena gazed around and Jack began staring at her trying to decide whether or not she was real.

"Jack what's wrong?" Siena asked

"Are you real?" Jack asked

"What?" Siena asked confused

"Are you really here or are you a figment of my imagination?" Jack asked

"Imagine this" Siena slapped him so hard he stumbled over

"What was that for?" Jack asked shocked

"Of all the cheek" Siena said angrily "How dare you treat me like this"

"Like what?" Jack asked innocently

"After all we have been through you ask me if I am real" Siena began pacing

"Oh stop, when you pace you're angry and that's bad for me" Jack said worried

"Piss off Jack you moron!" Siena shouted "Go on piss off"

"But I don't know what is real anymore" Jack said defending himself

Siena kicked him in the leg "That's bloody real"

"Ouch!" Jack cried holding his leg "What was that for?"

"A reality check, there you are alive" Siena was about to say more when she was interrupted by a door banging and someone rushing down a flight of stairs. It was the hunched figure of the goblin called Bramble, he was rushing out of the castle like his trousers were on fire.

"Bramble" Jack whispered

"Is he real?" Siena asked sarcastically

"Too right he is and travelled through a time portal to here" Jack replied

"So some of the vampires must have followed" Siena said noticing Jack still rubbing his knee.

"I am sorry Jack, but you annoyed me" Siena made an effort to apologise "And I have been traumatised by that thing that dropped on my head"

"Let's forget it and find out where Bramble is going" Jack said in a forgiving manner.

They followed Bramble into the woods and soon lost him, it was as if he knew they were following him and he found a hole to hide in. Siena and Jack decided to continue down the meadow to find Fargo, they had a feeling he would be in exactly the same spot that they originally found him in by stream sitting on a rock. Sure enough the giant was there and greeted them like old friends.

"My friends welcome back" he said smiling

"My dear Fargo how are you?" Siena asked

"I am well" he looked them both up and down "You both look well, but you have never grown"

"We need to know your secret Fargo, so that we can grow like you" Jack said looking up to him

"So what brings you back here, surely not me?"

"Much as we love you Fargo, we are looking for Lily" Siena said seriously

"Ah little Lily of course" He thought

"No big Lily she is twenty now" Jack said demonstrating her height with his hand in the air.

"Lily was small when we were here seeking the vampires" Siena said

"Think we need to find the tower of the lost poet, she was fascinated by his writing, I will travel with you" Fargo offered

"Have you heard anything about the vampires?" Jack asked

"Yes, people say they have been here at night and took people away" Fargo explained.

"So they are here" Siena said "We must stop them from leaving here"

"So that's what Bramble was up to, he was doing their work for them, searching for victims and leading the vampires to them".

"You must shelter here tonight and we can go to the poet's tower tomorrow" Fargo explained directing them to his cave which was surrounded by fresh garlic.

Fargo offered them supper and a comfortable place to sleep, it was so warm and cosy unlike the vampire castle that they had left behind in the future. But although they were so comfortable in bed together, Jack continued to thrash around in the night. Jack was dreaming about Natasha trying to seduce him, she was naked and teasing him by licking his ears and telling him that she loved him. Jack tried to control his desires and begged her to leave him alone, it was then that she exposed her fangs and plunged them into his neck sucking his blood. Jack tried to fight her and she changed into Siena, he pushed her away thrashing his arms in the air and waking up yelling "No!"

When he awoke Siena was on the floor holding her face and clearly in pain, he had hit her in the face during his struggle, Siena had tried to wake him in order to stop him from dreaming and was struck by him.

"Jack you idiot" Siena shouted

"Sorry did I hit you?" he said shocked

"Too right you did with your mad dreams of vampires" she replied

"How did you know that?" Jack asked her.

"You were shouting Natasha" she replied in disgust"

"Oh" Jack replied "Sorry"

"So what was this with Natasha, did you love her?" Siena asked jealously

"No, she kept trying to seduce me and bite me, she wanted us to be together" Jack admitted

"Why didn't you tell me?" Siena asked

"I did try to when we were going back to the castle with her" Jack said hoping his excuse would be enough to silence her.

"Well you didn't tell me which makes me think you don't care about me and would have gone with her" Siena said trying to mentally beat a confession out of him.

"No never, Siena I love you and I would never have ran away with her" Jack considered himself out of trouble but Siena was not going to let him off so easily, she was an ex vampire who never allowed her prey to get away.

"So, she wanted you to run away with her, the slag" Siena was fuming she got up from the floor and started pacing like a caged animal

"I would never have done that Siena" Jack said "Please come back to bed"

"I never trusted her, she was deviant and cunning, I true vampire" Siena said turning to face him "But you trusted her"

"She had a plan of the castle, she knew the layout of the castle" He looked into her eyes "You were a vampire"

"That's different I wanted to be human" Siena began to cry in frustration

"She told me that she wanted to be human, I would have asked for your help to make it so" Jack said

"She was using you to get to me and wanted to defeat the slayers" Siena said "She wanted to please Darius to kill him and take control of the vampires as leader, that was her plan" Siena had figured it out "She used everyone including you"

Jack sat speechless just staring into space, he knew that Siena was right but couldn't help feeling that Natasha was really fond of him. Siena lay beside him and they embraced, Jack felt her warm flesh touching his and they began to make love. The night seemed to pass quickly and before long Fargo had entered the area and nudging them to wake up; They got dressed and then joined him, he had prepared breakfast on a large table.

"Please eat" He said as they both sat near him

"Thank you" They both said

"I heard arguing last night" Fargo said

"Just a disagreement" Siena replied "Nothing important really"

"We are fine" Jack agreed

It was soon time to depart Siena and Jack collected all their weapons for the trip and headed through the meadow and into the mountains where the tower stood. There it stood in front of them high upon a hill the tower that they once visited with their friends a few years ago. John Gilbert Green the lost poet disappeared and was thought to be a ghost within the tower, writing unfinished compositions, a lonely man with little known about him but his fear of ghouls and monsters caused him to hide away in the tower. He was tormented by his nightmares he could never escape from them. The poet described himself as an image with a captured soul, he had died in the tower but his soul was with the vampires only free when they had been destroyed. They entered the tower and began the long walk up the spiral stairs to the top, not knowing what to expect when they reached the top. As they entered the room nothing had changed the table stood with the parchment a jar of ink and a quill, the curtain were the same and the image of the lost poet sat near the table. Suddenly there was a crashing sound as books fell to the ground and a figure ran towards a picture, she was slim with ginger hair and pointed eyes, wearing periodic a costume of the age. She had green trousers and a white blouse with a colourful pattern, her hair was platted falling down her back. Siena shouted to her in order to stop her from entering the time portal, she paused but failed to turn around, just maintained her pose.

"Lily" Siena repeated "It's me Siena, I need your help"

Lily remained motionless listening to what was being said to her, Siena moved forward as she continued to speak to her in an attempt to hold her back from the portal.

"Listen Lily the vampires are using the time portals to transport humans into the future for harvesting, they want blood to feast on human blood like yours" Siena felt as if she was failing to get through to her, at that moment Green the lost poet ghost appeared and he began to speak.

"Listen to Siena, Lily she needs your help to stop the vampires" Green said

Lily turned around and faced Siena, she walked forward and embraced her like a long lost mother, tears drifted down her cheeks.

"I never wanted to hurt anyone, but I wanted to find you" Lily said "You left me here and I wanted to be with you"

"You mean after Jack and I went home?" Siena was also tearful "Why didn't you say?"

"I was afraid to ask, I just thought you would take me" Lily explained "I faced the vampires they wanted to turn me into one of them but decided against it as they needed the time portals to travel and thought they would stop this if they changed my body, altered my human structure in any way" She looked into Siena's eyes "I travelled through time searching for you opening new time portals, but never found you"

"So, why did you collect the dolls?" Siena asked

"They were for you, gifts from the ages" Lily explained "Some could talk, some had microphones in them, so real and unique"

"Thank you for your kindness to me" Siena hesitated "So what do we do to close the time portals?" She asked

"The secret is in the paintings, I discovered it when I tried to get to you, each painting contains a trigger that activates as soon as you touch the painting" Lily explained.

"Lily you can live with us, come with us and we can return home after we have sorted out the portals" Siena said

"You promise, do you definitely want me?" Lily asked

"Yes of course" Jack agreed

"Okay, let us return to the future" Siena said "To Darius castle"

"This way" Lily showed them the picture to travel through

"Wait!" Jack shouted "I will go first in case the slayers shoot you"

Jack was the first one to enter the picture, followed by Lily and Siena

They reached the castle and as anticipated the slayers were ready to fire on them, Jack dropped to the ground and shouted.

"Stop it's me"

Lily came next and Siena close behind, fortunately Carina was with the slayers and ordered them not to fire helping Jack to his feet. Lily was used to the time portals and walked out of it normally helping Siena up and then looking at all the slayers.

"This is Lily" Siena said introducing her friend

"So what do we do now?" Carina asked

"Lily will explain" Siena said looking at her

"Take away all the pictures from the walls, but leave that one" she pointed to one picture "That will be our passage to the twenty first century"

"Remove the pictures" Carina instructed

"Take tem outside and burn them" Lily said "Then we shall return to the twenty first century and repeat this"

"But, what shall we do about cubicles and changing rooms?" Siena asked

"They is only one end of the time portal that has a picture this is the port of entry, the other is controlled by this one" Lily explained

"Please join us for dinner" Carina said

"Okay" Jack said "We are in no hurry"

"Actually we are" Siena said "We need to get back home and plan our search for the vampires"

"Then you will need these" Gareth offered them a small device "This will pick up the vampires"

"This will pick up the green protective substance in their suits and help you track them down" Carina explained

Siena led the way through the existing portal

"Take away the picture when we leave" Lily said as they left

Lily was wearing a hat to hide her ears, she seemed happy to go with Siena and Jack, perhaps it was because she was entering a new life and had a family around her at last.

They arrived in a changing room in the middle of a busy store during a hectic shopping day for most people. Siena left the changing room first, the shop assistants looked at their odd outfits with a surprised look, unable to comment.

"None of your clothes fit us" Siena remarked

"I decided to go for the seventh century look" Lily said smiling

"I am with them" Jack said following them into the crowd.

They headed out of the store and into a busy street, looking around them

“Now where do we go?” Jack said bewildered

“Let’s find out where we are” Siena said searching around with her eyes

“There” she pointed “A Birmingham bus going to Harborne”

“So we need to find a station to get home” Jack said

“Where do we go?” Lily asked

“Manchester” Jack replied

“Jack Clarke I hope you have money” Siena said

“Of course” Jack searched his pockets “My faithful flexible friend” he said showing them his visa card

They made their way back home to Manchester, arriving in Piccadilly station at night with people rushing around the platforms; suddenly Jack noticed a light flashing on his device.

“I am picking up a signal” Jack said “A vampire in the station somewhere”

“Walk forward down those steps” Siena said noticing a figure going swiftly down the stairs.

"The signal is getting stronger" Jack said walking down the stairs

Lily fell to the ground and appeared unconscious, a trickle of blood came down her nose, Siena attempted to wake her while Jack continued down the platform.

The area was dimly lit, as Jack continued down a platform hoping to catch sight of the vampire, suddenly a figure leapt out from the darkness, a man in armour with a green glowing light shining through it. Jack tried to fire his weapon but the vampire was right on top of him and knocked the weapon out of his hand, rendering him helpless. Jack wrestled with him but he was much stronger knocking Jack against a wall, Jack felt himself getting weaker but he was determined to beat this creature. Jack decided to fall limp onto the ground as if he was unconscious, the vampire exposed Jacks neck and showed his fangs ready to bite him, Jack reached out to where his gun had dropped and felt the handle. He managed to grip it enough to lift it up and aimed it at the vampire's chest, squeezing the trigger he managed to fire a bullet into him. The creature fell back with the impact and Jack shot him again in the chest and watched him disintegrate. Jack noticed another signal but it was fading, so he went back towards Siena and Lily, who by this time were both sat on a step.

"How are you Lily?" He asked

"I am alright just fainted sorry" she replied

"It's fine probably all the travelling" Jack said

But Siena looked oddly at Jack as if something was happening to Lily.

"I think we need to go home" Siena said

Jack never mentioned the other vampire as Siena seemed determined to get Lily home and get her to rest, Siena was concerned about her and felt that she would benefit from a good nights sleep.

Meanwhile in a warehouse in Manchester vampires were meeting together, Radius was leading them and appeared to be angry with them.

"Jack has found us, he has killed one of our vampires in a station" he said addressing his flock.

"But master he entered the time portal with Siena and Lily" a female vampire said

"Jessica, you should have stopped him" Radius replied

"But I had to warn you all" she replied "Besides he had powerful weapons from the future".

"We need Lily before she closes more time portals" Radius said "I want her alive" he insisted

"I am hungry" Jessica said dragging a woman from the corner of the room

“You are always hungry” He replied “Now go and find out where he lives”

Jessica bit into the woman’s neck, then cast her aside, watching her drop to the ground, she spoke to Radius through a mouthful of blood.

“I will find Lily and return her to you master” Jessica said wiping the blood from her mouth.

“The vampire race will survive and my children we will feast off these humans and once more hail supreme over the nations, I tell you all this that our race will be the most feared in history. Fear the darkness for we are in the shadows and hungry for blood, our bodies yearn for human blood and we will take by force, go out and harvest the city my children.

CHAPTER 7

HUNGER

Lily was the first to wake up in the morning, she walked into the bathroom and had a shower, she felt refreshed and ready to face the world until she looked in the mirror and noticed blood trickling down her nose. She was shocked at the sight of blood and began washing it away, at that moment Siena knocked on the door. Lily panicked and continued wiping away the blood, not wanting Siena or Jack to know, she thought they would send her home.

"Lilly are you okay?" Siena asked concerned

"Yes I am fine I just got my period" she said making up an excuse.

"Do you need anything" Siena asked

"No, I have things thank you" Lily was aware of using sanitary towels from recent travels to the twenty first century "I am good thanks"

"Okay, anything you need is in the cupboard by the sink" Siena explained

Siena used to be able to smell blood as a vampire, she could tell when a woman was in her menstrual cycle which made them easy to detect in the dark, and they became easy prey.

Siena and Jack sat eating breakfast waiting for Lily to come out of the bathroom, finally she appeared and joined them at the table.

"Lily are you okay?" Siena asked

"I must admit I am still tired and I don't feel like going out today" Lily replied

"That's fine but you know we have to find the vampires?" Siena said

"Probably safer for you to remain here Lily" Jack advised

"Okay I will rest and join you later, maybe get a meal out" Lily said yawning.

Siena and Jack left the apartment later that morning and headed towards the city centre, in search of the vampires, little knowing that they were also looking for them. Jack traced his steps back to the platform where he confronted the vampire, before long he was picking up a signal which led onto a train, a armoured figure was rushing through the carriages occasionally looking back to make sure that he was being followed. The train stopped at a station and the vampire left the train and began walking towards a trading estate, once he reached a warehouse he walked inside and kept his armour on and suddenly turned to face Jack, the place stunk of rotting flesh.

"Well done Jack you have landed in my trap" the vampire said clapping

"Whose trap?" came another voice as Radius appeared in the shadows.

"Jack what a pleasant surprise" Jessica said "Delighted you could make it"

"I am fully armed and ready for you" Jack said holding an grenade

"Tut! Tut! Jack my friend you are slightly out numbered and are they the only toys that Carina gave you?" Radius asked

"Not exactly" Jack replied looking around the room

"Well believe it or not we only want Lily" Radius said "But we can destroy you and find her quite easily"

The warehouse was almost in darkness so Radius and Jessica removed their helmets, as they did so Jack threw a grenade at one of the vampire and shot his gun into the roof.

"Bad shot Jack, so disappointing" Radius ridiculed him

At that moment a series of explosions occurred and the roof caved in Radius and Jessica put their helmets back on and dived for cover, Jessica flew on top of some crates while Radius searched around the ground for Jack. Siena appeared on the roof and climbed down to Jessica throwing grenades at the other vampires and exposing their green suits, Jack shot at them causing them to disintegrate. Jessica began to fight Siena with other vampires each brandishing swords, while Jack attacked Radius determined to defeat him. Siena managed to knock Jessica off some boxes, causing her to stumble badly to the ground, Jack was also damaging Radius splitting his armour with his weapon and then attaching a grenade to his chest, and then jumping away from him. The grenade exploded crashing his armour and while he was exposed he shot him in the chest. Jessica escaped with two other vampires and headed for Jacks apartment, while Siena and Jack were being kept busy with the remaining vampires. Jack realised that they were heading for his apartment but they were faster than Him, Siena and Jack could only rush as fast as they could back to the apartment. Suddenly Jack had a thought.

"They are going to use the time portal in the art gallery" He said

"Let's go there and stop them" Siena said "We must be close to that one"

They raced to the gallery as fast as they could hoping to stop them, but just as they arrived Jessica stunned the security guard in the gallery and pulling Lily into the time portal via the picture that Siena came out of a few years ago, when she first met Jack.

Jessica took Lily through the time portal unaware that she was so ill, they arrived in the room Siena had originally escaped from, Lily had scratched her arm on Jessica's armour and the blood from her gash was dripping on the floor. They walked out of the corridor and found the main entrance to the castle, Jessica was still holding Lily by the arm and pulling at her, trying to hurry her up, daylight was approaching and although Jessica was in her protective suit she was afraid Siena and Jack would catch up with them and kill her.

"Come on Lily hurry" she said

"Stop please!" Lily shouted "I can't go on" Lily was holding her head in pain

Jessica noticed her nose bleeding and let go of her, she paused for a while

"You're sick" Jessica said realising how ill she was

"I am dying" Lily replied "How did you find me?"

"That broach you are wearing has a homing beacon we have been tracking you with it for years, ever since you were captured at Count Vermont's castle and we realised about the time portals". Jessica noticed Siena appearing from the time portal and flew away with the remaining vampires.

Siena rushed towards Lily while Jack raced forward shooting at Jessica, managed to hit one of the vampires but Jessica escaped. Lily fell to the ground holding her head in pain,

Siena had followed her blood trail to the main door and realised her arm was injured, so seemed a little confused when she was holding her head.

Siena cradled Lily in her arms Lily began to cry, weeping silently against Siena's shoulder.

"I am sorry Siena" she said showing her the broach "They knew where I was because of this it has a homing beacon inside"

"What has happened to you?" Siena asked

"I became ill the last time we entered a time portal, I started bleeding I told you it was a menstrual cycle, so you wouldn't worry" she explained

"You need medical help Lily it could be temporal displacement, you could be seriously ill" Jack said concerned.

"No it's too late for me I know" she said shaking "I am so cold"

"But we can get you medical help back home, through the time portal" Jack said feeling helpless "We need to help you"

"It was the time portal that caused this I will never survive another trip" she explained "Please let me die" she said expressing pain with a grown and frowning "Please make the pain stop"

"I wish I could help you" Siena said with tears rolling down her cheeks

"I love you Siena" Lily said then looked at Jack "I love you too Jack" then she closed her eyes and passed away.

"Lily" Siena cried "I love you too Lily" She kissed her tenderly on the cheek "Don't die Lily please"

"Siena she is dead" Jack said touching her on the shoulder

"It's not fair, damn it" Siena said "Why did she have to die?"

"Siena we need to make plans" Jack said feeling tearful.

"No, I am not leaving Lily" she replied "I should never have left her"

"She was dying when we went hunting for the vampires, so don't blame yourself, that homing beacon told them where she was don't you see that?" Jack tried to explain "So what do we do now?"

"You go to Fargo and ask for his help, I am staying with Lily"

Jack never questioned her, but went as requested to seek Fargo in his usual place. After a short time Fargo hurried back with Jack and knelt beside Siena and Lily.

"I am so sorry Siena" Fargo said stroking Lily's ginger hair and toughing her right pointed ear "We have lost so much with Tom and Lily"

"I feel as if my heart has been ripped out" Siena said "We must rid this land of the existing vampires".

"Let us bury Lily first and then we will fight them" Fargo said "Take her to her home in the woods I will carry her home" Fargo said picking her up.

They travelled through the woods, to the cottage that Lily had lived as a child, she was buried beside a tree that Lily used to climb up looking over the meadow. Jack spoke a few words that were written by the lost poet John Gilbert Green and then they entered the cottage looking at the doll's that she had collected from various time zones. They left the cottage taking a few dolls with them and sleep over night at Fargo's cave dwelling. That evening they discussed strategies to attack the vampires.

"We need a plan" Jack said "We need help from the villagers in order to out number them and make sure no vampire escapes"

"The villagers will help, there are those who followed Tom" Fargo said confidently

"Great, so we will be well equipped and ready to fight as one army" Jack said excitedly

"No" Fargo said looking at Siena "They won't fight with her"

"Why not" Jack asked confused

"Because they still consider me a vampire, right" she said annoyed "Despite the fact I have killed countless vampires"

"They don't know that" Fargo said

"Well, can't you tell them?" Jack asked

"They won't believe it you must stay hidden, let us do the fighting" Fargo said

"Like that's going to happen" Siena said sarcastically

"He's right Siena you could get hurt and we don't want that" Jack said concerned.

"Sometimes I wish I had remained a vampire" Siena said angrily "The way humans treat me"

"We are concerned about you Siena" Fargo said trying to pat her on the back

"I am off to bed" she said shrugging him off "Alone" She said looking at Jack

Jack and Fargo remained by the fire discussing plan's of attack.

"Ignore Siena she is obviously upset about Lily" Jack said

"Yes, it is hard for her and I genuinely do like her, but the villagers would never understand or trust her" Fargo explained

Siena lay in bed clutching the broach that Lily once wore, her mind drifted back to happier times with Lily at the camp fire and the cottage. Then she thought about her dolls and travelling through time, the vampires and how they tracked her down everywhere. No wonder they could find their way to so many places harvesting the humans and feasting off their blood, she thought about what she said about being a vampire, but did she really want to live like that again besides she loved Jack and her life in the twenty first century did she really want to give all that up and live in hunger for the blood of humans?.

The next morning Jack and Fargo woke up, they had fallen asleep drinking wine and talking about many things, the fire had burnt down to a smoulder and both were snoring away. Jack awoke at the sound of Fargo yawning he jolted and opened his eyes widely, seeing the giants stretching and flexing his enormous muscles.

"Did you sleep well?" Fargo asked

"Not bad" Jack said scratching himself under the arms

"I wonder how Siena is today" Fargo said looking inside the cave

"I suppose I ought to wake the beast" Jack Said standing up

Jack walked towards the place where Siena had been sleeping but she was gone, he searched the cave but she was nowhere to be seen.

"Siena!" He called

There was no answer, she had gone during the night and somehow crept past the small ropes that would have tripped of an alarm namely tin cans tied to trees. She evidently was aware of them and avoided every trap, she could not have been abducted otherwise they would have been alerted by so much noise, and so Siena had decide to go.

A short while later Jack and Fargo went to the village and managed to gather a crowd together, they convinced a crowd of them to join in the fight to rid the land of vampires. Most of them were eager as they had experienced attacks in the night; some even spoke of green glowing demons snatching their children. One mentioned black vampires with white glowing fangs, some described them as six foot tall clad in armour.

Meanwhile at Count Vermont's castle Siena had been detected by Lily's broach and captured, it was as if she wanted to be caught, after all she knew the what the broach was used for and that the vampires would follow the signal and apprehend her. She was stripped of her weapons and armour and imprisoned in a room; she recognised the room as her own when she was in the castle with the other vampire women. The beige frilled curtains and four poster bed and oak furniture, she would now consider it as a dull room dark and un inviting, but then it was a wonderful place.

The door opened and Jessica entered the room walking gracefully in a black dress.

"Siena what a surprise" She said with Bramble creeping behind her

"Why have you brought that evil goblin with you?" Siena asked

"Be gone, creepy Goblin" Jessica ordered and walked closer to Siena

"You look so pale child" She observed

"And you are dark for a vampire" Siena said noticing her black skin

"Not all vampires are white my dear" she replied comparing her skin to Siena's

"So I gather" she replied

"You were once a vampire and now you're a human, how does that work?" Jessica asked

"I fell in love with a human" she replied

"Jack?" she asked

"Yes Jack" she replied

"So where is Jack now" Jessica asked "Have you fallen out child?"

"We have our differences" she replied reluctant to say much

"Do you miss being a vampire, living forever with your friends?" she asked

"Sometimes" Siena admitted

"Then let me help you" Jessica said "Come closer"

Siena walked towards her and Jessica began to stare into her eyes, she was trying to put Siena into a trance, making her feel out of control of her own body, and enticing her closer and closer until she was in her arms.

"That's good" Jessica said confident that she could control Siena "Now" she said gazing at the flesh on her neck "Let me kiss you"

Suddenly her fangs appeared and she proceeded to puncture her neck, Siena pulled away and felt blood trickling down her neck, she touched it with her fingers.

"No Jessica, I will never be a vampire again" she said looking around for an escape

"Don't be foolish child, listen to me" Jessica was angry "You could be a leader and fight the humans"

"No, I am human and I will fight you" she replied

"Fight me with what?" she shouted "You have no weapons"

"I have the greatest weapon of all" she replied "Gods love"

"So, where is your god now child?" she mocked her

At that moment a light appeared in the middle of the room and Jessica fled

"Faith" Siena said in relief

"I heard your prayers" Faith replied "Now be brave your friends are coming"

"Thank you Faith"

"Serenity is with them, now go and find your weapons and defeat this evil"

Siena went out of the open door and searched for her weapons, after a while she saw them on a table as if they had been placed there for her to find them. She grabbed the armour and put it on securing the traps and then grabbed her weapons and preceded towards the main hall, from the balcony she watched the slayers enter the hall from the door. Jessica ordered the attack and the vampires swooped down on them, the humans tried to break through their armour but found it impossible and so Jack began to throw grenades with Fargo and after half a dozen explosions weakened the vampires armour. Then Jack began shooting deadly bullets and one by one the vampires disintegrated, some of the humans used stakes killing more vampires until few remained.

Jessica attacked Siena they threw each other across the balcony, Bramble grabbed a speared and raced towards Jack trying to force it into him from behind but Fargo picked him up and with all his might dropped him onto his knee and snapped his back, his spine broke in two pieces and he lay helpless on the floor. Siena hit Jessica with her special blade splitting her armour and then Jessica managed to force Siena onto the ground ready to cut her throat, she brought the blade close to her neck and went to cut into it when a blast came from Jack's gun and she disintegrated. After this a human charged at Siena with a stake catching her side, Fargo picked the man up and tossed him over the balcony.

"She is a vampire" cried one human

"No She is human" Fargo shouted "See how the stake has merely scratched her"

"But she was once a vampire" another shouted

"No she is my sister" came another voice as Emma appeared out of the crowd and then went rushing up the stairs.

"She has fought vampires and proven to be worthy of forgiveness" Jack shouted

"Yes, my friends, we must thank her" Fargo said hugging her "And look she has a reflection in the mirror, isn't that proof enough"

"A vampire has no reflection" Jack said "Hold a cross to her forehead and she will not perish"

Emma had reached the top of the stairs and held up a cross "See I have a cross" she held it to her head "And see I have garlic"

"She was forgiven by god and changed back into a human to fight these vampires" Jack said

"Emma" Siena said "Thank god you are here with me"

"We have a lot to discuss my sister" Emma said

Siena spent some time with Emma discussing the past, but although the villagers were told about Siena and her reformed character they still failed to trust her and considered that she would one day betray them and change back into a vampire. So Siena and Jack returned to the twenty first century leaving fond memories as well as bad memories behind them. Soon after their return Siena announced that she was pregnant and eight months and eight weeks later she gave birth to a baby girl she called Lily. Amazingly enough she had ginger hair but not I may add pointed ears.

As for the vampire there were reports of sightings in various cities, but what do you truly believe?....

THE HARRINGTON CURSE

INTRODUCTION

The Harrington curse goes back a few generations and affected the Harrington family in a big way, it was said that Annabelle Harrington who went missing and cursed three mirrors before she disappeared. The mirrors were discovered in an attic and each given to three members of the family, it was then that horrific events took place that led to death itself. Horrible visions and blood curdling screams took place in Harrington manner where one of the owners of the mirrors called Emma. Emma was a descendant of Annabelle's Husband John Harrington who was Lord of the manor and the first member of the family to be cursed. John discovered that Annabelle was having an affair with the artist Ralph Bedford, so he pursued and murdered him. Annabelle went missing after discovering that she was pregnant by Ralph, it is there that the strange story begins, dare you read on. A number of crime investigators are from criminal world magazine are assigned to investigate the unusual activities of these mirrors and what lies between the death of one of inheritors Gladys Harrington. One such reporter called Samantha King is desperately trying to sort her own life out and believes the answer could come from her trip to Scotland on a dangerous search for the mystery of the mirrors.

CHAPTER 1

THE ARTIST'S MODEL

It was a midsummer day in a remote part of Scotland somewhere between Edinburgh and North Berwick near a small village called Aberlady, in a forest a man was walking on a dirt track dressed in a collarless shirt and a pair of brown corduroy trousers. He was carrying a shoulder bag and wore a hat with a brim that covered part of his face. He had a long nose and a small goat beard, he was fairly young and probably in his late thirties although he looked older due to his appearance and harsh skin. But what was more noticeable was his large staring eyes that appeared menacing at first glance. He travelled along a dirt pathway carrying a shoulder bag and walked over a stone bridge across a stream towards a group of rocks which were situated by a set of interestingly shaped trees. He then sat on a rock and produced a sketch pad and a set of pencils from his bag and began sketching the trees. He had been drawing for a while when a woman came walking towards him she crossed the bridge and walked up to him. She was wearing a hooded top and a pair of jeans, she removed her hood revealing a beautiful face with gorgeous large green eyes and a radiant smile.

"That's quite amazing" She said admiring his work

"Why thank you my lady" He said respectfully

She removed his hat and kissed him on the forehead "My clever Ralph" she said smiling.

"Why Annabelle be careful that no one sees us together" He said concerned.

"To hell with anyone else, we are all that matters" she said laughing.

"Well you are the lady of the manner and me a mere artist" Ralph said smiling

"You mean John, he either abuses me or neglects me, I don't know which is worse do you" Annabelle said with a tone of anger in her voice.

"Annabelle my love, you deserve more than that" He said squeezing her hand

"I have you and that's all I need, you are my true love" She said with sincerity.

"I will love you to my dying breath, you are my angel, my princess I worship you" He replied I

With that he packed up his equipment and they walked over the bridge and towards his cottage in the woods. The cottage was surrounded by wild flowers and bushes, the cottage roof had red tiles and white walls with leaded windows and a slatted wooden door. They entered the cottage and inside was just as inviting with its wooden furniture and colourful walls and beamed ceilings. They entered the kitchen and Annabelle noticed the crockery in the sink, with dirty pans on the cooker.

"Ralph really, you might wash up occasionally" Annabelle looked at him disgusted

"Well I am the only one here and I think why bother" He replied shrugging his shoulders.

"That's not the point, have some pride man" She said filling the sink with hot water and washing up liquid.

"Oh come on Annabelle leave it" Ralph said tutting.

But a stubborn Annabelle carried on washing up and ignored his plead, instead he decided to make a drink for both of them. When they had finished they went into the studio, Annabelle was admiring his work paintings, sculptures and wood carvings. He could bring anything he did to life with his artistic hands and mind, he was not just an artist but a creator who loved beautiful things. But his favourite subject was Annabelle who he sculptured and drew untiringly. Annabelle watched him preparing his art tools for the day, then became distracted by an object in the corner of the room covered in a sheet. She looked at the shape for a while and then went to peep underneath grabbing the corner of the sheet with her hand.

"Stop!" Came a loud hostile voice

At that moment Annabelle withdrew her hand and fell backwards, she looked at her hand which was covered in blood. The sight of it caused her to pass out and she fell to the ground with a thud, almost hitting her head on a picture. When she awoke Ralph was cleaning her hand and searching for the wound which was on the thumb of her right hand.

"Annabelle are you alright?" Ralph asked concerned

"Yes I think so, what happened to me?" She asked

"you cut your thumb, it needs a plaster or something, let me go onto the kitchen and fetch something" Ralph said heading for the kitchen

As he left Annabelle noticed something moving under the sheet, it was something large and seemed to be very active. Suddenly its head appeared it was a snake, it appeared to have yellow eyes that were looking at her, she then noticed its fanged teeth which could have been what caught her thumb she was petrified and froze with fear unable to speak. The snake slithered slowly towards her keeping its eyes trained on her and then opened its mouth to devour her.

As it struck out Ralph returned and it vanished as if it never existed, Annabelle passed out again and left Ralph bewildered by her actions. Again she awoke and looked at Ralph wondering if she had dreamt the entire events of the day.

“Annabelle I have dressed your thumb” He said looking at her with concern.

“Ralph what’s going on?” Annabelle asked with an angry tone on her voice.

“I don’t understand, I just didn’t want you to see my surprise for you under that sheet” He said innocently.

“Oh really, a snake is that my surprise?” Annabelle asked

“Snake?” Ralph said puzzled

“Oh come on Ralph I know a snake when I see one” She said angrily

“Mirrors” Ralph replied

“Mirrors?” She said puzzled

“I have got you three mirrors which are under that sheet and I am presently carving the frames” Ralph explained.

Ralph offered her a glass of water and smiled, Annabelle had the drink and sat quietly for a while. She was convinced that Ralph was lying as the snake had appeared and almost killed her, but why did he lie to her, what was he keeping from her and was it necessary to deceive her like that.

Not long after Annabelle left still bewildered by the snake and just wanting to go back to the stately manor where her husband John was waiting for her. He seemed very suspicious as to her whereabouts and questioned her repeatedly, he refused to give up until she admitted that she had been to Ralph's cottage. John knew that he was an artist and had many models posing for his work. But he suspected that his beautiful wife and Ralph had more going on that just art, so the next time she went there he followed her.

Annabelle met Ralph in the usual place in the woods and they went back to the cottage, Ralph had his hand bandaged up and blood was seeping out of the bandage.

"What have you done?" Annabelle asked concerned.

"Oh its nothing I slipped with the chisel while carving the frame for those mirrors" Ralph explained.

"Are they finished now?" She asked

"Yes do you want to see them?" He asked proudly.

"Of course" Annabelle was very excited

Ralph uncovered them and revealed the most attractive mirrors with their wooden carved frames, three of them each looking similar and with one flaw in them a blood stain not just on one but all three frames and in the same place.

"I tried to hide those stains but they keep re appearing, I don't know why really".

"Is some of it my blood?" Annabelle asked curiously

"Yes it is, it must be special" Ralph said jokingly

"So I am special?" she asked

"Yes" he admitted "So will you now model for me" he asked preparing his canvas.

"Yes do you want me to strip?" She asked

"Yes please, this is for a sculpture of you, for my exhibition" Ralph prepared his paint brushes.

While Annabelle stripped naked and lay across the settee, Ralph studied her form admiring all her curves and posture. She skin as smooth as silk and as pale as snow, he stood watching her for a while, then began to paint on the canvas. Annabelle relaxed but then thought about the last time they made love and began to blush, she was conscious of her body tingling with excitement and she naturally responded her body welled up inside the more that she thought about Ralph. She tried not to think about him so that she could pose for him comfortably but her body was telling her different and she began to fidget. Ralph picked up on her vibes and he was also responding, he dropped the brush on the floor and approached her, she wrapped her body around him and began kissing him passionately. She removed his shirt and kissed his chest then he removed the remainder of his clothes and made love to her. When they had finished, she lay beside him and looked into his eyes.

“I really love you Ralph” Annabelle said with tears in her eyes.

“I love you but what about John?” He asked

“I hate him, he is cruel and hateful” Annabelle said

“He will be angry when he finds out” Ralph said looking at the mirrors.

“So let’s runaway together, tonight yes tonight” She said also looking at the mirrors.

“Are you sure that’s what you want think of what your giving up?” Ralph said concerned

“I don’t care as long as we are together and happy” Annabelle began to cry.

“Alright if that’s what you want go and pack and we will go tonight” Ralph agreed.

A short while later Annabelle got dressed and left the cottage little knowing that John was outside, he watched Annabelle disappear into the woods and then entered the cottage.

“Have you forgotten something Annabelle?” Ralph shouted

He had his back to John and didn’t expect to be attacked, as John picked up a chisel from the table and plunged it into his back digging it deep and then twisting it. He pulled it out covered in blood and plunged it in again, he repeated this ten times until Ralph fell to the ground. He then found a pipe belonging to Ralph and lit the tobacco inside, then set fire to other items in the room. Before long the whole room was in flames then he left the cottage and ran into the woods.

When the fire brigade arrived the studio was burnt to the ground but amazingly the three mirrors were intact the wood wasn't even singed or damaged in any way. No one could explain it eventually they went to the Harrington manor and were displayed on the study wall. The servants witnessed a rough going on between Annabelle and John over Ralph so everyone soon knew about the affair, but nothing else that occurred.

The next day Annabelle had a black eye and a bruised right cheek, she remained silent and disappeared shortly after, her clothes were missing so the servants presumed that she had run away somewhere, one maid even thought that Annabelle was pregnant as she had morning sickness, perhaps she had ran away to have the child.

CHAPTER 2

EMMA'S STORY

John was said to have died a short while after Annabelle went missing, he had cut himself off the family and hidden the three mirrors away in the attic. Soon after he was said to have thrown himself out of one of the top windows breaking his neck in the fall. No one could say for sure why he did this as he never discussed what was going on in his head, but the servants had their own tale to tell about how he kept speaking to the mirrors and became tormented by his wife's disappearance. John's suicide meant that according to his will Gladys's being the next in line in the family would inherit the house, Gladys's was his eldest sister next in line was James and then Emma his eldest niece.

Gladys's moved into the house with Emma as she was her legal guardian, Emma's parents were killed in a car crash a few years before. Emma was already close to Gladys as she used to take her to play with another niece called Chloe in the Harrington household. John believed children should be seen and not heard and so he insisted they played in the nursery or in the garden, but the rest of the house was forbidden to them. But Annabelle used to allow them to join her in the study if John was out on business, they loved Annabelle but hated him. Annabelle wanted children but had a number of miscarriages due to the way John treated her, he wanted an heir to the estate and a figure head but hated children. Emma grew up believing that he was mad, although it was said that she in fact was mentally ill. She was said to be suffering from multiple personality syndrome or as it is known today as dissociate identity disorder, some even question whether or not this really exists in the field of psychiatry.

Gladys introduced herself and Emma to the servants and settled into the manor, all was quiet for a few years until James came to visit with his wife Margaret. James was very eccentric and Margaret was just a puppet that James controlled, answering to his every whim like she had no mind of her own or at least that's the way she presented herself to the family. Gladys was a real lady just like Annabelle so gracious slim and elegant with an air of superiority which was different to Annabelle. Emma was a little more down to earth and definitely not a lady but could still be gracious when she wanted to. She had long brown hair she was slim and in her twenties with large blue eyes, her cousin Chloe was very much the same but with darker hair. Chloe had a child a baby boy called Thomas she was also visiting Harrington hall happy that she was free to roam he house.

James and Margaret were like vultures looking for things to take as they had not appeared since the death of John and knew certain things had a lot of value. Most relative had come and gone as the will had been read and their was little left to anyone. Gladys even led them to the attic where many old things existed that were never considered nice or decent enough to exist around other parts of the house. This is where the three mirrors were propped against a beam gathering dust.

"I like them" James said admiring the mirrors.

"You may have one of them" Gladys insisted.

"Only one but they are a set" James said indignantly.

"We shall have one and Chloe can have the other" Gladys said sternly.

"But that's not fair" Margaret said looking at James.

"Of course it's fair, we can each keep one and that way it will stay in the family" Gladys looked at James then Margaret with a challenging expression on her face.

Neither questioned her but just picked up one of the mirrors and left the attic, Chloe picked up one of the others and Emma lifted the final mirror. It was fairly light considering the amount of wood round it. She was asked to take it to the study where the three mirrors once hung, Gladys then asked Albert the butler to hang it up above a decorative chair.

That night Emma heard a noise coming from the study, she opened the door slowly and entered with caution, she was drawn to the mirror by the sound of a muffled voice and to her horror saw the head of a woman. The features were hidden by a dark mist and it appeared to be a severed head as it moved from left to right as if it was swinging like a pendulum. Emma was transfixed on the object then saw blood dripping down the mirror and onto the floor. She let out a scream which alerted the servants and eventually her aunt Gladys. As they entered Emma was trembling with fear and began crying at the sight that she had seen, she was eventually consoled by her aunt. But when she described the experience and pointed to the floor where the blood had landed, it had disappeared with no trace.

"Come dear you must have imagined it there are no blood stains and the mirror is like any other mirror, you are tired and probably imagined that you saw something" Gladys said smiling.

"But it was there, a head and strange voice, blood everywhere" Emma insisted.

"Well its gone now isn't it" Gladys continued.

Emma went to bed thinking about her experience wondering whether or not she was imagining the image in the mirror or whether she was going mad like her dear aunt Annabelle. The following morning she rang Chloe and asked her if she had experienced anything strange with her mirror. Chloe said no and so she rang James and received the same response. That night she returned to the study and examined the mirror for herself, she was looking for a mechanism that would cause the mirror to make sounds or visions that would explain what she saw. Eventually she found something near to where the blood stain was that Ralph had tried to remove and cover up. Suddenly she felt something sharp and fell back onto the floor, she began to feel faint and to her surprise saw a big hairy spider crawl out of the mirror and onto the floor. It crept along the floor with its six feet approaching her, she began pulling her body backwards feeling blood dripping from her finger. But she never looked as she didn't want to take her eyes off the spider she had travelled as far back as the door and pressed her spine against it, in a desperate effort to find some kind of object to knock the spider away she searched around with her hands. But nothing was close she quickly looked around then back at the spider, she noticed heavy books close by and suddenly ran for her life to a book shelf and grabbed some books when she turned to grab one the spider disappeared. Lolled into a false sense of security she put the book down only to find the spider crawling up her body from her feet to her stomach. She let out a scream and picked the book up, knocked it off her and dropped the heavy book on top of it with some force. Again a servant came into the room and she pointed to the book, her arm was shaking.

"look under there, it's a spider big like a tarantella" Emma said her voice was quivering.

Albert lifted up the book cautiously, Emma had her eyes hidden by her hands and slowly took them away. But there was nothing under the book the spider was nowhere to be seen, not a trace just like the blood and whatever else she had previously seen. Now she believed that she was going mad who would possibly believe her now?, a mirror producing images that didn't exist. The next day Gladys advised that Emma stay away from the study and get plenty of rest. She rang Chloe with her tale but as expected was not believed, oddly enough James and Margaret visited acting very strangely. Margaret with her red tinted hair and bizarre dress sense like fashion gone wrong and James appearing as if he knew everything about everything in his arrogance.

"Of course you know she's insane" James said then went quiet as Emma appeared in the drawing room.

"As mad as Annabelle" Margaret chipped in.

"What was that?" Emma asked her

"Oh nothing" Margaret said turning her head to look at James.

"I am not mad!" Emma shouted "Tell them aunt"

Gladys shuck her head and looked at James and Margaret

"She is just a little upset in a new home and it wasn't long ago that she lost her parents" Gladys said in her defence.

"Oh god aunt don't tell them that, they want me locked up in some lunatic asylum, Emma the nut case, the fruit cake, well fuck you" Emma said and raced out of the door slamming it in her rage.

Emma lay crying in her room when she heard a knock on the door, at first she didn't answer then a knock again this time louder.

"Who is it?" Emma shouted

"Aunt Gladys" came the reply

"Are you alone?" Emma asked not wishing to see anyone

"Yes dear just me, the others have gone" Gladys reassured her

Gladys sat on her bed and hugged her tightly, Emma got up and put her head on her shoulder.

"Oh aunt sorry for swearing and losing my temper, but they got me so angry" Emma said sobbing "Oh child don't blame their stupidity after all you have been hurt so much, now dry your eyes and let's get something to eat" Gladys said standing up.

They went downstairs and headed towards the dining room where the servants had prepared food, soup and sandwiches. The days went by without any mention of the mirror or so called hallucinations. Emma seemed happy for a while until other events took place, this time others experienced things such as a servant and even Gladys.

Emma was looking in her mirror when it suddenly shattered, followed by the light bulb exploding. Emma was in darkness, she walked blindly across the room bare footed feeling glass under her feet. She felt around and kept walking until she hit the wall, then walked left holding the wall for support. Eventually she could feel the door but it was locked, so she yelled loudly.

"Help me, somebody I am trapped in this room" Emma shouted feeling scared and alone.

Then she felt something slimy crawl across her feet, it was moving slowly and then made an hissing noise like a snake.

"Oh my god" She shouted

Then the door handle moved and it opened slowly, a light appeared and the figure of a man looked into her. Emma pulled the door open and rushed out seeing Albert standing there, a sigh of relief was heard by Emma.

"Jesus thank god" Emma said

"Are you alright Madam" Albert asked concerned.

"Oh marvellous honestly" Emma said sarcastically.

"First my mirror breaks, then the bulb explodes, I have cut my feet and something crawled on me" Emma said annoyed.

"It's not just your room" Albert said trying to reassure her

"What?" Emma said in disbelief.

"Every mirror in this house has shattered all but one" Albert seemed upset.

"The one in the study" Emma guessed.

"Yes and other light bulbs" Albert said "And the clocks all went backwards I and others saw that"

"Backwards, you mean you actually saw them go backwards?"

"Yes and all stopped at 10.30 everyone" Albert said

"I have seen the image of the woman and heard her voice, I was also struggling in darkness for a while when the lights went out" Gladys said "You are no longer alone".

"Thank god for that, I really thought I was going mad" Emma sighed with relief.

"If you're mad then I am mad too" Gladys said smiling "The question is what do we do with the mirror?"

"Albert take it and burn it outside" Gladys instructed

"Yes Madam" Albert said taking it off the wall.

The next day Albert took the mirror to the gardener to burn on a bonfire, but as it stood in the middle of the rubbish, it never even caught fire instead it shot out of the fire and hit the Gardner who set on fire and burst into flames. He died of severe burns later in hospital and no one could explain how it happened. Not content with this Gladys had it buried in the garden deep in the ground it was missing for days, then it reappeared in tact on the study wall where it had been before just as if it had never been taken down.

Gladys thought that someone had dug it up and put it back, she could never believe that it was a cursed mirror, some believed that Annabelle was dead and haunted the mirror. Then one day Gladys was at the top of the stairs she shouted Emma to come to her and when Emma came she saw a swarm of wasps around her, she screamed but Emma was too late she had fallen down the stairs and when Albert and the servants examined her she was dead with her head turned round. Her neck was broken and there were no sign of wasps, no stings or dead insects. Instead Emma stood at the top of the stairs staring down at her in shock.

The police arrived and took Emma to jail then on to a mental health ward, where she remained for a while until a decision could be made as to her sanity. No one could confirm her story about the mirror or any other incident that occurred in the house her only real friend and defender of truth was Gladys who was dead. Now she had to find help from another direction. She went to university with Fiona from criminal world magazine maybe she could help her.

CHAPTER 3

SIMPLY MAD

Emma appeared on the ward, she was very calm but weary, she seemed to be aware of her environment knowing that she was on a mental health unit. Ruth the mental health nurse made her presence known to her.

"Hello Chloe I am Ruth the nurse who will be looking after you" Ruth said in a soft soothing voice

"Hello Ruth" Emma reluctantly replied.

"I need to ask you a few things if I may?" Rachel continued calmly.

"About my mental health condition, listening to mirrors, my hallucinations and paranoid episodes" Emma looked into Ruth's large hazel eyes "Look I know the jargon right all this is in the family".

"Mental health?" Ruth prompted Emma to continue

"Yes multiple personality or disassociated personality disorder" Emma said

"Yes I had a friend with that, go on" Ruth beckoned.

"Well I am not mad, but ok who gives a fuck" Emma said admiring Ruth's shinny hair.

"Give a fuck" Ruth said smiling.

"I'm sorry it's not your fault, your only doing your job" Emma said returning a smile.

"So let's start again Emma" Ruth said watching Emma fidgeting with her fingers.

"You have lovely long shinny hair Ruth" Chloe said looking at Ruth admiringly.

"Why thank you Emma, I was once a model but shush don't say anything" Ruth said looking round.

"Is that why you have lovely complexion and white teeth?" Emma asked

"Yes I suppose so, but enough about me, tell me your story" Ruth prompted.

"Well I kept seeing a head in a mirror and a Éire voice, then I saw a snake come out of the mirror and a large hairy spider" Emma mimicked a spider movement with her fingers "All the mirrors broke in the house and light bulbs blew up, I was so scared I was in darkness and the door was locked I felt something slither past my legs and feet. It sounds crazy but I felt like I was in a bog or quick sand being sucked down".

"It must have been terrifying for you" Ruth said with empathy.

"Simply mad" Emma said shrugging her shoulders

"Simply mad?" Ruth said looking oddly at her.

"Simply mad, an unexplainable phenomenon that not only I experienced by others like Gladys with her wasps and she saw the head in the mirror, but then she's dead so what proof have I?" Emma said sadly.

"Did the staff witness anything?" Ruth asked

"Albert did and the gardener was on fire due to trying to get rid of the mirror, it's like the mirror is alive, possessed or cursed it can't be destroyed, no matter what you try to do to it" Emma began to shake.

Ruth held her hands and felt her sweating palms, she could see the fear in her eyes and her anxiety, she had seen it before with people experiencing phobias. The fear of spiders as in arachnophobia or agoraphobia fear of open spaces, claustrophobia fear of closed in spaces. What had actually induced her fear was uncertain in Ruth's eyes, but whatever it was it was real to Emma.

"Seriously do you think I am mad?" Emma asked Ruth

"It is not for me to decide Emma, we have psychiatrists for that, you were brought here so that you would be far enough away from your home and would be able to think about things away from your district. I believe Chloe lives in Scotland have you spoken to her about this?" Samantha asked.

"Yes but she said that nothing has happened to her" Emma said

"I don't quite understand, happened as in what?" Ruth said confused.

"The mirrors" Emma said puzzled.

"You mean there are more than one?" Ruth asked

"Yes three identical mirrors the frames were carved by the same artists and only one belongs to me" Emma explained

"So who has the other mirrors?" Ruth asked intrigued.

"Chloe has one and Uncle James has the other one but nothing has happened with them" Emma said quietly, but my uncle may be lying as he wanted me in here".

"Why do you think that?" Ruth asked concerned.

"Both he and my aunt Margaret say I am insane and want all the inheritance" Emma explained "They think I am simply mad"

"I see, what about Chloe?" Ruth asked "Does she feel the same?"

"No I don't think so, we grew up together, then she moved to Scotland" Emma thought for a moment. "Can you contact her, she will be worried about me".

"Ok, let me do that for you now" Ruth stood up and walked out of the interview room to the office next door.

She tapped the number on the phone and waited, meanwhile Kathy walked in the office.

"Hi Ruth" she said

"Hi Kathy how are you?" Ruth asked then responded to a voice on the phone

"Hi is that Chloe?" Ruth asked

"Yes" came a voice on the other end of the phone

"This is staff nurse Ruth from the mental health unit I have Emma Harrington with me" Ruth said once she was certain that Chloe was listening, she then put her on speaker.

"How is she?" Chloe asked

"A little low, but alright" Ruth deliberately restricted her information on the phone.

“Ok tell her that I am thinking about her and my mirror is active” Chloe said.

“What do you mean?” Ruth asked hoping that she would elaborate on what she meant.

“I too have seen a head, it was trying to communicate but the voice was slurred and murdering, simply mad” Chloe explained “quite scary really”

“I am sure it must have been” Ruth said looking at Kathy.

“I know you don’t believe me, but it’s the truth and I have been in darkness that was scary the door was locked and I was alone” Chloe explained.

“Alright Chloe let me pass on your message” Ruth said terminating the conversation.

“Ok, send her my love, bye” Chloe said

Ruth looked at Kathy for support as they were old friends and colleagues they could discuss patients at ease, they were able to share thoughts and opinions.

“Now Ruth don’t re enforce Emma’s delusions and don’t get too involved please” Kathy said concerned.

“Kathy I purposely let you listen to that conversation so that you would hear what I heard about the mirrors, there are three and there is something odd about them” Ruth explained all about Emma and her dilemma, then she told the full story about the family tragedy. Making sure Kathy knew the facts and could advice accordingly as the senior sister. Kathy was ten years older than Ruth who was in her early thirties and who had been through her fair share of trauma and tragedy in her life. Kathy had fair hair and was a little plump or as she termed it cuddle, unlike Ruth who was slim and beautiful. Ruth also had to come to terms with her own sexuality she once fell in love with a patient called Pamela who was tragically murdered by Ruth's psychopath ex-boyfriend Malcolm. Kathy was heterosexual but understood Ruth at least most of the time, although some things that Ruth did appeared un orthodox at times. Kathy's life was more straight forward and unless she got involved with Ruth's affairs she lived an ordinary lifestyle.

Emma settled on the ward undisrupted until she experienced nightmares and became restless, some involved the mirrors or things associated with them. This included spiders, snakes being trapped or chased by Aztec Indians, she even dreamed of Annabelle and her violent husband.

Eventually she was visited by Fiona reporter from the crime magazine criminal world, Ruth recognised her and called her into the office.

"Emma said you would come" Ruth said acting a little distant.

"Yes she is a friend and once a fellow student at university with me" Fiona said removing her coat and adjusting her blonde hair.

"I wrote as accurate account as I could of you in my article '***Cracked porcelain***' I hope you believe that" Fiona said concerned by Ruth's response to her.

"Yes about the abuse Pamela and I experienced" Ruth agreed "It was a good article"

"So how are you now?" Fiona asked

"I am good though still wary about reporters, we also had bad press" Ruth said honestly.

"I agree not all reporters have a heart and some can be ruthless" Fiona admitted "But criminal world prides itself on good reporters who care for people's feelings.

"Well good for you, so do you want to see Emma?" Ruth asked not willing to divulge any more information due to patient confidentiality.

Instead Emma explained everything to Fiona from the Mysterious fire to the death of John Harrington and the so called curse of the mirrors. Fiona wrote a lot of information down and promised to send someone to be with Chloe and try to protect her. Emma knew that she could rely on Fiona to help her and put an end to the curse once and for all.

"Emma we need to get you out of here and go back to the manor, we also need to get Ruth to help us solve the mystery of the mirrors" Fiona explained.

"Will Ruth agree to this?" Emma asked eagerly

"I can be very persuasive" Fiona said confidently "I have already sent Daniel Harrison one of our reporters to James and Margaret's home under cover, so just keep that quiet and maybe we can find out something there" Fiona winked at Emma in order to reassure her all was well.

Meanwhile in the home of James and Margaret Harrington all seemed quiet Daniel Harrison was working undercover as planned he had successfully set up camera's and other equipment in order to catch the couple out with their plot against the other members of the family in taking their inheritance. Attempting to take all the mirrors was the beginning of their devious plan.

As far as they knew Emma had suffered a breakdown and was on a mental health unit. But Emma had been telling the truth about the mirror and was planning to prove it somehow. She was convinced that the other mirrors were a clue to some kind of tragedy and that something was keeping the mirrors apart and at the same time something wanted the mirrors to unite. In the James Harrington household things began with the breaking of mirrors and Margaret getting trapped in a dark room similar to Emma's experience. They were being drawn to the mirror for some reason led to a face and a garbled voice, then sent away for no apparent reason.

James sat in the dining room talking to Margaret.

Daniel Harrison was close by working as an handyman, he was busy listening to James and Margaret's conversation

"Look keep this quiet no one must know about this" James said in a low voice

"But I did experience things such as the horrid face in the mirror and a weird voice, but it was garbled and incoherent just like Emma said" Margaret admitted.

"Exactly as Emma said, can't you see she imagined it" James said trying to convince her.

"No James it was there as clear as I see you now" Margaret insisted.

"For god sake woman we need that inheritance, we need to prove that Emma is insane" James said sharply

"What about Chloe?" Margaret asked

"Oh she will be easy, she can't cope with her baby, she is probably suffering from post natal depression, don't you see it's in the bag, we have them all, all I ask you is keep a level head" James insisted.

"Fine maybe then we will be out of debt" Margaret said concerned.

"Yes the mirrors will see to that" James said confidently.

At that moment one of the butlers entered the room

"Phone call sir, it's your niece Chloe" He said

"Thank you Jarvis" James replied

James stood up and followed him into the study, he picked up the receiver and dusted it off with his handkerchief then cleared his throat and began to speak.

"Hello Chloe how are you?" He said jovially.

"Uncle James, have you heard from Emma?" Chloe asked concerned.

"No why?" James asks hesitantly.

"I heard that she was going back to the manor" Chloe informed him.

"Really" James said in a surprised manner "But I thought she was ill"

"Yes well one of them is a mental health nurse and the other is a reporter, they are staying with her" Chloe said awaiting his response.

"Well evidently they think she is normal, although I can't think why" James said with disappointment in his voice

"Define normal Uncle, compos menus or simply mad, those are lay man's terms a little non descriptive don't you think?" Chloe was trying to expose her uncle by teasing him.

"So you haven't experienced anything with the mirror then?" Chloe prompted.

“Not at all, it’s ridiculous” James insisted “Why have you?”.

“Yes I have seen the head, not clearly but it was there and I heard a voice it was horrible and muffled very scary” Chloe admitted.

“Well perhaps you should tell someone and let it known” James encouraged her in order to show that she was also insane.

“Oh I have someone called Samantha King, she is staying with me soon” Chloe explained.

“Oh where is she from?” James asked curiously.

“A Crime magazine called criminal world, she’s a reporter like Fiona at Emma’s home, it’s because of these mirrors they have raised much interest” Chloe said hoping he would take the bait.

“That’s good tell her everything and don’t hold back explain about the haunted figure and the blood coming down the mirror, the spiders and big snake”. James sounded very excited “Listen Chloe I am being called I will phone you later bye for now”.

James put the receiver down and hurried out of the study; he entered the drawing room and re-joined Margaret who was eager to hear the news.

“Well what did she say?” Margaret asked impatiently.

"She like Emma is walking right into our trap, it's a matter of time and we will be rich". James said excitedly.

"Really, so have they kept Emma locked away?" Margaret asked

"No but they have reporters going there and they will prove that they are insane" James said confidently. "They are both experiencing the same things, both Emma and Chloe" James continued

"How very odd" Margaret said looking towards the mirror.

"So don't mention about your experiences" James advised "I don't want you locked up"

"No of course not, but we need to get rid of the mirror" Margaret said "It gives me the creeps"

"Fine, we can take it to the antique shop and sell it" James said in agreement.

CHAPTER 4

CRIMINAL WORLD

Criminal world is a magazine dedicated to investigating crime all over the world; the reporters and photographer gather details of crime from victims, police records and criminals themselves. The team take steps to ensure that the public are provided with detailed accounts of events with graphic pictures that questionably cannot be compared with any other crime magazine.

Fiona Ellington is one of the reporters who are strong-minded and a force to be reckoned with as she immerses all her energy into finding a good story. Her life is criminal world and anything else in life takes a back shelf including love and marriage. Although she did lose a boyfriend during her time in New York, he was shot in action.

Samantha King is a reporter who joined the team from the Australian office of criminal world. She is courageous and determined to get what she wants despite upsetting a few people on the way. She can be outspoken using her beauty to her advantage. She is known to offend people with her bad language which she often says she's working on.

Stuart Elliot was a photographer who spent a few years as a wedding photographer and then ventured into the world photographing models moved into the area of crime when he found himself actually photographing a murder as it happened.

Daniel Harrison another reporter that used to work in war zones, he had a history in the army and used it to help him on location in remote areas. He achieved many things in his younger life recognising an opportunity for a story an every moment. He was said to even sleep with a notepad in his bed.

Many other people worked for criminal world of course and the main offices employed computer experts and retired scientists surprisingly enough. It was a thriving concern and the connections with other areas of expertise helped to make the magazine more accurate and credible. The World Wide Web or internet serves as a valuable asset for criminal world in order to receive vital information for the magazine.

Samantha sat opposite Fiona sharpening pencils, organising her papers and measuring each pencil checking that each one fit into her neat box.

"Sammy what are you doing" Fiona asked.

"Tidying up why" Samantha replied

"Because you're getting on my nerves must you do that?" Fiona asked aggravated by Samantha's habits.

"Sorry but I can't help it" She said continuing to measure the pencils and sharpen them even more.

"No wonder you have trouble with men" Fiona said laughing.

"Well men are just Dick heads who think of one thing" Samantha said laughing.

"Oh Sammy that's a sweeping statement" Fiona said playing with her blonde hair.

"It's fucking true Fi you know it is" Samantha said taking the bobble out of her hair and looking for her brush.

"So what about Scotland, are you looking forward to that?" Fiona asked

"Oh yes being in some creepy manner like that fucking castle, yes of course I am" Samantha said finding her brush and using it on her long brown hair.

"Ashley Manor will be nice and not at all creepy, besides you will be looking after Chloe" Fiona explained.

"Oh some nut job who talks to mirrors and spooks herself silly" Samantha said tying her hair up

"Sammy she is nice and has a baby, you like children don't you?" Fiona said smiling

"You know I don't it is all about commitment and all that" Samantha replied knowing that Fiona was teasing her.

"You are going to Harrington manor with that mental health nurse, I feel more sorry for you with the lesbian" Samantha was responding to Fiona tormenting her by making her own remarks.

"Oh how homophobic is that Sammy" Fiona replied.

"I am not but from that article you wrote about her and Pamela, what was it called? 'Cracked porcelain' she deserved what she got messing about with patients".

"I thought you liked it?" Fiona said disappointedly.

"Oh Fi I am only playing you up" Samantha said laughing "I loved the article"

"Anyway pack for a week, I believe it is chilly in that part of Scotland" Fiona continued "Have you read up on the mirrors?"

"Yes about the things they have supposedly seen and heard" Samantha said.

"Good we need someone with an open mind and you and Elliot will be just the right people" Fiona said confidently.

"Wait did you say, Elliot?" Samantha said frowning.

"Yes Elliot will be going too" Fiona said surprised by her reaction.

"You are fucking joking of course" Samantha said angrily.

"No we need him to get photos of the place and camera equipment as evidence of paranormal activity" Fiona explained.

"Rubbish you just want to freak me out even more, fucking with my head I call it" Samantha said clearly annoyed by the idea.

"Sammy you need to curb your language and deal with your issues with Stuart" Fiona said seriously.

Samantha went quiet which usually meant that she was sulking; she began reading a magazine which was another indication that she was upset by what Fiona had said. Fiona recognised that she had upset her.

"Sammy you're a good reporter and friend please do this for me" Fiona gave her the look that no one could resist as if she was pleading "Please Sammy for me".

"Ok Just for you, but if he upsets me can I have your permission to slap him?" Samantha asked.

"Yes that sounds reasonable" Fiona agreed.

"I will try not to swear" Samantha agreed.

At that moment Elliot walked in to the office, he was dancing and full of life as he approached them.

“Hello ladies so we are going to Scotland then Sammy?” He said pointing to a map on the wall.

“Yes I believe so” Samantha replied trying to contain herself.

“Just like the McGregor castle nice and creepy” Elliot was trying to annoy Samantha and Fiona was watching her waiting for Samantha to react.

“Me and you again” Elliot continued “Like old times”.

“Elliot it was last year” Fiona said

“My word only a year, down them creepy corridors in a murder mystery with you my love” Elliot said laughing.

“That will do Stuart, leave her alone” Fiona jumped in.

“Like she left me alone, all over me like a rash” Elliot jumped quick as he noticed a book being hurled in the air towards his head.

“You fucking conceited bastard, don’t speak about me like that” Samantha said angrily.

“Go Elliot please” Fiona said pointing to the door” Fiona said

“Sorry Fi but you saw what happened” Samantha said

“Look you can swap with me have Ruth and Emma” Fiona offered.

“The rampant lesbian no thanks I am safer with Elliot, I can handle him” Samantha said smiling.

“Ruth is a nice woman and so kind, she really is nice” Fiona said in Ruth’s defence.

“Yes but it’s the patient thing with Pamela, hey alarm bells and hello forbidden territory”.

Samantha said “No offence but that’s going too far, out of order”.

“Sorry you feel so strongly” Fiona said disappointed.

“And Emma is definitely a fucking Nutter believe me with the mirror thing, like you said we will be gathering evidence to show there is no such thing as a haunted mirror”.

“Maybe, we will see” Fiona said

“You don’t seriously believe in this nonsense” Samantha said

“I like to keep an opened mind” Fiona replied.

With that Elliot re-entered the office like a tornado

“I am just going to pack, anything you need Sammy, flick knife or a sledge hammer?” Elliot said laughing.

"Fuck off Elliot" Samantha shouted

"Isn't she wonderful, beautiful with a nice figure and a mouth like a sewer" Elliot said tormenting her.

"That's really funny Elliot, go fuck yourself" Samantha said looking back into her magazine.

"She is at it again, moaning, swearing and giving me grief" Elliot went on.

"Look Elliot I am not apologising for anything so forget it" Samantha said not even giving him eye contact.

"Ok I can live with that I will see you at two o'clock" Elliot actually left the room without another word.

Later they set off for the north east of Scotland near Edinburgh; Samantha remained quiet listening to Elliot's favourite classical music which eventually sent her to sleep. This was probably a plot by Elliot to keep her quiet while they travelled miles up north. When she finally woke up Elliot was admiring the scenery and driving around the smaller roads through the mountains and valleys of Scotland.

"I love the scenery, the heather and the hills" Elliot said noticing that she was awake.

"Really" Samantha replied.

"Oh here we go with the attitude" Elliot said

"Tell me Elliot was it your idea to come together" Samantha said

"No why?" Elliot said with surprise

"So you don't want to fuck me?" Samantha said bluntly.

"Nothing further from my mind" Elliot said innocently.

"Like at the McGregor castle experience" Samantha said

"Oh that again don't you ever forget?" Elliot said

"You obviously do so was I that bad?" Samantha said prompting him.

"Look you came on to me, not the other way round" Elliot insisted.

"No I didn't how dare you, stop the car" Samantha insisted

"What are you serious we are in the middle of nowhere" Elliot said

"Stop the fucking car now!" Samantha said becoming rigid.

Elliot stopped the car and looked at her puzzled.

"Now get out" Samantha was frowning again.

Elliot got out of the car and slammed the door, Samantha got out the other side and they both stood for a while looking at each other.

"Right get this straight it was a mistake never to be repeated" Samantha shouted pointing her finger.

"But you came to my bed and made me feel as if I had done wrong" Elliot said in his defence.

"Only because I was scared and you took advantage of me" Samantha started pacing up and down.

"That's bloody rubbish and you know it" Elliot said.

"Anyway I don't want to talk about it" Samantha said turning her back on him.

"But you brought it up" Elliot pointed out.

"Just fuck off" Samantha said dismissing him

"Look we have to work together, that means getting on" Elliot said trying to reason with her.

"Ok" Samantha took a deep breath "But let's forget the incident" Samantha said walking towards the car.

They continued their journey to Ashley manor saying very little to each other and then when they arrived Elliot offered to carry Samantha's bags. Samantha refused and struggled to the door almost falling over. As she reached the door the butler stopped her and carried them in looking disgusted at Elliot, Elliot was surprised at the butlers response as he struggled in with his own luggage. Once inside the staff took their luggage upstairs and one of them showed them into the drawing room where Chloe was waiting for them.

Samantha entered the room but there was a delay before Elliot finally entered the room.

Elliot clumsily entered the room "Sorry I am late" He said sitting on a seat beside Samantha

She merely gave him a look of disgust and began talking to Chloe

"So tell me about the mirrors, from your point of view" Samantha said in a professional manner.

Elliot looked at Samantha and then at Chloe "No pressure of course"

"Thank you Elliot" She said frowning at him

"Can I ask, are you two married?" She asked

"No" Samantha said shocked "Why do you ask?"

"Nothing, you act like it that's all" Chloe said smirking.

"Me with her I don't think so" Elliot said laughing.

"Look can we get on" Samantha said obviously irritated by Elliot's reaction.

Chloe explained about the mirror "At first everything seemed normal and then the trouble started" She paused to think for a moment. "I was in the study looking around the mirror when I felt around it hearing what Emma had said about cutting her finger, it was then that as I felt around it cut my own finger, then things started happening such as seeing the image of an headed that seemed to sway from left to right, then a horrible voice that wasn't at all clear".

"Muffled you mean?" Elliot asked

"Yes she didn't even sound English" Chloe explained "Then I heard weird noises like wild monkeys and tropical birds like I was in a jungle".

"Strange how did you feel" Samantha asked.

"Dizzy and weak, I began using the feelings in my body" Chloe explained touching her body "I saw swinging from the hair, it was cut off in a rough manner as the skin seemed to hang down in strands, the voice was definitely not audible and as I said seemed to be foreign".

"It sounds creepy" Samantha said shuddering.

"Do you want to see it?" Chloe invited.

"Yes of course" Elliot said excitedly.

"Come, follow me to the study" Chloe offered.

They entered the study after Chloe struggled with the door, the door was very stiff and the door itself seemed to be too big for the frame.

"The door seemed to be sticking" Elliot observed.

"I got stuck in here, the light went out and I was in darkness I felt trapped away from my child and heard jungle sounds, then my feet seemed to sink as if they were in quick sand. I felt like I was dying I couldn't breathe, my heart was beating out of my chest as if I were having a panic attack" Chloe said holding her chest and her eyes widening mimicking her actions.

Elliot walked up to the mirror and gazed into it, then he had a cheeky look on his face as he spoke into it.

"Mirror mirror on the wall, who is the fairest of them all" He paused "Samantha he replied to himself in a deeper voice "She is the fairest in the land".

"Stop it Elliot you prick!" Samantha shouted.

"It's only a mirror" Elliot said mocking her "Are you afraid?"

"I was traumatised as a child by Snow white and the enchanted mirror, my mother thought it was the wicked queens who turned into a witch, but it was the enchanted mirror Samantha explained.

"It was just a Walt Disney cartoon nothing more" Elliot went on.

"Not to a child" Chloe said sharply

"I was only joking" Elliot said innocently.

"Well don't it's really not funny" Chloe said in Samantha's defence "Fears like phobia's can be real you know".

"Ok, point taken I will just continue admiring the mirror" Elliot said looking around the frame

"I suppose you both want to settle down and rest" Chloe asked

"Yes I need a shower" Samantha said.

CHAPTER 5

MIRRORS

That evening Samantha and Elliot were shown their rooms, Samantha's room was opposite Elliot's and next to Chloe's room the nursery was a few rooms away. Samantha unpacked and went into the bathroom to have a shower. Elliot was in his room examining his new camera playing with the aperture and adjusting the lens. He focused on a picture on the wall, it was a portrait of a woman so beautiful and yet her eyes were sad. It was a portrait of Annabelle painted by Ralph Cornell the artist the more Elliot looked at the portrait the sadder he felt.

Samantha was enjoying her shower when she thought she could hear a voice, she stood still and listened, but all she could hear was the water coming from the shower. She continued to wash and again heard a female voice, this time she turned the shower tap off and listened. Again she heard nothing so she grabbed her bath robe and put it around her. She walked into the bedroom and looked around "Hello" she said baffled.

"Is somebody here?" she struggled her shoulders "Can't be anyone" she said to herself

She took her make up case and removed a mirror from her bag, she then lined her make up neatly across the dressing table. She noticed that a mirror was missing from the dressing table, observing the wood that supported it. Suddenly her mirror shattered in front of her and her make up flew into the air as if it was alive. She jumped and then stood up looking around her, she put on a pair of knickers and pink pyjamas. And then she returned to the dressing table, to attempt to pick up some of the fragments of the mirror from the table and on the floor. Suddenly the light went out and she was in darkness, she tried to move but felt splinters of glass under her naked feet. Cautiously she walked away from the dressing table feeling cuts to her feet "Ouch fuck" she said walking with her hands in front of her.

"Elliot!" she shouted "You better not be fucking pranking me"

"She could feel something around her feet, it felt warm and slimy, she stopped and listened "What the fuck, okay keep calm" she told herself "Your nearly at the door Sammy, come on its not a snake they are silky". Samantha reached the door and felt for the handle "Why are all the doors either stiff or locked?" she asked herself.

She continued pulling the handle down and trying to open the door then she felt something touching her face and she screamed, at that moment the door opened and she ran into the corridor. She continued into Elliot's room, the door was open and she looked around.

"Elliot!" She shouted then heard a scream that seemed to be coming from downstairs.

She ran down the stairs leaving a trail of blood on the landing and stairs, she immediately headed for the study and found Chloe with her hands over her mouth and Elliot on the floor.

"Elliot!" Samantha shouted then knelt beside him

"Oh god is he dead?" Chloe asked.

"No I don't think so Chloe he has just bumped his head" Samantha said examining him

Elliot opened his eyes and focussed on Samantha, "An angel" He said holding his head.

"Fuck off Elliot" Samantha said checking a slight cut on his head.

"Is he hurt?" Chloe asked.

"Not as much as I would like him to be" Samantha said harshly.

"Well, that's a bit much" Chloe said shocked at her reaction.

"Sorry just my humour, besides I have had problems of my own" Samantha replied showing Chloe her feet "Here help me up with him" Samantha said trying to get Elliot to his feet.

"Ouch my head" Elliot complained.

“Get me a cold wet flannel please” Samantha asked.

“I will arrange it” Chloe said pulling the servants bell.

“So what happened?” I was examining the mirror and photographing it when I felt something hit me on the head, it came from behind me” Elliot explained.

“Well it wasn’t me” Samantha said laughing “I was too busy fighting off slimy creatures in my room”

“Well I saw a head in the mirror and heard a voice” Elliot said “Just as Chloe said earlier.

At that moment a servant entered the room, she looked surprised at seeing them.

“Can I help you madam?” she asked

“Yes get me a cold compress” Chloe asked.

The servant looked puzzled at Chloe

“A cold wet flannel, face clothe for the man’s head, quickly” Chloe ordered.

“So how are you Elliot” Samantha asked

“Like you care” Elliot said grumpily.

“Oh that’s not fair I am concerned you know” Samantha said sympathetically.

"How's are your feet?" Elliot asked.

"Could be better, I need to soak them make sure all the glass is out" Samantha said checking her feet.

Two servants returned with a compress and Chloe applied it to Elliot's head then Chloe arranged for a bowl of water to bathe Samantha's feet. Some of the servants who lived at the manor assisted them. They then retired to bed, Chloe checked on her baby before she settled down.

The next few days were uneventful then Samantha began to hear the voices again, she did not hesitate this time and dressed in her pink pyjamas she headed towards Elliot's room. He didn't seem surprised to see her and commented.

"By the way, the door is open" Elliot said sarcastically.

"Elliot" Samantha began

"Yes Sammy" He said sitting in a chair and reading a book.

"Can I stay here?" Samantha looked frightened "please".

"In here with me?" She asked.

"Yes" Samantha nodded.

"Is this because you're frightened?" Elliot asked.

"Maybe or maybe not" Samantha said hesitantly.

"Oh for god sake Sammy make your mind up, why don't you give me a straight answer" Elliot said

"Ok I am alright" Samantha admitted

"Ok well there is room on the chair" Elliot teased.

"Er I don't think so, I get the bed" Samantha demanded

"No way it's my room" Elliot insisted.

"I am joking we can share the bed if you behave" She said smiling.

"I know how to control myself, you came onto me remember" Elliot said reminding her of the McGregor castle experience.

"Not that again, forget all that lets have a truce" Samantha insisted. "She put her hand out to shake his hand.

"Agreed" Elliot said shaking his hand.

"They both got into the bed then Samantha started making noises demonstrating that she was clearly not happy, she kept looking at Elliot and continued making noises.

"Ok, what's wrong" Elliot asked.

"Can I sleep next to the window?" She asked smiling at him.

"I suppose so" He agreed moving over.

There was a moments silence and then Samantha broken the silence with a random comment.

"I didn't enjoy the sex you know" She said with her back to him

"Sammy" He said grumpily.

"Sorry I won't mention it again" he said smiling to herself.

After a while Elliot could feel her fidgeting and shaking, she put her feet on his legs and yelled "Ouch"

"You're shaking" He said feeling her cold feet on his bare legs

"That's because I am fucking cold" She replied

"Oh so you're not frightened?" He asked

"No" she thought for a moment about what Elliot said about being indecisive "Well a little maybe".

"Sammy a straight answer please" Elliot said irritated by her reply.

"You feel warm at least your legs are" she said pressing her feet against his legs.

"What was that?" She said

"What?" Elliot asked opening his eyes

“The bed moved and I heard something” she said lifting her head.

She turned round and faced Elliot’s back, then she clung to him tightly, I heard birds not just birds but tropical birds, does that sound silly?” Samantha asked him.

“Elliot!” she continued “Wake up”

“What Sammy?” Elliot was getting irritated by her behaviour.

Samantha then put her arm around him holding his chest, you are cuddly just like an hairy bear.

“Roar!” she said teasing him.

“For god sake Sammy what is wrong with you?” He asked.

“I enjoyed the sex really Elliot” She said kissing his neck.

“Oh good” Elliot said sarcastically.

Elliot could feel her breathe on the back of his neck, then her hand began rubbing his chest.

“Elliot” Samantha whispered

“What Sammy” Elliot replied also whispering

“Hold me” She said eagerly.

Elliot held her hand that was drifting around his chest, he really wanted to stop her hand wandering as he was tired and avoiding what he considered was her advances.

"No turn around and hold me" she insisted.

He turned around "If I hug you and keep you warm will you let me sleep?"

Elliot could see her brown eyes looking at him, they looked like Annabelle's eyes so sad but kind and yearning, she was wearing her pink pyjamas but the top few buttons were unfastened revealing her tanned skin. Her hair hung down the sides of her face and her soft cheeks seemed to glow from a nightlight outside.

"Hello" She whispered her thick lips moved with a moistness that covered both lips as she spoke, she moved closer to him her body pressed against him, then pressed her lips tenderly against his and kissed him tenderly. Elliot felt the warmth from her lips as she used her tongue to wet his mouth. Suddenly the woman that she found hard to bond with was showing him affection.

"Oh Elliot kiss me back" She said continuing to kiss him

"Sammy" He said confused at her advances.

"Elliot" She said still whispering.

"Can't you call me Stuart?" He asked.

"Ohhhh Stuart" She whispered kissing his neck.

Elliot began to kiss her back and felt comfortable with her for once.

"Are you sure you want this Sammy?" He asked her.

"Yes you idiot I do" Samantha said pushing her hand down his shorts.

He copied her by pushing his hands down her pyjamas and stroked her buttocks, Samantha climbed on top of him unbuttoning her pyjama top and then revealing her breasts, her body tingling with excitement, she leaned over him thrusting her breasts in front of his face. Elliot cupped them in his hands and he began playing with her nipples between her fingers, she lifted her head back and gave a heavy sigh. Her skin was like velvet compared to his masculine rough hands. Samantha a ran her fingers through the hair on his chest and her head moved forward again and her hair covered her face. She removed her pyjama trousers and they kissed again as she pulled down his shorts and then removed her knickers, they were getting a little more wild and hot as they made love for hours. Eventually they stopped and lay down together until they both drifted off to sleep.

The next morning, Samantha woke up first finding herself naked lying on top of Elliot.

"Fucking hell" She said in shock

"Morning Sammy" He said looking into her eyes.

"Elliot" she said

"Sammy I said call me Stuart" Elliot insisted.

"Why?" She said confused

"Because that's my name" He said puzzled.

"No, why did we do this?" She asked.

"Don't tell me you regretted it again" Elliot said still puzzled.

"No sorry Stuart I am fine with it" She kissed him on the lips "But you really don't understand women do you" Samantha said.

"Why do you say that?" He asked

"Oh god Stuart you think I didn't want you?" She said

"You said that or at least you implied" Elliot said

"I didn't want commitment or complications" Samantha said concerned.

"I see" he thought for a moment "No I don't" He was certainly confused.

"I want love yes, but as for something more complicated I mean more of a commitment; you know the trimmings, marriage and children". Samantha said smiling.

"Sammy no pressure whatever you want" Elliot agreed.

"You mean that?" she said in disbelief.

"Yes of course" Elliot said kissing her.

"Well I have never really been loved or understood, just because I am attractive it doesn't mean I am any more loved at least for the right reason. Samantha explained.

"So tell me Sammy what do you really want?" Elliot asked

"To be noticed and loved not for my looks or my body, but for me" Samantha said "After all love runs deeper you know".

"I don't know what to say" Elliot really didn't understand women especially Samantha.

"Just tell me how you truly feel, without complicating matters" Elliot said smiling.

At that moment they heard a scream, they looked at each other and then both leapt out of bed and got dressed into their pyjamas and rushed out of the door. They raced down the stairs and immediately headed for the study. They tried the door but it was locked and they could here a baby crying.

"Quick Stuart kick the fucking door down!" Samantha shouted

"Stand back" Elliot shouted as he stepped back and kicked at the door, with one great shove hey both managed to push the door open and fell onto the floor. Chloe was holding the baby in her arms. "He's not breathing" she shouting.

Samantha took the baby off Chloe and rendered first aid, giving him mouth to mouth resuscitation, then chest compression with her fingers. Elliot held Chloe and tried to comfort her, she was trembling and trying to keep calm. Eventually Samantha got him breathing and had stabilised him, she then handed him back to Chloe.

"Thank you Sammy, you are marvellous" Chloe said holding her baby.

"Chloe what happened?" Elliot asked

"Something came out of the mirror and landed on his face, it was like jelly but covered his face and was suffocating him" Chloe said in disbelief.

"Strange, very odd" Sammy said looking back at the mirror.

"Speaking about what happened, what is this with you two" Chloe asked noticing how close they were. Samantha and Elliot looked at each other and smiled.

"Well we decided to get together" Samantha said smiling.

"I see" Chloe smiled

"What do you mean?" Samantha asked knowing what she meant.

"I knew it Sammy, I am happy for you" Chloe touched Samantha's arm with affection.

“Thanks Chloe” Samantha said happily.

“Children next” Chloe said looking at her baby.

“Hey, let’s not go too far” Samantha said laughing.

“Let’s get out of here, that mirror gives me the creeps” Chloe said looking across the room.

“I know the feeling” Samantha said.

They all headed upstairs and Chloe watched Samantha and Elliot enter his room

“See you later lovers” Chloe said teasing them.

While Samantha, Elliot and Chloe were experiencing problems at Harrington manor James had been busy selling his inheritance or the third mirror. He had travelled to a distant shop in a remote village hoping to obtain a fair price, but was offered a minimal amount. Never the less he took the money, however when Margaret and himself returned from their journey on entering the study they received an awful shock. The mirror was back and in exactly the same place as before, James looked at it and appeared completely baffled.

“Margaret!” he shouted angrily “Come quickly”

Margaret entered the room and was equally as shocked “The mirror, but that’s impossible we just sold it” She said gasping. “Stay there I will ring them right now”.

"Wait, leave it after all they robbed us anyway" James insisted.

"You mean by not giving us enough money?" Margaret asked.

"Exactly so we keep the mirror and the money" James said watching two of the servants pass the door "I bet they took it as a joke".

"Not everyone is as crooked as you dear" Margaret said in a serious manner.

"Someone had to have brought it back, it can't have got here by itself" Margaret said puzzled.

"Well only us two knew about it and we didn't" James said feeling around the frame

"What are you doing?" Margaret asked.

"Looking for wings" James replied "Well it can't just appear here like magic"

"James" She said annoyed by his remark.

"Well isn't it obvious I am searching for any clues that its been tampered with in any way" James said continuing to search.

"It's only a worthless mirror" She replied.

James suddenly jumped and held his left hand, he was bleeding.

"God damn it that was sharp" James said in pain "Don't just stand there get me something to stop the bleeding".

"What do you need?" she said looking round

"A damp towel or something like it, from the bathroom" James said panicking.

Margaret left the room and James started feeling dizzy, he started to see a spider come out of the mirror. IT crawled along the floor and then a snake appeared just as menacing. James looked across the room and saw a shotgun on the wall, he picked it up and watched the snake moving across the room. He searched the cabinet below for cartridges, they began spilling out on the floor. Desperately he tried picking them up, keeping an eye on the snake, then the spider moved closer until it was close enough for James to see all its features, from it's six legs to its eyes as it gazed at him ready to attack. It then seemed to pick up speed as it headed towards him moving onto a nearby table. James turned the shotgun around and using the butt he began hitting it and crushing it's head and body, he could hear a strange high pitched screaming sound as he hit the spider several times. He also heard a crunching sound and saw slimy yellow matter coming from it. Then he noticed the snake charging at him with large fangs and a gaping great mouth, so he turned the shotgun around and shot it in the mouth. During this time the room seemed to be in a mist, this was beginning to clear, but to his horror his wife lay across the table with her head crushed and the butler lay on the floor with a hole in his head. James dropped the rifle and began yelling and then sat on the floor, Harrison and the servants stood watching him in disbelief. Blood was everywhere up the walls on the floor, James had been hallucinating and murdered both Margaret and the butler. The police soon arrived and began questioning everyone no one was above suspicion although it was clear that James was mentally ill judging by his behaviour and the fact that he spoke about hearing voices and seeing spiders and snakes. Harrison kept quiet about the camera's and bugging devices as he wanted to continue with his surveillance of the house and mirrors.

Meanwhile at the Harrington household, Emma was experiencing more visions this time she was subjected to bind weed which wrapped around her hands and feet. She yelled out to Fiona and Ruth who ran into the room, by this time it was wrapped around her neck and strangling her. But all they could see was Emma thrashing about on the bed and her face changing colour from red to white. Ruth grabbed hold of her and shouted

"Emma what is it" She said looking at her

Just then she stopped and looked round, she noticed that the weed had gone and sighed with relief.

"Oh thank god, that bind weed had got me and I was being strangled" She said in a serious tone.

"Well, its gone now" Fiona said reassuringly.

"We had better stay close by from now on" Ruth advised.

“Good idea we need to bring beds in here” Fiona said “Or at least mattresses”.

“I am used to nightmares, but I guess you too are not” Ruth said seriously.

They arranged for mattresses to be brought into Emma’s room that night and all slept in the same room.

The following day they were informed about James.

Emma relayed everything to Fiona and Ruth who were sat at the dining room table, Emma didn’t appear shocked and continued having her breakfast. Harrison also informed Chloe and the others at Ashley manor.

“Oh my god that’s awful” Chloe said.

Samantha and Elliot were also at the dining room table, Chloe beckoned Samantha to the phone.

“Hi Dan how are you?” Samantha said putting the phone on loud speaker

“Hi Sammy, I am fine which is more than I can say for Margaret” Harrison said concerned.

“Well the police are here at the moment, but I can say that James started hallucinating and killed Margaret and the butler”. Harrison continued.

“What did he see?” Samantha asked

"Spiders and snakes coming out of the mirror" Harrison explained.

"He smashed Margaret's skull in and shot the butler in the head, blew it apart" Harrison explained in gory details.

"You don't have to be so graphic" Elliot said looking at his tomatoes.

"Sorry but it was awful, I actually felt sorry for both of them" Harrison continued.

That evening Samantha and Elliot were lying in bed, Samantha was wearing her pink pyjamas while Elliot wore a t shirt and shorts. They spoke for a while then Samantha began to get nervous again and lay on top of Elliot, wrapping her arms around him. Before long she was sat on top of him and removing her Pyjama top as she had done before, she then pounced on him like a tiger after her prey. Elliot was still sore from the previous time that she lay her claws on him, making scratches on his back. She made a roaring sound and began kissing his neck, then held her head back removing the rest of her clothes. Elliot removed his and Samantha began making love to Elliot wildly and passionately, he felt very subjective as Samantha took complete control. Elliot felt a little uneasy but allowed Samantha to have her fun, he did enjoy the experience but something was wrong. As she tilted her head back and gave her usual sigh, she brought her head forward and her head was replaced by Annabelle's decapitated head. The face was the one on the painting but her eyes were evil and yellow, there was also blood on her neck. Elliot yelled out and pushed her away, he then fell on the floor and began gasping for breath.

"For fuck sake Stuart" Samantha shouted "Jesus fucking Christ"

Elliot was almost blue and still gasping for breath, he was hardly breathing when Samantha realising he was having a asthma attack rushed to the bedside table by Elliot. She opened the draw looking for his ventolin inhalor; a few items came out of the draw.

"Where the fuck is it? She continued frantically searching until she realised it was in his trouser pocket. She raced back to him and opened his mouth and pushed it in squeezing the top to release the spray "Breath for fuck sake" She said spraying again.

Elliot started to breath still staring at the ceiling.

"Come on Elliot speak to me" Samantha said anxiously.

Samantha felt helpless but continued to attempt to get a response, she continued yelling at him.

"Stuart come on please" She said repeatedly then slapped his face hard.

"Oh god Sammy" Elliot said

Samantha smiled and said "Thank god, are you ok?"

"Yes but why did you slap me?" Elliot asked holding his cheek.

"Two reasons, one you knocked me off the bed and the other in order to make you respond, oh and I am still trying to think of a third reason" she said smiling.

"I saw a severed head on your shoulders" He look round at Annabelle's painting "It was her".

"Oh how horrid" Samantha said frowning.

"But her eyes were horrible and evil" Elliot said "Unlike your lovely eyes".

"Oh my poor Stuart, in that case I am sorry". She said feeling guilty for slapping him.

"Yes well you can certainly slap" Elliot said smiling.

"I had tough brothers who taught me to fight" She replied she hugged him then realised they were still naked "Oh look at us" she said smiling back.

"Shall we try again" Samantha said kissing him on the lips

"You bet lover girl" Elliot replied eagerly.

The next morning Samantha and Elliot sat at the dining room table with Chloe and her baby sat opposite, Chloe was breast feeding the baby. Elliot seemed a little uncomfortable with this, although he had seen her do it many times it did rather put him off his porridge.

"Did you sleep well?" Chloe asked.

“Oh yes thank you” Samantha replied kicking Elliot under the table.

“Yes thank you” Elliot said and smiled at Samantha.

“Very comfortable and cosy” Samantha smiled back like a love struck teenager.

Chloe couldn’t help noticing a scratch on Elliot’s right cheek and a bruise on Samantha’s forhead.

“Are you sure you two slept?” She asked suspecting activity in the bedroom.

“Oh yes I am sure” Elliot said unsure exactly what she was referring to.

Samantha realised straight away as she had looked in the mirror and seen her bruise, she also noticed the scratch on Elliot’s cheek. She gave a smile to Chloe and began playing with her hair then tucked it behind her ears in order to eat her breakfast.

“Mmmm coffee delicious” She said sipping from the cup “I love a nice cup of coffee”

Samantha seemed to be over emphasising her enjoyment for her drink and teasing Elliot by removing her shoe and playing with his leg with her foot. Then sending her bare foot up his leg which was easy from her position at the table, Elliot just smiled not knowing how to respond. He was about to drink when Samantha reached a vulnerable area making him jump.

“Oh Stuart did you miss your mouth?” She said laughing.

“Of course it’s all in the beans” Chloe said also laughing.

“Obviously, go for the best I say choose the best and hit the right market, where it counts” Samantha continued teasing Elliot “Isn’t that right Stuart?”

“You sound like a bloody coffee commercial Sammy” Elliot said fidgeting.

They were interrupted by the phone ringing, Chloe walked over and picked up the receiver, she remembered to put it on speaker.

“Hello Ashley manor” She said politely

“Is that Chloe?” Harrison asked eagerly.

“Yes what’s wrong Chloe said noticing his anxious tone

“I have spoken to Fiona and Ruth they suggest we get these mirror together and find out if there is some truth about a message” Harrison said eagerly awaiting her response.

“I don’t know what does Emma say?” Chloe asked

“She is in agreement but she said it’s up to you” Harrison replied.

"I agree there is something in what you say, but I am concerned something may go wrong" Chloe said concerned.

"I say do it Chloe we need answers and who knows what we may find" Samantha said looking at Elliot for support.

"Well we can't just sit here wiggling our thumbs, lets see what happens, besides enough has happened what else can go wrong" Elliot said looking back at Samantha.

"Ok I head for Harrington manor at around midday see you on route" Harrison said

"See you on the road Dan" Elliot said "Drive carefully"

"As usual Stuart" Harrison replied

Chloe replaced the phone on the receiver and returned to the table, she was about to eat her toast when the phone rang again.

"Hello Ashley manor" She said a little abruptly, putting the phone on speaker

"Chloe this is Fiona are you all there" Fiona asked

"Yes all having breakfast" She said continuing to eat her toast

"Oh sorry, but I need to know about the mirrors" Fiona said concerned.

“Daniel has just rang and mentioned it, we are all meeting at Harrington manor where it all began” Chloe explain.

“Good see you here later” Fiona said “How’s your baby?”

“Sammy is holding him, she has got used to his vomiting and smelly nappies” Chloe said laughing

“That’s amazing for Sammy” Fiona said laughing

“I still don’t want any” Samantha shouted to Fiona “Not that he isn’t a cute one”

“Watch this space Sammy” Fiona said “See you all soon”.

By midday Harrison was ready to depart, he has put the mirror in the boot of his car with no resistance and started on his journey to Harrington manor. He was driving at a fairly fast pace listening to the radio when he heard a loud scream which seemed to be coming from behind him possibly from the boot of the car. He ignored it and carried on driving thinking he may have still been tired from the night before, he then heard the sound of hissing and saw a snake in the passenger seat. He tried to slow down so that he could sort out the snake but instead he was taken by surprise as it attempted to bite him. Harrison swerved in the road a few times then slowed down, but landed in a ditch as he swerved a third time. His head hit the door and then he slumped forward. He must have been there for a time unconscious when Elliot pulled up in his car, he and Samantha rushed to Harrison’s car.

"Dan are you alright?" Elliot shouted.

"Dan can you here us?" Samantha asked.

"Yes, I am" Harrison said holding his head "Help me out of this thing"

Both Samantha and Elliot helped walk Harrison away from the car, then they helped him down by a grass bank.

"The mirror" He shouted

Samantha walked towards the car, suddenly it exploded and she was thrown in mid air and landed by a tree, she was motionless her body was limp and lifeless.

"Sammy!" Elliot shouted "Oh no".

He raced towards her not knowing what to expect as he lifted her head up and watched her eyes open.

"What the fuck" Samantha exclaimed.

"God are you alright?" Elliot asked

"Ouch my head" Samantha said holding the back of her head

"God you flew about fifty foot in the air" Elliot said knowing he was exaggerating.

"Get me up" Samantha insisted.

Elliot helped her back to Harrison who was still dazed, they sat for a while then Harrison remembered the mirror.

"I bet the mirrors gone now" He said disappointed.

Elliot walked towards the car, then cautiously open what was left of the boot.

To his surprise the mirror was in tact, so he tried to extract from the boot. The others heard a great shout and a cry of pain as Elliot grabbed the painting.

"Elliot!" Samantha shouted

"God damn it, I have burnt my hands" He shouted

"Stuart you might have known that would be hot" Harrison shouted

"Stuart you fool" Samantha said rushing to him.

Harrison found the strength to go to Elliot's car for a fire extinguisher and a bottle of water, He passed Samantha the water and bandages and then headed to his car with the fire extinguisher. He sprayed the mirror then wrapped a blanket around it, then picked it up and carried it to Elliot's car. Samantha and Elliot struggled to the car and sat in the back seat together. Harrison drove the car heading for the main road to Harrington manor, They continued to hear banging and shouting now they had two mirrors. They were a mile away from Harrington manor when a woman appeared at the roadside she was young and beautiful wearing a hooded coat.

"Can I help you?" Harrison asked

"Yes could you take me to Harrington manor?" She asked

"Of course get in" Harrison offered.

Harrison glanced at her in disbelief then concentrated on the road, Elliot and Samantha remained quiet.

"Are you going to visit there" Harrison asked.

"No I live there" She replied

"I thought Emma lived there" Harrison said finding it strange that the others were quiet.

"Yes she does now and so do many others" the woman said.

"May I ask who you are" Harrison asked.

"I am the one you seek and the one you wish to free" The woman said mysteriously.

"I don't understand" Harrison asked feeling very cold.

"Put the mirrors together and find out" She said "The answer is in the mirrors".

"I really don't get it you want us to bring them together?" Harrison said

"Stop, I will walk from here" She said

Harrison opened the door and the woman walked into the woods then vanished.

"Jesus Dan" Elliot shouted

"What's wrong?" Elliot asked.

"That woman did you know who she was?" Elliot asked.

"A hitchhiker" Harrison said surprised at Elliot's behaviour.

"It was Annabelle" Elliot said shaking

"Are you sure?" Harrison said smirking

"Oh yes it was her notice her neck was bloody and her voice a little strange?" Elliot said nervously.

"Yes but I didn't think it was Annabelle" He replied unperturbed.

"A ghost has been travelling with us, I don't believe it" Elliot said looking at Samantha who was asleep.

Two of the mirrors were placed in the library temporarily until they could be united with the other mirror in the study, but while they were sorting this out Samantha decided to enter the study looking for Fiona. Instead she saw Ruth sat at a table reading one of the many books out of the book cabinet.

"Where's Fiona?" She asked

“I don’t know” Ruth replied sensing hostility in Samantha’s voice.

“No of course you don’t” Samantha said sarcastically.

“What’s that supposed to mean?” Ruth asked.

“Nothing, I mean you haven’t tried to make a pass at her then?” Samantha said “I mean she is pretty”.

“Look just because she’s pretty it doesn’t mean I am going to fancy her” Ruth said in her own defence.

“She’s blonde like Pamela, but she’s straight shame isn’t it” Samantha said rudely.

“Look just because I am a lesbian it doesn’t mean I like every beautiful woman” Ruth said angrily. At that moment the mirror began to glow and blood poured down it. But Samantha and Ruth were that busy arguing they hadn’t noticed any activity.

“Why have you got to knock gay people? Ruth asked.

“It’s you I don’t like, my god you think you invented sex especially lesbianism”.

“I stand up for my own kind, what’s wrong with that? Ruth asked

“No you flaunt it and throw it in peoples faces, both you and Pamela did that on fashion shows” Samantha said in disgust.

"Just because it was on television and radio, we were hounded by the press" Ruth explained.

"Fucking exhibitionism if you ask me" Samantha said

"Not at all everyone was against us, we merely defended ourselves, against religion and political extremists" Ruth replied "We had to challenge them".

"No you didn't that's a lame excuse" Samantha said beginning to pace up and down.

"So you think the likes of priests are perfect, those who abuse young boys, they are so fucking untouchable, so righteous" Ruth was getting angry

"How can you say that?" Samantha asked

"Why don't you read the papers or magazines?" Ruth said pointing to a newspaper on the table.

"I do they are inaccurate and lie to sell the paper" Samantha said folding her arms in defence.

Like criminal world, I mean you as a crime reporter?" Ruth was referring to all reporters not just criminal world's staff.

"Just keep your lesbian ideas to yourself" Samantha said looking away from her.

"What are you afraid of?" Ruth asked

“Nothing” Samantha replied swiftly.

“Yes you are that’s why your against me, your frightened of something, perhaps things that you don’t know about” Ruth said realising that what Samantha was referring to ran deeper than she would care to admit.

“That’s fucking rubbish” Samantha said refusing to give Ruth eye contact.

“I have touched a nerve haven’t I Sammy” Ruth said trying to get her to look at her.

“No I am not gay or anything” Samantha said in disgust.

“You don’t attack someone for no reason and you said your not homophobic, so what is it” Ruth said probing her.

“Fuck you” Samantha said unable to answer properly.

“I will find out I am not being hated for nothing, you must have a reason, so what is it” Ruth was determined to find out the truth.

“OK your right” She turned and looked at Ruth “My sister committed suicide because she was a lesbian, her girl friend and her had a fight and her friend left her. She said it was due to watching you and Pamela on television that convinced her that she was gay. She followed your story and when things went wrong she took her own life”.

“I am sorry” Ruth said sincerely.

"No I am sorry, I blamed you but I can see now I was wrong" Samantha admitted

At that moment the room shuck and books started to fly in mid air, They were both dodging the books and then noticed a snake slither out of the mirror. Ruth pushed Samantha to the floor as a series of poison darts flew in the air and pinned Ruth to the door. Samantha got up and managed to block a dart with a book as it was flying towards Ruth's head, then the snake travelled towards Samantha with it's mouth wide open. At that moment Pamela appeared and grabbed the snake and threw it back into the mirror, but only Samantha saw Pamela who smiled at her before she vanished.

The mirrors were becoming more intense as the evil seemed to consume each mirror, it would appear that nothing could stop them. A cycle of murders had inevitably influenced the mirrors or the evil that caused the initial murder possessed all three mirrors. The force was undeniably strong and had the power to control, influence and possess the mind. Pamela appeared and captured John's spirit binding him securely with a rope, he struggled but was unable to break free.

He had little power when Pamela and Annabelle were involved, especially with all their personalities combined, John had become weak and helpless.

Annabelle assisted her in throwing him into a dark room and then the audience assembled in the study and witness the mirrors come to life.

By this time the others came in with the other mirrors, John appeared but was taken away by Pamela and Annabelle who bound him and put him in a dark place. Once the mirrors were up Annabelle's other personalities were freed and the host personality appeared to everyone. Each person sat down and watched as Annabelle appeared in the central mirror. She had strange eyes at first and blood on her neck.

"Thank you for freeing me from the darkness that dwells within these mirrors, my personalities have joined their host, the real me and I am one again. Please don't be alarmed by my head as I will explain it all to you keep watching these mirrors as I convey the story of how became imprisoned in the mirrors" Everyone looked at each other in disbelief, it was like watching a movie of Annabelle's past.

"Here lies the mystery of the mirrors which will astonish and shock you as I tell the tale. The story will unfold and you will be enlightened by your experience although no one will believe where you have heard the story from, I am Annabelle. Although I cannot offer you evidence of this experience I can provide you with reassurance that nothing else will happen to you on your journey of enlightenment".

"Thank god for that" Elliot said then looked at the others "Sorry" he said apologetically.

"It all began at here at Harrington manor I was the lady of the manor and I lived with my husband John Harrington who was lord of the manor, we had no children as I had numerous miscarriages probably due to the way I was treated. John was a cruel and jealous man who beat me and locked me away in a dark room, sometimes I was missing for days. I shouted but nobody heard me, I banged at the door and tried turning the handle but it was no use. I could feel things crawling on me and screamed eventually I was set free from my captivity. John used to humiliate me and mock me in front of the servants, I felt trapped even outside the dark room. John encouraged the maids to flirt with him and even had sex with some of them, usually when I was pregnant or sick of him raping me. I used to go for walks in the woods this was my freedom away from the manor and his family who considered him perfect. It was during one of my walks in the woods that I met an artist by the name of Ralph Baxter, he was kind and courteous, a true gentleman who treated me nice. He was sat drawing pictures of the trees near a stone bridge, at first I was a little shy and perhaps nervous of him, but then I got used to him. I used to wash my hands and face in the stream that ran under the bridge; Ralph was amused by this and used to gasp at my beauty. He eventually invited me into his cottage and offered me tea and cake just to be treated like this was nice".

The silence was broke by Samantha who was sobbing to herself, comforted by Elliot.

Annabelle continued with her story her face kept changing in complexion and she was looking like she looked when she met Ralph. Ralph could not take his eyes off me, he told me that he was captivated by my beauty. It was then that he asked me to model for him; I was shy at first as I posed for a portrait and he painted me on canvas. He started with a head and shoulders painting using oils, then as I became more comfortable with him I undressed and posed naked. He was observing my beauty spending hours perfecting all the curves and crevices of my body, just like when he was drawing the trees. At this point we must have fallen in love and made love together for the first time, it was a wonderful experience unlike John; Ralph was gentle and treated me like a lady. Although his hands were rough from his work and he was so strong, he treated me as if I were a fragile object or flower. After this day we met regularly and I was so in love, I felt my heart flutter and my whole body tingled in his presence, I believe he felt the same although he was a man of few words. He did announce that he loved me so many times and not just when we made love". Annabelle's voice began to change as she began to speak about the next events, she sounded upset as her voice quivered.

"It was a warm summers day when I went for my usual walk in the woods, John and I had been arguing, he wanted to try for a baby, but his very presence began to repulse me and I left the house. I was unaware of him following me, he had evidently realised that I was having an affair and wanted to find my lover. I met Ralph in the usual place wearing a hooded top and jeans, Ralph was sat smoking his pipe on a rock by the bridge drawing the stream and bridge that we liked so much, close by was a wishing well. He warned me to be careful as the well was deep and could be dangerous, I noticed he had a brown leather bound book at his side. When I asked him what it was he became defensive as if he was keeping some sort of secret from me. We then went inside the cottage to his studio where I observed some souvenirs from South America and other exotic places. I noticed a sheet covering something large and asked about it, he explained it was some kind of gift for me. Out of curiosity I moved part of the sheet and something pricked my finger, I collapsed and when I awoke I saw a snake coming towards me. It was enormous with a large mouth that was trying to devour me. At that moment Ralph came into my room like a knight in shining armour, the snake simply disappeared and Ralph said that I was imagining things. The only thing under the sheet was three mirrors that he had as gifts for me; he had been carving the wooden frames".

Annabelle indicated the blood stains on each frame "These blood stains belong to Ralph he told me that much had he tried he couldn't remove it. He did it on a chisel when carving one of the women's heads, apart from women's heads there were animals that he had seen in jungles and deserts everywhere. I felt better after a glass of water and Ralph's soothing words, I went home and returned the following day I was followed again by John who by now knew about Ralph and myself. I posed for him naked as usual and this time Ralph and I made love in the studio, little knowing that John was watching from outside. After my visit I walked the usual way home and John entered the studio, he was so quiet Ralph was unaware of his presence. Ralph was relaxing smoking his pipe with his back to the door admiring his painting of me. He grabbed a chisel which was already blood stained from Ralph's accident and plunged it into his back right up to the handle, he then pulled it out and sent it back into his back then trust the final blow into his neck. He had evidently hitting an archery as the blood spurted out everywhere. He then took his pipe that was on the floor and emptied the contents on the floor. He took a match then lit a few inflammatory objects and started a fire. The studio was burnt to the ground, but amazingly the mirrors remained in tact not even a scorch on them, even the glass was in one piece".

All Annabelle's audience sat with mouths open unable to comment at this point allowing Annabelle to continue her gruesome tale.

"It was then that John planned my disappearance, he had brought the mirrors to the manor and displayed them on the study wall and they were strategically placed as they are now. He had locked me away as usual but before doing told me about Ralph's death and how he knew about our affair. I was so upset that he had not only followed me, but also murdered Ralph in cold blood. I needed to tell someone about everything, but when John set me free he murdered me by stabbing me with that same chisel from the studio and not content with that he got an axe and cut off my head".

Fiona reacted as well as Samantha this time and even Elliot was forced to use his inhaler, each person reacted to the story in some way even Ruth who had witnessed many things.

"He had sent the servants away, saying how upset he was that Annabelle had been unfaithful and had gone missing, he said I had run away in shame. Once he had severed my head from my body he held it up from my hair and boasted to the mirrors 'See the bitch that dares to fornicate and commits adultery, Ralph behold your lovers head' with that he put my head in a brown sack and took it to Ralph's well and dropped it down followed by the chisel. As for my body that is buried by the rocks beside the stream you will also find the leather bound book in a hollow part of a tree in a plastic bag. As for John he called back the servants to clean the house and always liked Lucy a young maid. John committed suicide not by choice I might add, but when he was so remorseful and sad about my death, he was making love to a maid when my head appeared on her shoulders he was so shocked that he threw her to the floor and ran to the window. Lucy lay injured and he threw himself out of the window. That is the full story of my life at Harrington manor I will now rest in peace knowing that you know the truth".

Annabelle faded away leaving everyone to think about what they had heard and seen, but nobody was able to convey anything to anyone. But at least Annabelle was at rest having told her tale, her spirit was at peace at last. As for the mirrors they suddenly set fire and despite all effort to save them, they disintegrated as they should have done originally in the studio fire. Amazingly nothing else was damaged not even the wall, only the mirrors that had kept a secret hidden inside them.

"Well follow that" Harrison said completely baffled.

"So tragic" Fiona said, shaking her head in disbelief.

"The poor woman" Ruth said looking at Emma "Who simply nodded.

"I am really shocked" Samantha said wiping the tears from her eyes.

"What the hell are we going to tell the police about Annabelle's body?" Elliot said confused.

CHAPTER 6

ON REFLECTION

Now that the three mirrors were finally together it was thought that they would either consume the manor or in one mighty wave cause a massive explosion of energy, or it would endeavour to reveal the secret that has been locked away for so long. Whatever happens has a purpose and the meaning so clear to those seeking the truth. As it happened the truth was revealed and a mystery unravelled no matter how strange it happened.

"So what do we have as evidence that these mirrors even existed and what proof, if any that they were haunted or possessed in some way?" Fiona said leading the discussion.

"Well we all saw Annabelle's image and she relayed a story to us" Emma said confidently "I also saw Pamela's ghost, now I have not met her before but I described her and Ruth said the description was accurate".

“Thank you Emma, but this would be classed as circumstantial to most people” Fiona said eventually chairing the meeting.

“The pricking of the finger on the corner of each mirror located by the old blood stains” Samantha said pointing to a photograph of the mirror “I understand that a hole was discovered in this area containing a small cylinder resembling a bullet, inside was a substance that was analysed and found to be some sort of illegal substance that caused not only hallucinations but temporary paralysis”.

“Safe to say that a number of people pricked their finger and became exposed to this drug, they then became subjected to all kinds of hallucinations and delusional ideation” Ruth added.

“No doubt the work of James and Margaret Harrington who not only tried to get their hands on the inheritance but also defrauded hotels and many people on the internet with their evil schemes using charity work as their front” Elliot said producing paperwork as evidence.

“I used camera’s and bugging devices as further proof of their fraud, I did try to gather evidence of supernatural activity but the sounds were muffled and visibility limited” Harrison said disappointed.

“So what has happened to James Harrington?” Fiona asked.

“He was transferred to a mental health hospital on a secure unit, he was said to be delirious seeing a headless woman and then monkeys around the cell” Harrison said smiling.

"James was said to have continued to tell his story about his wife being a spider when he killed her and the servant was a snake who he shot in the head and chest" Ruth said looking at Samantha for support.

"Yes Ruth is correct and clearly perceptive with her explanation" Samantha said smiling at Ruth.

"It would also seem that without steering away from the facts that people had a combination of hallucinations and imaginative ideas that were a little confusing. Annabelle herself had a mental illness known as multiple personality syndrome or dissociated personality syndrome which due to past trauma caused her to have an individual personality in each mirror, this needed to be brought back together in order for her to converse with us using the host personality or her real self. Arguably this is a real mental health condition and is very difficult to treat, usually it is done through therapies" Ruth paused looked around then continued "Coupled with another personality questionably haunting the mirrors who is suggested to be evil may be down to John who evidently influenced James, although I would deem James as a sociopath who has no conscience and will probably spend the rest of his life in psychiatric care" Ruth finally took a breath

Samantha began clapping encouraged others to join in Fiona was astonished by Samantha's sudden change in views and her opinion towards Ruth. Samantha even winked at Elliot which was clearly seen by Fiona who was sat beside her. She leaned and whispered to Elliot hoping Samantha wouldn't see her.

"What on earth did you do to Sammy and did it involve drugs?" Fiona smiled.

"Elliot shrugged his shoulders and he whispered back "God knows but I hope it lasts".

"I have something" Chloe shouted and came forward "I have been to the cottage and discovered a diary tucked inside a tree" She produced a book approximately Six inches long by five inches in width, it had a brown leather cover.

"An entry on the Fifth of July 1975 says that he was in the Amazon jungle when he discovered a cave, inside the cave was a series of paintings some seemed to relay a story of a tribe like the Aztecs who had discovered an odd shaped mirror with an image of a woman's head severed from a body, she was said to be some sort of sorceress and slain by warriors for putting a curse on their family" She looked at her audience who seemed to be in a trance. "Shall I go on?"

"Yes Fiona" said curious

"This is freaky" Samantha said nervously.

"Go on Chloe" Elliot beckoned.

"Well, other entries are similar until I reached the part that mentioned Ralph being bitten by a poison snake, he was helped by a tribe of people who related to him how he was delirious and calling for help as he was attacked by wild monkeys and fell into a swamp".

Chloe passed the book to Harrison who examined it.

"I am amazed at this even in my army days I have never come across anything like this" He opened a page on a passage about the glass in the mirrors "I Have ordered the glass mirrors from here as the glass is made from minerals in the jungle and I am looking for wood from the trees in the forest" Harrison looked at his colleagues "So that's what he was up to and he is suggesting the curse is from the jungle, a so called sorcerer.

"Well thank god the mirrors have been destroyed" Elliot said sighing with relief.

"So all those jungle sounds and experiences were from the Amazon jungle?" Samantha asked.

"Yes it appears so Sammy, but then we are dealing with facts and not fiction" Fiona reminded her.

"Of course but you know what we heard and saw it offers explanation to me" Samantha said glancing at Elliot and back at Fiona.

Elliot smiled "Yes no doubt about it Sammy is right, we did hear and see a lot".

"Stuart you know we deal in facts for crime reporting, conjecture or fiction has no bearing or credibility in selling our magazines" Fiona said sternly

“Come on Fi, you know as well as me that sometimes what we see can’t be explained even in the best surroundings where we visualise many things, I refer to ghostly places such as castles and haunted houses.” Harrison said

“Thanks for that Daniel” Samantha said “You really know how to make a girl feel at home”.

“Well we have little solid evidence judging by my camera’s and Stuart’s photo’s all seem very grainy and even inferred doesn’t show much” Harrison said disappointedly “In fact I have seen better on that television program ‘most haunted’.

“Without the over dramatisation you mean” Elliot said laughing.

CHAPTER 7

A NEW START

Once everything was over Emma left the manor and joined Chloe at Ashley Manor. They were happy together and soon forgot the event that took Place at Harrington manor, at least that was the what they told each other. But they both had occasional nightmares of past events and could never forget Annabelle's severed head displayed in the mirror. No body ever looked at mirrors the same again without thinking that something was going to jump out at them, grabbing or clawing at them in a frenzied attack showing no mercy.

Elliot was driving home with Samantha, he was listening as usual to his classical music which Samantha loved so much.

"Oh come on Stuart this is funeral music" Samantha said rolling her eyes.

"You have no idea, this is quality music" Elliot said

"Music to sleep through" Samantha said complaining.

“So have a sleep” He advised.

“I don’t want to” She replied in an aggravated manner.

“Ok you win, put something on you like” He said keeping the peace.

Samantha looked through her bag and removed a compact disc from its case, she let put it in the player. That’s what you get by Paramore began to play.

“There we are real music” She said jigging around in her seat.

After they had been driving for a while Elliot was feeling tired, he swerved to miss what he thought was an animal on the road, which made Samantha think of Harrington hall and Annabelle’s tragedy.

“What the fuck was that?” She asked

“I don’t know I couldn’t make it out” Elliot said continuing to drive

“Stop!” Samantha said alarmed.

“Here we go” Elliot said

“Stop the fucking car now” Samantha said angrily.

Elliot stopped the car in a lay by and got out knowing what to expect from Samantha.

"I don't believe you Stuart Elliot" Samantha said pacing up and down.

"What do you mean?" Elliot said confused

"You really don't care do you?" Samantha said flapping her arms about "That poor creature could be injured and you just don't give a shit".

"What's this really about Sammy?" Elliot said knowing there was something else wrong with her.

"It's you, you're so insensitive at times, not a thought for others and god you annoy me" Samantha was getting tearful again.

"Oh come on that's not fair" Elliot said "I have helped you and been close to you, now I am insensitive".

"Yes" She paused "No, I don't know"

"Indecisive Sammy again" Elliot said trying to get Samantha to say what she truly felt.

"I can't help it Elliot, I mean Stuart, I mean god knows what" She said putting her hands over her face. "I can see Annabelle every time I close my eyes and it's so sad, why couldn't be happy with Ralph, its not fair, why Stuart?"

"I don't know but your wearing the grass out beneath your feet" Elliot said trying to make her smile.

"Take us for instance enjoying each other having casual sex, no ties" She said ignoring what he said. "We are happy".

"Well I am" He said still trying to get a reaction.

"So why couldn't she be happy? Samantha continued "What?" she said realising what he said.

"I said I am happy" Elliot waited a moment for her to react.

Inevitably she did react by slapping his face, and then thumping him repeatedly on the chest.

"Elliot!" She shouted in a fit of temper "I love you"

She then held him and cried uncontrollably, She remained in his arms for a considerable time until they both returned to the car. The radio played 'strange magic' by ELO which seemed very appropriate for the occasion regarding the mirrors and how it brought them together.

CHAPTER 8

CURSED

In a market in South America a man was selling an assortment of mirrors with hand carved frames similar to Ralph's mirrors. He seemed keen to sell them and explained that they were designed to look like Aztec tribes, he was quite convincing and foreign tourists did buy them. They were exported around the world and displayed on walls in houses unknowing that these mirrors had the same Aztec curse that Ralph's had recently. The glass contained a wicked spirit that would cause problems for many people, but no one was aware of this or the sorceress that curse them.

Back in London, England the criminal reporters and photographers of criminal world magazine involved with Harrington curse story got together in order to discuss the story. As so much had happened and things needed clarifying each person involved needed to sort out fact from fiction. A lot of amazing things had occurred that involved investigation from the team, even from the idea of hallucinations and factual occurrences would have to be discussed in detail before a proper story could be written.

Samantha and Elliot were sorting out the story from their perspective while Fiona was clarifying things on the phone with Ruth, Harrison had collected evidence from his sound and camera equipment, he had also had Ralph Baxter's diary and researched Aztec history.

Fiona sat in as chairwoman in the absence of her father who was playing golf in Scotland with Gordon MacGregor his Scottish friend.

"Ok folks, let us begin this meeting" Fiona said confidently "Now I realise we discussed this at Harrington hall, but we really need to get clarification about what we saw and what evidence we have to substantiate our find".

Each of them looked at each other in turn, then they nodded in agreement.

"So let's begin with you Sammy" Fiona said looking at Samantha

"Oh yes well" Samantha paused looking at Elliot for support "We witnessed many things but have little concrete evidence, mostly visions and sounds which were said to be hallucination's".

"Yes I agree" Elliot said producing photographs that only showed shadows and blurred images.

"Not much in the way of facts, I am afraid all we have for sure is our own statements".

"Well Daniel, the floor is yours it seems" Fiona said very much in control of the meeting.

Other journalists were present and eager to here what Harrison had to say, they were hoping that

"I realise that we are discussing mainly about the Harrington curse myth or fact, however I must explain about the origins of these mirrors that most people didn't know about. For instance are you aware of an earlier curse on these mirrors that goes back in history. In around 1511 an Aztec sorcerous was killed by the Spanish who had invaded Mexico, she was stabbed and beheaded because the Spanish army feared her. She was then dropped into the volcano hoping to destroy her powers, instead she became more powerful and put a curse on the Spanish and their descendants through to today. Ralph's diary revealed that he had Spanish blood, but so did John Harrington thus the continue of the curse today.

"What about the jungle sounds and such?" Samantha asked

"Well Ralph used to travel a lot and one of his favourite places were south America and Egypt, although his best known place was Mexico. He studied Aztec history particularly Tenochtitlan's who were known for their markets visited by countless people supporting their economy. The Aztec were also highly developed socially, intellectually and artistically" Harrison showed a number of pictures on a screen from his laptop.

"This is all fascinating but what about the mirrors?" Samantha asked

"I am coming to that, bear with me" Harrison said "The Aztecs worshipped a number of gods like Huitzilopochtli a god of war and of the sun, the Aztecs made human sacrifices, they practiced divination using the surface of a bowl of water as a mirror. Some mirrors were fashioned from obsidian used by English alchemist John Dee, these mirrors of black obsidian are a type of shiny volcanic glass these played a central role in their mythology and religious rituals of the Aztecs and Mexicana. Tezcotlipoca means smoking mirrors thus the mist seen by James when he murdered his wife Margaret mistaking her for a giant spider. It all gets involved as the mythological story tells about the smoking mirror replacing the foot of a god as he battles against an earth monster But Aztec magicians would divine the future while looking into the obsidian's reflection's".

"So what your saying is that some of the things we experienced with the mirrors go back to the Aztecs and the sorcerous head was the same as Annabelle's? Samantha asked "Does that also mean that the Sorcerous cursed the mirrors".

"I am saying it is a possibility that's all, I have no evidence of this, also the voice could have been talking in the Aztec language and that's why you couldn't understand her. As for the snakes and other creatures you know about, they were to do with the desert and jungles of Mexico and South America I am merely offering suggestions for the hallucinations. The sacrifices made by the Aztecs to their gods were because they believed that the gods were nourished by living hearts and that this made the sun rise the next day. Sacrifices ceremonies varied from small to large according to the mightiest of the god. This explains the type of people they were and their obsession for worship. The Spanish army wanted to destroy the Aztecs and probably feared their beliefs as the Spanish were Catholics and considered witchcraft and sorcery as evil. The sorcerous was threat to them and so they destroyed her by stabbing her to death and then severing her head from her body. They then threw her into the flaming fire in the volcano and destroyed what was left of her. Her spirit was said to have remained and entered the obsidian thus cursing the mirrors afterwards when they began creating them".

"So the mirrors were cursed?" Elliot asked

"It appears so if you believe the legend" Fiona replied.

"So she caused all the problems at the Harrington household?" Samantha asked.

"That may be a contributionary factor but it all seems a little difficult to believe" Harrison said

"Well let's get this thing wrapped up and present a story for our readers" Fiona said eager to begin a new story called 'The Harrington curse'

Meanwhile in Mexico mirrors are being packaged for export all over the world and in England in one stately home a lady is brushing her hair ready to go out when suddenly a thin hand with long sharp nails grabs her by the throat and throttles the life out of her. Her body lies on the floor covered in blood and an image appears in the mirror looking like the Aztec sorcerous.

OPERATION BRAINSTORM

SIMON ROBERT SINCLAIR

ACKNOWLEDGEMENTS

Thank you to Amy Brindley for providing and giving permission for the front cover photographs. Thank you to my prove reader Rachel Day for her valuable input. Thank you to Gemma Louise Sutton, Jennifer May Sutton, Michael James and Daniel Robert Sutton. I wish the readers to consider the points made about mental health and try to think about those less fortunate than ourselves, having a little knowledge of mental illness may help one to appreciate other peoples predicament. One day brainstorm maybe a reality and then we can hope that certain types of mental illness or brain disease could be irradiated, who knows what lies ahead in our future.

INTRODUCTION

In the 21st century the world had hit a crises with mental health, the demands for caring for people with mental health conditions were dire. Few people wanted to take responsibility for anyone with any mental health problems, in the United States of America alone people with serious mental health conditions were falling through the cracks in the system. Victims had very little sympathy shown to them and often landed in emergency rooms, county jails and on the city streets. The so called 'lucky people' were ending up in the morgue according to U.S.A today, a popular newspaper of this time.

It was the year 2180 the world had changed as technology had advanced and scientist were inventing things that would have been thought impossible in the 20th century. However one of the most amazing inventions came from a Norwegian scientist called Jon Ulrichsen, he had created a machine that was capable of analysing and curing brain dysfunctions. Ulrichsen along with his daughter Kristina with assistance from other scientists put together an invention that Kristina named 'brainstorm' it was like a scanning machine but did far more than this, it became multi functional and even cured such things as Alzheimer's type dementia, vascular dementia and repaired brain damage. The invention was revolutionary but it appealed to not only scientists and surgeons but terrorists who planned to steal the equipment and kidnap the scientists so that they could use the equipment to take over governments all over the world. It was decided by the world powers that Brainstorm was too dangerous and had to be destroyed along with the scientist. Both the Americans and the Russians form their own strategies to destroy the equipment and the American called the mission 'Operation Brainstorm'

TERRORIST ATTACK

It was a cold winter's night in Norway; the snow lay thick on the ground and clung to a forest of pine trees in a remote part of the country. A long and winding road ran through the middle and tracks were visible from a recent convoy of heavy trucks evident by the track marks that were heading south to a secret army location.

It was the year 2180 science and technology had advanced to such a degree that the whole shape of some vehicles were so well equipped to cope with the severe weather conditions in Scandinavia and could resist heavy bombardment from enemy weaponry. Also some vehicles were able to hover over the land without contacting the ground which enabled them to move quicker and more effectively. They also had the use of robots to infiltrate areas undetected, entering small places and placing minute devices such as, cameras, explosive and other objects in buildings. The Droid was such a robot these and androids served as most effective in military operations, they were programmed to perform many tasks. However in the wrong hands this could be problematic and with a team of highly skilled terrorists, they could easily infiltrate any complex almost undetected.

On the 3rd February 2180 such a problem occurred, this operation was led by an ex General Matt Murray from the United states army who was paid to take an army of men and equipment to infiltrate an army installation. The area it up as one explosion occurred followed by another strategically placed in order to divert attention away from the Southside of the building all the guards were alerted and concentrated their attention on the north side expecting a full scale invasion.

This was led by Lieutenant Gerald Deakin and Sargent Sam Harris who organised the northern attack and followed with the southern aspect of the base. The object was to enter the building undetected and to steal equipment for a future operation. They began to disarm the lasers and destroy observation cameras.

"Send in the first druids" Deakin ordered.

"Sergeant Holmes here sir we have disabled all contact within the base and heading forward with the androids" Holmes said confidently.

"Good man Holmes remember what your going for and report back when your out" Deakin said. "Sergeant Harris report please"

"All is well, Sergeant Alison Foster will report soon" Harris replied.

A hologram appeared, it was Murray who looked a little upset.

"Deakin I hope you are in control of this mission, we need the equipment as soon as s

"We have already used the explosive and infiltrating the premises sir". Deakin replied the first druids have entered the building".

"If you are on the Southside, who may I ask is in charge of the north side?" Murray asked

"Sergeant Alison Foster of ninth division" Deakin replied confidently.

"A woman is in charge of the attack force?" Murray said

"Yes sir but she's good" Deakin said in her defence.

"She had better be a lot depends on this mission" Murray's hologram image disappeared.

Sergeant Alison Foster was leading the attack at the north entrance, she continued the deception that they were being defeated and on the retreat. Alison had short blonde hair and blue eyes; she was slim but she had big bones making her look butch also she was athletic spending long hours in the gymnasium working out. She was fierce with a constant stern look on her face; she was a determined woman who wanted to succeed no matter who she trod on modelling her persona from such historical women as Joan of Arc, Queen Elizabeth the first and Boudica. She had a way of smiling and making people feel in secure by her very presence with her deep voice and penetrating eyes.

“Let show these geeks how we do business in the terrorist world” She looked at her attack “Give them hell boys”.

The entire area on the north side lit up with laser fire and explosives, it appeared like a full assault on the building but happened to be a successful decoy for the men on the south side as they infiltrated the building and stole equipment from within. The entire operation took an hour which included escaping to a secure location in another area of Oslo. All the equipment was hidden until they were ready to use it; this was just the beginning of the terrorist plan to rule the earth.

INTRODUCING BRAINSTORM

In the laboratory one morning a child was brought in, he was brain damaged from a car accident. His mother was distraught and stood waiting while her son was prepared for his operation conducted with the help of brainstorm. After hours of surgery the child came out of the machine with a fresh look on his face, alert and able to communicate. His mother couldn't believe her eyes; she had her son back as he used to be before the accident thanks to brainstorm.

A similar experience happened to a young girl who was brain damaged through a similar accident. Her parents were grateful and praised the scientists behind the brainstorm project. It was a five year success program before being publicised in a Norwegian paper the next thing would be to announce the success of brainstorm in a public lecture with fellow scientists, surgeons and reporters.

It was a day of operations after which the scientists and surgeons were mentally exhausted. The anaesthetists sat talking to other specialists, some were joking about social events, no one discussed the operations as they had been involved in so much activity surrounding these events. Scientist's John Phillips and Sven Anderson shut down brainstorm for the rest of the day, checking all instruments were operational before shut down. Sven was a realist while John Phillips was an optimist between the two they balanced ideas of a brighter future with brainstorm. Curing people from all over the world with top brain surgeons like Brian Steiner and Jon Gregg so many patients would be helped regardless of their financial status. Thousands of people of notoriety funded such projects in order to improve society, creating a caring race of individuals that want to improve the future for all brain diseases and defects.

After years of trial and errors, experimental procedures Ulrichsen machine brainstorm was ready for the world to see and demonstrate its full potential in the field of medicine and science. It was time to look at the many issues raised about mental health and expose any myths or discriminatory ideas of mental health conditions which have been passed down through generations. The negative views recorded throughout history can finally be discussed, the thoughts of lunatics running about causing havoc in society and being locked up in lunatic asylums. Brainstorm ended such problems reoccurring, leaving such things in a dark and distant past never to relive in generations to come. At least that was the plan Ulrichsen, Phillips and Anderson had in mind when they cured twenty thousand people of their mental health conditions. But what would the world think of such a machine given the fact that some religious leaders would question the ethics of such operations and drug manufacturers had invested a lot of money into stabilising mental health conditions.

Norway August 3rd 2180 in a science convention somewhere in Oslo at the science forum in a lecture theatre at the university of Oslo (UiO) people present would be scientists, surgeons and other medically trained individuals. The media were also invited along with fund raisers, charitable organisations and governmental representatives from most nations.

The chairman opened the meeting by discussing some of the more recent studies and research from around the world. The chairman then seemed very excited about the latest project called 'brainstorm' and introduced the inventor doctor Jan Ulrichsen a leading Norwegian scientist. Ulrichsen stood up and made his way to the stage. He was applauded by the large audience in the lecture theatre, they were a very mixed group made up of scientists, students, the media and others.

Ulrichsen was a tall man in his fifties; he had thick black hair with grey natural highlights. He looked very studious with his silver framed glasses, which rested on the end of his thick shapely nose. He was a quiet man as a rule and liked to work on his own in his laboratory; however he is sometimes joined by his daughter Kristina.

She was a twenty five year old with dark hair, slim and strikingly beautiful.

Ulrichsen took a deep breathe before making his speech, he glanced across at the audience and noticed Kristina sat at the front row of the theatre in order to support him. He firstly spoke in Norwegian.

“Velkommen til vårt nye prosjekt som vi kaller ‘brainstorm’. Jeg håper at dette vil ende problemet med hjernesykdom”

Translation

“Welcome to our new creation called ‘brainstorm’ I hope that this will end the problem of brain disease” The many languages were being filtered into a set of elaborate headphones which were connected to a type of visor. Each individual could switch a button and scroll up and down with a dial to receive their chosen language. The languages ranged from Norwegian of course, English, Swedish, Japanese, German, Spanish and so on.

“It is my pleasure to be able to introduce you to our new discovery which is simply called ‘Brainstorm’. Ulrichsen was reading from a handful of notes, which he was gripping tightly in his hand. “We hope to help many people in this world who will definitely benefit from such an invention”.

Ulrichsen then looked behind him as a photograph of the machine was projected onto a large screen. It appeared three dimensional diagrams showing how ‘brainstorm would work in practice, it was a virtual tour of the brain. The audience wore the helmets with visors and sound fitted into minute speakers within the helmet as previously mentioned, over twelve languages were heard in these speakers controlled by a remote hand set according to the persons own native tongue. A Frenchman heard the lecture in French while a German beside him heard it in German.

French 'Bonjour bienvenue sur remue méninges'

German "Hallo willkommen bei brainstorming"

Swedish "Hej, och välkommen till brainstorma"

Spanish "Hola bienvenido a una lluvia de ideas"

This was just a few languages introducing Brainstorm

'Brainstorm' is simply a concept that was discovered to unravel many mysteries of the mind during this process we hope to rid the world of such terrible diseases of the brain. We are looking at mental health conditions as well as tumours and other brain defects. It is named brainstorm after working on it in the laboratory when we discovered its potential my daughter and I noticed it was raining outside and a storm filled the skies, thunder and lightening and with the sound of the machine and flashes s like lightening Kristina called it 'brainstorm'

Ulrichsen paused and watched the photo change on the screen, Kristina smiled she was obviously proud of her father as proud as he was of her.

"'This machine is capable of probing the brain, reaching areas of the mind that was were once considered impossible to find. In the process it is possible to look into persons thought process and discover just how powerful the mind is. The mind can be capable of many things this can be achieved by the use of 'brainstorm'. At last we can reveal secrets never before thought possible; in the last five years we have seen the effects of this discovery. It has already helped so many people and looking ahead we can see the benefits of 'brainstorm'. So is the future this is brainstorm.

Its primary function is cure certain types of mental illness by probing the mind and reaching the vital spots that cause the most problems. It has the ability to remove any blockages in the blood vessels, renew damaged tissues and repair any area caused by accidents" Ulrichsen pointed to the screen where the three dimensional program was making a journey through the brain. "Ladies and gentlemen I provide you with fact and not fiction, what you see here is reality it is the here and now". Ulrichsen glanced at his daughter Kristina who helped to perfect the idea. "We believe in this and want you to believe in it too, this machine will save lives and improve peoples quality of life. I want to share it with you and provide you with a purpose to understand those who suffer from brain damage understand them and help them understand you".

"Now let's take the journey together into the brain entering the frontal lobe where we find the seat of personality, thinking and intellect. We will now travel through the various labyrinths of the left hemisphere of the brain that controls complex movements and voluntary movements note all the blood vessels and nerves that surround us as we journey towards the parietal lobe responsible for pain, touch, temperature and pressure. Here we experience sense of touch, choice of words and awareness. We now enter the occipital lobe responsible for vision control you will notice a fluctuation of light or electrodes at this point as the brain is fully active. We travel briefly into the cerebellum a muscular area, breath in at this point I don't want you to be crushed. Now we enter the medulla oblongata or spinal bulb, this is the control centre for breathing, the heart, and blood pressure, better not linger here it could upset the patient. Now we are in the temporal lobe area of the brain, here we find the smell centre, hearing centre and choice of thought from here we re-enter the frontal lobe area at speech control. We leave the brain at this point I hope that you enjoyed your journey and are now ready to experience brain operations in order to experience brainstorms true potential".

Ulrichsen received a rapturous applause before demonstrating the operations performed by brainstorm.

"Now watch as we perform an operation to remove blood clots, repair severed and trapped nerves and repair cell damage. You will now witness the curing of vascular dementia, Alzheimer's and Parkinson's disease" Ulrichsen looked happy as his audience watched amazing surgery.

Ulrichsen looked at the investors "This is our future an inheritance for your children, it is the alpha and the omega for us to cherish welcome it with open arms I do say you will not regret this believe me".

Ulrichsen's word echoed around the lecture theatre this was followed by a rapturous applause even he was surprised at the response. The video sold the idea but Ulrichsen sold the entire program.

Kristina looked proudly on at her father's performance as if to say that's my father there and he is helping the world with his invention.

Ulrichsen introduced his daughter to the stage.

"May I now introduce my daughter Kristina to the stage, the one who named this discovery 'Brainstorm' ladies and gentlemen my daughter Kristina".

Again the audience applauded

"Ladies and gentlemen, fellow scientists may I say that it is an honour to be here with my father and share 'Brainstorm' with you. It has been a struggle to do this as so many people thought the idea of curing brain disease impossible, many scientists touched on a formula which could slow down the process of such problems as dementia, however what we have achieved in just ten years has revolutionised science. It has also given hope to many families around the world, patients can now be cured of such diseases and illness as Parkinsonism, Huntington's, schizophrenia, by polar and many brain damaged conditions. I am proud of my father and his idea to save mankind with the creation of 'brainstorm,' I sincerely hope that you are too".

Ulrichsen stood up and embraced his daughter, and then he addressed the press.

“Are there any questions?” Ulrichsen asked reluctantly as he never trusted them, they were often guilty of twisting things and finding the bad in good things.

“Dr Ulrichsen by creating this machine won’t you be putting drug manufacturers out of business?” One reporter commented.

“May I ask you sir, what is more important a cure for brain disease or a company being put out of business?” Ulrichsen seemed angry by the question.

“What if the machine gets in the hands of terrorists?” Another member of the press asked.

“I must tell you that there is a self destruct mechanism within the program that will set of an explosion when the program is activated”. Ulrichsen explained knowing that it would also require five scientists’ individual codes to enter the program.

“Don’t you think that you are playing god and messing with a natural creation?” a woman said.

“No I don’t I feel that I am assisting him to repair the mind” Ulrichsen replied “No one can be god, but if we possess the knowledge to do good by using what god has create within us then we should do so. An artist uses his gifts from god and creates beautiful picture, as does a writer of poems and so on”. Ulrichsen knew he was right

Brainstorm had to work in order for the human race to survive people were dying slow and horrible deaths due to brain damage and people with mental illness were suffering unnecessarily when such cures as brainstorm existed needing sponsorships to continue the project successfully.

The sponsors were whispering to each other in a small group on the left hand side of the theatre while a man who looked so out of place sat on the right hand side. A small thin man with small glasses lingering on the end of his long nose partly covered his small beady eyes, he had large teeth that were yellow and nicotine stained as were his long thin fingers on his right hand. He taking notes and attentive to every detail like a reporter, his clothes were creased and nothing really matched as if he had dressed in a hurry not considering how he looked. This would suggest that the man was single because if he were married a woman would have dressed him properly and not allow him to go out in such a state. He also sat away from everybody else as if he was reluctant to mix with either students or anyone else in the audience; this suggested that he wasn't a lecturer.

After the lecture ended he hurried out of the door, he looked back and the found the exit. He seemed nervous and uneasy as he was waiting for the sky train constantly looking around clutching hold of a briefcase that contained his notes.

The sky train docked on the hanger and he entered still looking form left to right as if he was crossing a busy street, he sat down and the vehicle took off from the flight pad across a busy flight path.

He arrived at his destination disembarked from the sky train and walked towards a large building; he entered the door and walked into an elevator pressing a button to the seventh floor. He then proceeded down a corridor and entered a door, a large man nodded to him and he continued into a second door where a older man sat looking at him.

"Well what news Dawson?" General Murray asked

"Oh you will like this" Dawson replied, "He has exactly what we need".

"Brainstorm is real then?" the man asked

"Yes sir it is real and operational"

"My god, I have waited for this for a long time" Murray said in a cunning voice.

"It is everything we dreamed of and more, it is capable of mind manipulation" Dawson said smugly

"Can you operate it?" Murray asked

"I don't know I think we need the scientist Ulrichsen and his daughter at least" Dawson said dreading Murray's response.

"If that's what it takes lets kidnap them all starting with Ulrichsen" Murrays evil eyes gazed at Dawson "You worked with him so arrange it".

Back in the laboratory Ulrichsen was working with his daughter, preparing brainstorm for the next day, they had a full day of operating on patients and needed to get the equipment ready. They had to check all systems and ensure all was operational.

"Is the world ready for brainstorm I wonder, after all the technology is so advanced and I have already been verbally attacked by religious leaders suggesting that I am playing god" Ulrichsen said feeling let disappointed by these religious people.

"Father you must realise not everyone is like you, some are not honest and don't consider others". Kristina seemed upset.

"Kristina I know that, but you have to trust some people and allow yourself to be loved" Ulrichsen wanted his daughter to find someone and marry one day.

"I am married to my work I have told you many times" Kristina said abruptly.

"I want you to marry and have children who will grow to continue our work"

"I will continue the work without children" Kristina said tapping in the code to brainstorm.

"We have cured brain damaged people and done good things" Ulrichsen insisted

“But I don’t want our creation getting into the wrong hands” Kristina seemed agitated.

“Like who?” Ulrichsen noticed her behaviour

“People like terrorists, mad men or any of the world governments”. Kristina explained

“You have quite an imagination, nothing will happen honestly” Ulrichsen said checking the controls.

“I wish that I could share your optimistic views Father” Kristina said trying to smile.

THE KIDNAPPING

"Hei, dette er Jan Ulrichsen, kan jeg hjelpe deg"

"Hvem er dette?"

Translation

"Hi this is Jon Ulrichsen can I help you?"

"Who is this?"

No one spoke on the other end of the phone, instead there was an Éire silence

Ulrichsen left the building and walked towards the car park, he was conscious of being followed but carried on walking. Suddenly a car stopped beside him and a man asked him the way to the science building, as Ulrichsen began directing him someone came from behind him and stabbed him in the neck with a needle. Ulrichsen fell to the ground and remained there until he was put in the boot of a car.

When Ulrichsen came round he found himself in a room with photos of him on the wall, other photos were of Kristina and other scientists with brainstorm.

Ulrichsen found his hands were bound in some form of handcuffs and he was lying on a settee.

"Doctor Ulrichsen my dear fellow" Murray said.

"Who are you?" Ulrichsen asked.

"General Matt Murray of the united states marines" Murray replied in his deep gravely voice "But you can call me Matt"

"Well Matt why am I here?" Ulrichsen asked anticipating the answer.

"Why to help me of course" Murray said knowing the difficulty he would have getting Ulrichsen to cooperate.

"I want you to help me set up your machine, what's it called brain breeze"

"Brainstorm!" Ulrichsen shouted

"Whatever" Murray said sarcastically "I want to use brainstorm"

"Why would you need brainstorm?" Ulrichsen asked

"To control minds and manipulate thoughts and then to kidnap world leaders and control the world" Murray said flinging his arms about like a madman.

"You are clearly not normal" Ulrichsen commented "Perhaps you need to be in the machine".

"Doctor I was in your machine and it didn't help me, I was suffering from a form of post traumatic shock from the war and you fried my brain" Murray became angry.

"I trusted you and what did you do to me?"

"The damage must have been too severe and besides I do remember that you had by polar". Ulrichsen reflected back to the event and remembered complications at the time.

"I tried to help you but there was a lot of damage to tissues and we were at the early stages of our scientific discoveries". Ulrichsen explained

"So I was a guinea pig, a trial for your brain machine?" Murray was pacing.

"We had to start somewhere and I have offered to help you now" Ulrichsen suddenly felt vulnerable watching Murray pacing and seeming agitated.

"Anderson!" He shouted

Alison escorted short grey haired man into the room with a fat younger man who was gripping his arm. The older man had a black eye and fresh burns to his face, he seemed in pain and looked at Ulrichsen for help.

"Sir he refused to talk despite my efforts" Alison explained "So Mr Bowles tried"

"Sven what has happened to you?" Ulrichsen asked

"The same thing that will happen to you if you fail to cooperate" Alison said

"Torture" Ulrichsen said concerned about Anderson.

"Yes and your daughter Kristina when we find her" Murray said shaking his finger

"You are clearly mad" Ulrichsen deduced.

"Yes driven mad by you and others, so I will get my revenge and ultimately rule the world" Murray seemed very dramatic as he through his arms in the air.

"Do you recognise your science assistant Mr Bowles?"

The fat man smiled and waved at Ulrichsen then he proceeded to thump Anderson in the face making his nose bleed.

"Doctor Ulrichsen you fired me, but I was there to hear your speech about brainstorm" Bowles said with a cunning grin.

"You became too friendly with my daughter and tried to rape her" Ulrichsen said angrily.

"Oh dear" Bowles said tutting then thumping him too "Manners Doctor and she loved it, I felt inside her coat at her breasts so firm and young, she pulled away and hit me on the head with a spanner the silly bitch".

Ulrichsen tried to struggle free in order to hit him back, but the handcuffs were too tight. Bowles went towards him in order to attack again but this time Murray hit him and the fat man fell and broke a table.

"Sorry doctor but I hate men disrespecting women" Murray said sincerely.

Bowles got up and rushed towards Murray with his eyes blazing and fists clenched he had almost reached Murray when he was stopped by a number of laser blasts from Alison and two androids guards. His fat body fell crashing down onto a glass table.

"I hope we didn't need him doctor?" Murray asked.

"No" Ulrichsen said struggling to get his words out in view of the shocking activity.

"Now to business doctor" Murray said "How can we get brainstorm to work?"

"You never will" Ulrichsen said confidently.

"And why is that?" Murray asked

"Because you need the codes from each of us scientist who worked on brainstorm before you can get started" Ulrichsen seemed calmer by telling Murray the facts.

"So very clever doctor and I suppose that it is tattooed on each scientist?"

"Correct, I presume that you noticed it on Sven when you were torturing him?" Ulrichsen said.

"Yes a Norwegian song bird and numbers" Murray said smiling "It's a matter of time before we find the other scientists and Kristina and then you will cooperate".

"Alison organise the search immediately" Murray ordered.

RESCUE

Kristina was having a shower, she felt at ease as she let the water pour down her face and body. She then poured shower gel into her hands and rubbed it on her silky body, then she shampooed her long dark hair gathering a lather and being careful not to get any shampoo into her large green eyes. At that moment she could here the house alarm sounding; she hurried out of the shower and put her bath robe on. She ran into the bedroom and picked up the intercom.

"Alex hva som skjer"(Alex what is happening?) She asked in Norwegian

"Opphold hvor du er Madam, ikke forlat rommet" (Stay where you are Madam, don't leave your room) Alex insisted.

"Men hva er det?" (But what is it?) Kristina asked concerned

"Du er i fare, bo der hvor du er trygg" (You're in danger stay there where you are safe) Alex replied anxiously.

Following this there was a big bang and the sound of lasers firing, Kristina was frightened and remained in the bedroom as advised. Her heart was pounding in her chest and she began to perspire, she frantically looked for somewhere to hide. She began to tremble as the door handle began to move, she began looking for an object to use as a weapon such as a vase or a chair. But before she could do this the door was blasted open and the figure of a man was standing in the doorway, he had a laser in his hand that was pointing up towards the ceiling. He edged for ward lifting his visor and putting his finger to his mouth instructing her to remain silent. At that point another figure tried to enter the room so he fired his laser at his chest, then grabbed Kristina by the arm.

"Be quiet and follow me" He instructed.

"Who are you?" She asked

"My name is John Stone a government agent working for MI5, I'm here to rescue you" Stone said leading her out of the door.

"Where are we going?" She asked

"Just follow me and trust me" He said "Follow my instructions and you will stay alive".

He led her across the landing towards the stairs

"Get down" He shouted firing his laser at figures racing in various directions. Lasers were being fired and bodies falling flashes of light and laser blasts everywhere. Eventually Stone led Kristina down the stairs and out of the building where he was joined by other agents who fought in their defence. Stone led Kristina into a vehicle and raced away at great speed followed by the other agents in their vehicles. They seemed to travel miles until they stopped in a quiet area and Stone pointed to the back of the vehicle.

"In here are clothes and a blonde wig, you need to disguise yourself so that we can get away undetected". He instructed "We can find a safe place for you to change and continue to Sweden".

"Why are we going to Sweden?" Kristina said confused

"That's just the beginning of the journey" Stone said

"Really?" She said surprised

"Yes we are going to England in a round about way with others dressed like us as a decoy".

Stone waited outside the vehicle while Kristina got changed into other clothes and blonde wig. She looked stunning as she appeared in her new outfit, Stone could not believe his eyes as he gazed at her beauty.

"Well, do I look the part?" Kristina asked

"Absolutely" Stone replied

"So stop staring and lets go" Kristina insisted

They travelled over to Sweden and travelled to a train station Kristina spoke in Swedish when she was in the station purchasing her ticket.

"Jag har två biljetter till göteborg?" (May I Have two tickets to Gothenburg?) Kristina asked

"Vill du ha tillbaka biljetter?" (Do you want return tickets?) The lady asked

"Inte bara enstaka biljetter vänligen" (No just single tickets thank you) Kristina said searching through her purse

Kristina waited and began fidgeting nervously with her fingers and looking from left to right.

The lady returned with her tickets and seemed a little odd as she gave them to her, as if she was trying to tell about something or warn her of danger.

"Tack och ha en säker resa" (Thank you and have a safe journey) She said writing a on a piece of paper. 'Din betraktat' (your being watched)

Kristina looked shocked but tried not to show anyone that she knew about being observed.

"tack så hemskt mycket" (thank you very much) Kristina replied

Kristina left pulling Stone by the arm and whispering, "We are being watched"

"How do you know?" Stone asked

"The lady said at the ticket booth" Kristina said

"Ok you go through the gates first" Stone suggested staying behind

Kristina began walking towards the gate and Stone observed, He recognised Andrea Buckley the terrorist waiting by the gate. Kristina stopped at the gate and then spoke to a member of the station crew; she looked back and then went onto the platform. Stone walked forward towards the gate expecting trouble, but he was told to carry on.

"Gör om du" (carry on please) the man said

Then he shouted "stopp!, Där har ni?" (Stop, where are you going?)

"Gothenburg" Stone replied

"Du behöver plattform 2 över bron" (You need platform 2 over the bridge) The man said

"Thank you" Stone replied

"You are English?" He said

"Yes why?" Stone asked suspiciously

"No reason continue over the bridge ahead of you" He said smiling

The man looked across at Andrea and nodded, she acknowledged him and walked through the gate followed by others. Stone walked over the bridge and was immediately fired upon, people began to scatter and run. Stone removed his gun from his coat and fired at one of the figures which exploded, it was an android. He was almost hit by a laser blast and stooped low before firing back, after a while he hit another android. He continued over the bridge and was again fired upon this time by Andrea who was hiding behind a post. Stone saw the train ahead and decided to run for it, he made one great effort to jump and landed inside the train doorway just in time for it to depart. Stone knew that he was still not safe and began to walk down the train in order to find Kristina, he felt eyes on his back as if someone was close behind him. He was puzzled by the fact that despite efforts to disguise both Kristina and himself, he was still being followed. Then he realised that Kristina was wearing a bracelet on her wrist when they were at the house, she may still be wearing it despite getting changed. This may have had an homing device concealed inside it, therefore they were being tracked by the terrorists.

Stone was almost in the last carriage when he noticed Kristina with two men; he had to act fast before the train reached the next station. He pulled an emergency cord and everyone standing fell to the ground. He had a clear shot of both of the men and fired his laser hitting the first man, then the second, both fell to the ground. He grabbed Kristina and pulled her to the front of the train, looking back he noticed other men running forward. They began firing at Stone, he fired back at them while Kristina hid in a corner.

“They are a little persistent Mr Stone”

“Yes they are and would you mind removing that bracelet” Stone insisted.

“Why?” Kristina replied holding the back of her head and shielding the sprays from laser blasts ricocheting off the nearby wall.

“It has some kind of homing beacon inside” Stone replied continuing to shoot at the terrorists.

“Really?” Kristina said surprised

“Yes really” Stone said annoyed

“It was a gift something special” Kristina added “Sentimental”

“Well that sentimental thing is about to get us killed” Stone said shooting one of the terrorists.

“Here take it” Kristina said passing it to Stone who was still shooting at terrorists.

“Throw it out of the window” Stone shouted.

“Which window?” Kristina said looking around her.

“Anyone it doesn’t matter” Stone said impatiently

Kristina threw it out of the window but it bounced off something and landed by her feet.

"Whoops" She said watching it land.

"For god sake Kristina throw it out" Stone said impatiently

"I am trying" Kristina said picking it up.

"Very trying, now throw it" Stone shouted

Kristina threw the bracelet once more this time it disappeared out of the window.

"Remind me never to give you any grenades to throw" Stone said killing the last cabin and terrorist.

Stone headed to the driver's made sure they missed a few stations by insisting the driver had a rest for a while. At least a brief sleep helped by a drug which he kept by for such occasions called a sleeping draft, this would usually last a few hours.

Once they reached Gothenburg they were met by another agent who took them safely to a boat and they travelled to Denmark and across Germany to France. They reached England weeks later and continued to London and caught a train to the north of England.

Eventually they reached a safe house and Kristina was able to relax for a while without fear of being recognised. Stone met Sylvia at the apartment and introduced her to Kristina; she was a dark haired slim lady in her thirties with a generous smile and what could be termed as the gentle touch. She was kind and sincere with a heart of gold, she was used in the field of espionage for her communicational skills and being supportive in a crises. She was attractive and often dressed to kill, usually she killed fashion, Sylvia was not the type to follow fashion but dressed according to mood. If Sylvia wore yellow or green that was good, but if she wore brown it was bad news for others around her.

Kristina became friends with Sylvia they spent evenings playing board games, discussing fashion and discussing England and Norway. Kristina discussed some of her experiences with brainstorm and how it would benefit mankind.

"I have seen so many people recover from such disfiguring illnesses, I have seen people walk again, talk again and their eyes come alive gain and the joy on the relatives face as they recovered in front of their eyes. It was like a miracle spoken about in the bible, performed by Jesus giving sight to the blind and raising the dead. Perhaps that sound a little profound but it's the only way that I can describe it, my father never professed to be a god or work miracles but he cured people". Kristina explained.

"He is a clever man" Sylvia said "I am sure many people are grateful to him for his help and compassion".

"You are a kind and wise woman Sylvia" Kristina said smiling

"I am just me, plain and simple" Sylvia replied

"No far more than that, you are deep and loving" Kristina said thoughtfully.

"I do my best in life and no one could ask more" Sylvia replied humbly.

"I sometimes wish that I was someone else with no responsibility, A person that could go home from work and relax, forget about the job and be a wife with children".

"You mean work in a shop and go out to the cinema at night with your family?" Sylvia said in a understanding manner.

"Yes exactly" Kristina agreed.

"That's not you and the life that you were destined for". Sylvia spoke as if she had known Kristina years.

"Your probably right, my life was mapped out and I was supposed to help others" Kristina had given it some thought, Sylvia had recognised a pattern of success and a journey that many people would have loved to have taken. Katrina's journey was far from over and she could help many more in the future given the opportunity.

OPERATION BRAINSTORM BEGINS

At the American headquarters in Washington troops had been selected for a mission, each one chosen for a particular task. A large man with grey hair sat at a desk with other officers he stood out because of his size and decorations on his tunic.

“Gentlemen”, he looked round at the women present “And ladies”

“We have reached a dilemma; our problem in case you don’t know is brainstorm. The revolutionary brain machine that cured brain disease has been stolen along with the inventors Jon Ulrichsen and his daughter Kristina. Now I don’t need to tell you what this means for mankind, the risk of it being used against us in war, the terrorists will stop at nothing to use this machine as a weapon against us”.

“General Lewis does this mean what I think you mean?” Another officer asked.

"Jeremy Let me tell you that I propose that we not only destroy the brainstorm machine but also the scientists behind it all, that way we can guarantee that this wild dream that turned into a nightmare ends for good". Lewis said trying to convince the other officers.

"American agents are already on it" another officer reported.

"I am preparing a briefing with my marines to find these scientists no matter where they are and get rid of them" Lewis said confidently.

"So are they all going to die?" Another officer asked

"Operation brainstorm will happen and brainstorm will be history" Lewis announced to the officers.

On the 5th November 2180 a briefing was held at marine base in New York, U.S.A, it was chaired by non other than General Lewis. The room was filled with U.S marines who were awaiting their orders for 'Operation brainstorm' and their mission details.

Andrea was present posing as an American agent trying to gather information for Murray about the operation.

"Okay troops this is are mission, as you know brainstorm has been taken by terrorists. It is a dangerous weapon because it is capable of mind control and so we must seek it out and destroy it. As for the scientists, who have been using it, I want them to be assassinated, killed, wiped out or whatever other term that you wish to use". Lewis said looking around the room at his potential killers.

"Are you suggesting we murder scientists General Lewis?" One of the officers said.

"I am not suggesting murder, but I do say kill" Lewis said looking around at the marines. "We have no choice, we have to act for the good of mankind this machine brainstorm is dangerous and so are the scientist's our government does not reach this decision lightly but after careful consideration looking at all the facts. Brainstorm is a weapon and the scientist can use that weapon against us man is not safe while they or the very idea of brainstorm survives". Lewis looked at his fellow officers "Any questions?"

Everyone sat quietly; the odd cough or clearing of throats broke the silence. The soldiers looked at each other speechless unsure of their own commitments, trying to decide whether it was right to kill someone in cold blood who's sole purpose was to help their fellow man. If they were heart surgeons would they still be ordered to kill them, they were faced with a moral dilemma that questioned their own conscience, was it right or wrong. Had Lewis and the governmental establishment got the right to give such orders that would require the execution of scientists who were working for the good of others.

"I trust all of you to carry out this mission unquestionably for your countries sake, don't let us or yourself down" Lewis said coldly.

The news reported that so many scientists had been shot in various locations of the world, this included Doctor Phillips who was in Germany when an assassins bullet struck his head while he was in a park. Others died in similar ways in public places and leaving their grieving families bewildered by the bloody attacks.

As for General Lewis who had been instrument in their deaths, he lay in pain awaiting the diagnoses of his severe headaches. He received the news that he had Infact got a inoperable brain tumour and would not be expected to live long. The only hope for him ironically would have been brainstorm and the scientists that he had ordered to be executed. He lay ion his death bed regretting what he had done, he suffered the pain and discomfort that he bestowed on innocent people and few people attended his funeral, even his own family were discussed by his actions and refused to have any contact with him.

Kristina was having a nightmare about the misuse of brainstorm, seeing zombies walking out of the laboratory, their minds had been altered by brainstorm and soldiers stood shooting them. It was a complete reversal of the work that her father and her had accomplished, a sad, cold place with no clear hope for the future. She awoke in a cold sweat, looking at the cold blue walls of the safe house with nothing to remind her of home. She was a long way from Norway; her family were so distant as she lived in an existence and not the life she was used to. She thought back to the log cabin and the boat trips through the fjords, with its magical settings where her father once told her tales and in her mind adventures took place. Sylvia had become a good friend but her aunty Kari was her closest friend who used to help her escape from her work. She thought about her life and at twenty eight she was still young enough to do many things like cruising along the Baltic sea to Estonia or Russia. Kari would talk about this or visiting Florida or California for a holiday away from the pressure of work occasionally with her father.

CLOSING THE NET

After living in England for a few months Kristina was really missing her father and all their time together in Norway. She was watching the world news reports on hunting down the scientists and resent reports of deaths in various countries of those scientist suspected of being involved in 'brainstorm'. Kristina was thinking of her family and if they were safe in Norway. Stone was resting on a chair and fidgeting with a pen, he was aware that Kristina was home sick but felt helpless as his job was to protect her from harm.

"I want to go home" Kristina insisted

"You can't its impossible" Stone replied

"You can't keep me here against my will" Kristina shouted

"I am protecting you" Stone explained

"I am a prisoner" Kristina insisted

She rushed into the bedroom and slammed the door, at that moment Sylvia came in and heard Kristina crying in the bedroom.

“What’s going on?” She asked concerned

“Oh she is on about going back to Norway again” Stone replied

“You have to understand her situation John; she is separated from her father and feels lost. They are very close and as you know he brought her up after her mother died, they have hardly ever been apart”.

“I realise that Sylvia but it’s too dangerous to go to Norway and we are protecting her” Stone said concerned.

“Okay let me speak to her while you check what’s happening with brainstorm” Sylvia said positively.

Sylvia Knocked on the door and waited for a reply

“Go away leave me alone” Kristina shouted

“Kristina it’s Sylvia” Sylvia said softly

Kristina opened the door and wrapped her arms around Sylvia “I have missed you”

“I have missed you too Kristina can I come in?” Sylvia asked

“Yes of course you can” She replied

They walked over to two chairs situated near the dressing table, both sat down and Sylvia began to speak.

"I know that you want to go home, but things are bad there at present" Sylvia explained.

"Really, that's what John said" Kristina replied sadly

"He is only thinking of your safety, I understand your point of view too" Sylvia empathised with her.

"You do?" Kristina looked sad at Sylvia

"Yes wanting to be near your family but I am sure you are in their hearts and minds"

"Yes I suppose so and I was a bit harsh with John, he was only trying to help" Kristina said understandingly.

"So dry your eyes let me make a nice hot cup of tea and come out when you're ready"

Sylvia said getting up and walking towards the door.

Kristina went into the bathroom, got undressed and entered the shower, she was feeling better but still wanted to hear a Norwegian voice. Once out of the shower she switched on the radio and picked up the phone. She dialled an international number.

A voice answered, it was her Aunty Kari in Oslo, Norway and spoke in Norwegian.

"Hei Kari, hvordan står det til" Kristina asked

"Takk bare bra men hva skjer? Jeg har hatt militæret her" Kari replied

"De søker etter deg på grunn av 'brainstorm', et prosjekt tilhørende min bror, din far".

"Så de søker etter meg i Norge?"

"Ja og de er veldig ivrig etter å finne deg"

Kari, jeg savner far og trenger å komme tilbake til Norge".

"Men du er i fare!"

"Jeg vet at jeg er i fare men jeg må hjem".

"Kristina, tenk på hva du holder på med for du er ikke trygg"

"Hør her, jeg må gå. Jeg er i en tryggbolig i England".

"Vi snakkes Elsker deg"

Which translated means

"Hi Kari how are you?" Kristina asked

"I am fine, what's happening we have had the army here?"

"The army! why have they come to you?" Kristina asked concerned

"They are searching for you because of 'brainstorm' a project of my brothers your father" Kari explained

"So they are searching for me in Norway" Kristina asked

"Yes they were very keen to find you" Kari said concerned

"Kari I miss my father, I need to come back to Norway" Kristina said with a quivering voice

"But you're in danger" Kari said

"I know I am in danger but I must come home" Kristina pleaded

"Kristina think about what you are doing, you are not safe" Kari tried to explain.

"Listen I have to go, I am in a safe house in England, speak soon, love you" Kristina put the phone down quickly as Sylvia knocked the door.

"Kristina your tea is ready" Sylvia said politely.

Kristina came out of the room dressed in a white blouse and dark trousers, let her hair flow free and appeared happy.

"Hi Kristina you look happier" Sylvia said watching her smile

"I am Sylvia thanks to you" Kristina replied

"You need a man by your side" Sylvia said pouring the tea.

"I have always wanted a relationship but I am scared, I have only ever dated geeks because I felt safe with them. I thought of them as not so much of a challenge". Kristina explained "Does that seem fair?"

"Well I never thought of that but I suppose you felt comfortable with them" Sylvia said feeling awkward

"You mean because I am a Geek?" Kristina said jokingly.

"No, you're different somehow" Sylvia said hesitantly

"It's okay I know I am no catch for a real man" Kristina said looking down

"Kristina you are beautiful and you have the world ahead of you" Sylvia said touching her hand.

"I am a scientist I have worked on brainstorm, I have seen miracles occur before my eyes and still can't believe it" Kristina admitted.

"I know brainstorm is marvellous it has cured many people, I heard of it a few years ago, it's a big hit in various places around the world" Sylvia said excitedly.

"Yes we have helped people with various types of brain conditions, I have seen people come to us in a vegetative state and become fully functional human beings in a matter of hours" Kristina said proudly.

"I heard this and live normal lives afterwards" Sylvia said happily.

"But what is to become of it now, years of research and successful stories to see it destroyed, one assistant scientist who tried to rape me called Bowles I think, hated the work we did and thought brainstorm should be scrapped" Kristina said sadly.

"Now that's being negative, you need to look forward and see what's ahead it could still work" Sylvia said positively.

At that moment they heard gun blasts and the door opening, Sylvia told Kristina to hide while she headed to the door. A man stood in a trooper uniform, so she raised her weapon and pointed it at his helmet. He lifted his visor and spoke to her in a reassuring manner.

"Sylvia it's me John, we are in danger" Stone said concerned "They have found us"

"But how did they find us? Sylvia asked

"I don't know, a signal from a phone or some other means" Stone explained

"But no one used a phone" Sylvia said confused

“It was me, I have phoned Norway” Kristina admitted “I brought them here when I phoned Kari”

“Why do we bother to protect her when she does something stupid like this” Stone said angrily.

“I’m sorry” Kristina said upset.

“She couldn’t help it John, she wanted to speak to her family” Sylvia said in her defence.

Activity continued outside the door with laser fire and troops moving around.

“We have to move from here” Stone said

“Okay what’s the plan” Sylvia asked

“We shoot our way out” Stone said holding his weapon firmly in his hand.

“That’s your plan?” Kristina asked Stone with a worried expression on her face.

“Do either of you have a better plan” Stone replied sternly

Both Sylvia and Kristina answered together “No”

“Okay, we go on three you all have weapons, blast your way out” Stone said edging his way near the door. “One, two, three go”.

Stone opened the door and began firing at the enemy, and then they began to move forward blasts from the enemy guns ricocheted off walls banisters and doors. Alison was seen organising the troops to fight the agents, men were falling everywhere. Suddenly a shot was fired that sent Sylvia out of a window, glass shattered and Sylvia was gone, out of sight. Kristina tried to go after her, but Stone held onto her in order to prevent her harming herself in any way.

"No Kristina we have to carry on" Stone insisted.

"But we need to help her" Kristina shouted

"The fall may of killed her" Stone shouted back.

Stone led Kristina out down the stairs, out of door and onto the street where the battle continued. Eventually Stone managed to wound Alison as he fired his laser and hit her body, the force from the blast was enough to make her fall to the ground in pain, she eventually passed out. Stone stole a vehicle and escaped.

It was shortly after Alison had led the attack on Kristina and Stone that they made the decision to return to Norway. Kristina was insistent and Stone realised that he was unable to stop her, she had decided and he had to agree if he wanted to help her and protect her from harm. He knew that if it was his family in the same situation, he would try to help them and Sylvia would have gone with them too.

A QUESTION OF LIFE OR DEATH

The journey was hard as Kristina and Stone headed into France and then entered Germany, Denmark, Sweden and finally Norway. After a long arduous two week journey across the various countries they arrived in Oslo were Kristina was discovered by Deakin and Harris who found her near Kari's house trying to contact her aunty; Stone had shot Harris when he was pulling Kristina by the arm, Deakin had moved up behind Stone and knocked him unconscious. Kari and her family were injured in the attack but survived; they were transferred to hospital soon afterwards.

Stone recovered and continued to the enemy base disguised as an American soldier joining with other soldiers to find the terrorist base. He was carrying a device that would alert his agency of his presence this was like a homing device. Kristina was reunited with her father and managed to update him with activities, she was allowed to remain with her father as the terrorist considered they might obtain more information, if they kept them in the same room and monitored their conversation. A Norwegian interpreter listened in on them hoping to discover a part of the conversation that would give them a clue to the operation of brainstorm. Shortly after they had been there a battle started between the terrorists and army troops, amongst others wanting either procession of brainstorm or its ultimate destruction. They had began fighting outside and then took the battle inside, the atmosphere consisted of laser lights and explosions. Katrina and her father hugged together hearing all the sounds from inside their cell room. Then the sound of someone blasting their door, it was army troops trying to get in.

Once they had entered the room one of the troops held his laser up and aimed it at Ulrichsen. Kristina ran forward and shielded him, there was a sudden blast and both of them fell to the floor. The entire room lit up as lasers were being fired everywhere, after a while they stopped and Kristina raised her head and opened her eyes, Bodies lay everywhere in various army uniforms. A soldier in a green uniform and visor stood with his laser aimed at her.

Kristina stood frozen on the spot and watched him raise his visor.

"John"

"Hello Kristina" John replied smiling

"It's good to see you" Kristina smiled

"Are you hurt?" John asked concerned.

"No we fell to the ground when the shots were fired" Kristina turned to watch her father getting up "Er du ok far" (are you ok father) she said helping her father up.

"ja, selvfølgelig" (yes of course) Ulrichsen replied.

Ulrichsen looked Stone up and down "You must be John Stone" He said.

"Yes I am" Stone replied

"Thank you for looking after her, you're a very brave man" He smiled at Stone

"Father whatever do you mean?" Kristina asked.

"I pleased to meet such a great man" Stone said addressing Ulrichsen.

"I am not great, I just want to do the right thing for the right people" Ulrichsen insisted.

"Well you certainly have done that" Stone replied

Another soldier appeared lifting his visor

"John we need to get out of here" Sam advised.

At that moment Sam fired his laser at Ulrichsen, his body was forced across the room and Stone immediately responded by shooting Sam.

"Why Sam, after all we have been through" Stone asked confused.

"I had to make it look convincing so that you can shoot me and escape" His friend said "So go get away" with those words he seemed to drift into unconsciousness.

Ulrichsen stood up and brushed himself off he looked at Kristina and Stone

"I am fine" Ulrichsen said

"But papa you have been injured, look at your leg" Kristina said concerned

"Only a flesh wound, I need to show you an escape route" He pointed ahead

"Look an escape route?" Stone asked.

"Yes we must go right now" Ulrichsen insisted.

He led them behind a glass screen and asked them to wait while he activated it.

They waited for a while and then a series of troops arrived, Stone prepared his laser but Ulrichsen placed his hand on the top of the weapon and whispered 'don't fire just watch and trust me'.

All the troops past without even looking over at where they were, he then used a remote control device creating voices from the next room. So the troops would proceed to investigate.

“What a clever device this is” Ulrichsen said smiling.

“But I don’t understand how did you do it?” Stone asked

“It was simply the use of false imagery with camouflage and sound effects simple stuff that fooled them”. Kristina said confidently.

“Yes while I was waiting to be rescued I began working on ways of escape” Ulrichsen said smiling.

“I would never have thought of that” Stone admitted

“Now for the next plan, we get into army suits and get away”. Kristina suggested.

One Kristina and her father had suited up, they headed towards the door, and it was at this time that Stone saw the brainstorm machine.

“Is that what all the fuss is about?” He asked “This enormous brain object”

“Yes this is brainstorm” Kristina said

“The thing that should have saved the world” Ulrichsen said.

“My god it’s like a massive scanning machine” Stone said in disbelief.

"Like an ultra sound or MRI scanner" Kristina said.

"It has to be destroyed, inside this machine is a self destruct mechanism that I am going to activate, so you two carry on while I activate it".

"But father you could get hurt" Kristina said concerned

"I will be fine believe me" Ulrichsen insisted he then spoke in Norwegian to Kristina

"Jeg elsker deg, stol på meg" (I love you, trust me).

Kristina smiled "Jeg elsker deg"

Kristina and Stone left the room and headed down a long corridor, troops were everywhere all heading for the exit.

Ulrichsen prepared the machine for destruction, altering the timing device and pressing a number of switches. Kristina kept looking back hoping to see her father coming through the door, and then they heard a mighty roar that shook the building, followed by an explosion.

Kristina turned back and Stone gripped her by the arm, she pulled away and started to run back, Stone ran after her.

"Papa" She shouted "Jeg forstør ikke" (I don't understand)

She fell onto her knees and began to cry, some of the troops returned to see what was happening.

"Is everything alright" One of the troops asked

"Yes of course" Stone said helping Kristina up "She lost a few colleagues in that last explosion".

"Come trooper, man up we have more work to do" Stone said squeezing her arm.

"Yes sir she shouted, I am okay" Kristina began racing with the others out of the building and once they were out the entire building exploded.

Stone headed for an army vehicle and told the others that their unit had been destroyed so he was heading for the next base. In reality he was going elsewhere to plan the future. They went into the forest and arrived in at a log cabin where they remained for a few days, Kristina was grieving for her father but when he asked her to trust him she was a little confused.

She sat beside an open fire and stared into it, deep in thought, Stone walked over to her offering her a warm drink. Sit with me John here on the rug, I want you close to me". Kristina had tears in her eyes.

Stone remained silent and did as she said, he sat close to her and she lowered her head onto his right shoulder. They both felt the warmth from the fire and from each others flesh, Stone could feel Kristina's tears dripping onto his neck and felt helpless as she cried.

"I wish that I could find the words to comfort you Kristina" Stone said stroking her head. "Feel so helpless in these situations after all its not in our agents manual".

"John I feel like I have known you forever" Kristina gripped hold of the hand that was stroking her head. "Your kind and considerate, a true gentleman, you have never taken advantage of me and I respect you for that".

"I must confess I have thought about it" Stone admitted.

"Yes but you haven't until now" Kristina said kissing him on the lips.

Stone kissed her back, Kristina tilted her cup and the contents went onto her dress.

She removed it and continued to kiss him passionately, Stone responded by removing his clothes and exposing his naked chest. Kristina was now naked and hugging Stone tightly; he could smell her perfume and a natural smell from her body that told him she truly wanted him. But he still had to ask her after all was it him that she desired or comfort from her bereavement.

"Kristina are you sure about this?" Stone asked

"Of course, why don't you want to do it" Kristina said with disappointment in her voice.

"Yes I do" Stone replied

Kristina pushed Stone down to the floor and climbed on top of him; she squeezed her thighs into him and rubbed herself against him. Her naked breasts moved about in front of his face and he caressed her hard nipples and gently massaged her breasts. She continued to rub her genitals against his and became excited making groaning noises. Stone then penetrated her body with his penis and she yelled out in ecstasy, she became more and more passionate and they made love in various positions.

Once they had satisfied each other they both lay down beside each other closely then Kristina lay across Stone and began kissing his hairy chest.

"I could easily fall in love with you John" Kristina admitted

"I could easily do the same" Stone confessed.

"I could live the rest of my life with you" Kristina continued "Here in this place with no one to disturb us".

"Me too never having to see anyone again" Stone said looking into her eyes.

The next morning they awoke covered in a blanket from the settee, Kristina awoke first and kissed John on the forehead. She then got up put some of her clothes on and went upstairs. She had filled a bath with water and foam. John entered the room as she sank into the water.

"Come and join me" She offered

Stone did so and they lay opposite each other in the bath, Kristina began teasing Stone with her feet touching him in certain areas.

“I like bubbles don’t you?”

“Yes so soft and stimulating” Stone agreed.

At that moment they heard a noise from downstairs, Stone jumped out of the water

“Stay there” He ordered

“Yes okay” She agreed.

Stone kept into the bedroom and put on some clothes, then he grabbed a weapon and proceeded downstairs. As he reached the foot of the stairs he noticed troops there, “Drop the weapon” one of the troops said.

Stone realised that he had no choice but to obey the command, so he threw down his weapon he turned around and faced two androids.

“I must compliment you Commander Murray on you finding this place” Stone said turning back towards Murray “And this must be Alison the double agent Alison Hager”.

“Oh well done John Stone what a good agent you are” Murray said removing his helmet.

“Spot on Stone” Alison said removing her helmet.

“How did you find us?” Stone asked

“It was easy, look at Kristina’s wrist?” Murray said smiling.

“A bangle perhaps small but effective” Alison said showing him her bangle.

Murray nodded to Alison “Go and get the girl and we can go”.

“Tell me Murray what do you need Kristina for if you have lost brainstorm?” Stone asked

“To create a new brainstorm that will infiltrate mind and manipulate thought patterns” Murray explained. “But I have no use for you Stone so you can die”.

“Stop!”, Shouted Kristina “I will do nothing without John”.

“Okay, lets go” Murray insisted.

However when they left the building shots were being fired, one of the androids exploded then the other. Shot were fired in all directions Murray and others tried to escape, but each one were stopped by laser blasts. Stone jumped on Murray and they began to fight on the ground meanwhile Kristina fired a laser at Alison. Alison fell off a wall and landed badly on the ground hitting her head. Stone and Murray continued to roll around the floor fighting until a trooper shot Murray in the head. She removed her helmet and watched the last terrorist die beside her.

“Sylvia!” Kristina shouted

"Darling" Came cheery words from Sylvia's mouth

"I thought Andrea had killed you in the house raid" Kristina said

"Hardly darling she couldn't hit a barn door at close range" Sylvia laughed.

Kristina hugged her "It okay we are going to surprise you now" Sylvia said leading her to her vehicle.

"What do you mean Sylvia?"

"Come on you will see" Sylvia said excitedly.

They went in a small shuttle craft then Sylvia suggested that she removed the bangle, but Stone advised them to drop it mid-flight over the Baltic Sea before they entered Sweden. They landed amongst trees where a building suddenly emerged, once they had left the shuttle they noticed the entrance guarded by androids. They entered the building and walked down a long corridor towards a laboratory. When they entered to their astonishment was 'brainstorm' the magnificent machine with scientist's milling round her.

"My god is it real or am I just dreaming" Kristina remembered a young girl asking this question as she came back to normality from a brain operation performed by brainstorm.

"Yes it is the original and guess what?" Sylvia said pointing to one of the doors

"Papa?" Kristina said in astonishment "But how?"

"I faked the explosion and that was not the original brainstorm, I remember what you said about trust and had the original one sent here days before the raid, they stole a copy. But in order to carry on the important work, we made two more which are located in two other isolated areas in the world. We can work separately for a while and John can help you".

"Yes papa brainstorm lives on thanks to you; we will accomplish your dream". Kristina said looking at John.

"But, what about my work, as an agent?" Stone said

"You are retired from duty John" Sylvia said "Enjoy your new life".

The idea of being involved in a new project thrilled Stone immensely, not only was he given a good job as head of security, he also married Kristina and they had two daughters called Kari and Sylvia after the two most influential women in Kristina's life. The brainstorm project was a success and years later millions of people were cured from brain damage and brain diseases; this led to more research and followed on with other operations that included all parts of the body. Brainstorm revolutionised the technology of medicine to such a degree that Ulrichsen was awarded the Nobel peace prize years later.

FOR THE LOVE OF CHARLOTTE

INTRODUCTION

It all began in Rome as Charlotte from Manchester met Harry from Brooklyn, New York in May 2000. Their romance grew until they became inseparable and in May of 2001 Charlotte moved in with Jack. All went well until the September of 9/11, Harry was working in the World Trade Centre Twin Towers when a plane went crashing into one of the buildings. The question was would he have been one of the fatalities there or did he survive, also was Charlotte killed as she went to search for him?

While writing this fictitious love story I was mindful of people's feelings and whilst researching the facts I endeavoured to make the story as real as the tragic moments that actually took place. This was one of the most tragic events in America's history and still raw for numerous people. Many people will never forget the tragic events that took place on the 11th September 2001, I can only imagine what people must have felt like; I watched it on television and couldn't believe what I was seeing. I hope in my approach to this sensitive matter that I have not offended anyone. I went to O'Hara's bar near Ground Zero and saw their book of remembrance; I also went to St Paul's Church in Manhattan and visited their memorial. Ground Zero has two fountains where the Twin Towers once stood with plaques on each side with all the names of the victims inscribed on them. It is an eerie place, close by outside another building is a screen with a key pad, you tap in a name and a picture of the victim appears, with details about them. Some people come from across the other side of the world in order to pay respects to their friends or relatives, some of us visit because we feel for their loved ones and for the victims that died so bravely. Please read the dedication at the end of this book, thank you.

MANCHESTER 1996

Charlotte Haywood was a nursing student based at the University of Salford for her theory and who was placed at Royal Oldham Hospital for most of her practice work. Charlotte was quite a shy girl, but was so confident when it came to hands on nursing. To look at Charlotte she appeared ordinary, she had blonde hair and wore silver framed spectacles, which hid part of her beauty. Her eyes were bright blue with a fair complexion she was slim but shapely her skin was soft and unblemished.

It was a Saturday in Manchester, which meant that the city would be crowded especially around the shopping areas and central park area known as Piccadilly Gardens. Charlotte had gone into what she called 'town' with her University friends and her sister Abigail tagged along. Abigail was slightly larger in proportion than Charlotte with darker hair; she was more out going and dressed more elegantly. Charlotte was the type to dress in jeans a white t-shirt and a black jacket or a Kaori long coat, she often had slogans on her t-shirts or badges to demonstrate her disregard for conformism or to show how she felt about society.

Charlotte had just left the Arndale Shopping Centre and crossed the road to another store; they had no sooner entered the building when they heard a loud bang and the building vibrated. Glass shattered and spread and the force threw them all to the ground it all happened in slow motion, mannequins went in all directions along with clothes. Charlotte noticed Abigail and her friends lying on the floor, Abigail had blood on her leg, Charlotte felt a trickling down her face and realised that she too was bleeding. Her eyes blurred and she collapsed and fell onto Abigail's body. When she awoke her friends had gone, leaving her and Abigail in the building.

She looked at her and suddenly shouted "Abigail are you alright, Abigail speak to me." She got no response.

Charlotte staggered out side shouting "Help me!"

When she noticed a lot of people rushing about shouting and screaming, an ambulance crew, police and fire brigade were helping injured people on the street. After a while one of the ambulance team came forward to help her, she noticed her friends further down the street and told the medic about them and about Abigail in the store. Fortunately that day there were no fatalities and the injured people were taken to a local hospital and their injuries were attended to effectively. It was later discovered that the IRA (Irish Republican Army) had planted a bomb in a van right next to the Arndale Shopping Centre this caused damages streets away and took months to rebuild the area.

Charlotte had her head injuries attended to and her sister Abigail had scars on her leg where the glass had penetrated her flesh from knee to toe. Her friends suffered shock and minor injuries; they had left the building to seek help for Charlotte and her sister. They carried on studying at Salford University but had to go around the outskirts of the city in order to get transport anywhere. The whole outer perimeter was sectioned off until the city could be cleaned up.

Charlotte visited a clairvoyant with her sister, hoping to find answers to her future and keep her mother happy with news of romance and possibly children, maybe this would quieten her down for a while Charlotte thought. The clairvoyant seemed odd dressed with her wild hair and badly matching clothes pinks with blues and everything baggy despite her being such a large lady.

"Come in," came an odd voice that easily matched her clothes.

"Are you the clairvoyant?" Charlotte asked hoping she would reply no I am the cleaner or something.

"I am the clairvoyant," she replied a little disgruntled at her and scratching her matted nest. "Please sit down," she said pointing to a badly stained seat.

Reluctantly Charlotte sat as requested, but thinking that she would rather stand, she observed as a cat stepped into a litter tray and performed a bowel action.

"So you must be Charlotte?" she said watching the bored expression on Charlotte's face and realising that she didn't really want to be there. Obviously she had been coaxed to come and would rather be in a pub or protesting at some march for Green Peace.

"Well to begin with I can see that you love nature and fight for what you consider right," she was doing what psychologists would term a cold reading, observing the subject and commenting on what they see. This is not difficult as long as you have a keen eye and state the obvious.

"Yes I do care for everyone and everything," Charlotte replied.

"I suppose you're in the caring profession?" continued the clairvoyant.

"Yes I am a nurse," Charlotte said proudly.

"You are well travelled and you have been to some very nice places," she said looking at the badges on her coat of Japan, Sweden and other countries.

"I get around," Charlotte said realising that she was observing her clothing.

She then removed a pack of tarot cards from the draw beside her chair and asked Charlotte to shuffle them for her, and then layer them on the table in some form of pattern. She then turned one over and looked surprised, she glanced at Charlotte and then back at the card.

"Oh you're going to cross water," she said coughing and clearing her throat.

"Oh that's a surprise!" Charlotte said sarcastically.

"No you don't understand this is to meet a man," she described a dark haired man with a foreign accent.

After finishing with the tarot cards she looked at the palm of her hands, it was then that she began saying really odd things.

She raised one arm "A lady is waiting to greet you in a foreign land with her one hand held high and the other holding a book, but I also see tragedy in this place buildings on fire and heart break for many," she bowed her head then lifted it, tears were in her eyes "Such sorrow and a place to avoid on the 9th month."

"People are going to die?" Charlotte said surprised.

"Yes don't be there then my dear," she said "But I also see a child in your life, a boy and the apple of your eye."

"Am I only having one child?" Charlotte asked disappointedly.

"Yes that is so, but bear in mind my warning, tragedy bestows the place you are going to visit and two numbers come to mind nine and eleven, the ninth month and eleven," the clairvoyant seemed very disturbed.

Charlotte left the room bewildered, Abigail entered confidently after her, to have her reading, she seemed a lot happier with hers than Charlotte. After it had finished they both left and discussed their readings with each other although neither seemed completely happy.

“So what was that all about?” Charlotte asked in bewilderment.

“I don’t know but she must have been talking about someone else,” Abigail said.

“Some woman holding her arm up and hanging on to some book!” Charlotte said deep in thought, “It’s nobody that I know.”

“I have to avoid some place because of a pending disaster, must be Manchester or somewhere, but she did say across water.” Charlotte said with an expression of doubt on her face.

“New York silly, she saw the Statue of Liberty, it has to be,” Abigail said showing Charlotte a photograph.

“So it is well I never,” Charlotte said in surprise, “But I’m not going there!”

“Well you never know, in years to come you could do,” Abigail said confidently.

“What if I do meet someone?” Charlotte said after a moment’s thought.

“Cricky Charlotte give it neck will you, you never have done yet!” Abigail said.

“No I’m not mithered either way,” Charlotte said shrugging her shoulders.

WHEN IN ROME

It was a bright morning in the beginning of May 2000; Charlotte woke up to Abigail singing out of tune to her favourite pop song. Charlotte put her hand over her ears hoping to drown out the sound but even this didn't work, so she placed her spectacles on and dressing gown and walked down the stairs.

It was no quieter in the kitchen with all the banging and clattering about, but the smell of freshly cooked bacon and percolated coffee was inviting.

"Hahaaaaa!" said her father, "So nice of you to join us," he said sarcastically.

Charlotte sat at the table and frowned at him "It is Sunday and I am not at Uni," she reminded him.

"I get up at 5.30 every morning rain or shine," her father said.

Charlotte was mimicking him as she had heard the words so many times before.

"Henry we can't all be like you," her mother replied.

"Yes I am not like you Dad!" Charlotte insisted.

"You should be working earning money," Henry went on.

"I'm a student nurse Dad, I have a career!" Charlotte said surprised at her father's attitude towards her.

"Yes your princess is going to be a nurse," her mother said defending her.

"I thought you wanted her to get married and have children?" Henry said spreading butter on his toast.

"I do more than anything else but a career is a career," her mother said.

"Married me!" Charlotte said choking on her coffee.

"Mary I think the shock nearly killed her, bless her," Henry said laughing

"I'm a free agent like my dad was," Charlotte insisted.

"You're stubborn like him," Mary said.

"I am not stubborn I just stand up for my rights!" Henry said.

"We are both stubborn dad admit it," Charlotte said laughing.

At that moment Abigail came down the stairs continuing to sing out of tune.

“Now she’s like you mother!”

“Charlotte when do you travel to Rome?” Abigail asked.

“On Friday why?” Charlotte asked.

“Can I sleep in your room?” Abigail wanted to know because her room was larger.

“I suppose so but don’t use my stuff,” Charlotte was referring to her make up and clothes.

“Ok I won’t,” Abigail always said she wouldn’t but did.

“Suppose you’re going alone as usual?” Mary asked.

“Of course,” Charlotte said confidently.

“Don’t you feel vulnerable?” Mary asked concerned.

“No I love it alone and free, I meet people there,” Charlotte explained.

“But it’s dangerous,” Henry said concerned.

“Oh and Manchester isn’t?” Charlotte said thinking of the bombing and countless gang wars.

“She has a point Dad,” Abigail said showing him the local news paper about crimes in Manchester.

The time came for Charlotte to travel to Rome, she had packed the night before and was all prepared for her journey.

She had booked a taxi to the airport and said her goodbyes to her family before setting off from her home. Once at the airport she was waiting at the departure lounge thinking about her many journeys from the very same airport. She had been to Japan, Thailand, Canada and Sweden. But she had a feeling this was going to be a special journey with life changing events; she sat on the plane and continued to think about Rome. She arrived in Rome and caught a taxi to the hotel; she was admiring the scenery en route when she noticed a man running across the street with a camera, a car narrowly missed him and he fell beside the taxi. She jumped out and helped him up, he swept the dust from his trousers and spoke to her.

"Thank you, my name's Harry."

"I'm Charlotte can I take you anywhere?" She said pointing to the taxi.

"No its ok I'm only going across the street."

He walked away and left Charlotte thinking, she had let him go, he was slim, dark and handsome and she had let him go. She got to the hotel and couldn't stop thinking about him; it was fate she was supposed to meet him. But she had no phone number or address the moment had come and gone, she was so annoyed with herself a moment wasted never to be repeated. A few days passed and Charlotte was sight seeing at the Coliseum she was about to take a photograph when she heard a man with an American accent.

"Nice view isn't it?" the man said.

"What?" Charlotte said surprised realising it was Harry.

"The view I love Rome don't you?" Harry said.

"Have you been here before?" Charlotte said struggling to make conversation, as she felt nervous in his presence.

"I came here last year with my ex-girlfriend," he said realising who he was talking to, she was the girl who helped him.

"It's you, Charlotte!" Harry said smiling.

He remembered my name Charlotte thought, but said nothing about it, obviously he must like her to remember her name.

"So you split up with your girlfriend?" Charlotte said crossing her fingers behind her back.

"Yes it didn't work out," Harry said.

"Sorry to hear that Harry," Charlotte said feeling relieved that she had a chance to be with him.

"So have you got anyone special?" Harry asked.

"No I haven't" Charlotte replied trying not to sound desperate.

"So did you come here alone like me?" Harry asked.

"Yes I often do," Charlotte replied wishing she had not said those words.

"My word you're brave" Harry said impressed by her bravery.

"No I prefer to be alone, I like my own company," Charlotte wanted to kick herself because her mouth was working alone out of her control.

"Oh sorry, do you want to be alone?" Harry asked disappointedly.

"No it's ok," Charlotte said quickly hoping not to put Harry off.

"So why don't we sight see together?" Harry suggested.

"Well I don't know!" Charlotte was now playing hard to get.

"Oh, I didn't want to seem pushy you have probably got other plans!" Harry said confused at her reaction.

"Look if I didn't want you to be with me I would simply say do one!" Charlotte said smiling.

"Do one?" Harry seemed even more confused by her comment.

"Yes it's a polite word that means piss off!" Charlotte said cringing underneath.

"Ok so you mean we can sight see together?" Harry said.

"Yes! Okay what about the Trevi fountain?" Charlotte suggested.

"Okay the Trevi fountain it is" Harry said.

They travelled to the Trevi fountain and both threw a coin in and made a wish, it was the same wish of course - to be together.

They went from there to the Vatican, Caesars Palace and many other attractions. On their final day together they went to an Italian restaurant, the evening was warm and clear. Charlotte had bought a special dress for the occasion as she had not packed one. Harry however did have a suit and he looked very smart, he was stunned by her appearance she looked so beautiful, wearing a green dress with small flowers on it.

"Well I have had a great week with you," Harry said.

"Me too, but I don't even know what you do for a living," Charlotte said inquisitively.

"I work for a company in New York at the World Trade Centre, Twin Towers," Harry explained.

"I'm a nurse, I work in Manchester, England," Charlotte said eager to tell him more. "I work in a hospital on a medical ward," Charlotte continued.

"That's nice, you are an angel I think!" Harry said joking.

"An angel with clipped wings," Charlotte replied. "I am no angel Harry."

"I shall miss you Charlotte," Harry admitted.

"You will probably forget about me after this week," Charlotte said with a sad face.

"No way, I think you're wonderful and I can see a future for us," Harry was quite sincere and having found her he didn't want to let her go.

"I think so too," Charlotte said feeling exactly the same.

"Well here's to us," Harry said raising his glass of wine.

"To us," Charlotte said clinking her glass to his.

They left the restaurant and headed to the hotel where Harry was staying, Charlotte and Harry spent the night together making passionate love almost all night long to some amazing music. In the morning they woke up together snuggled up to each other.

Then next night was a little different as Charlotte wanted Harry to see her true colours, or rather for him to meet the real Charlotte, not the meek and mild, innocent girl, but a wilder more promiscuous woman that lurked beneath those sparkling blue eyes and pearly white smile.

This time Harry visited her hotel only to find that Charlotte had a surprise for him, when she opened her door she was dressed in a leopard bikini. She pulled him inside and led him straight to her bedroom. She started to undo his shirt buttons very methodically then kissed his neck and started to work down his chest, she then began to lick him like a cat, stoking his back with her claws.

It was then that he realised that she had a vivid imagination and liked to play out fantasy parts, animals usually, like tigers clawing and biting their prey.

Harry rather liked the tiger role but didn't like her being too rough, especially when he struggled to walk afterwards. He had scratch marks on his back from when they were making love, she had unintentionally drawn blood. Her tiger mask was the best feature as she could hide behind it and be whoever she wanted to be and not care.

She had stripped him naked bringing him to her level, she was the permissive one and made him the submissive on this occasion. This increased her power and put her in control, Harry was ordered to do as he was told and she would fulfil his fantasy. She found some oil and rubbed him with it, massaging his chest, arms and legs, then began clawing at him and stroking his body. He moved forward and she pushed him back then began kissing him and rubbing the inside of his thighs against his stomach. She then removed her top and shook her breasts at him, he remained silent and appeared to be a little embarrassed. She was clearly in control and loving it, she was also able to tease him and he was powerless.

She pulled at his pants until she had removed them and then played with his penis, watching him lose control of his feelings. Then she removed her bikini bottoms and allowed him to make love to her, enjoying her game and feeling on fire, hot and passionate. She was in control for most of the night, Harry had thought that he had met another woman and never expected such a passionate night, even though it was rough and he was injured.

Charlotte and Harry had a more relaxing day, this may be because Charlotte had given him an adventurous night to remember. But that evening Harry invited Charlotte back to his hotel, Charlotte offered to meet him in his room and with her poor memory forgot the number, he was in 223 and she thought it was 232. She was dressed up under a thin coat as a nun, she knocked the door to this room and noticed it was open.

"Harry," she whispered. "Where are you?"

A man was lying on the bed, his body was straight and his arms at his side. The lights were low, so Charlotte crept up to him.

"God Harry what's up its Charlotte come on let's get you going!" Charlotte said trying to rouse him. "Have you got a stuffy?" she said laughing.

She slid down beside him and then began to kiss him. "God Harry you're cold, let me warm you up."

Suddenly the light went on and a woman screamed, "Who is she and why is she in bed with my dead husband?"

Two men grabbed her, "Get the fuck off me!" Charlotte shouted.

"What are you doing here?" one of the men shouted.

"I was after Harry," Charlotte replied.

"This is Harry!" The woman shouted.

"Not him I don't do stiffs! She shouted. "At least not like this!"

"Get out of here, you're a disgrace to your faith," the woman continued.

"I don't make a habit of it!" Charlotte said. "Anyway he's old!"

With that she left the room and ran back to her hotel a few streets away, but left her coat behind. She got changed as a nurse and went to find Harry's room this time the body was being taken into the elevator, Charlotte tried to hide her face, but was spotted by one of the men.

"Oh nurse can you please look at my mother she has had a terrible shock?"

Charlotte nodded then cringed when she saw who it was, the grieving widow of the man she shared a bed with as a nun.

"You look familiar," she said peering at her and speaking with a posh accent in the Queen's English.

"No not me I don't come from round here, I'm just at a nurses convention," Charlotte said examining her.

"So you're English?" she asked.

"Yes from Manchester with some other nurses," Charlotte face became bright red, something that often happened when she lied.

"Charlotte there you are," Harry shouted.

"And doctors are attending," Charlotte quickly added. "Well you certainly seem fine now," she said turning to see Harry.

"What the hell!" Harry said shocked.

"I need a doctor, young man you will do," the woman said.

"What?" Harry said surprised.

Charlotte winked at him and whispered, "Go along with it I will explain later."

"But!" Charlotte put a finger on his mouth.

"Yes well, what seems to be wrong?" Harry said confidently.

"Well you tell me doctor!" the woman annoyed.

"Well are you sick?" Harry said puzzled.

"I've lost my husband then some nun was in his bed trying to make love to him!" she said angrily.

"Oh I can see why you are upset, gosh yes," Harry was trying to put two and two together but didn't get four.

"Are you American?" she asked.

"Yes mam I am," Harry said happily.

"Oh at an English medical convention?" she continued. "Rather out of your way aren't you?"

"A special invitation," Harry quickly added.

With that the woman went with the rest of her party, her son thanked her and Charlotte and Harry entered the elevator and after a few seconds started laughing.

"You were great Harry," Charlotte said. "A fucking natural!"

"Well if you've got it" Harry boasted. "So speaking of which how do you make it with a dead man?"

"Let me come to your room and I will show you!" Charlotte said laughing uncontrollably. "Shit!" she said stumbling.

"What's wrong?" Harry said concerned.

"I've just pissed myself!" Charlotte said holding her groin.

As they left the elevator they met a man in the corridor who noticed Harry holding her.

"Is she alright?" he asked.

"Yes. She's a nurse," Harry said supporting her down the corridor.

Their holiday was all but over as Charlotte was due back home in the morning. It's true that she could do a lot in this time, Charlotte being the person she was but could Rome handle such a woman! Harry was certainly exhausted although he did say he wanted to see her again, he even gave her his phone number and address which she put in the travel bag of her hand luggage. She put it inside a little side pocket last minute when she was packing. Harry had Charlotte's address too at one stage, she wrote it on a receipt from a shopping trip.

Charlotte was at the airport with Harry, they had a final embrace before she went through security.

"Well I will miss you," Charlotte said smiling.

"I will miss you too Charlotte," Harry said. "Now you have my address?"

"Yes of course, it's in my hand luggage right here," Charlotte said pulling the paper out of the side pocket. "See."

Harry smiled and kissed her tenderly on the lips, he could taste her lipstick.

"Hmmm cherries!" he said laughing. "I am glad you didn't do anything at the Vatican!" Harry said joking.

"Oh I would have dressed up as a little devil," Charlotte said wickedly.

"Now that would have been worth seeing," Harry said amused.

"Believe me you haven't seen anything yet!" Charlotte said laughing as she left Harry waving to her.

BACK HOME

Charlotte returned home to face her family and tell them her news; she was so excited about her news about Harry. She hoped that her family would take the news well and eventually meet Harry; she wanted her family to accept Harry and get to like him as she did. When she arrived back home all her family were there so she decided to tell them straight away.

"While you are all here let me tell you about Harry," Charlotte said excited.

"You have actually met someone?" Henry said surprised.

"Well yes, he is wonderful," Charlotte said watching the reactions on their faces.

"Where is he from?" Mary asked.

"Brooklyn, New York," Charlotte replied.

"Not English then?" Henry said in a sarcastic manner.

"No, he is American and he works in the World Trade Centre" Charlotte explained.

"That's good," Abigail said. "So have you got his address?" she said inquisitively.

"Of course it's in a pocket in my hand luggage, let me show you," Charlotte began looking in the pocket of her hand luggage.

Charlotte began to panic, as she looked deeper in the pocket, then opened the bag and took everything out carefully examining each piece of paper.

"I've lost it, I don't believe it!" Charlotte said getting upset.

"Charlotte, how did you manage to do that?" Abigail said then watched her sister repeat her search.

"Surely he has your address doesn't he?" Mary said concerned.

"Yes he has so he can call me," Charlottes face lit up and she began to smile again.

"So stop worrying if he likes you he will contact you," Mary said reassuringly, kissing her on the forehead.

"Ok thanks Mom," Charlotte said smiling.

A week went by without a word, no letter, and no emails absolutely nothing. Months went by and still no word, by now Charlotte was beginning to think that he didn't care. Maybe he had found someone else, and so she had to move on, sometimes life can be very cruel. Charlotte approached her family and friends for advice hoping that they would have the answer to her problem.

"Charlotte you know where he works and his full name so get in touch with there," Abigail advised.

"That's what they said at work," Charlotte said.

Charlotte began to take steps to contact Harry by phone; she managed to reach the World Trade Centre South Tower and tried each department from the eighty third floor upwards. Eventually she was successful in contacting one of his work colleagues who was at his desk when he spoke to her.

"This is Charlotte Brooks I am trying to contact Harry Trent?" she had her fingers crossed.

"Hi Charlotte this is Geoff Mason I work with Harry he has been talking about you for a month or more, he couldn't get hold of you are you ok?" Geoff said relieved to hear her voice, Geoff was about ten years older than Harry heavy built with short cropped hair and a moustache.

"Geoff it's so good to hear from you, I lost his details," Charlotte explained.

"Gee must have cost you a fortune to find him," Geoff said concerned.

"Well it's worth it to find him," Charlotte said relieved.

"Well he will be back shortly so give me your phone number and I will pass it on to him ok," Geoff said searching for a blank piece of paper.

Geoff wrote down the number and then left the office, he began walking down the corridor and passed a woman who had her dark hair up in a bun and wore glasses.

"Hi Jackie," he said politely.

"Oh hi Geoff, have you sorted those papers for me?" Jackie asked, she was slim and walked very straight backed acting very official.

"Yes they are on the desk," Geoff replied.

Jackie entered the office and picked up the papers including Charlotte's phone number that Geoff had written down.

Harry entered the office and Geoff had returned from the restaurant with some food.

"I got the last cake on the stand," Geoff said smiling.

"Geoff you know I've lost my appetite since Rome," Harry said sadly.

"Well I have news for you," Geoff said. "She has been in touch."

"When?" Harry said excitedly.

"About an hour ago, I have her phone number here somewhere," Geoff said searching for it.

"Geoff you need to seriously sort your desk out it looks just like an earthquake has hit it!" Harry said assisting him to look.

"Jackie was here she took some papers, she could have picked it up with them," Geoff said pointing to the door.

"I will phone her, no I will go there to her downstairs," Harry said excitedly.

"Upstairs next floor up," Geoff pointed up to the next floor.

"Geoff you're a life saver, next floor up?" Harry needed clarification.

"Yes quickly before she throws it away," Geoff advised.

Harry rushed outside and caught the elevator to the next level, Harry was a fit man and usually ran up and down stairs rather than use an elevator that was usually occupied or broken down. But he was in so much of a hurry to get the number off Jackie. As he entered her office she had just found the phone number and Charlotte's name and was on the phone to Geoff.

"Have you lost a phone number belonging to Charlotte Brookes?" Jackie asked watching Harry approaching through the glass in her door.

"It belongs to Harry, hang on to it he's on the way," Geoff said relieved that she had found it.

"He's here now," Jackie replied.

"Jackie have you got…." Jackie was holding up the message and stopped Harry in mid conversation.

"You are amazing Jackie!" Harry said kissing the message.

"I do my best," Jackie replied shrugging her shoulders. "Besides I am all for true love and all that," she said laughing.

"She is amazing and we want to be together," Harry said dreamily.

"My god where's my bucket I want to throw up!" Jackie said jokingly.

"I have got to ring her now," Harry said eagerly.

"It will be late in England," Jackie said alarmed.

"Why how many hours difference?" Harry asked.

"At least five hours, she will be asleep right now," Jackie said concerned about disturbing Charlotte.

"Phone her in the morning and for god sake, don't lose that number," Jackie said although she had already copied it into her cell phone in case he did lose it.

However Charlotte was awake and kept looking at her phone in case she had a message or he was trying to ring her. She hardly slept that night, she was thinking of Harry and imagining that he had got the message and was not bothered about contacting her, even though Geoff had said that Harry could not think of anything but her. She had convinced herself that their relationship was over and that he desired someone else who was probably more his type, attractive and intelligent, who was more than likely American bearing in mind the location of where he lived and worked. Perhaps her life was all about travelling and meeting guys around the world, having incredible sex and moving on. Had Charlotte got a brick for a heart and had no feelings maybe she could have brief romances and then tell men to 'do one'. But Charlotte was much deeper than that she was so sensitive and had a heart of gold, or was it glass because it broke so easily. Charlotte was up early the next morning getting ready for work, she went down for breakfast and sat quietly eating toast, at least she was pecking at it like a bird!

"Honestly Charlotte you need to eat your almost anorexic now," Mary said concerned.

"I can't eat I feel sick" Charlotte said staring into space. "Anyway I can't be mithered."

"This is about Harry again isn't it?" Mary said angrily.

"Oh mother you know how I feel about him," Charlotte replied.

"Forget him he is obviously not bothered about you, why chase after him?" Mary said worried about her feelings for him, she wanted to protect her from harm and felt that Harry was a lost cause.

"So he's made the effort calling you, that's right all for the love of Charlotte!" Mary said sarcastically.

"Don't say that, according to Geoff he does love me," Charlotte shouted.

"Then why hasn't he phoned?" Mary asked. "That's because he doesn't bloody care."

"You don't know him, he's sweet and kind, handsome and a gentleman." Charlotte was being to get upset sobbing into a tissue.

"Darling I don't want to hurt you, just make you see sense," Mary said trying to comfort her.

"You should meet him then you will know, I love everything about him and he loves me," Charlotte explained.

"Yes but it was a holiday romance, a brief encounter that's all," Mary tried to reason with Charlotte.

It was eight o'clock in the morning when the home landline rung, Charlotte looked at her mother.

"I am late for work," Charlotte announced and put her coat on holding a piece of toast between her teeth, dropping crumbs on her nursing uniform.

"Wait!" her mother shouted. "It's him."

The toast dropped out of her mouth and onto the floor, she headed towards the phone and looked in a mirror adjusted her hair and checked her make up.

"Charlotte he can't see you," Mary reminded her. "And put your bloody specs on!"

"Hiya!" Charlotte shouted putting her glasses on or bins as her mother called them.

"Oh for god sake, he's not deaf either," Mary continued.

"I miss you too, it seems like ages since we spoke last," Charlotte said still sounding upset.

"No, I have been scriking," Charlotte said in her broad Manchester accent.

Her mother tutted and then walked out of the room in order to give her some privacy.

"Scriking, you know, crying," Charlotte explained, "just upset about something, mom was vexed and," Charlotte had to explain herself again. "Vexed, angry,"

"You're coming here, well all right I will mention it to me Mam."

Harry got off the phone a little confused with the conversation and her accent, however he seemed much happier and able to get on back to sleep for a while before going to work.

When Harry reached the World Trade Centre South Building he went through security and spoke to one of the guards he knew.

"Morning Arnie," he said in a jolly manner.

Arnie was his nickname because he resembled Arnold Schwarzenegger; his real name was Douglas or Doug. He seemed to throw his body around as he walked finding it hard to adjust properly. It was said that this was due to his army days when a shell exploded in close proximity affecting his hearing. His balance has been compromised since this time and he often becomes clumsy. Even so he is reported to be one of the best security officers in the building, a well-respected man who is dedicated to his job.

"Hi Harry," Doug said. "How are you?"

"On cloud nine," Harry replied.

"So you got in touch with your girl?" Doug replied.

"Yes, her names Charlotte," Harry said smiling.

"Charlotte, true love hey Harry?" Doug said seeming pleased for Harry.

"Yes I would do anything for the love of Charlotte," Harry said starry eyed.

"God Harry I have never seen you like this before," Doug said laughing.

"Well I guess she does that to me, I'm planning a trip to England to meet her family," Harry said happily.

"Well good luck with that one Harry!" Doug said sincerely.

Harry walked to the elevator and noticed John and Janice standing inside, they seemed eager to see him and greeted him warmly.

"Hi Harry, how are you?" Janice said.

"How's it going Harry?" John said greeting him like a long lost friend.

"Hi, I'm fine and you too?" Harry asked.

"Can't complain," John said, "how was your trip to Rome?"

"Oh it was good," Harry replied not wishing to expand on it as he had mentioned it so many times before.

"Just good?" Janice asked expecting a longer explanation of the trip.

"Okay, well it was more than good, I met someone," Harry said.

"No you old dog what's she like?" John asked.

"A bit different, sort of attractive and a really nice personality," Harry said trying to explain about her.

"I heard you had found a nice girl and was trying to locate her in Manchester England," Janice said inquisitively.

"Well I found her and I am going to see her in England," Harry said when in reality he wanted to shout her name from the hilltops or the highest point in New York, the Empire State Building.

"Well good luck Harry, you deserve good luck," Janice said smiling.

"Yes good luck Harry, John said watching Harry leave the elevator.

Janice and John were like the parents that Harry never had they always invited Harry around for dinner on Sunday and were disappointed when Harry declined on occasions. But Harry didn't want to burden them and often felt guilty having their food even though he took a bottle each time and chocolates for Janice.

Charlotte phoned Harry once a week, Harry phoned Charlotte more often and so between them they were constantly in touch. Even with miles between them they grew closer together, they spoke about many subjects from movies to recent news and world affairs. Strangely enough Harry never mentioned his family only work colleagues, the very idea of acknowledging anyone outside New York was unthinkable. Charlotte thought this strange but nevertheless went along with Harry's wishes, if he wanted to discuss the subject he would have done.

After a few months passed Harry was beginning to miss not seeing Charlotte, although the internet had become a great tool for keeping in touch. The web cam was a useful item too enabling them to see each other although computers were quite basic back then and prone to crashing. Charlotte used to find Harry amusing as he began falling asleep in front of the screen almost falling off the chair. Harry was quite comical under his hard business exterior, often amusing his colleagues and Charlotte at the same time during his break. Charlotte loved American humour she watched many funny movies and situation comedies that had been exported to England. It was suggested that '***Friends***' and '***Frazier***' may have been the most popular at the time, amongst others.

Music was another thing they both shared although Harry ventured on the more classical music and lighter pop music, while Charlotte liked more heavy metal and earth moving to her mother and fathers dismay. Anything that caused the ceiling tiles to drop down or the nails to loosen from the floor board was worth listening to according to Charlotte.

"Turn that bloody row down," her father would shout up to her.

"It is down," came the reply.

"You must be deaf," her father shouted.

"No I like to feel the sound under my feet," Charlotte shouted back.

"They can feel that in Bolton and think it's an earthquake!" her mother said tutting.

In the August of the year 2000 Harry made his first trip to England, he was excited about meeting Charlotte again after a few months, he had done nothing but discuss her with some of his closest colleagues such as Geoff and John, Frank and Jackie. He was about to meet Charlotte's family and stay in Manchester, England. Harry boarded the plane from New York to Manchester; he was nervous about flying and experienced turbulence on the journey to England. He was also nervous about meeting and staying with Charlotte's parents. The flight seemed long and uncomfortable in economy class, a few screaming children and people moving about like they were on the pavements of a busy New York street like Broadway. Harry was pleased to exit the plane and get through security in Manchester airport.

Charlotte was waiting at the airport arrival area with a board and written on it was the words 'Welcome my Yankee friend, Harry come and meet Charlotte' I suppose that was typical of Charlotte who never failed to surprise people with her wit. Some people were amused at the sign others seemed quite offended, but Charlotte couldn't care less either way because she was the type of girl to make a statement, offend or not that was Charlotte.

She stood waiting dressed in a rather loud red, purple and pink t-shirt, a pair of jeans cut of at the knees and with designer holes here and there. She had sandals on her feet and her blonde hair just over her ears; she wore large glasses that seemed to be worn more for design than to adjust her vision.

Harry finally made an appearance and glanced around looking for Charlotte, as if it wasn't obvious where she was!

"Harry!" came the excited voice of a girl who was acting as if she had seen a pop or movie star.

Harry was wearing a grey suit and less obvious apart from his good looks, his eyes lit up like stars in the sky as he noticed Charlotte in the crowd.

"Charlotte well you look good, I hardly recognised you," Harry said sarcastically.

"Well, Harry look at you in your suit, my word you stand out," Charlotte had made her own attempt of sarcastic humour.

A cough came from behind Charlotte and a rather large woman emerged, she looked like a mixture of a wrestler and a body builder to Harry. He was a little apprehensive but Charlotte did warn Harry that she was a little scary on first appearance, Harry found this to be an understatement. He had visions of a small petite lady who was slightly reserved;

Charlotte had indicated that although northern men thought they were king of their castle, this was a misconception and that the women ruled.

“I’m Charlotte’s mother Mary,” Mary said introducing herself and shaking him firmly by the hand.

Harry’s thoughts were that if this was Charlotte’s mother god knows how she will end up, as slim as she is at present. Also what must her father be like, probably a champion wrestler or car mechanic, after all they are usually big.

When they got outside Harry breathed in the Manchester air, then coughed

“So this is Manchester,” Harry said looking around.

“No, it’s not really, just a small part, the real city you will see later,” Charlotte said smiling.

Charlotte’s father Henry was waiting by the car, he was smaller in stature than Mary and Charlotte was more like him.

“Hiya you must be Harry?” Henry said putting his hand out to greet Harry.

“Hi Mr Brookes,” Harry said politely.

Charlotte laughed “Mr Brookes?” she looked at Harry in disbelief. “Mr Brookes are you serious!”

"Now Harry, call me Henry," he said loading the cases in the boot of the car.

"Charlotte, Harry was just showing respect," Mary said embarrassed.

"I don't mind her teasing me, she's always doing it," Harry explained.

"Well as long as you're not offended," Mary continued. "Charlotte don't forget to show Harry all the sights."

"Oh I will do that alright!" Charlotte said laughing.

"I don't get it, what sights?" Harry asked.

"Museums, art galleries and theatres," Mary explained.

"Night clubs, pubs and the gay village more like," Charlotte said excitedly.

"Harry wants a history lesson not a culture shock," Mary said frowning at her.

"Well I don't mind really," Harry said looking at the expression on Charlotte's face, she was rolling her eyes and smiling at Harry.

Harry read her expression realising that Charlotte had her own ideas about fun in Manchester and remained silent, while Charlotte and her mother continued discussing their itinerary.

On arrival Harry noticed a set of terraced houses and opposite a row of semidetached houses this was typical of the more traditional buildings in Manchester. Harry had reached a working class area where minors once lived, he was to experience true life in the rural districts of Manchester warts and all.

Here a spade is a spade and people say what they think, nothing is wrapped in paper and decorated in ribbon. But as they say in Manchester you seen what you get and like it or lump it, offend or please. Harry gathered this from Charlotte and the way she was no heirs or graces, she was straight talking, but had a heart of gold.

Once they arrived home Charlotte took Harry straight to her room, she opened a few draws for him to place his clothes in.

“Welcome to my room, your clothes can go in here, unpack and make yourself at home,” Charlotte said showing Harry a tidy room.

Harry looked round at posters and a very feminine room, he noticed a dressing table with makeup neatly placed in a box. The room was painted partly in a pale green colour and wallpaper on one wall. She had a double bed with a green patterned bed spread and cuddly toys on her pillows.

“Nice room Charlotte,” Harry said unpacking his case.

“It’s okay I suppose,” Charlotte said watching him unpack.

Harry took a pair of shorts from his case and Charlotte began to laugh

"Harry, you have to be kidding, I mean are you serious?" Charlotte seemed to be mocking him.

"You don't like them?" Harry said offended by her remarks.

"They are hideous and what's more the weather here is not exactly the weather for shorts right now," Charlotte took them from him.

"Oh Harry I am going to have to dress you?" Charlotte held the shorts tightly.

"Come on Charlotte give them back," Harry insisted.

"Come and get them sexy," Charlotte teased him.

Charlotte started running around the room; Harry perused her as she jumped onto the bed and off the other side. Finally after a few minutes he caught up with her and they both fell on the floor. Charlotte dropped the shorts and began kissing Harry on the lips, Harry returned the kiss and they were fully embraced. Charlotte looked back at the open door, with one fast leap she managed to close and lock the door, she then closed the slats to the blinds.

Harry was undoing his shirt, while Charlotte removed her t-shirt, they began kissing again, tenderly and passionately. Charlotte removed her glasses and placed them on the dressing table. Harry removed his trousers while Charlotte pulled down her jeans and folded them neatly on the floor. They both lay on the bed and cuddled up together, both of them were stroking each other's back. Charlotte removed her bra and allowed Harry to caress her breasts, she then stroked his buttocks and he did the same. Soon they were both naked and it was just like their experience in Rome, as they began to make love but this time without the soft music in the background. They had to imagine moving to the rhythm of the beat and the magic moment of their warm and naked bodies being entwined. Harry could feel Charlotte's warm silky skin, soft and tender against his and her breath as she heaved in and out, moaning and groaning in ecstasy.

Harry too was making excited noises as his muscular body was moving rhythmically pushing his thighs against her, penetrating her body with his penis.

They made love for an hour and then lay beside one another, neither speaking for a while just enjoying each other's presence. The silence was broken by a knock at the door, Charlotte jumped up and spoke.

"Yes?" she shouted.

"Hiya Charlotte its Abigail," Abigail shouted back.

"Oh, hiya Abigail we'll see you downstairs in five minutes," Charlotte replied.

"Okay, hiya Harry," Abigail shouted teasing them.

"Hi Abigail," Harry shouted back unaware that Abigail was teasing them.

"Well what a tease," Charlotte said folding her arms.

"Really!" Harry said smiling.

"Oh yes that's my sister for you," Charlotte said starting to stand up.

"So you don't like my shorts?" Harry said laughing.

"Don't start that again, you're as bad as Abi," Charlotte said attacking Harry and knocking him out of the bed. They both landed on the floor and once again started kissing each other, Charlotte's soft warm lips were moist and her tongue entered his mouth sending a tingle down each other's spines. It was like an electrical current travelling from one body to the next, but instead of pain came a spasm of absolute delight, purely orgasmic.

After a while both Charlotte and Harry went downstairs, no one reacted to their absence, but Abigail kept smiling at Charlotte in a wicked manner.

"So is this Harry who we have heard so much about?" Abigail asked.

"Yes this is Harry all way from New York," Charlotte said proudly showing off her boyfriend.

"Yes, I work for a company of traders called Emblem Mechanics its one floor, and a great bunch of guys work there including my best buddy Geoff who Charlotte spoke to, in fact Geoff was the one who kept telling me to get in touch," Harry said happily.

"I bet you didn't need much persuading right," Henry said prompting Harry to say more.

"No after I initially met your daughter I kind of knew I loved her, back in Rome we saw all the sights together including the Vatican," Harry looked at Charlotte, "I guess we were meant to be together."

"Oh how romantic, isn't it Henry?" Mary said she had already picked the hat for the wedding.

"Mother really!" Abigail protested. "She has just met him and you have them married off!"

"Well true love and all that," Mary said looking at Harry and Charlotte snuggled together on the settee.

"Anyway tater ash for tea," Mary said confidently.

Harry had no idea what she was saying but bravely nodded in agreement, then looked at Charlotte hoping for a logical answer.

"What did she say?" Harry asked her when they were alone.

"It's a local dish with corn beef and potatoes," Charlotte explained, "she may do Lancashire hot pot tomorrow that's minced meat, potatoes and gravy."

"Abigail lay the table please," Mary instructed wanting her to set the table out for tea.

"Henry get some drinks please," she shouted from the kitchen.

Henry left the room and joined Mary and Abigail in the kitchen, she looked at them both.

"Well what do you think of him?" Mary asked.

"He's nice," Abigail said.

"Yes he is nice, a good honest worker," Henry said.

"He certainly loves Charlotte you can tell," Abigail said confidently.

"A chance meeting in Rome how romantic," Mary said happily. "Do you think they will get married?"

"Yes I think so maybe in Central Park!" Abigail said jumping around the kitchen.

"But that's America isn't it?" Mary asked.

"Yes but imagine that getting married there and maybe a wedding reception in Manchester", Abigail said thrashing her arms about with excitement.

"Have you both been on the brandy or wacky backy," Henry said laughing.

Tea was ready and the family were gathered around the table, Henry sat at the head of the table, while Mary sat the other end. In the middle were Harry, Charlotte and Abigail. Normally they were more informal and sat in front of the television with their food on trays, but as Harry was there they decided it was good to eat at the table. The course of conversation was firstly about food and Charlotte was right about tomorrows dish being Lancashire hot pot, Harry was pleasantly surprised by how delicious the food tasted as it seemed very unusual.

The following morning Charlotte awoke first and spent time staring at Harry while he was sleeping. She was imagining them together in New York at his apartment. Charlotte had such a vivid imagination and even as a child could invent a whole new world for herself based usually on romance. She imagined having a baby boy and would name him different names just as she had done with her cuddly toys. One teddy was called Alice and a bunny rabbit with floppy ears became Tatty, she always liked the name Daniel or Michael and often called her baby dolls by these names. She continued to observe Harry as he slept on, at this point she could only think of him and felt that they would be together forever.

She had no idea where they would live and what she would do for work, she was a qualified nurse and loved her job but whether or not she could remain a nurse depended on a lot of things. Did they need nurses in America or would she be a housewife bringing up children? The future was certainly not mapped out. Having said this Charlotte believed in fate and she strongly believed that fate had brought Harry and her together; whatever destiny had thrown at her she must accept it. Perhaps her job had infused such thoughts into her, dealing with death brings things home, such as when your time is up then you must accept it and meet your destiny. Harry was different he could never accept death and the loss of his parents in a plane crash brought him to the conclusion that you must do anything to defy death. Two conflicting ideals and who can say who is right and who is wrong, no one has the real answer.

Charlotte watched as Harry opened his eyes and focused on the room, he looked around and then noticed Charlotte staring at him.

"Good morning Charlotte, how's my angel?" he asked.

"I'm fine and it's nearly midday dear," Charlotte said amused.

"You mean you let me sleep?" Harry asked in surprise.

"Yes well you were snickered and you must have needed it," Charlotte said.

"I was dreaming of us," he said kissing her forehead.

"Well that's okay then, you big softy," Charlotte said kissing him back.

"Well what shall we do with the rest of our day?" Harry asked inquisitively.

"You mean after sex?" Charlotte said squeezing his testicles.

"God Charlotte do you think of anything else?" Harry asked curiously.

"Not much but then I have an incredible sex drive!" Charlotte admitted.

"That's true and I am not objecting, but you mean more to me than sex, I want you to know that I love your heart, soul and mind," Harry explained.

"Yes well so do I, don't want you just see me as a rampant nymphomaniac Harry darling," Charlotte said kissing his chest and working her way down his body.

Later they ventured out into Manchester city centre, Charlotte took Harry to Piccadilly Gardens and all the surrounding shops including the Arndale Centre where the bombing took place years before. Harry was amazed at all the shops and even a big wheel by the shopping centre.

"Let's go up there?" Charlotte suggested.

"I would rather not," Harry said nervously.

"Oh come on Harry it will be fun," Charlotte teased knowing how he felt about heights.

"I will be with you it's quite safe honestly," Charlotte said reassuringly.

“Okay I will try it” Harry said bravely.

They went on the wheel which was enclosed with a glass cover so they were protected from the weather conditions, Harry sat nervously beside Charlotte, she could feel his sweaty hands on her arm they reached the top and stopped.

“We’ve stopped what’s wrong?” Harry said looking at Charlotte for reassurance.

“Oh its okay, they’re just picking more people up and probably wiping the puke up from the seats!” Charlotte laughed teasingly.

“You mean people vomit?” Harry said concerned.

“Oh yes, vomit, faint or have horrific nose bleeds!” Charlotte turned away and grinned.

“My god that’s awful,” Harry said shocked.

“Harry you’re so gullible honestly,” Charlotte said watching Harry’s colour drain from him.

“Oh my god you look awful, you’re going to puke your ring up aren’t you?” Charlotte said realising she had gone too far.

“Gosh I feel ill,” Harry admitted.

“Hold on we are going down,” she got up and sat opposite him.

“Please don’t move,” Harry said trying to hold her hand.

"Not bloody likely! You're not puking on me" Charlotte said pulling herself back.

"But princess!" Harry said pleading.

"Sorry Harry I don't do vomit," Charlotte said frowning.

When they finally got down Harry had managed to contain himself until they got out and reached a grassy area. He then vomited until he had emptied the contents out of his stomach. Charlotte stood cringing and then offered him some water, she felt guilty about tormenting him but tried not to get too close to him.

"Are you alright?" Charlotte asked concerned.

"Like you care!" Harry said angrily.

"Harry that's not fair, I'm sorry," Charlotte flashed her blue eyes at him and smiled sweetly, "I am really sorry forgive me babes."

Charlotte had one of those faces that you couldn't be angry with for long, Harry soon found it in his heart to forgive her and they spent the remainder of the day going around shops and museums. Charlotte tried not to tease him again that day. The only other incident that took place was when a car back fired and Charlotte nearly jumped into Harry's lap.

"God Charlotte your shaking are you alright?" Harry asked her.

"Yes, I think so," Charlotte said clinging to him.

"But you're trembling" Harry noticed her sobbing. "And you're crying!"

"It was that bang I thought for a moment that I was back at the shopping centre during the bombing. Charlotte looked up and noticed all the people staring at her.

"It's okay, you're safe now," Harry said comforting her.

Charlotte sank her head into his chest, hidden away from public view; some people commented others asked if she was alright. Harry just nodded to them and stroked her head and kissed her forehead.

They arrived home just in time for tea, but neither were hungry, Charlotte had learned a valuable lesson about respecting other people's feelings, she had also realised just how much Harry cared about her. They both went upstairs for a shower and jumped in together, washing each other down and making the most of their time together. Harry was experiencing a kinder partner who seemed to understand him more; she seemed more gentle and loving than before. Once they finally left the shower, they both lay on the bed and just snuggled together sharing each other's warmth.

"You know Harry I don't mean to upset you, I just wind people up, it's all part of me, but I will try to consider you more I promise," Charlotte said sincerely.

"Oh okay, because I was going to return to New York and never see you again!" Harry said seriously.

"You were?" Charlotte said surprised.

"No, I was what you call winding you up," Harry admitted laughing.

"Oh you," Charlotte said slapping him on the arm, "you really had me going then".

"Seriously though I must explain about the bombing," Charlotte said, "have you ever been in an accident?"

"I can't say I have, just bad situations like that woman who thought I was a doctor back in Rome, you remember you slept with her dead husband?" Harry said laughing.

"Now don't remind me of that," Charlotte said laughing back. "No I mean like the bombing here in Manchester?"

"No I don't know what I would do in that situation," Harry admitted.

"Well when I said that everything happens in slow motion," Charlotte explained.

"Yes, why is that?" Harry asked inquisitively.

"It's known as slow motion perception it happens to the victims of accidents not onlookers who merely witness it. It's known as a subjective perception of time, things are perceived as passing by slower than normal. Your brain concentrates on the situation trying to process a lot of information the rate increases going up, so the brain perceives it for a longer time due to the concentrated information in the interval, neurons are said to expand and take longer to take in all that information. In other words things slow down as they did when the bomb blew up and shattered that glass in the store."

"God and no one was killed?" Harry said surprised.

"No, but there were a lot of injuries including me," Charlotte said looking at Harry.

"I'm trying to imagine slow motion!" Harry said. "You were very lucky".

They stayed in most of that evening watching television and chatting to Abigail, Mary and Henry. Harry had begun to realise how polite people were in this particular part of Manchester. Neighbours had called into meet Harry, and Abigail introduced her friends to him, they went to the local for a 'quick drink'. Harry soaked in the atmosphere and local conversation that seemed to be predominately about football.

Charlotte took Harry to Old Trafford home to Manchester United; they explored and were given a tour through the Theatre of Dreams. Harry was really impressed with seeing one of the world's most famous football teams in

Manchester. It was like seeing his favourite baseball team in New York, he was 'gobsmacked' and pleasantly surprised.

It would seem that Charlotte was not the only person in the family who could wind people up (trick or torment people) Abigail was also like this but not as bad as Charlotte. Harry was sat on the settee when Abigail was in that sort of mood to play Harry up.

"Hey Harry, has Charlotte done her party piece yet?" Abigail said smiling.

"What's that?" Harry asked inquisitively.

"Has she dressed up as say a tiger, or cat woman?" Abigail went on.

"Yes, she must have told you about the nun caper too!" Harry said wondering what was coming next.

"Oh yes, but then that's usual for her!" Abigail said chuckling wickedly.

"It is?" Harry said nervously.

"Yes she has done many things with outfits, chains, creams and things!" Abigail was getting excited about teasing Harry.

"She has more power tools than Black and Decker and costumes galore," Abigail looked up at the bedroom. "In fact she is preparing her next party trick right now for you, it's called Mr Dentist!" Abigail was trying to keep a straight face.

Harry took a gulp and licked his teeth, at that moment Charlotte called him to her room.

"Harry come upstairs," she shouted.

"You had better go up Harry dear," Abigail said turning her head away.

Harry went up the stairs nervously then heard the sound of a drill, Abigail watched him stop and then continue up the stairs. He opened the door slowly and entered the room with his eyes virtually closed.

"Harry what's wrong why are you squinting your eyes?" Charlotte said holding a drill and wearing a white coat.

"I am not playing your games anymore," Harry said seriously.

"What are you talking about Harry you numpty," Charlotte tried to approach him and he moved backwards hitting his head on a wooden shelf.

"Now look what you have done, I need help with putting a shelf up, Dad wants to drill into the wall, I put this white coat on to protect my clothes," Charlotte explained.

"Hiya Harry," came a voice in the corner.

"Oh hi Mr Brookes, I mean Henry," Harry said feeling a little more relaxed.

Later Harry explained all about Abigail winding him up and he felt embarrassed when he knew the truth.

A week passed and Harry had been educated into the Manchester way of life, he had been so close to Charlotte and at every opportunity indicated how much he loved her. Symbolic gestures such as buying flowers and chocolates, clothes that she never considered wearing before such as a nice dress or blouse. He also started wearing t-shirts something he would never usually do. They were both changing and adapting to each other's ways. Harry used the odd phrase from the area and Charlotte said the odd word from Brooklyn which sounded odd with her accent, just as it did when Harry used local terms. After three weeks Harry was due to leave and return to work in New York.

"Well God what can I say it's been a real experience visiting clubs, pubs, museums and just being with you Charlotte it's been fun," Harry said smiling.

"Well I aim to please and yes it has been fun Harry really," Charlotte said smiling back.

"So call me okay," Harry said opening his arms to embrace her.

"Okay I will once I get used to the time difference," Charlotte said remembering that she woke him up a few times in the early hours thinking it was late morning.

They had a lingering kiss and seemed to embrace for a while. They were both a little tearful before parting and then Harry disappeared through security.

Charlotte headed back home partly exhilarated and partly upset by Harry's departure, she felt lost and alone and wanted him back. She continued with her work on the wards but things didn't feel right as she went from patient to patient dealing with their needs. She was taking a patient's blood pressure when she suddenly thought about the corpse in the bed and his screaming wife. She burst out laughing and the ward sister rushed up to her in order to see what was wrong.

"Sorry Sister," she said embarrassed.

"Charlotte come with me," the sister insisted.

The sister led her away from the ward into a side room.

"Now Charlotte what's so funny?" she asked.

"Well Trudy listen to what happened to me in Rome," Charlotte said telling her the full story of events in the hotel back in Rome.

Trudy began to laugh uncontrollably and said that she could just imagine her dressed as a nun and feeling her way round in the dark. Before long most of the hospital knew of Charlotte's capers and made references to her nun's experience. People even left posters on the wall saying 'Nun required with experience of dead people' and other cartoons and references. Charlotte became a legend in her own lifetime due to her practical jokes and amazing true stories of her life.

NEW YORK, NEW YORK

It was Charlotte's turn to visit Harry in New York; she was so excited knowing she was visiting him in his own home in Brooklyn. She would be overlooking his place of work, seeing the skyline with the World Trade Centre's Twin Tower in the foreground just across from the Brooklyn Bridge. She enjoyed the flight over unlike Harry she actually liked flying, but perhaps his fear stemmed back to his parent's death. The plane landed in New York and Charlotte entered security, she was amused by one of the questions they asked 'was she there for business or pleasure' definitely pleasure she replied cheekily.

Harry made a point of making a banner which read "If you're a good looking blonde English girl by the name of Charlotte come with me." This was in response to the banner that she made for him, but Charlotte appreciated his humour and the pay back remark.

Charlotte ran up to him and gave him a lingering kiss on the lips, he responded by kissing her back and almost taking the lipstick off her lips.

"Harry I have missed you," Charlotte said.

"I have missed you too Charlotte," Harry admitted.

"So here's my friend Geoff," Harry said introducing Geoff to Charlotte and vice versa.

"Charlotte you're as beautiful as I had imagined you," Geoff said smiling.

"Why thank you Geoff," Charlotte said politely.

"Shall we go to the car?" Harry suggested.

"Sure let's meet the others," Geoff said leading the way.

"Others?" Charlotte asked.

"Oh yeah we're meeting colleagues from work before going home," Harry explained.

"But Harry I need to freshen up after the flight over," Charlotte said a little disgruntled.

"You're fine as you are, say did you only have one bag with your clothes in?" Harry asked.

"They don't call me Mary Poppins for nothing you know," Charlotte said laughing.

They arrived at the car and Geoff headed for the driving seat, Charlotte and Harry sat in the back, with the luggage in the spare seat. They travelled straight to Manhattan, Harry was pointing to places of interest on route to the restaurant, but Charlotte was finding it difficult to concentrate due to being tired.

On arrival Geoff parked the car, while Charlotte and Harry carried on to the restaurant. Inside Jackie, and John were sat waiting for them, Geoff and Frank joined them soon after followed by Alice and Graham who all worked at the World Trade Centre some in the North Tower others in the South Tower. John took to Charlotte straight away as if she was their daughter, Charlotte was always considered the girl next door by most people.

She sat beside Alice and they were talking for hours, until Charlotte began to yawn.

"Oh my dear we have been talking all this time and you must be exhausted, Harry you must take her home to sleep," Alice insisted.

Everybody said their goodbyes and Charlotte, Harry and Geoff left the restaurant and all headed towards the car. Harry was supporting Charlotte who was struggling to walk she was so tired, Geoff was pleased to see Harry helping her and glad to see Harry so happy.

Once they arrived in Brooklyn Geoff said goodbye and watched them enter the apartment safely.

"Have a nice vacation both of you!" he shouted.

They both waved and walked inside, Harry checked his mailbox then they walked up the stairs. When they entered the apartment Charlotte noticed that he was not as tidy as she was, she observed the odd clothing on the settee and the odd pot as she called the cups, and a plate left on a table. But

Charlotte was too tired to mither with such matters and just wanted to rest on the settee.

She soon fell fast asleep and Harry being the gentleman he was, just covered her in a sheet and allowed her to sleep. The next morning she awoke to find him staring at her sat in a chair opposite drinking coffee and eating cookies.

"Good morning princess," he said sweetly.

"Oh morning, did you make me a brew?" she asked referring to his hot beverage.

"A what?" Harry asked confused by her choice of words.

"A cup of coffee, has it been so long since we met that you have forgotten what I call things?" Charlotte said concerned.

"I am truly sorry it has been a long time," Harry admitted.

"God I missed you," Charlotte confessed.
Harry put down his drink and approached her; he knelt beside her, kissed her on the lips and hugged her.

"I have missed you too princess, I wish you were here forever," Harry said.

"You do?" Charlotte said surprised.

"Yes I can't live without you," Harry admitted.

"But I would have to give up my work and move from my family," Charlotte said concerned.

They both snuggled together and remained quiet for a moment, both of them finding it hard to make a decision.

"Harry?" Charlotte said in a soft voice. "I want to be with you."

"You mean it?" Harry said excitedly.

"Yes I do, I want to spend the rest of my life with you," Charlotte kissed him tenderly on the lips.

"Let's see how this week goes and if you still want this then I will arrange it," Harry said hoping things would work out.

Later that day they travelled into Manhattan and Harry gave her a tour of the city from museums to the Empire State Building. They travelled by car, subway and taxi in order for her to experience New York by day during a busy time.

They finished their trip by visiting the restaurant at the top of the World Trade Centre's North Building. The sight from the Empire State Building was incredible and seeing the city from the North Tower was just as good.

"Wow what a sight!" Charlotte said. "It's so amazing."

"Yes I look out the window at the South Tower and get this view," Harry pointed to Brooklyn. "Right over there is my apartment."

"Really you can see it?" Charlotte said surprised.

"Yes and I can see this place from my apartment, its breath-taking," Harry said.

"That's nice waking up to the sight of the World Trade Centre," Charlotte said amazed.

"Shall we eat?" Harry asked her.

"Yes I would love to I'm starving," Charlotte admitted.

Harry looked at the menu and passed it to her, at that point Geoff walked in.

"Harry good to see you and Charlotte I hope that you've recovered from your journey?" Geoff asked concerned.

"Yes thank you Geoff but how did you know we were here?" Charlotte asked surprised.

"Because Harry is predictable!" Geoff said laughing.

"I am predictable, unlike Charlotte who is spontaneous," Harry explained.

"I like the element of surprise, I also like surprises and I am also romantic," Charlotte said glancing at Harry.

"I think Harry is too honey," Geoff said winking at her.

"I agree with that Geoff, he buys me flowers, chocolates and is so loving," Charlotte said squeezing his hand under the table.

"You are my princess," Harry replied squeezing her back.

It seemed all too amazing seeing all this from the North Tower. She did think that other people took the view for granted and didn't seem to appreciate this fine view. But this would only be like people living near the Trafford Centre and taking that place for granted. I suppose we all do it and no matter how spectacular a place is, people will take it for granted if they see enough of a place.

However one of the most spectacular places to visit had to be Central Park, it was truly amazing and one of the world's most romantic places to see, with its lakes, fountains, statues and entertainment. Places to meditate, sketch, and spend time alone to think, or with your partner, people just did what they wanted to do. Horse and carts travelled through passing bikes, joggers, young and old couples, people playing ball games and people singing happy tunes.

Charlotte and Harry went around the park in a horse and carriage, imagining that they were married and on their honeymoon. Needless to say this was all Charlotte's idea, but Harry was willing to go along with her fantasy if it made her happy. Harry was pointing out all the attraction with his one free arm his other arm was wrapped around her waist. They travelled around the park seeing lakes, fountains and street performers playing instruments, singing or doing acrobatics. Some performers juggled or were mime artists;

there were art stalls and other interesting attractions. Once they had completed their journey they went on a boat on the lake. They both seemed so happy together, then they walked a while arm in arm and rested on the grass. Harry had brought a picnic and laid out a blanket so they could spread their food out on it. Harry watched as Charlotte laid the sandwiches out on the paper plates.

"Jam and ham butties," Charlotte announce. "This will be followed by tasty apple pie."

"Charlotte you do have a unique way with words babe," Harry started to laugh.

"Are you taking the piss out of the way I talk?" Charlotte said. "Do you want a face full of pie?" She said holding it up.

"Hey no, its fine Charlotte I love the way you talk honest," Harry said not wishing to lose the pie.

"Good cos I like the pie too and I don't want to waste it on your face thank you!" Charlotte laughed and took one of the sandwiches.

"Can I have a butty please?" Harry asked politely.

"Just grab one silly, they are for both of us you know," Charlotte insisted.

Charlotte was less conscious of her broad Manchester accent than Harry was, she carried on talking and Harry unscrambled the words in order to decipher the English words that were obviously there somewhere. Despite this he did find her use of words endearing and in total contrast with his own American tongue. He felt out of his depth in Manchester just as Charlotte found it awkward in New York, but this was partly the attraction between them. Harry had found an interesting Mancunian girl and she had discovered an American from New York.

Harry opened a Tupperware pot revealing fresh strawberries, and then searched about in the picnic basket.

"Go on magic the cream up then," Charlotte said laughing.

"Okay," Harry said producing a container of whipped cream and squirting it at her.

"God Harry where on earth did you find that?" she asked.

He put it down and she decided to attack him by spraying the cream onto his chest.

"Charlotte we will have none left, this is the Charlotte special you know," Harry explained.

"Well it's very nice and I appreciate it." Charlotte said humbly.

"Strawberries and champagne, that's your favourite, right?," Harry asked searching through the picnic basket once more.

"Tell me you haven't got champagne?" Charlotte said waiting for the bottle.

"I haven't got champagne," Harry announced. "But I would have done."

"How about soda?" Harry said producing a few bottles of coca cola.

"I suppose we can use our imagination," Charlotte said a little disappointed.

They went from the park to O'Hara's and spent a short time in there; Charlotte began drinking vodka which really didn't suit her.

They returned to the World Trade Centre South Tower and when they eventually got through the strict security system manned by Doug and some other guards. Harry took Charlotte and John up to the 83rd floor.

"Good to see you again Charlotte," he said embracing her.

"Hiya, nice to see you too," Charlotte said, feeling a little suffocated from his presence, and even worse from the tight embrace.

Charlotte was a little winded, but tried to disguise her feelings in case he took offence. They spent a while talking and then Harry offered to take her to the top of the Empire State Building as Harry was afraid of heights.

It was at this time when Charlotte took Harry by surprise by climbing the railings and threatening to jump if he didn't propose to her.

"Well shall I jump?" Charlotte announced.

"Hey lady come down," a security guard shouted.

"Yes Charlotte come down," Harry pleaded.

"I don't hear those words," Charlotte said hanging over the edge.

"For god sakes if you love her tell her!" the guard said.

"Okay, will you marry me?" Harry said.

"No!" Charlotte said bluntly and stepped down.

"What?" Harry said in disbelief.

"Oh, I was just testing you," Charlotte said laughing.

"That was not funny, you could have fallen, all of this just to humiliate me!" Harry was very annoyed with her. "I really don't believe you Charlotte."

"Sorry it was just a joke, don't be like that," she said looking at him and the security guard and realising what she had done.

"Oh god I'm sorry really," Charlotte said. "I need to crawl up my own arse don't I?" Charlotte said looking down at her feet in shame.

She then looked up to see the reaction on Harry's face, he looked at the guard then back at Charlotte.

"You're drunk Charlotte," Harry said realising that she had been drinking at O'Hara's.

"We are sorry," Harry said to the security guard.

"It's okay just getting her out of here," the guard said pointing to the door.

They went down in two different elevators; Charlotte remained silent and hoped that Harry would forgive her. By the time they reached the lobby Harry was speaking to Charlotte.

"How can I stay mad at you, with those sparkling blue eyes and that cheeky look on your face," Harry embraced her. "God knows I do love you Charlotte."

"And I fucking love you Harry," Charlotte said kissing him.

They left the building and Harry hailed a cab, he told the driver his address in Brooklyn and they travelled home.

When they entered the building Harry explained to Charlotte that he was afraid of losing her and told her how much she meant to him.

"Charlotte I don't need you to hang off a building and threaten to jump so I can propose to you," Harry explained.

"I told you I was just messing," Charlotte said. "And I told you I was sorry."

"You don't understand, I do want to marry you," Harry said holding her.

"I think I'm going to be sick," Charlotte announced and ran into the bathroom.

The next morning Charlotte couldn't remember the incident at the Empire State Building and anything that followed.

"God I feel rough," Charlotte announced from under the sheets.

"No kidding," Harry said sarcastically.

"What happened to me?" she asked.

"You mean you don't remember anything?" Harry asked.

"I remember the park and meeting Janice and John at the South Tower." Charlotte was struggling to remember anything else.

"So no recollection of the Empire State Building or trying to get me to propose to you?" Harry explained.

"Oh know really, I don't believe it, not me!" Charlotte hid her head away from view.

"I am so sorry, I would never ever say or do those things normally," Charlotte said remaining under the covers.

"Come out," Harry insisted.

"No the shame and humiliation my god," Charlotte held on to the sheets.

"Come on Charlotte it's happened and it's over and I did propose to you later," Harry admitted.

"When?" Charlotte said pulling the sheets off her head.

"Back here at the apartment," Harry looked at her messy hair.

"And what exactly did I say?" Charlotte said worried.

"You vomited," Harry said smiling.

"I puked," Charlotte said horrified, "I puked in response to you proposing?" Charlotte returned under the sheets.

"Charlotte you had been drinking," Harry was trying to make excuses for her actions.

"Fuck, I well and truly fucked up," Charlotte went quiet.

"Charlotte please comes out of there," Harry said, "for Christ sake Charlotte!"

"Let me die please," Charlotte said in a muffled voice.

"No you can't die we have things to do," Harry said amused at her behaviour.

"A quick death followed by a resurrection to normality," Charlotte pinched his behind and listened for his reaction.

"Get me something for my headache," She said pinching him again.

"For god sake that hurts," Harry said jumping.

"Do it or I will snap your cock okay?" Charlotte said laughing in her usual teasing manner.

"Okay I will just don't do that ok?" Harry said leaping out of bed and opening a cupboard.

"You know I wouldn't really do that don't you?" Charlotte said emerging out of the sheets. "I haven't got the strength at present."

Later that day they went exploring around Manhattan, the subject of marriage was never mentioned for the remainder of their holiday. Charlotte had got quite attached to Janice and John, she had also got close to Geoff and Harry's other friends and colleagues. In turn they warmed towards her and got to know her ways, some a little strange but that was Charlotte she never failed to surprise anyone. She was certainly one of a kind and even her family didn't understand her sometimes, her father Henry perhaps knew her better than anyone. Although Abigail was the one she really confided in about most things, especially sex and serious relationships.

Charlotte is in Harry's apartment dancing to the music of Bruce Springsteen, Born in the USA, using Harry's guitar pretending to play it. The music was that loud especially with the window open that she had managed to draw a crowd. Harry returned from work seeing the crowd and hearing the music.

"I will deal with it," Harry said.

"I hope so," one woman said angrily.

Harry entered the apartment and saw Charlotte dressed in a long t-shirt and jogging bottoms.

"Hiya Harry," she shouted.

Harry turned down the music down.

"Do you know they can hear this music in Manhattan?"

"Do you think they like it?" Charlotte said.

"Charlotte for god's sake."

"Oh come on Harry, let your hair down!"

"Well I have to live here," Harry said.

"Sorry Harry," Charlotte said, "But I love this music, I like to feel the beat!" Charlotte said laughing.

"So do the neighbours," Harry said.

Charlotte walked out of the room and into the bedroom slamming the door in temper.

Charlotte knew she was in the wrong and soon apologised, realising that if Harry and her were going to make a go of being together, she needed to calm down.

Harry was lying beside Charlotte in bed. She was holding him and he was looking at her, finding it hard to understand how the wild woman from earlier could be so quiet and calm. But this was Charlotte she could change like the weather. Stormy one minute and then settled the next.

If anyone could keep Charlotte's feet on the ground it was Harry with his laid back attitude to life. Charlotte was once free as a bird, but now she wanted commitment, her life was changing and she was ready to take on more responsibility. She just needed to free herself of the wild side of her personality to a much more responsible role, as a wife and eventually a mother.

Harry was a patient man but Charlotte could try the patience of a saint sometimes. However his love for her kept him sane and tolerant of her behaviour.

Charlotte was taken on a boat trip seeing Manhattan from a different angle; she was quite calm - for Charlotte until she saw the Statue of Liberty.

"Oh my god look the lady with the book, she's holding a torch." Charlotte said remembering what the clairvoyant said to her.

"That's the Statue of Liberty one of America's finest monuments," Harry said proudly.

"I know it's the lady that the clairvoyant pointed out!" Charlotte seemed so pleased to see her, and then remembered the clairvoyants warning.

"Disaster is going to occur right here," Charlotte said like an old Roman soothsayer.

"You're not making sense Charlotte," Harry said confused.

"It's not important really just some silly old woman telling me about a disaster occurring here," Charlotte said dismissing it.

"Things are quite safe here, I think she may be on about somewhere else," Harry said confidently.

Charlotte spent most of her time with Harry, but also got to know Jackie, Janice and John, Doug the security man and of course Geoff who became fond of Charlotte, Harry had younger friends such as Frank and his wife Amy. Amy worked in the pub near the World Trade Centre called O'Hara's a place Charlotte wanted to forget after her vodka incident.

Amy and Frank lived in a place at Long Island and commuted in together each morning, Amy was very hard working behind the bar and often invited Charlotte for lunch either at the pub or at a local diner in the area.

This enabled Harry to go to work at times and help Geoff with a difficult project.

Charlotte was in O'Hara's the one day when Amy wanted to discuss the future with her.

"Charlotte do you love Harry?" she asked her directly.

"Yes of course I do why?" Charlotte seemed surprised at her question.

"I just wanted to know because Harry has been hurt in the past," Amy explained.

"Who by? A relationship?" Charlotte said concerned.

"By me, we were once together and I broke his heart," Amy admitted.

"So why tell me you didn't have to?" Charlotte said a little bewildered.

"I don't want him to get hurt again, he told me about you and how he feels about you, I am glad that you feel the same."

"Hey love let me tell you I love that man and don't plan to lose him." Charlotte said rather defensively.

"Hey honey I like you, don't get me wrong you're real nice," Amy said smiling and clutching her hand.

"Well you're ok too for competition!" Charlotte said smiling back.

"Another drink?" Amy asked.

"Yes why not," Charlotte agreed.

Charlotte and Amy really became friends after this day and spent a lot of time together before Charlotte was finally due to go home.

The time came for Charlotte to go home she had spent the final day with all her new found American friends at a restaurant near Times Square. It was a good day and a lot was said about Charlotte returning to visit again, but both Charlotte and Harry were thinking of a more permanent arrangement in Brooklyn. This was kept between them although Charlotte did confide with Amy on this matter after their little chat in O'Hara's pub restaurant bar.

SEPERATED

As the months passed both Charlotte and Harry were missing each other, they felt lost and empty being apart and both knew the only solution was to be together. The question was where they would be together was it to be in New York or Manchester, it was such a hard decision to make and no one could make it for them. Charlotte had her family and friends in England, while Harry had his friends and colleagues in New York. Charlotte discussed it with her family, breaking the news to them gently, but she ended up being as subtle as a flying mallet.

"I want to move to America!" she announced to them all at teatime. "I want to be with Harry."

"Oh now, tell her Henry," Mary said concerned.

"Tell her what that you want me to stay, that I am being foolish?" Charlotte was waving her arms erratically and shouting. "We love each other doesn't that mean anything to anyone but Harry and myself?"

"Charlotte are you sure you know what you're doing?" Henry said agreeing with Mary.

"Yes, it's my life and I can do as I like, you can't keep me locked in a cage like an animal!" Charlotte said looking at her sister for support.

"She's made her mind up Mum," Abigail said looking at Charlotte.

"It's my life I want to be with Harry in Brooklyn," Charlotte said angrily.

"Charlotte we know you love each other but think about this," Henry said concerned.

"You don't understand any of you, I simply can't live without him," Charlotte turned to face Abigail. "Please tell them Abigail."

"Charlotte maybe you do need to think about it, you are very young," Abigail said concerned.

"Charlotte we love you and don't want you to make any mistakes," Mary said trying to attract her attention.

"Mother no matter what you or Dad says I am going," Charlotte insisted.

Mary looked sternly at Charlotte but then she could see a stubborn streak which came from her whenever she wanted to do something.

"Okay we can't stop you," Mary said. "We love you and want you to be happy."

"Yes your mother is right, we do love you and want you to be happy wherever you are," Henry said putting a hand on her shoulder.

"Thank you all I'll go and pack," Charlotte said excited.

While she was packing Charlotte reflected on her past, she thought about her happy childhood with her sister Abigail. She also thought about her parents, living with the good times and all of the arguments about various things. She remembered the conversation about getting married and having children which made her more determined to travel to New York. Charlotte's decision to travel to America was not on a whim despite her parents feeling this way. Charlotte had planned it to detail which was so out of character for her, she had the tendency in her life, to let everything around her change causing her to get caught up in a romantic whirlwind and remaining in mid-air. Her life had certainly been turned around; it was what her mother described as a romantic turmoil of events. Charlotte questioned herself at this point, "Was she doing the right thing or was she in fact being reckless and foolish?" The answer was she was chasing a dream, after all we all dream, some people never chase that dream, others chase it and fall short of achieving it and others actually get somewhere. But if we never try we never achieve, this is the difference between having a dream and acting upon it. Yes Charlotte may have had a vivid imagination but she knew the difference from imagination and reality, she at least knew how to live and enjoy herself to the full.

Harry was explaining the same thing about living together to Janice and John at work, he could hardly contain himself.

"You know that I've been seeing Charlotte, I've stayed with her in England and she has stayed here," Harry tried to explain.

"Come on Harry tell us," John said impatiently.

"John let him tell us in his own time," Janice said patiently.

"Get to the point Harry," John insisted.

"Well Charlotte wants to move here," Harry finally told them but made it look as if it was her idea, when in reality it was a joint decision.

"Harry that's wonderful, but what do her parents think?" Janice asked from a parent's perspective.

"I don't know," Harry said puzzled.

"Well how do you know they're going to approve?" Janice was looking at the practical side, knowing that Harry really wanted this.

"I don't know she's telling them tonight," Harry said defensively.

"Harry, you know we think of you as a son and that's why we worry about you. You have to consider her parents and their love for Charlotte; they may fight to keep her there."

"I know but I will fight for her affections if it means her living here, I would do anything for the love of Charlotte," Harry said looking at them both.

"Well we shall support you both, when is she coming?" John asked.

"I don't know yet, she will let me know," Harry said smiling.

"We need to plan Christmas, it will soon come round," Janice said looking at John for support.

"Yes Christmas holidays in New York," John said smiling at Harry.

You could take Charlotte ice skating and show her how beautiful New York is at Christmas," Janice said obviously thinking of the Christmas's her and John had had in Manhattan.

"She would love it," John agreed.

"Yes, you're right she will love it," Harry said positively.

Back in Manchester Charlotte was packed and ready to travel, all she needed was her new passport and an Esta Visa waiver from the American Embassy. She continued to work in hospital knowing that she would be leaving. Her colleagues knew nothing about her plans and just knew that she seemed happy at this point, they never questioned her about her love life. She only ever discussed pop concerts or gigs that she attended locally, or even the Leeds festival which lasted a few days. She was a good nurse who loved her job and often attended courses in order to improve her skills, she was due for promotion but she was never a career girl. Charlotte was a fun girl and loved life, she was very sociable, caring and probably a little selfish at times. At one time you could have considered her self-centred as she used to get self-absorbed. Her mother thought that she never considered anyone else's feelings especially when it came to moving to America.

A week passed and Charlotte was on pins, her passport hadn't arrived but she had sorted her ESTA, she was getting very irritable and snappy. She went downstairs and walked up to the front door.

"Mum!" she shouted.

"Yes Charlotte," came the reply from the kitchen.

"Any post yet?" Charlotte asked.

"No not today unless he's late," Mary answered.

"God no bloody post!" Charlotte said entering the kitchen.

"Are you still waiting for your passport?" Mary said.

"God mum, I've been waiting for weeks now and I want to go," Charlotte said taking her sisters toast from her plate.

"Hey that's mine!" Abigail shouted.

"Correction it was your toast," Charlotte said laughing.

"I heard the letter box," Abigail said pointing to the front door.

Charlotte jumped up and ran to the door, when she got there she found nothing.

"Abigail!" she shouted. "You wicked bitch you tricked me!"

"Oh Charlotte would I do that?" she said laughing.

"Yes you pinched my toast," she said pointing to her plate.

"Oh would I do that, my name isn't sweet and innocent Charlotte!" Abigail said.

At that moment the letterbox made a clattering sound that was like heaven to Charlotte's ears, she ran with Abigail to the door. They both looked down at the letters and parcels that were piled at the doorway. Neither moved but remained like statues in a park, finally Mary passed them and picked them all up.

"Well if you two are just going to look at the post, I will pick them up," Mary said.

"No Mum, let me have them," Charlotte insisted.

"No mum let me" Abigail also insisted.

But Mary took them into the kitchen then went through each one methodically, watching her daughter's expressions. Finally she noticed a package that was obviously from the passport department and passed it to Charlotte.

"For you Madam," she said smiling.

"Oh my god, it's here!" Charlotte said opening the parcel.

"So this is it, you're leaving?" Abigail said grinning at Charlotte. "I get your room."

Mary hit Abigail on the arm and looked at Charlotte who was crying.

"What you skriking at you got what you wanted," Mary said sharply.

"Yes Charlotte what's the problem, I was only joking about the room it will always be yours," Abigail said trying to comfort her.

"You don't understand, neither of you, I feel like I am torn apart half of me here and half in New York with Harry," Charlotte said running out of the kitchen and up the stairs to her room.

Mary became tearful and looked at Abigail who was also upset, Mary was not one to make a big fuss or to hug people even those close to her, but even she hugged Abigail.

"Mum," Abigail said surprised by her reaction. "What is it?"

"I suppose I have seemed distant to you, after all I am not the affectionate type, I don't go in for hugs or cuddles it's not me, no flannel Mary they used to call me. But when it comes to losing one of my own and her living so far away," Mary wiped her nose on a tissue.

"Well mother it's not like she isn't coming back, she may not even like it there and she may not stay with Harry, if they fall out she will be back in her old room and arranging a new holiday to Rome or somewhere and may meet a new man! "Abigail said reassuringly.

"And I thought Charlotte had a vivid imagination," Mary said smiling.

"Now enough of this silliness go and get Charlotte please," Mary said adjusting herself and wiping the tears from her eyes.

"Charlotte," Abigail shouted going up the stairs to her room.

Charlotte was lying on the bed looking at a poster of the New York skyline.

"Charlotte," Abigail repeated.

"Come in Abigail, I was just thinking about New York," Charlotte said looking at Abigail.

"You've been crying, why?" Charlotte asked tapping the bed for her to join her on the bed.

Abigail put her arm around her younger sister

"The same reason as you, I am going to miss you," she replied.

"But I am still with you in spirit and you will feel my presence," Charlotte said dramatically.

"Honestly Charlotte you don't half come out with some stuff!" Abigail said laughing.

"What do you mean?" Charlotte continued. "I believe in a spiritual place where our thoughts converge and where all the living and the dead merge and discuss world affairs, this is some sort of happening it occurs at disaster sites and such."

"Charlotte really do you actually believe this, is this even possible?" Abigail said doubting her.

"Yes, I believe that anyone who died during the bombings in Manchester, that their ghosts will remain there until they are happy to cross over. Abigail we could have been those ghosts, we could be meeting in the shopping area discussing why it happened!" Charlotte was totally sincere in what she said.

"Well I never thought of that, so if people loved each other and died together they would return together at the place where they died?" Abigail asked trying to rationalize it in her own head.

"Yes you've got it Abi, it's merely a suggestion but food for thought," Charlotte explained.

They went downstairs and Mary was stood by the window, she was looking out into the street. It was busy with a lot of traffic and so much going on, police cars, fire engines and ambulances. Children returning from school all the things that you expect in rural districts around Manchester nothing changes. Charlotte spent her entire life in the area, although she ventured out to other places this was her home. She attended local schools, clubs and bars, but life was more adventurous around the world.

Mary turned to look at Charlotte she had a stern look on her face; it was a look that both Charlotte and Abigail were used to.

"So Charlotte you have made up your mind to go?" Mary asked.

"Yes I have," Charlotte said looking into her eyes, beneath that hard exterior she could see a gentle woman who had been broken hearted in the past.

"Very well, I won't say another word about the matter," Mary put her arms out to her.

Charlotte looked shocked at her and approached her slowly as if to expect something else. But to her surprise she actually hugged her, squeezing her tightly as if she didn't want to let her go.

"My dear Charlotte what will we do without you?" Mary said.

Charlotte had never felt the warmth from her mother, not like this, how she longed for a moment like this. She had thought this would never happen, her mother experienced a rough life, and abandonment was a common word to her. She was orphaned as a child and promised things and then had them taken away from her. She was chastised and her foster parents were strict, her schooling was rough too corporal punishment was used back then, so the use of the cane for minor crimes was common place. You learned to be tough or you didn't survive, it was a matter of sink or swim for want of a better expression to describe the situation. Mary decided to be tough and survive in her own way, so hugging was the last thing that she thought of, no love and hugs just being tough and direct with people.

Charlotte counted the length of time her mother was holding her it was at least ten minutes. She would have broken her record in one minute or even less, but Charlotte felt good and wouldn't question this rare act of affection.

"Now, time for tea," Mary said breaking away.

If Mary never hugged her again Charlotte had the memory of this moment, she would be able to say in the future that her mother truly loved her.

Charlotte left home a week later; she had a leaving party with her nurse colleagues at some local venue and made it a night to remember. Her colleagues made a fuss of her and made her promise never to forget them; she had worked with them for a few years and had happy and sad moments with them.

She was especially fond of Ward Sister Trudy who was her mentor and long suffering friend along with Julie, Andrea and Stacey. Each one could tell a good story of Charlotte but they all loved her. One such story was when a male nurse played a trick on her by sowing the pockets of her long sleeve coat and stuffing the pockets full of rubber gloves. So in retaliation she found his uniform, a white coat, sowed the sleeves up and filled a pair of gloves with water and tied them up. She then dipped them in talc and placed them in the pockets. The next day the nurse appeared on the ward with a smart clean uniform which puzzled Charlotte. It was time for ward round and the young doctor was missing. When he finally turned up the senior doctor said. "Where have you been?" in which he replied "Sorry sir I had trouble with my uniform, somebody had sewn it up and done something to the pockets."

Despite what Charlotte called 'prancing' or playing practical jokes, Charlotte was really caring and kind, and she was also very clever and lacked confidence in her own abilities as a nurse. Yet she had saved lives and often patients left her flowers when they went home, but she considered herself part of a team and always shared what she had with her colleagues. She could deal with death but often cried when she was alone or with some colleagues, showing that she was only human.

Andrea and Stacey went out drinking with Charlotte one evening; Andrea was bigger than Stacey and Charlotte she was dressed in a white dress with a blue pattern all over it. Andrea was very outgoing and sociable; Stacey was sociable but could get moody when she'd had a few drinks.

"So Charlotte I can't believe your moving to America!" Stacey said glancing at Andrea.

"Yes, you will be missed," Andrea said sincerely.

"Well my heart is there," Charlotte said happily.

"So what if it goes wrong?" Stacey asked clutching her bottle of booze.

"It won't I know Harry and its true love," Charlotte said positively.

"Oh come on Charlotte true love, give me a bucket so I can puke!" Stacey said joking.

"That's not nice, Charlotte is in love and we have met Harry he's nice," Andrea said smiling.

"Yes I know and I wish her all the happiness in the world, I'm only saying if it did go wrong we are here for you," Stacey said leaning on the table for support.

"Yes we are Charlotte we are with you, even in spirit," Andrea said holding her glass up.

"Andrea your pissed! Stacey said laughing.

"I think you're drunk than me!" Andrea replied.

"Now ladies I've got the advantage because I drank a bottle of wine before I came out," Charlotte announced. "In answer to your question if things went wrong I would return to my friends of course."

Other friends joined Charlotte that evening including Abigail and her friends, everybody had a good time pub crawling around Manchester. Eventually they all went home and Charlotte was violently sick, sitting on the floor and clinging hold of the toilet as if it was going to escape.

Two days later Charlotte had fully recovered and went to the airport with her family, Mary didn't really want to go, she hated goodbyes and it wasn't as if Charlotte was going to return in a few weeks, she was going to live with Harry.

"Well Charlotte this is it," Mary said sadly.

"God Mum, I am going to visit you and call you each week," Charlotte said looking at her mother.

"I know but you will be missed and you will always have a home here," Mary said hugging her.

"Yes Charlotte we love you," Henry said waiting to hug her.

"Me too Charlotte, love you sis," Abigail said smiling. "You're room will always be here."

"Thanks Dad," Charlotte said hugging him. "And you Abi miss you and love you lots." Charlotte hugged Abigail as the tears began to flow.

Charlotte waved to them and disappeared through a doorway, she went through security and waited for her plane in the departure lounge. At that point she thought about what she was leaving behind, her friends her family and her career. But Charlotte was prepared to lose all that for love, she knew Harry would make her happy and she would live a good life in New York.

By August of 2001 Charlotte was taken by surprise by an unexpected visitor. Her sister Abigail had come to visit her in Brooklyn. She was less courageous than Charlotte and travelled over with her boyfriend Mike, he was a slim man in his late twenties. Mike was a nice hard working man who was sensible and totally the opposite personality to Charlotte or Abigail. They stayed for a week and this time Charlotte showed them around, she knew exactly where to take them. Their whole agenda was full and that included a trip on the boat. It also included a journey up the Empire State Building and a number of shopping trips, to places such as Bloomingdales. They eventually relaxed in Central Park where they had a picnic with Harry and a leisurely carriage ride through the park.

Charlotte was happy and had settled into New York with Harry and she was beginning to make her own friends too. Gina became her best friend, she was the same age and was a nurse at the local hospital. All seemed to be going well for Charlotte until she became sick one morning, she thought at first that it was food poisoning or a virus, but Gina suggested that she thought that she was pregnant.

Charlotte suddenly thought of many things like was she still a Mancunian or a New Yorker? What would happen to the baby and its nationality, but what was more important was how her parents will react to the news. She had to tell them, but she hadn't even said anything to Harry.

9/11

It was the 11th September 2001, the sun was coming up that morning and all indications were that it was going to be a nice day. Harry was up early for work knowing he had a busy day ahead, while Charlotte decided to have a lie in bed.

They had fallen out over the fact that Harry was reluctant to take her over to meet his relatives in Washington DC. Harry said he had to finish his work load and did not want to disappoint Geoff by going away and leaving him to all the work. Geoff was on Charlotte's side and thought Harry needed a rest, he also considered it important to meet them as they had wedding plans to sort out.

But both Charlotte and Harry were stubborn and nothing was going to prevent him from working that day and Charlotte was not prepared to speak to him, in fact he went in earlier to prepare everything. Charlotte wanted to tell Harry about being pregnant, she had done more than one test and both had showed positive, somehow she was convinced that she was having a boy. At 06.30 Harry was sat at the table drinking coffee, he decided to clean his teeth before leaving for work, but Charlotte was occupying the bathroom. She came out looked at him, and then turned away in disgust; this was all part of her stubborn pride. She usually made Harry's packed lunch but decided not to this morning, Harry entered the bedroom to kiss her goodbye, but she had her head turned away from him so he kissed her tenderly on the forehead and went out the front door. Charlotte's eyes welled with tears she was convinced in her heart that she was right about seeing his relatives, they could have been there today explaining about the wedding. Harry only needed a day or two off Geoff didn't mind after all it was important, Charlotte felt awful and was vomiting in the toilet, evidently morning sickness she really wasn't prepared for this, not now when all these other problems were occurring. After, she began to feel a little better she had a shower, once she was out it was 08.15 by the digital clock beside the bed. Harry had decided to given Charlotte a call but she missed it while she was in the bathroom, so she tried to ring him back. Instead Geoff answered he seemed bright and cheerful and happy to talk to her.

"Oh hi Charlotte, how are you?" Geoff asked.

"Okay," Charlotte replied. "Is Harry there?"

"No he's gone for breakfast, have you been arguing again?" Geoff asked her concerned.

"Why has he said anything?" Charlotte asked.

"A little but you know Harry never really vents his feelings, you need to sort it out Charlotte you're a nice couple" Geoff said.

"That's why I rang, will you let him know that I rang and I need to speak to him urgently?" Charlotte said crying.

She put the phone down and put her hand to her face, she began to get dressed then prepared lunch for Harry and herself.

Harry reached the office just after Charlotte had rang.

"Right here I am sorry I got delayed, I had to get Jackie's coffee and donuts, I reckon she is pregnant don't you," Harry said without taking a breath.

"Harry!" Geoff shouted.

"What Geoff what's wrong?" Harry asked.

"It's Charlotte she's….!" Before Geoff could finish Harry butted in.

"What's wrong with her?" Harry said concerned.

"If you will let me finish, she's very upset you need to ring her," Geoff insisted.

"She's just upset over not going over to see my family, I told her that we were very busy and we could go next week," Harry explained.

"Nonsense you can go today, we can do all this later, now call her up and sort it out". Geoff passed him the phone.

"Okay, she can come here and we can travel as soon as she gets here," Harry explained tapping out the number to his landline.

"She's not answering," Harry said impatiently.

"Keep trying, she may be asleep or in the bathroom maybe," Geoff said considering the options.

"I suppose it is my fault, I proposed to her, we got engaged, had our get together and I said that I would take her to meet my family. Damn I should have done more to please her but I was thinking of our workload and I didn't want to abandon you." Harry said feeling guilty.

"Look Harry you're young and have a lot to learn, so has Charlotte. It's no good making rash decisions just consider each other, I am older the majority of my life is behind me, I have a wife and children who I love dearly but work doesn't come in the way of them," Geoff said hoping to get through to Harry.

"You're right Geoff. I will keep trying to get through to her," Harry said feeling better after talking to Geoff.

"Charlotte means the world to me, I love her so much," Harry admitted.

"Harry you're going to marry her, I hope you love her?" Geoff patted him on the back laughing. "Now get that call made."

It was 08.45 (13.45 in the UK) Charlotte phoned her mother in England.

"Hiya Mum it's me Charlotte, I've got some news for you, we're engaged!" Charlotte said happily.

"That's great news, let me tell Abigail," Mary said.

"Yes but Mum I think I'm pregnant!" Charlotte said anticipating a negative reaction.

"You're pregnant that's wonderful news," Mary sounded positive but she had reserved judgement not wanting to upset Charlotte.

But while Charlotte was on the phone to her mother giving her the good news she was glancing out of the window at the Twin towers when she saw a plane crash into the North Tower.

"Oh Christ, oh my god no!" Charlotte dropped the phone and put both hands over her mouth.

"No it's not happening!" Charlotte shouted.

"Darling what's wrong?" she said concerned.

"Mom the North Tower has been hit by a plane, it's crashed right into the building!" Charlotte said panicking.

"Mother it's still bad and who knows where Harry is I need to be with him," Charlotte insisted.

"But wait it might be dangerous," Mary said concerned.

"But Harry doesn't know I'm pregnant!" Charlotte said frantically.

"I have to go, love you," Charlotte said putting the phone down then picking it up again.

"Is Harry there Geoff?" Charlotte asked frantically.

"No he went to see Jackie," Frank explained.

"Have you seen the North Tower?" Charlotte said.

"Yeah a plane crashed into it must have gone off course or something," Frank said alarmed. "What a god damn mess," he continued.

"I'm coming over," Charlotte insisted.

"Wait, do you think that's wise Charlotte honey you could get hurt?" Frank said concerned.

"Well I'm sorry but I need to see him!" Charlotte said grabbing her bag.

"I'll let Harry know you rang," Frank said.

Charlotte got into a taxi and was heading along the Brooklyn Bridge when she saw a second plane travelling towards the South Tower. The driver stopped the car and looked on in horror as it hit the South Tower. Charlotte got out of the taxi and ran down the rest of the bridge towards the area hoping that Harry was not in the building. When she arrived in the area she was horrified at all the devastation. All the surrounding buildings were damaged. Even the bar that they used to go to was damaged, rescue teams including firemen were racing about and helping people. There was a lot of dust about Charlotte could see silhouettes but could not distinguish anyone, she could only tell the fire fighters because of their helmets. The whole situation was insane and no one could understand why it happened, not until the second plane hit the South Tower and half an hour later President George Bush made a statement on television stating "We have had a national tragedy. Two aeroplanes have crashed into the World Trade Centre in an apparent terrorist attack on the country".

This was broadcast across the world watched by millions of people, who were saddened and shocked by the news. Some had relatives in the building others had friends and colleagues, but most people just looked in horror as the second plane hit the South Tower.

It was 09.03 when the second plane hit the South Tower when Harry said goodbye to Janice and John at the lift as usual, then Harry could not believe his eyes as a plane was coming straight towards him heading for the building. It was just like Charlotte said your brain slows everything down in such situations it seemed as if the plane was in slow motion then until it suddenly changed course and hit the floors above. Harry felt the building shake as the plane crashed into the floors above, his first thought was for his friends in the lift travelling up on the next floor.

Down below Charlotte had reached the area and hoped that Harry had left the building.

"Oh my god no!" came the cry of one woman who had gone out of the building to a shop nearby, another lady beside her who had been late for work.

Frank was already heading down the stairs to escape; he seemed to be in shock as he ran frantically down the steps missing a few en route. People passed him down the stairs and some fell, but a lot of people were helping each other.

Geoff remained in his office, he was even tidying up and then reality hit him and he stopped.

"This is it isn't it Harry?" Geoff said staring at his desk.

"What do you mean?" Harry asked looking at the expression on his face.

"Here, now all of this, it's over!" Geoff looked at Harry.

"We have to go Geoff," Harry advised.

They noticed people jumping from the North Tower then bodies passing the window from the above floors, some were people they knew.

"That's the only way out," Geoff said approaching the window.

“Geoff wait don’t jump!” Harry shouted.

“What choice have we got, stay here and be crushed by this building?” Geoff replied.

“There must be a way out, please can we just try?” Harry pleaded.

“Harry for Christ sake there is no other way, come with me now this is a better way to die!” Geoff insisted.

“No I won’t die like that please doesn’t do it Geoff,” Harry said desperately trying to grab his arm.

Geoff hesitated as if he was having second thoughts, then he pushed Harry away from him, “Sorry Harry if you want to die in this place……” he said and jumped out of the window to his death.

Harry stood for a while feeling sad and numb wondering how many more friend he would lose before the day was out. People were jumping from various storeys of the building he even saw a few pass by the window falling tragically to their death. Yet here was he trying to escape, he wondered whether or not to jump but as he didn’t the question was could he be classed as a coward? Who was there to judge him but himself and in his mind yes, his friends were brave maybe they knew best but still he was convinced there was a way out.

Harry found his way to the staircase hoping to escape, but other people had thought of this, as he entered through the door he was not prepared for the horror that lay ahead as he trod on glass and marble segments from the offices above. Bodies mangled and twisted with limbs missing, blood and skin decorating the walls and floor like a horror movie of some sort of massacre. It was so horrific it made Harry physically sick, he vomited in a corner then fell back against a wall.

"No, no, why?" he shouted beating the back of his head on the wall behind him.

It was at this time that the true horror of all the events began to affect him, the crash and then all that was to follow, burnt and disfigured bodies. He touched one of the severed limbs with his foot, it was someone's leg.

"Shit!" he shouted. "This is all insane."

He looked down the staircase some areas were filled with smoke which seemed to drift through an opening and Harry could see outside. More jumpers passed and descend down to their death trying to avoid the smoke filled rooms prepared to die from the fall rather than suffocate from the smoke. This time he was about to jump himself and was stopped by someone grabbing his hand, he turned to see who it was and to his surprise there stood Jackie.

"Jackie you're alive?" he said hugging her.

"So are you, so stay that way," Jackie said leading him down the stairs.

Others joined them as they continued down the stairs, most of them had cuts or bruises, they were all ages ranging from 19 to 70 some really struggling to move but all deciding to escape from the building. Suddenly the stairway was blocked by rubble, there was too much to move even with ten or twelve men.

"What now?" Jackie asked.

"Find the nearest door," Harry said.

They went up one flight of stairs and found a door, when they entered they had entered a hallway between offices, Harry led them to the next stairway behind another door, it was darker and part of the way they had to feel their way. They felt bodies and the warm dampness of fresh blood, people were moaning in pain and screams could be heard from a distance. It was Jackie's turn to start feeling the urge to jump; she was beginning to doubt that there was a way out after all.

"Think we should consider ending it all and joining the jumpers?" she said her voice beginning to tremble.

"No Jackie don't think like that, I have lost too many friends not you too," Harry said grabbing her.

"But how are we going to get out of here?" Jackie asked.

"If these stairs are blocked then we find more stairs," Harry insisted.

Sure enough the stairway ended with no way down, pipes had fractured and water was gushing out making it hard to maintain their balance. People were slipping some fell down the stairs, ceiling tiles dropped on their heads Jackie became hysterical and screamed, and she stumbled over a body and went on screaming. Harry slapped her waiting for a reaction but Jackie stood silent and hugged Harry. They stood for a while then heard a rumble, the building shook causing them to find a door back into the offices then the building shook again, a Coca-Cola vending machine exploded and glass bottles went in all directions.

As they moved across the floor with the others the floor began to move, items of furniture began to slide and crash into people. Jackie screamed as she was hit by a desk, at the same time Harry was knocked over by a cabinet they both recovered but were then were swept down surfing down floors. This went on for a while; they were travelling fast down and down unable to stop. The journey seemed to last forever down to almost the basement, until finally they landed some never made it, some were crushed by masonry. They assumed that they were still high up but they had landed in some kind of pit. It was fairly dark all but for a glimmer of light; Harry was lying next to a metal pole or pipe, while Jackie was lying next to an African business man called Isaac. He was brushing off the masonry from his dark skin and trying to move.

"Man I think my leg's broke," he said holding his leg and frowning in pain.

"Mine too," Jackie said holding hers.

"My shoulder is injured," Harry said in discomfort.

Jackie tried to move then felt a warm trickle as she held her stomach, as she pressed she felt it trickle through her fingers.

"Oh my god, I'm bleeding from my stomach," Jackie suddenly yelled out in pain.

"I can hear something outside, sirens and shouting," Harry said

"You're imagining it Harry," Jackie shouted.

"I heard a siren," Isaac said.

"I need to get their attention" Harry said searching for a metal rod or something else to bang the pipe.

Eventually he found something, a thick stick lay on the ground so he began banging, he did this for about ten minutes then stopped then began again. After a while Isaac took over until they were all exhausted, Harry tried keeping Jackie awake by talking to her.

"Jackie stay with us," Harry insisted.

"But I'm in so much pain," Jackie said holding her stomach.

"They will hear us eventually," Harry said confidently.

"Face it Harry we're going to die," Jackie said. "I really should have jumped."

"No not that," Harry said upset.

"I wouldn't be in so much pain," Jackie said becoming weaker.

A few days passed and still Harry banged at the pipes, by this time both Jackie and Isaac were weaker and only Harry was able to move about. He sat beside Jackie and tried to comfort her but her pain was now uncontrollable and she could hardly speak. Isaac had been discussing his family back in Africa and managed to describe his village and educational background. Suddenly the rescuers who had placed sound equipment in the area heard Harry banging the pipes and responded to them.

"Jackie did you hear that they know we're here!" Harry was laughing hysterically.

"Jackie they are coming," Harry continued then realised that he could no longer feel her breath on his face, he put his face closer to hers but she was cold.

"No don't die on me. Not now they're here," Harry said weeping.

Charlotte was near the South Tower at 09.59 when it collapsed, and was seen by Frank who had been rescued by firemen. He was convinced that both Harry and Charlotte had died and that two of his favourite friends were no more. He saw the towers fall first the South Tower then at 10.28 the North Tower collapsed. But what Frank didn't see was Charlotte running away from the area. But the question remained did she survive with so much happening - nobody knew for certain!

Charlotte saw Frank and ran up to him; he seemed dazed and didn't seem to acknowledge her being there.

"Frank it's me, Charlotte," She shouted.

He seemed to look right through her and stood still as if he were in a catatonic state.

"Frank where is Harry, is he dead?" Charlotte shouted hysterically. "Frank for god sake tell me!"

At that moment firemen and other rescue team shouted.

"Run for your lives the South Tower is collapsing!"

When she was told to run from the immediate area, she did so at great speed and didn't stop until she reached St Paul's Church a few blocks away. She was hit by a car but seemed to recover, she stood, clinging to the railings and yelling, she was covered in blood but most of it belonged to other people as she had been helping so many casualties. She was pulled off the railings by two police officers one male and one female both asked if she was alright, Charlotte said yes just to avoid going to hospital then entered the Church. A clergyman asked if she was alright and she broke down, she explained who she was and told him all about Harry. Then she went to Harry's apartment by taxi over the Brooklyn Bridge and never looked back. When she arrived she had a shower and changed her clothes, she then phoned the airport and arranged a flight home. When she got back she was admitted to hospital in Manchester suffering from delayed shock and minor injuries, her breathing seemed laboured, she was also informed that she was pregnant. Nobody mentioned Harry until Charlotte was willing to say something, even then things were difficult due to the circumstances of Harry's apparent death.

9/11 MEMORIAL

It was ten years later when it was announced that the anniversary of the 9/11 was due to take place at the site where the World Trade Centre Twin Towers once stood. It was named Ground Zero; two fountains were made within the places where the Twin Towers had stood. Around the fountains engraved on metal plaques were the names of those who died in the towers and in the aircrafts. Charlotte searched desperately for Harry's name where the South Tower once existed. But she found nothing and so she went around again, she was accompanied by a ten year old boy who looked a little bored. She glanced across to the other fountain and suddenly her face went sheet white, she clung hold of the boy who looked at her with concern.

"Mum what's wrong?" he asked.

"Oh nothing, I thought I saw a ghost!" Charlotte said looking at a man who resembled Harry.

The man vanished and she continued walking across to a new building that had a computer built into the side of it sheltered from the weather. She tapped in his name and still nothing came up as if he didn't exist, so she tapped in the name of all his colleagues each one came up in turn with photographs. By this time she was getting frustrated and called a security guard to the computer. He too had no luck finding him which didn't make sense if he was buried alive he would still be mentioned somewhere. At that moment she heard a man's voice speaking to her and the security officer.

"Could you please find Charlotte Brookes for me?" the man asked.

Charlotte went cold and felt faint, she began to stagger and almost fell to the floor she felt a hand holding her on the left which was her son and a larger hand on her right. Slowly she turned and looked at the man, it was that moment that she realised that she was neither dreaming nor hallucinating.

"Harry!" She said in disbelief.

"Charlotte!" He replied also surprised.

"Mum who is he?" the boy asked.

"Daniel this is your father," Charlotte explained.

"But you told me he was dead!" Daniel said confused.

"I thought he was, I mean I thought you were," Charlotte said not knowing how to respond.

"And Frank told me that you were killed from falling rubble," Harry said unable to take his eyes off her.

Eventually they embraced then Harry shook Daniel by the hand, and they walked away from the area and found a café nearby. Charlotte explained how she was told to run away from the area when the South Tower fell, she said that she arrived at St Paul's church. But Harry's story was more astonishing.

"Three of us were buried in rubble Jackie, a man called Isaac and myself, we thought that we would die in that pit. But then as I banged on a pipe someone heard me, it was the firemen and other people, some volunteers. They got us out but unfortunately Jackie had died from her wounds, Isaac survived and I lived to tell the tale." Harry looked at them listening intently to his story.

"So then what?" Charlotte said impatiently.

"Well I went to hospital and then my family came and took me to Washington where I stayed for a while. When I returned your things were gone, I assumed that someone had collected them for you. Frank said you were dead so what was I to think Charlotte?" Harry asked dreading her reply.

"Well ten years on and where are we now?" Charlotte asked.

"I still love you Charlotte, I have always loved you," Harry admitted.

"So are you married now?" Charlotte asked inquisitively.

"I was but I never loved her, not like I did you," Harry seemed very sincere.

"Well I have always loved you, but I am married," Charlotte said with a guilty expression as if she had committed adultery.

"Charlotte you moved on which is good, I would have expected you to," Harry said trying to relieve her of her guilt.

"Oh god I wish I had known about you surviving 9/11." Charlotte said tearfully.

Harry stretched out his hand and placed it on hers, he was also tearful as he explained further.

"We have both been robbed as everybody else has by the 9/11 disaster, people have lost their loved ones, some from the Towers, some from the firemen who died trying to rescue people from the Towers and those who were passengers in the planes," Harry looked at Charlotte's sad face.

"My god it's such a mess," Harry pondered for a moment. "Do you think that we would still be together if it wasn't for the 9/11?"

"Yes of course why do you say that?" Charlotte asked confused.

"I often think of that and wonder about our life together, getting married and living here in New York," Harry seemed troubled.

"I went to a clairvoyant and she told me about 9/11, avoiding a disaster and having a boy." Charlotte explained.

"A fine boy too, so why didn't you say anything about what she said?" Harry asked.

"Because you would never have believed me," Charlotte said anticipating his response.

"Probably not," Harry admitted.

"So where do we go from here?" Harry asked feeling uneasy.

"Christ Harry how can I reply to that, you suddenly appear and throw my life upside down, how the hell do I deal with that?" Charlotte banged her coffee cup on the table. "Really, I don't believe you Harry you expect me to just drop everything and run back to you, as if I have no life in Manchester!" Charlotte stood up and went to leave.

"No wait I'm sorry it was wrong to expect you to give up your life there," Harry was standing looking so pathetic at her.

"I don't know what to say or do, please tell me!" Harry pleaded.

"Well for one thing you're a father and another I still love you even now you idiot, so I have the problem not you," Charlotte admitted.

Harry stood speechless looking at Charlotte and Daniel, he was deep in thought and could only imagine them together living in Brooklyn.

"I will be here for a few days we can spend the time showing Daniel the sights as you showed me back in 2001," Charlotte was desperate to find a solution to the situation. There had to be an answer but only one came to mind and that was to leave her husband, she didn't want to do that to him as he had been loyal to her. But she did love Harry and wanted to be with him as she should have been ten years ago; she had days to think about things.

Charlotte's dream came true when she finally married Harry all seemed to go well until they both decided to revisit Ground Zero, maybe for the last time as it held such painful memories for them both. Harry relived the events in his mind trying to find a reason why he survived, by now the Freedom Tower had been built and a museum to visit and remember the day in a positive way. Thinking about all those who perished but building a future for the survivors. Charlotte also revisited the events in her mind, those moments watching the second plane hit the South Tower and realising Harry was in the building and may have been killed. Then as the Tower fell she ran for her life, but suddenly things seemed different, as she was running she was crossing a street and was hit by a car she was close to the railings by the church but not holding them. She was covered with blood, but it was her own, she was lying on the pavement hearing a voice and seeing two police officers looking over her.

"Is she alive?" said the male officer.

"I don't think so," said the female officer.

"She just ran out I couldn't stop," the driver said. "I'm sorry."

Someone covered her over with their coat and waited for the ambulance crew evidently Charlotte did die that day. All that happened since was in her mind and even to the point of not seeing Harry on the plaque on the side of the fountain, she was in denial and didn't realise that she had died. As for Harry he too thought that he had survived and yet he died and Jackie survived he was the one that was badly injured but due to wanting to survive considered that he had actually lived. There was a baby but it died with Charlotte, as for the meeting they were both ghosts. Occasionally they did meet at Ground Zero where they both met their fate, so all events from the Nine Eleven forward were Charlotte's own desires and not real.

There were many ghosts at Ground Zero all present to see their families and friends mourning, if only they could communicate and say we are with you and safe.

Two ghosts stood in the mist holding hands and looking up to a building that would symbolise new hope for the city of New York following one of the bleakest days in American history. Charlotte and Harry were two of the many victims of that day, lives that ended senselessly because of a terrorist attack. Charlotte took her love for Harry to the grave, and Harry had loved Charlotte so much that he would have done anything for the love of Charlotte.

AN AFTERTHOUGHT FOR READERS

Please remember this is a purely fictitious story although the disaster was very real and a lot of research has gone into writing the facts the characters remain fictitious and the story not based on anyone in particular.

DEDICATIONS

I would like to dedicate this book not only to friends and family, but to the brave people such as firemen and other rescuers involved in saving people's lives during the 9/11 disaster. It was through their heroic work that so many people were saved; some even lost their own lives while attempting to save others. On my last visit to New York I experienced personal sadness at seeing the exhibition at St Paul's church, looking in the Visitors Centre, but mainly seeing Ground Zero for myself. I got an eerie feeling as I walked around the fountains where the Towers once stood. Reading the names of the victims really brought home to me just how tragic it must have been for those involved, I would suggest that anyone wishing to visit there should be prepared to be upset. My heart goes out to the friends and relatives of the 9/11 tragedy. Although my book is fictitious I would hope that by doing my research it was accurate to events. I even went into the local pub O'Hara's in order to find out more about that fateful day, this is why I included it into my story. I was pleased to see the Freedom Building being constructed and the mast from the North Tower on the top, I also saw the start of the construction of the Museum which I believe is now finished.

I recommend anybody to visit Ground Zero just to pay their respects for all those people who tragically lost their lives there. This is a part of history which will be remembered as one of America's biggest tragedies, and will never be forgotten.

FURTHER READING BY SRS BOOKS

CRACKED PORCELAIN- THE FULL STORY (cracked porcelain & cracked porcelain too)

DOUBLE EXPOSURE

STORIES BEYOND BELIEF

CONFLICT OF FAITH

ULTIMATE PURPOSE

FOR THE LOVE OF CHARLOTTE

NOTHING IS REAL

CURSED

30693900R00366

Printed in Great Britain
by Amazon